MW01504192

The
Blood of a Stone

A Monsoon Series

Richard Braine Jr.

Proof reading agency: PaperTrue
(www.papertrue.com)

Cover designed by DAMONZA
(www.damonza.com)

For my beautiful wife, Tamitha.
Thank you for your endless support.
I'm sorry I killed your character.

PROLOGUE - RAIN

Rain splashed at Ember's feet as she ran across the street to club Faceless. The wicked summer storm had finally subsided as it chased the sunset west. An annoying drizzle and a cool breeze were all that remained. Ember stopped under the overhang at the club's entrance just long enough to read the Kate's Mind concert poster tacked to the door.

The band was new to Ember. The first time she heard their music was an advertisement on a local Tulsa radio station the previous day. She was hooked after just one song; their unique lyrics and melodic guitar riffs were a rare find in today's rock music. The concert seemed to be a good way to kill Saturday night and celebrate her acceptance to the university next semester; plus, a night of careless fun was long overdue. This was Ember's eighth campus tour in as many weeks. Education had been her addiction for as long as she could remember. She graduated from some of the most elite schools in the country, which included Yale, Harvard, Brown, and MIT. Luckily, she never had to worry for tuition or traveling expenses—she had more money than a person could spend in a lifetime, though it was impossible to discern just by looking at her. She didn't look a day over twenty-one, and she rarely ever used her private jet.

Ember opened the door and was immediately struck with a wall of cigarette smoke riding a wave of loud, rhythmic rock music pumping from the inside. She handed her ID to the bouncer. The muscular bouncer shot Ember a sideways look, as if the ID was fake.

Judging a book by its cover is challenging and often dangerous. Ember's close-fitting black dress exposed a tattoo on her shoulder—a petite, gothic fairy with a trail of stars following behind her. The diamond at the center of her pendant, worth more than the entire club, enhanced her sapphire eyes. Her dark hair and innocent smile added to the illusion, and that made it extremely difficult to decode the real Ember.

Ember knew she didn't have to worry, fake ID or not, the bouncer would let her into the club knowing guys will buy her expensive drinks.

The bouncer handed the ID back and stepped aside.

Faceless was set up like any other club. The dimly lit building was packed with rock fans, and a gigantic sound system pumped out loud music, keeping the crowd dancing between bands. Half a dozen semi-clothed push-up bra wearing bartenders worked behind the main bar. Each girl wore a tight, black tank top with *FACELESS* in white letters printed across their chests to make their cleavages stand out for bigger tips.

Ember ordered a Cape Cod—her signature drink—as her eyes followed the stairs next to the busy bar up to the high ceiling and the balcony that circled the entire club for a great view of the stage. A rather tall guy squeezed in rudely beside Ember, making her nearly spill the drink. The guy's friend wedged his way in next, forcing the tall guy even closer to Ember. She knew what was about to happen even before a single word was uttered.

"Hey sugar," said the tall guy, "we haven't seen you in here before."

Any guy who referred to Ember as "sugar" was not the type of guy she was hoping to attract.

"That's probably because I haven't been in here before," she replied with a hint of sarcasm. "You're very observant."

The tall guy and his friend were definitely not her type. They were both clearly intoxicated before the headlining band could strum a single chord. The tall guy stood eye to eye with Ember, and his shorter, heavyset friend stood right behind him. They both wore biker vests with *Lucky 13* patches embroidered and ball caps with a large number thirteen at the center. Ember had been to enough clubs around the country to know she didn't want anything to do with these wannabe motorcycle club guys.

The tall guy continued hitting on Ember.

"How about we buy that fine ass a dri—"

"Not interested," Ember interjected, turning away.

A smile appeared on the bartender's face as she gave Ember her change.

"Screw her Marty!" said the short guy, elbowing his biker buddy in the ribs as Ember walked away.

Ember had a feeling it wasn't the last time they'd try that tonight. She sipped her drink as she wove through the crowd toward the stairs going up to the balcony.

Rain had been watching the two guys from across the bar. He saw them hitting on the stunningly beautiful young girl from practically the moment she walked in. They were fast movers. He saw the two joke with each other as the girl shot them down and walked away.

Rain had not missed a Kate's Mind show since attending the band's concert for the first time at a Chicago music festival four years earlier. Since then, he had seen practically every one of their shows, from New York City to Seattle and every venue in between. Rain found it odd that someone as attractive as this girl was out alone tonight. He ran his tongue over his deadly sharp fangs, wondering what her blood would taste like, as his eyes followed the girl making her way up the crowded stairs.

Rain turned his attention back to the local motorcycle club. One thing he had observed on his trips to Tulsa was that Lucky Thirteen motorcycle club's main mission was always trouble. Depending on the night, the club ranged anywhere from ten to twenty members. The amount of trouble intensified with the number. That night, they were in full force at the end of the bar, poking fun at the guy who just got shot down by the blue-eyed mystery girl. A few of them were even attempting to coax the tall guy to give it another shot.

Rain sat waiting patiently for the band to take the stage. *Those fools will never learn*, he thought.

Ember found an empty spot along the railing of the balcony and sipped her drink. She scanned the crowd below and saw the two drunken bikers laughing it up with their buddies at the bar.

"Jerks," she whispered to herself.

Rain silently agreed with the mystery girl's observation.

The stage lights went out, and the crowd erupted in excitement. Ember heard the guitar amps click on and noticed the silhouettes of the band members moving around on the stage. Her heart pounded with anticipation. The energy of the crowd grew louder as the guitar feedback ramped up through the massive sound system. The stage lights turned steadily brighter. The lead singer, Jimmy, and other guitarist were in front of their amps, their guitars in hand and their backs to the crowd. The drummer began a nice, slow groove that the bass and the guitars matched perfectly. The music intensified with every measure, and the volume slowly crept louder and louder.

Ember's heart raced to keep pace with the beat.

Rain could feel Ember's anticipation as her heart pounded away.

The music stopped, and the speakers went silent as Jimmy stepped up to the mic. He brushed a few long, dark strands of curly hair out of his face and smiled. He yelled, "Pick it up Tulsa!"

The whole band kicked back in with perfect time. The crowd cheered as the band jammed out a few measures. They were absolutely amazing. They had sharp guitar riffs and perfect rhythm, all led by possibly the best front-man Ember had ever seen. She was blown away, to say the least, and the band hadn't even finished their first song.

After several songs, Ember headed down the stairs to buy herself another drink. She quickly scanned the crowd and saw that her secret biker admirers were down at the far end of the bar. She made it a point to order from as far away as possible.

The bar was packed, possibly over its capacity. It took an entire song for Ember to get another drink. She grabbed the glass from the bar only to discover she stood once again face to face with Marty, her new biker friend.

Marty immediately got too close for comfort. "How about we buy you that drink now?" he said with half a sly smile.

Ember could smell the alcohol on Marty's breath. "Looks like you've had your share," she said irritably. "And I already have a drink. Those observation skills are hurting your game."

Ember sidestepped to walk around Marty.

"Come on. What happens in Tulsa stays in Tulsa," the shorter guy said with a grin, stepping in Ember's way.

"That was original," she replied, rolling her eyes as she read the name on his jacket. "Did you and your playmates come up with that in your tree-house after school, Shorty?"

Ember was annoyed; she didn't want to miss the rest of the band's set because a couple of drunken jerks couldn't take her hint.

"Damn, honey," Marty said arrogantly, "you've got a bad little mouth to match that nice little ass."

Marty was now tucked up close behind Ember. She shuddered from the touch of his hand sliding up her thigh. The crowd was too thick for anyone else to notice what was going on, and the music was loud enough that no one else could hear their conversation—almost no one.

Ember knew they weren't going to take no for an answer. She wasn't the first and won't be the last girl they hit on. Ember looked toward the main entrance for the bouncer, but he was no longer there. Reluctantly, she turned to face Marty with a fake smile on her face.

"You have no idea of the things I'd do to you, *honey*," she mocked, running her hand down his chest.

Marty grinned at his buddy who was now behind Ember. Ember didn't think twice; she raised her knee hard, and hit Marty right between his legs. He went down instantly.

Ember retreated. She needed to get to an open space, and she needed to get there fast. She headed straight for the closest exit, which probably led to the alley beside the club. It didn't matter; she just needed open space. She headed for the door, bouncing side to side off people in the crowd until she hit the door and practically tumbled outside. The cool air was refreshing compared to the thick smoke inside the club. The door shut behind her as she reached for her purse. It was gone! How could she have been so careless? Her most valuable possession was in that purse.

"Dammit!" she exclaimed, turning back toward the door.

Drumbeats and bass guitar poured from the club as the door suddenly opened from the inside. The alley was dark at this time of night, and Ember knew it wasn't the bouncer at the doorway. She saw the short biker step out with two more of his club members. As the door slammed shut behind them, it muffled the music from the inside.

Ember guessed they weren't out for a breath of fresh air.

Shorty walked over to a line of parked motorcycles. Each bike had a green spade and number thirteen painted on the black gas tank. He grabbed what looked like a hammer from a leather saddle bag straddled on the back fender.

The bar door swung open again as Marty limped out with two more guys. He was still holding his groin after Ember's knee.

"Hold her!" Marty shouted with pain in his voice as the door slammed shut behind him. "I'm first!"

Ember needed her purse. Now!

The guys circled around Ember, blocking her from fleeing. Shorty and another biker grabbed her by her shoulders and shoved her against the brick wall soaked from the rain earlier.

Ember could hear the clink of metal as Marty limped closer unbuckling his belt.

The door opened a third time and shut back just as fast. Ember strained to twist her neck around and watch. She could barely make out the silhouette of a man in a dark T-shirt and shiny black leather pants standing in front of Marty. The man stood still, almost like a statue.

"This ain't a peep show friend!" shouted Marty. "Invitation only! Keep moving!"

"Nice jacket," Rain said calmly. "Lucky Charms. Isn't that the little kids' cereal with fun, colorful marshmallows?"

"Hey friend!" snapped Marty. "Do you know who you're messing with? It says Lucky Thirteen, dick!"

Rain took a step forward, closing in on Marty.

"The Lucky Thirteen Dicks?" asked Rain. "Nice name for a bunch of not-so-tough Tulsa bikers. Of course, I say that solely based on the fact that it's taking four of you to hold down one lovely young girl who was clearly just trying to enjoy a nice night out for some live music."

Marty had enough of this distraction. He threw a punch.

Rain moved like lightning, shifting left to dodge Marty's fist. Marty swung again with the same result—a miss. Rain grabbed Marty's arm midflight, and in one swift move, bent it the wrong way, breaking it right at the elbow.

Marty shrieked out in pain.

"And my name's not *friend*. It's Rain," he said, lifting his head slowly as his lips curled into a thin smile. Rain's dark eyes narrowed as the other bikers circled around him.

Free from the bikers' grasp, Ember spun around, throwing herself back against the wall. She was frozen in place, too terrified to run. Her eyes followed Rain. He was strikingly handsome and appeared to enjoy the challenge of saving her without so much as messing his perfectly styled dark hair.

Shorty was the first to attack.

Without even looking in his direction, Rain shot his arm out, grabbing Shorty by the throat and lifting him off the ground, as though he was weightless. Rain turned his head to the flailing biker and flashed his deadly fangs. A wet spot formed on the crotch of Shorty's jeans. Terrified, the other Lucky Thirteen members stumbled backward, turned, and ran back inside the club. So much for loyalty.

The hammer clanged on the pavement as Rain squeezed Shorty's neck. Ember could hear the agonizing sound of bones shattering under his powerful grip. Shorty gurgled his last word, more of whimper, as Rain hurled him through the air like a rag doll straight into the line of motorcycles, knocking them down as if they were a line of dominoes.

Rain casually walked over to where Marty lay sobbing from the pain of his broken arm. He grasped Marty's hair and yanked his head back. A thin stream of blood trailed behind Rain's finger nail as he sliced deep through Marty's flesh.

"Do *you* know who you're messing with, *honey?*" Rain said, twisting Marty's neck.

Ember, now in tears, cringed from the repulsive sound of more bones breaking, similar to someone stepping on dry twigs.

In the blink of an eye, Rain moved to Ember. He lightly brushed the hair away from her eyes. Tears rolled down her face as her lips parted to say something; although nothing came out as Rain gently wiped away another teardrop. The touch of his hand felt cold against her warm cheek.

Rain held out a small cloth pouch that was laced shut. "I believe those men stole your purse," he said, handing the pouch to Ember. "This was inside."

Ember reached out and snatched the pouch—her dust. She parted the laces, took out a pinch, raised her hand above her head, and closed her eyes, letting the dust fall over her body. It sparkled down her frame like a shower of tiny diamonds.

Rain stepped back amazed. Ember was now only six inches tall and floating in front of him. She had the most amazing set of miniature black wings that complimented her petite black dress perfectly. Her eyes were bright as little, blue stars. She was a mirror image of her fairy tattoo.

Rain had heard stories of fairies before, but he had never actually seen one.

Likewise, Ember had never seen an actual vampire until then.

With a motion too swift for even Rain's eyes to follow, she flew forward and planted a tiny, gentle kiss on his cheek. Then, she flew back away from Rain, just as fast, and with a flicker of her wings, she was gone.

ONE

The officer guarding the crime scene's front entrance peered at my FBI identification and back to me for a second time. He was right to question the validity of the identification, considering that it was, in fact, a forgery. Not having the time to find a proper suit to fit the stereotypical FBI wardrobe didn't help sell me as an FBI agent. It's not every day you see a federal agent investigating a murder wearing jeans and a tee and ridiculously messed up hair that was more rock star than special investigator. Trivial things like shopping for a suit and looking in the mirror were not high on my priority list. I had to work the scene quickly. The actual clean-cut, suit-wearing FBI couldn't have been more than a couple hours behind me.

"Hey!" an officer yelled at a news crew van parking in front of a fire hydrant. "You can't park there!"

The officer waved me through his checkpoint and took off toward the news crew.

Three other local news vans were scrambling to find parking outside Madison's Rock Shop where two people were brutally murdered last night. Each reporter was hoping to get the full story before another. The national news teams were most likely on their way, since someone had already leaked that these two victims were similar to nine other recent homicides from across the country. The FBI linked the homicides together and labeled them as a serial killing spree, even though they were yet to establish a motive or uncover a single solid lead. It's almost as if the killer was a ghost, and just as a side note, I don't believe in ghosts. I had my own suspicions to the motives; though I'd be locked up myself if I even tried to break it down for them. Let's just say there aren't many things that frighten me in this world, and that day, a chill ran down my spine that didn't even come close to the full meaning of the word "terror".

Was there any good news? It was late June, and the sun was shining in Madison. The wicked Wisconsin winter snow was still months away. I would consider that as possibly the only good news of the day.

I tucked my fake ID into my belt and removed my sunglasses as I entered the rock store. The shop was fairly small, maybe only a couple hundred square feet. The creaking of the old wooden floor and the layout gave the shop a vintage feel. Numerous unique rocks filled glass display cases and a few tall wooden shelves. The other shelves were scattered with unique gift ideas and rocks cut in half, revealing amethyst-colored crystals inside—geodes, I think. A security camera, more than likely a fake one, was mounted in the far-right ceiling corner. Another decoy camera blinked a little red light from the diagonal corner.

A man and a woman, both wearing ironed suits, appeared from the back room. I took a wild guess that they were local detectives. The woman flipped her small notebook shut and glanced down at my badge. I hoped my imitation ID wasn't too good to be true; my forgery skills aren't what they used to be.

"We've been waiting for you," she said, extending her hand. "I'm Detective Kasiah Johnson, and this is my partner, Detective Damien Tone."

"Special Agent Mike Wesley from the Seattle field office," I introduced myself, shaking both their hands. I was still getting used to my alias. I intended to keep my real name, Erone, as far away from this case as possible.

Damien was tall, with a clean-shaven head and a firm handshake. He had a straight to-the-point attitude in his voice when he said hello. I suspected his smooth, direct movements and his discipline were courtesy the U.S. military.

Kasiah's Midwestern accent made her sound a bit sweeter than I guessed she really was. Her brunette hair would fall just below her shoulders if it wasn't pulled back and out of the way. I could see the edge of her contact lenses around her deep dark brown eyes. Her closet probably had at least a dozen of those sleek black suit jackets and matching pants. I doubted the weapon making the slight bugle at her right hip would offer sufficient protection against the person who committed these gruesome murders.

"We've been expecting the FBI for a few hours now," said Kasiah, insinuating that I was late.

"I apologize, Detective Johnson," I replied. "I was on a plane to Seattle from Chicago when I got the call. I was back in the air within an hour after landing. I was actually surprised to even get a flight out to Madison this quick. It's amazing what this shiny badge can do."

I may have left out the part about having my friend Tara use her magic cyber wand to delay the FBI's flight a couple hours. I highly recommend everyone having their own hacker; and Tara was mine. I've actually never met Tara, and I don't even know where she is; although when I require an internet pirate, she's the one I call. I laughed at Tara's comments on how easy it was to hack into the flight database and take control of the passenger lists and seating. I was sure the FBI would use their own tricks to bump someone from another flight.

Kasiah looked past me out the front window. "Damien, please go outside and make sure the officers keep the news crews as far back as they can."

"Yes, ma'am," Damien said as he quickly went outside, pointing his finger down the street and shouting at the news crews.

Kasiah was obviously in charge.

"What would you like to see first?" she asked.

"Two victims?" I questioned, looking toward the rear of the store.

"Yes, that's correct," she confirmed, flipping open her notebook. "The owner and one of his employees were the only ones in the building at the time. The owner was male in his late forties, and his employee was a local college student in her early twenties. Both bodies have been transported to the local crime lab. I was instructed to wait here and brief the FBI upon arrival. We'd typically investigate the murder as part of our precious stone theft case, but these victims apparently match the M.O. of your killer. This is your crime scene now, Agent Wesley."

I sensed a hint of sarcasm in Kasiah's voice when she said *your killer*. She was used to calling the shots. I was also pretty sure she did not approve of my attire; she looked at me as if I was one of those 'these rules don't apply to me' agents. She was right.

"Precious stone theft?" I asked out of curiosity.

"Yes. There have been multiple thefts across the country involving some of the rarest stones in existence—some worth millions. None have been recovered so far."

This got me excited. I was on the right track.

"I wasn't aware something was stolen during the murders," I continued. "This is the first time the killer has taken something from the scene other than blood."

"I'll give you the short version to bring you up to speed," Kasiah said, obviously annoyed that her precious stone theft wasn't more important than a cross-country serial killer. "My team was originally notified by the local P.D. because of what was stolen from the shop—one of the world's rarest geodes. Actually, the correct term is 'nodule', which is a geode with a core of solid crystals. This particular nodule is priceless, and one of only two halves ever discovered."

Kasiah pulled out several photographs from her suit jacket and arranged them on one of the glass display cases.

"The full nodule," she said, pointing to one of the photos, "was approximately the size of a basketball when discovered. The internal crystal is of a bright cobalt color, which glows an even more intense blue when placed in the dark. Nothing like it had ever been seen before or again. One half of the nodule was donated to the Smithsonian in 1998 by a geologist from Arizona. From what we've learned, the geologist is the daughter of the shop's owner, Kevin Harding. Mr. Harding's daughter gave him the second half as a gift. It's been on display here at the rock shop ever since. Mr. Harding refused to sell it no matter what the offer was. While interviewing Mr. Harding's wife, we learned that that some offers were over a quarter million dollars and that the nodule immediately boosted business. Geologists have come from all over the world to view this rare find."

Kasiah collected her photos and placed them back in her pocket.

"Madison's White-Collar Crime Unit had been watching this particular piece for the past six weeks," she continued, "ever since Mr. Harding received several death threats. He was afraid someone would eventually steal the nodule. We were actually hoping someone would try, so we could catch the thieves red-handed. I'm sorry to say we hadn't anticipated this type of violence. The theft occurred around seven this morning, and Mr. Harding's wife discovered the bodies around eight. I phoned my supervisor and described the nature of the wounds on the victims' necks. He immediately instructed me to stop everything while he contacted the Bureau—an order we reluctantly obeyed."

I listened closely as I followed Kasiah across the shop, checking my watch and wondering if the FBI's flight had touched down. Time was running out.

Kasiah flipped a few more pages of her notebook before adding, "It's apparent on the security camera footage that the murders were not planned as a part of the theft. They only occurred as a result of being surprised while stealing the nodule. However, my superiors still insisted we hold the investigation for the FBI."

I don't admit it often, but I was caught off guard by what Kasiah had just said.

"Did you just say you have the killer on a security camera?" I asked as calmly as possible.

Kasiah looked up at one of the two security cameras in the main shop area. "Yes," she said. "These two are dummy cameras visible in the main area. Each of these cameras have a battery-powered blinking LED light but no actual video recording capability. Both the cameras would fool your average shop-lifter. We had four of our own micro cameras on the property focused on the entryways and nodule's night safe."

I took a breath and waited a few seconds before asking the next question. I didn't want to sound desperate. "May I review the footage?"

"That can be arranged once we get back to the local office and download the footage. I can take you first to the coroner's office at the crime lab, so you can verify the wounds are similar to the others."

5

"No," I said more aggressively than intended. "We have not yet caught this particular killer on camera or have a single living witness. I need to review that footage as soon as possible."

Kasiah motioned for Damien to join us. She asked for his phone as she reached into her pants pocket. She pulled out a flash drive and plugged it into the bottom of his phone. Kasiah toggled through several menus and stopped at a file with today's date. She pushed play and fast-forwarded to 7:14 am.

I love modern-day gadgets like these; I remember a time before Edison had even thought of inventing the light bulb. At that time, everyone was terrified of new things, especially electricity. More than just a few early scientists were burned at the stake as witches for predicting modern inventions like telephones, airplanes, computers, and the internet. Although, I don't necessarily miss those days.

The micro camera that recorded the footage appeared to be mounted on a drain pipe near what must have been the rear door. It was aimed parallel to the rear wall and directly at the door. The video played for a few seconds, when a man suddenly appeared from what looked like out of nowhere. His movements were a blur, almost as if he was moving too fast for the camera to actually record the movement. He stopped at the door only long enough to grab the handle and pull it open.

"The rear door was unlocked?" I asked.

Kasiah paused the video. "No, the door is an industrial strength steel door with two dead bolt locks. He broke both the locks as if they weren't even there. They must have been precut before the break-in."

Kasiah pressed play again. The video didn't have a very good shot of whoever opened the door, even though there was a light directly above. The view was of the man's back. All you could see was a full-length black leather trench coat and short dark hair. He vanished inside as soon as the door opened.

"Is there footage from inside?" I asked.

"Yes, but they didn't capture much. The cameras inside the building only caught Mr. Harding removing the nodule from the safe two minutes before the killer entered through the rear door. The killer wasn't seen on any of the

THE BLOOD OF A STONE

inside cameras. He must have walked right past the camera that has a view of the entire back room away from the rear door."

I glanced at my watch again. "Does he leave from the same door?"

"Yes, he leaves almost exactly ninety seconds after he enters, which is amazing, considering he had to surprise Mr. Harding and his employee, kill them both, and steal the nodule." Kasiah pointed to the tiny screen. "Here, you can see him leaving."

The steel door opened as if it was struck by a truck. It swung open, hit the wall, and came flying back shut. The killer was out the door and gone even before the door completely swung shut.

"Can you rewind that and step through each frame?" I asked excitedly.

Kasiah moved her finger over the small function buttons on the phone. "Yes, we did that, but you can't really see a clear shot of his face. I guess some is better than none."

Kasiah rewound the video and started playing it forward frame by frame. It took only ten frames at twenty-five frames per second for the door to swing open. The killer emerged from the building and was in view for only several frames. Kasiah was right when she insisted you couldn't, in fact, see his face. However, the little I could see was enough. I instantly recognized him. His facial features hadn't changed a bit; his movements and the timeframe in which the two victims were killed was enough for me to know without a doubt.

Kasiah picked up on my fear. "Is something wrong?"

"No," I lied.

Like I said, there aren't very many things that frighten me in this world. I emphasize *in this world* for a reason, because I'm not from this world, and neither is this killer. What sends a chill down my spine and top the number one spot on my fright list? Well, I had just seen a Shadow Vampire for the first time in almost a century. Not just any Shadow Vampire; this was Atmoro, a Shadow Vampire rumored to be dead for decades. And by the way, I still don't believe in ghosts.

TWO

I was positive of what I had seen, no matter how impossible it seemed.

"Are you OK?" Damien asked. "You look like you've just seen a ghost."

"Ghosts don't exist," I retorted. "This footage is a huge break in the case. It's the first piece of solid evidence of any kind the bureau has recovered. This killer has been incredibly careful. To have an image of his face is the break we've been looking for."

"Does he look familiar to you?" asked Kasiah.

I honestly don't try to make a habit of lying, but there's no way I could have told them, "Oh yeah, that's Atmoro, one of the oldest and strongest Shadow Vampires to have ever existed. He's only the most skilled killer your world has ever known. Decades ago, he broke a few major Shadow laws and jumped to the Light World, and now he's killing people and stealing priceless stones just for fun!"

"No," I said, lying again. "It's just an adrenaline rush to finally put a blurry face to the case. Is this the only copy of this footage?"

Kasiah unplugged the flash drive and stuffed it back in her pocket. "Yes, we haven't had the chance to download it to the servers back at the office."

I gazed blankly at nothing in particular. There was no way I could leave the contents of that flash drive in someone's hand, or pants for that matter. Atmoro didn't exist in their world or on any of their databases, but if they start plastering his face on national news stations, more people from my world would see it and immediately recognize him.

I turned to Kasiah. "What other information can you give me about the nodule that was stolen?" I didn't need her to tell me. I just needed to act interested to keep on her good side and get that flash drive. I knew this nodule was from the Shadow World; yet I had no idea why Atmoro would need this stupid rock. In my world, they're a dime a dozen and primarily used as a light source within homes. It was probably brought here by a jumper, then lost or traded afterward.

Kasiah and Damien started toward the back door for a waiting black SUV. The vehicle was straight out of a CSI-type TV crime show: black exterior, chromed wheels, tinted windows, and low profile LED emergency dash lights.

"We don't know much," Kasiah explained, "except that it's rare and apparently attracts serial killers. The one thing we do know, however, is that the other half of the nodule is set to open on display here at the University of Madison on Monday as part of the American Geologist display from the Smithsonian that's touring around the country. The display will be here for two weeks."

"So, this isn't a coincidence," I said, thinking out loud. "The thief knows both halves of the stone are going to be together for the first time since its discovery."

"Yes," she nodded. "The American Geology Society is funding the display and has been notified. They're willing to continue the display at the U.W. under our supervision and surveillance."

"When does the nodule arrive?" I asked, though I was sure Atmoro would not wait long before trying to retrieve the other half. I still had no idea why he wanted this stone, how it was tied to the killing spree, or why he stole one half when the other half was on its way to the same city. Why not wait till the same night, grab both pieces, and then get the hell out of town?

Kasiah glanced down at her notebook. "All of the items for display are scheduled to arrive on Friday afternoon at Dane County Regional. They'll have an escort from the airport to the university campus. We're already setting up cameras on campus where the display will be held. We'll have our team in place as staff members when it opens on Monday."

"If you're watching the campus," I said, anticipating Atmoro's next play, "then so is the killer. He may run if he notices your people setting up security. How sure are you he's not going to meet the convoy halfway, or just wait for the nodule to return home to the museum?"

I could tell Kasiah was annoyed with me questioning her abilities.

"All of the items for display have been accumulated and stored at the Smithsonian. The security there is fit for the White House. We don't anticipate the thief to travel nearly a thousand miles for the other half when it's on its way here in two days."

I had to admit Kasiah was right. Why would Atmoro go to a heavily secured museum when the nodule is being hand-delivered here to a college campus with a few rent-a-cops? Although, why did he want the damn thing in the first place, and why did he take the first half this morning? He must have known it would bring in the Feds. Unless, of course, if that's what he wanted.

Kasiah opened the door of the SUV. "Follow us to the morgue," she suggested, "and we'll see what the coroner found with the two bodies. Then we can go to the station and make a copy of the video footage."

I tried to be nice and interested in her poor attempt to forge a plan to catch Atmoro, but I have other ways of getting what I want from Kasiah. I was growing tired of the whole fake FBI agent charade anyway. It was not as much fun as it looked on TV, especially since I knew my hunch was right and there's a rogue vampire on a killing spree. I no longer needed to play the nice FBI agent. The FBI and CIA together couldn't catch a Shadow Vampire. I'm going to need help from someone who can make the FBI and CIA look like a bunch of third graders trying to figure out who ate the last cookie.

I could have easily just turned and walked away and let life play out. I had no interest in tangling with a Shadow Vampire. Regrettably, I couldn't live with myself seeing this devastation continue, knowing all the while no one from this world could to stop Atmoro.

"That sounds like a plan," I said eagerly. Then, I took one intentionally close step toward Kasiah to catch her eye. She was now no more than an arm length away. I focused my gaze deep into her eyes and spoke quietly, so

Damien could not hear. "You want to reach into your pocket, remove the flash drive and hand it to me," I instructed.

Compulsion is an amazing tool when used correctly. It's a suggestion placed strategically into someone's mind; it is not mind control, which is what most people believe it to be. The only down-side, other than taking years to master the techniques, is that not everyone is susceptible to compulsion. It's very rare to find someone capable of using compulsion on a Shadow, but most humans are fair game. However, the human brain processes billions of pieces of information every minute, and that makes it difficult to get in and *plant* your suggestion. It's also a little dangerous; it's like playing with a bomb—when you accidentally cross the wrong wire... boom! Any type of mind manipulation has long been forbidden in the Shadow World. It is one of the laws that, when broken, will get you banished to the Forgotten Shadow City, which is the San Quentin of the Shadow World.

Many years ago in our first warlock trainings, my father secretly taught my sister and me the art of compulsion. He knew the risks of teaching his children an outlawed practice, but he was willing to take his chances to prepare his children to protect themselves. As our minds grew and our powers increased, he pushed us to our limits to remember as many spells as we could manage. My sister's natural control over fire still amazes me to this day. The only thing that limited us was the amount of energy we could draw in to cast the spells. If we weren't careful, we could easily become drained and powerless, so our father stressed how important it was to manage our powers and use them only when necessary. We were gifted to have such a knowledgeable warlock that our father once was.

I had a fifty-fifty chance compulsion would work on Kasiah. The risk paid off. Kasiah slowly removed the flash drive and handed it over. The breeze blew just enough for me to catch a hint of her perfume; flowery, but unique. I couldn't place it. The scent intoxicated me none-the-less. I took the flash drive and quickly stuffed it in my pocket.

"Is that all?" Kasiah asked.

11

"Yes," I smiled. "It was nice to meet you, and I look forward to working with you to catch this guy."

Kasiah will forget we had ever had this conversation. Unfortunately, she will have some explaining to do when she can't find the flash drive.

I asked Kasiah and Damien to wait there while I went to fetch my rental car. I quickly walked back to the car and drove in the exact opposite direction—away from the crime scene. I only had until tomorrow to put a plan together and figure out how these nodules were tied to the murders. I needed some help and knew just where to find it. I followed my GPS out of town down I-94 toward Milwaukee.

THREE

Watching from across the street, Jake was certain that the FBI agent had just used compulsion on the Madison detective; and that meant the agent was a Shadow. Jake didn't know much about Shadows other than what Atmoro wanted him to know. He knew compulsion wasn't a human trick and that warlocks were the only ones who could ever master the complex art of mind manipulation. He also knew it was best to stay away from warlocks—compulsion wasn't their only skill. Atmoro had warned him of their powerful minds many times.

Jake, once a promising law student at NYU, was adjusting to his new vampire life quickly. He was only turned less than a year ago. The memory of exactly how he became a vampire had faded to the back of his mind. He could no longer separate his nightmares from reality. He recalled walking home with a girl he had met at a bar that night. The girl's name had escaped his memory—Sarah sounded right. They were on a shortcut through the park on their way to Jake's apartment for a drunken one-night stand. Sarah giggled and stumbled along the way, and Jake continuously steadied her. They were both too busy flirting to notice the man blocking their path. Before either could react to the apparent mugging, Jake was knocked unconscious from a single blow to his head.

The attack had happened too quickly for Jake's memory to record more than just bits and pieces; his brain possibly decided to misplace the worst parts of that night. He recalled his vision getting blurred and seeing the man holding his mouth against Sarah's neck. He tried to scream, but his lips wouldn't respond. Then, he blacked out.

When Jake came to his senses, he noticed Sarah lying next to him. Her eyes were wide open in a permanent state of shock. It was obvious she was no longer alive; her throat was literally half torn out, and the volume of blood sickened him.

This was when Jake blacked out a second time.

The next time he awoke, he was lying on his back in pitch-black darkness. Disorientation had taken over. He wondered about the girl and wanted to yell out her name, but he couldn't remember it. Jake struggled to regain control of his mind and emotions.

A man's voice slowly faded in. "You will be thirsty," he said. "Try to control it before it controls you. Breathe."

The voice sounded calm and relaxed to Jake. *Perhaps a doctor*, he thought.

"My name is Atmoro," the man continued. "I am from an ancient world you have never known. I have taken your friend's life to preserve my own, and in return, I have given you a gift that will lengthen yours indefinitely. The transformation side effects will diminish and your mind will clear shortly."

Jake tried to wake up from the nightmare. His senses weren't working properly. He was frozen, unable to think straight. His neck ached and his head pounded in pain.

Atmoro, now looking down directly into Jake's eyes, spoke as if it was an everyday conversation. "You will do as I say," he demanded, "or I will sever your head from your shoulders."

Having comprehended only half of what Atmoro had said, Jake had trouble focusing his eyes. His brain was running at half speed. *What gift?* Jake thought to himself. *What the hell is this crazy man talking about? Why did he kill whatsername?*

Jake finally sat up, dizzy, his mouth begging for a drop of water, the little voice at the back of his mind telling him to run without looking back. He had to get away from this maniac as fast as his legs would carry him. He may have listened to that little voice only if his legs would have carried him.

Beneath Jake's hands, the ground felt like cool dirt. The two windows above his head were black, and only a sliver streak of moonlight found its way through the glass. He was in what appeared to be a shed or a small barn. Jake listened for any sign that could tell him where he was being held. The last place he remembered was New York City. The comforting car horns, sirens, and voices were all gone; it was completely silent.

"It will take some time for you to get used to your sharpened senses," Atmoro said, startling Jake. "Feeding will help you regain your strength and complete the change. Animal blood shall keep you alive, but you will need fresh human blood to maximize your new abilities."

Jake's mind continued to struggle to understand what he was hearing. *What abilities?* he wondered.

A soft thumping on his right caught Jake's attention. As if programmed to do so, he turned his head, and he searched for whatever was producing the sound. The thumping intensified. A powerful scent excited his sense of smell, and his mouth began to salivate.

Suddenly, Jake's strength returned. He stood up and focused on the sound, it grew louder and faster with every passing second. His vision cleared. It was the middle of the night, and yet it might well have been a bright sunny day at the beach. Jake ran his tongue along his teeth. They felt sharper than before—pointed and sharp enough to puncture his tongue. The blood didn't taste coppery, like the time he got punched in eighth grade for making out with the quarterback's girlfriend; instead, it tasted sweet, sweeter than the sweetest chocolate he'd ever tasted. He wanted more—he had to have more.

Stepping toward the sound, Jake came in view of a young woman pressed against the corner with a gag tied across her mouth. Her wrists and ankles were bound with thick rope, and her eyes were filled with fear. She appeared dressed for a night out with her friends, wearing enough glittering necklaces, bracelets, and earrings to open her own jewelry store. Her tight, blue mini-skirt was dirty and torn. This certainly wasn't the night she had planned while giggling in front of the mirror with her friends as they prepared to go out on the prowl.

The girl was pressing her bare feet into the dirt in front of her, trying to push her way right through the wall. Jake's mind clicked; it was the girl's heart beat that was making the sweet rhythmic beat. The beat was beckoning to him, and Jake could literally see the blood flowing through the girl's veins at every beat of her heart.

Jake could hear, see, and smell everything—all of his senses were intensified by ten.

The girl's wrists were bleeding at the ropes; they had cut into her skin. Jake closed his eyes and let her blood's scent fill his lungs. He inhaled slowly and smiled. The scent was intoxicating. He opened his eyes, and with his peripheral vision, Jake noticed Atmoro moving like he did when he first attacked.

"I brought you your first meal," Atmoro said, standing next to Jake. "As a vampire, you will have to learn to find your own nourishment."

The girl's eyes switched swiftly between Atmoro and Jake. It was obvious she heard what Atmoro had just said, and it became clear to both her and Jake—he was a vampire, and she was his meal.

Jake snapped back to reality and the task at hand in Madison. Atmoro had given him specific instructions to observe the scene at Madison's Rock Shop until the FBI arrives. He had his video camera set up on a small tripod at the window of a house across the street behind the shop. Jake was proud of his amateur footage. He hoped Atmoro would like this new turn of events.

Jake removed the camera and collapsed the tripod. He debated whether he should finish off the young girl on the couch. She was maybe twenty-two years old, and Jake could tell by the family photographs and older furniture that the girl lived there with her parents. She was probably a college student living at home. Unfortunately, just like in the movies, she was in the wrong place at the wrong time.

Jake sat down next to the girl's motionless body, caressing her naked breast, pushing his fangs even deeper into her neck. The girl had long passed out from the sight of an actual vampire in her house and the fact that she had lost entirely too much blood. Well, it was not lost; Jake knew where it was. He turned the girl's head to see her face. It was a shame he couldn't keep her. Atmoro would never allow him to have such a magnificent prize all to himself.

The girl's heart finally beat its last beat.

Jake was still thirsty. "So many college girls and so little time," he said to himself as he stood up. "But what Atmoro doesn't know won't hurt him."

Jake poured gasoline around the living room. "The coroner will have to use dental records to identify your lovely face," he said, laughing to himself, splashing the remaining gasoline on the girl's nude, lifeless body.

Whistling casually, Jake walked to the back door. He flipped open and lit a small, silver lighter, then tossed it into the room. The gasoline vapors exploded in a ball of fire. Jake stood in the back doorway, savoring the dancing fire, and just before the flames could reach him, he was gone.

FOUR

I spent most of the two-hour drive to Milwaukee trying to make sense of the nodule theft and murders in Madison. I asked Tara to surf the net to try and find something linking all the victims. She was able to dig up one connection the FBI had either overlooked or intentionally left out of the case notes. All the victims' names where related to precious stones or gemstones: *Amber* Johnson, Tiffany *Sapphire*, Tommy *Silverstone*, *Jasper* Long, Jennifer *Aventurine*, and Melissa *Topaz*. Three of the victims were born in February—birthstone *Amethyst*. The unusually similar names didn't help answer why Atmoro stole the nodule. They only confused me even more as to what Atmoro was planning or why he seemed obsessed with the blood of stones.

It was well past eight by the time I arrived at Summerfest. The sun was setting over Lake Michigan as I purchased a ticket and entered the concert grounds.

I've attended this music festival on the shores of Lake Michigan for the past ten years. It's promoted as the World's Largest Music Festival, and believe me when I say this, Summerfest isn't your mom's music festival. Every year, more than seven hundred bands perform on eleven separate outdoor stages. The festival lasts ten days, spread across late June and early July, and has an annual attendance just under a million fans. I have heard every kind of music here, from country and rock to rap and soul. I have seen Jamaican drum acts, Scottish bagpipes, and even just a few locals jamming on their acoustic guitars. You can see a dozen of the most popular touring rock bands all in one day.

Yes, this is where I come when I need help slaying a vampire.

Just as I passed the northern gates, I heard Breaking Benjamin playing *Dance with the Devil.* The lyrics almost seemed like sound advice. I'll remember that when my throat is ripped open for getting between a Shadow Vampire and whatever the hell he's after. I had to repeatedly remind myself why I was pursuing Atmoro: the main reason—the Light World is my home and has been so for nearly a hundred years. Shadows refer to this world as *Light* because of all the natural light from the sun. The Shadow World is hidden deep inside the Light World, where the sun's rays are never seen. Most of the light in my world comes from forests of sapphire trees, with their glowing brilliant blue leaves. I miss the natural beauty of that world every single day of my life.

There are others like me here in the Light World. By others, I don't mean warlocks, but other Shadows that have escaped the now corrupt Shadow Council. We've found a new home here in the Light World. It's a constant struggle to keep our existence a secret, and for the most part, we've succeeded. Every now and again, the actions of a Shadow threaten to reveal our kind to the Light World. I had never seen a skilled and disciplined Shadow Vampire go on a rampage. This is a new one for me, and it could turn deadly any second.

The one thing I can guarantee, Atmoro is not looking to cure cancer or help the homeless. Shadow Vampires *turned* by the Shadow Council are trained from creation to be hunters. Vampires are not the only inhabitants of the Shadow World, but they are trained with a single purpose—protect the Shadow World like the knights of medieval times.

Shadow Vampires have incredible strength, and all their senses are enhanced tenfold. They have eagle-eye vision and can outrun most modern sports cars. Their bones are normal and can break just like humans; however, they heal very quickly. You could drain every drop of blood from one of these elite vampires, but it wouldn't die. Its body would simply be immobile, and unless it was burnt to ashes, the vampire will be as good as new once

19

blood begins to flow through its veins. The only real weakness Shadow Vampires have is the Light World's sun. All vampires are sensitive to sunlight and can only tolerate direct sun rays for a very short time. It doesn't burn them to a crisp like it's told in stories; it makes them incredibly weak by draining their energy. Although, it doesn't take long for them to recover once they are out of the sunlight.

What does all this mean? Let's just say vampires created in the Shadow World are very hard to kill permanently.

The main task of a Shadow Vampire is to hunt down anyone who jumps from the Shadow World into the Light World without permission from the Shadow Council. They hunt down the jumpers and bring them back, dead or alive. Basically, they are highly skilled bounty hunters without any rules.

The vampires that inspired most horror stories were once mortal humans from the Light World who had been turned by a Shadow Vampire. These vampires are simply clones of the original and don't have the same control over their thirst as Shadow Vampires have. These vampires have nearly as much strength and the enhanced senses of Shadow Vampires, but they lack the centuries of skilled training that make Shadow Vampires the most dangerous predators to have ever walked the Earth.

Most scary stories told around campfires or to children to keep them out of the woods at night are true. Yes, they've been elaborated upon over time, but their origins are still very true. Vampires, werewolves, warlocks, goblins, and demons do exist. Yes, there are monsters in this world.

I hung around the stage for Breaking Benjamin for two more songs. I left after *Give Me a Sign,* which I took as my sign to get moving and find my soon-to-be accomplice.

I couldn't have asked for a better night for a summer concert. The sun had by then fully set, and a slight breeze was blowing off the lake. Unfortunately, one couldn't see many stars due to the bright Milwaukee city lights.

I checked the festival program for the list of bands playing tonight. My finger ran down the list, stopping on Mandi Perkins's new band, Of Verona. They were scheduled to headline at ten o'clock after Pop Evil—that's where I'll find my vampire-slaying sidekick.

I grabbed a gyro on my way across the festival grounds. Summerfest was especially packed that night. I contemplated catching the sky-ride that runs on cables high above the crowds from one end of the seventy-five-acre festival to the other, so I could avoid some of the madness, but I'm only going halfway, and someone would surely notice a man floating down from the sky ride.

Numerous street performers were scattered across the festival performing magic tricks or juggling acts for tips. I stopped at a large crowd circled around one of the performers. At the center was a young man getting ready to juggle several fuel-soaked torches that he had just set on fire. He had an old-school, unique look, with tattered dark suit pants, a bright white dress shirt with suspenders, and a derby hat. The crowd built with anticipation as the juggler prepared for his act.

The juggler tilted his head back and easily balanced one flaming torch on his chin and one in each hand stretched far out to his sides. His head tilted forward, and as the torch began to fall, he immediately tossed the other two in the air into a full-blown cascade of flaming torches.

The crowd cheered loudly with excitement.

The juggler's pace increased every few cycles. Several times, he sent one torch flying behind his back or tossed another high out of sequence to make the crowd "ooh" and "awe". He stopped only for a second to grab a fourth torch and began his act all over again. Each time, his juggling seemed to get faster and the torches higher. He started tossing two in the air at a time, holding two and tossing them while catching another two. Amazing.

The crowed kept applauding throughout the act. The "oohs" and "awes" seemed to energize the juggler. For the grand finale, he walked over to a large plastic ball positioned near the edge of the circle. He tossed one of the four torches into a waiting bucket of water and hopped up onto the ball. He effortlessly controlled the movement of the ball with his feet, circling the crowd once, all the while juggling the three flamed torches. He finished with a back flip off the ball to a huge uproar from the crowd.

The crowd cheered as the juggler walked around the circle collecting tips with his tattered hat held out. The whole act was stunning to watch. I wondered if he was from the Shadow World. I wasn't sure how a fire juggling act could aid my vampire slaying plan, though I knew where to find one if needed.

I moved on before the rest of the crowd could clutter the festival walkway once again.

Pop Evil had just started their encore song *Monster You Made Me*. Mandi Perkins was coming up next, and my soon-to-be accomplice was somewhere in the crowd. She's never missed a Summerfest festival, and Mandi Perkins was one of her favorite artists. I knew she was there—I could feel her presence.

I scanned the crowd standing next to the massive stage. The band was halfway through the song when someone yelled in my ear.

"WHAT BRINGS AN FBI AGENT TO THE WORLD'S LARGEST MUSIC FESTIVAL?"

I have to admit, I jumped a little when I heard Kasiah's voice, and my astonishment prevented me from thinking of a better response than what came out of my mouth.

"I heard the food here is worth the drive."

Kasiah moved forward to stand next to me. She had traded-in her stock detective attire for blue jeans, a white tank top, and a slim brown leather jacket for the night breeze. Her hair was let down, and her perfume filled my nostrils. I still couldn't quite place the sweet scent. I noticed the holster making a slight bulge at her right hip.

"Did those fake credentials get you free admission?" Kasiah asked with a smirk.

It's not every day that someone catches me off guard. I quickly sorted through my mental spell book for something to get me the hell out of there before my wrists could be clasped in cuffs. There were far too many people there to pull off any wizardry. We needed to move away from the stage.

As Pop Evil finished their set, the crowd started chanting, "*One—more—song... One—more—song!*" The roadies poured out onto the stage for set change, and the lights turned bright white. The crowd realized the band wasn't coming back out, and the chant switched to *"Mandi—Perkins… Mandi—Perkins… Mandi—Perkins!"*

"I'm sorry! I can't hear you!" I yelled back, pointing to my ear. I motioned for Kasiah to follow me.

We weaved our way around through the chanting crowd to the corner of a large merchandise tent that blocked most of the sound.

"I'm surprised to see you here," I said.

"I bet you are," she replied sarcastically. "I want to know what you're doing here."

"To see Mandi Perkins," I said jokingly, thumbing toward the stage.

"Mandi Perkins? Did you want to show her your fake badge as well?"

"Excuse me?" I asked, knowing what she meant.

"Agent Wesley, that fake badge wouldn't fool a five-year-old. Now, tell me what your involvement is with this case, or I'm taking you back to Madison in cuffs—real ones."

I accidently laughed a little. Kasiah squinted her eyes and opened her jacket enough to place her hand on her pistol. I was pretty sure she had used it before and was fully prepared to do it again.

"Milwaukee is out of your jurisdiction," I reminded Kasiah.

"There are a hundred Milwaukee officers working this festival," Kasiah said without taking her eyes off me. "It would only take one call from me to lock this place down. I'm asking one last time: what's your involvement with this case, and why are you impersonating a federal agent?"

The energy around me began to intensify. I could sense help had arrived.

"That's it," Kasiah said, grabbing my arm. "You're coming with me."

Then, in a flash from behind Kasiah, a woman's arm swung over her shoulder. From the opposite side, a small blade pressed against Kasiah's throat.

"Give me one good reason why I shouldn't spill your blood all over this festival and smile while doing it," the woman said, pressing the knife harder against Kasiah's skin. "Oh and take your hand off that gun before you shoot yourself in the foot."

Kasiah held her place and remained calm, this clearly wasn't the first time she'd been in a situation like this.

"Do you really think this is the best way to introduce yourself," I asked the knife-wielding maniac.

"You can thank me later when you're not spending the night in jail," she spat back.

I shook my head. This was going from bad to worse.

"Just let her go, so we can have a proper introduction," I said, realizing it was a poor attempt to pacify the situation.

"Oh yeah, so this little rent-a-cop can shoot us both?"

"You're going to be calm and not shoot us, right Kasiah?" I raised my hands slightly, as if I was calming a child.

Kasiah bobbed her head up and down.

"OK, let's put the knife away before Kasiah's blood ends up outside her body."

"You're going to need to do better than that, Erone," she said, tightening her grip on Kasiah.

"Listen," I said, still trying to calm her down. "People have been killed. They've been drained of blood. Kasiah's a local detective who's helping with the case. They're close… *real close*… to catching the killer. We need your help."

My pleading seemed to be working. The knife was slowly removed from Kasiah's throat, and she released her death grip.

Kasiah spun around quickly and took a few hasty steps back. Her right hand dashed to her holstered gun. She didn't draw the weapon because of the crowd, but she was all too willing to do so.

"What the hell is going on here?" demanded Kasiah.

"Feisty, isn't she, Erone?" the other woman said, her lips curling into a smirk.

Kasiah didn't relax or remove her hand from her weapon.

"Kasiah, meet my twin sister, Aerona."

FIVE

Kasiah pulled out her phone from her pocket and began dialing, keeping one hand on the butt of her gun.

"Um, no calls, sweetie," Aerona snapped.

"You," Kasiah retorted, removing her hand from her gun to point at Aerona. "Don't move."

Aerona crossed her arms and ignored Kasiah. "Erone," she said, "control your little pet before I do."

My twin sister is tall and thin like me and has long, dark hair and sharp, threatening sienna eyes, which she often used as a weapon to control the opposite sex. As usual, she had on an inappropriate tight black T-shirt meant to attract attention. The shirt's white letters read "Who Needs Tits… When You Have An Ass Like this." Aerona dresses like a harmless twenty-something rocker chic, but beware, she's capable of beating the hell out of a dozen marines without breaking a sweat. She's also lethally trained in virtually every known form or fighting technique, and her knowledge of weapons is extensive—courtesy her Shadow Vampire ex-boyfriend. Her sarcasm toward Kasiah was just one of the many complicated layers of the warlock known as Aerona.

"Just give me a minute. I need to get my partner over here," Kasiah offered, waiting for Damien to answer her call, "and we can work this out."

"Tall guy with shaved head?" Aerona asked.

"Yes," Kasiah answered uncomfortably. "How did you—"

"He's not going to be answering his phone anytime soon," Aerona said, cutting her off and giggling. Only Aerona would do so at a time like this.

Kasiah's hand flew back to her holster only to find it empty.

"Looking for something?" Aerona joked.

I was growing impatient with my sister; she knew better than to use magic around humans. "OK! Enough games!" I shouted. "Aerona, what did you do to Damien?"

"He's fine," Aerona said, waving off any concern. "Well, he will be fine."

My sister and I have a bond. It's difficult to explain it, but we can feel each other's presence and emotions, which was not always a gift we wished we shared.

"I felt your presence here at the festival," Aerona explained, "and wanted to surprise you before you could surprise me. So I made my way over to the side of the stage behind the beer tent, and that's when I noticed you walking up and scanning the crowd. Little miss trigger-happy over here snuck in behind you. She was totally focused on you." Aerona flashed Kasiah a smile. "Way to blend in," she mocked.

"Hey!" Kasiah shouted at me, clearly not amused by Aerona's observation. "You've been using a fake name, have forged FBI credentials, and have a knife-wielding maniac for a sister! For all I know, you two are the killers! If I don't see my partner in the next twenty seconds—"

"Hush," Aerona interjected, raising her hand and forcibly shutting Kasiah's mouth with her mind. "As I was saying, I also noticed she wasn't alone. I saw her partner back her position up by settling in near the bathrooms."

Aerona has the ability to perceive the world in slow motion. She could manipulate her perception of reality without adjusting real-time. She's not a time manipulator in the sense that she could stop time for everyone, but she does have the ability to increase the speed of her mind and movements, making everyone else appear slower to her. This ability gave Aerona a unique advantage; she saw Kasiah and Damien's subtle movements out of time from the rest of the crowd. Her rare skill could be rather useful in a fight, since she could practically predict her opponent's moves by speeding up her perception of time and essentially slowing down their actions.

Although we both have amplified hearing, Aerona could probably hear Kasiah and Damien's conversations on their phones since she was focused on them and I was not. I had no idea they were near me. Their conversation blended in with the rest of the crowd.

"WHERE. IS. DAMIEN." Kasiah demanded, blending aggression with her Midwestern accent, which I found increasingly and curiously attractive.

"Calm down," Aerona reassured her, "He's passed out in a restroom stall nearby. He'll be fine… well, besides a slight headache."

Kasiah's anger flared up. "You little bitch!" she yelled.

"Let's move this cat fight somewhere else," I suggested, looking around to see if anyone else had noticed us.

"I'll move when I have my gun," Kasiah said sternly, "and answers."

"You're right" I said, trying to calm Kasiah, "I'm not who I say I am, but you need to trust me."

"Trust is earned, not demanded," she spat back, glaring at me. "My gun. NOW!"

I pointed to Kasiah's holster. "Look," I said, "Your gun is at your side, and you can use it later if you don't like what we have to say."

Aerona and I started walking toward an exit gate. We must have sparked Kasiah's curiosity; she fell in step behind us as we walked away.

"So, we're going to ditch her and go have a beer, right?" Aerona asked, only half whispering so Kasiah could still hear her.

I only had to say one word: "Atmoro."

Aerona understood. Her mood changed from playful and happy to aggressive and alert. Her eyes moved back and forth, scanning the faces of everyone around us. She used her gift to slow the world around her, or rather, she sped herself up. I already felt more comfortable having her by my side.

We made our way back to my rental car. Kasiah refused to get in unless Aerona and I sat up front. She finally gave in and sat in the back with my car keys in her hand.

"Who are you two?" Kasiah asked. "I don't think I have to tell you that impersonating a federal agent is a felony, even if you use a poorly forged FBI badge."

"You have a fake FBI badge?" Aerona asked excitedly. "Sweet! Can you get me one?"

"Yes," I said in a low and embarrassed voice, "but apparently my forgery skills are a little lacking lately."

"I'm Erone," I said, turning to the back seat, "and this is my twin sister, Aerona. I don't work with the FBI, but I have more interest in solving this case than they do. You and the FBI don't understand the destruction this killer is capable of. By the way, how did you find me?"

Kasiah gazed at me for a moment before answering. I wondered if her response was honest.

"You never showed up to follow us back to the morgue," she answered. "So, we called all three rental car services at the airport until we found the one you used—or Mike Wesley used—and requested your car's GPS tracking information. We were only ten minutes behind you all the way to Milwaukee."

Out of the corner of her eye, Aerona gave me a disapproving look for my carelessness for being followed. I made a mental note to disable the GPS tracker on any future rental cars.

"You need to tell me why you're impersonating a federal agent," Kasiah demanded for a second time.

I looked at Aerona. "We have to tell her something," I said, wondering what that something would be, "or she's not going to help us. We need some inside help on this one."

"This is your decision, little brother," she warned. "The weight is on your shoulders."

I have always hated it when Aerona called me her little brother. She had used our age difference against me a thousand times over the last hundred years, and she still finds it amusing. Yes, Aerona was born a whole two minutes before me, which only makes her older— and more annoying.

"You know what you'll have to do when we're done…" Aerona said, turning her face away.

I knew what she meant. If I chose to give Kasiah any information about us or the Shadow World, I would have to erase her memory. The process wouldn't be pleasant for her, and I can't simply poke around in Kasiah's brain and remove specific memories; I would have to remove her entire memory. She wouldn't even remember her own name. When people wake up with amnesia, it's usually because their memory has been erased by someone like us.

"I'm aware of the consequences," I said hesitantly. "Kasiah, I know who is responsible for the homicides. This isn't someone you or the FBI are capable of stopping. Whatever he's after—whatever he wants—he's going to get it, and he's not going to let anything get in his way."

"More lies," Kasiah said, shaking her head. "How did you make me give you that video?"

I ignored Kasiah's second question and instead, took a few minutes to bring Aerona up to speed with the similarity of the victims' names, the crime scene in Madison, the surveillance video, the nodule, and the display set to open at the University of Wisconsin.

Kasiah's phone started vibrating in her pocket. "Here's Damien," she said, answering the call. "Yes, I know… No, don't worry about that right now. I'm with them. Yes, them! No, everything's fine. I'm in Wesley's car. OK. See you in ten."

"I need to know what you know, Erone," Kasiah said, putting her phone away, "or I'm taking you back to Madison where we can finish this conversation with the real Feds."

Aerona let out a quick *hah* and smiled.

"This is a two-way street," I said to Kasiah. "If we're sharing information, then I need to know what you have. Once you're involved, this isn't something you can simply walk away from."

Aerona shook her head. She knew as well as I did that Kasiah and Damien could never take us back to Madison. I didn't want to admit it, but we needed help, and Kasiah drew the short straw—whether she knew that or not.

I turned to Kasiah and looked right in her eyes. "The killer's name is Atmoro," I stated, "and he's a vampire."

SIX

"A vampire?" Kasiah questioned, raising her brow.

Kasiah's tone implied I was joking, and she didn't look very amused. Her accent thickened as her anger and frustration intensified.

"You two need to start getting real serious," Kasiah warned, "or you can spend the rest of your lives sharing a cell with other people twice as crazy as you two put together."

"This isn't a conversation we should be having in the parking lot of a rock concert," I said, turning to Aerona. "Do you have a hotel room?"

"Yes," Aerona replied, "a suite at The Hampton. It's not far."

"Kasiah," I said, spotting Damien stop a few cars away, "you and Damien should follow us to Aerona's hotel, so we can discuss this."

Keeping my car keys, Kasiah got out of the back seat and spoke to Damien. He shook his head several times, but Kasiah was in charge. She returned to the back seat and handed me the keys.

"Don't try anything," she said. "Damien will be right behind us."

I started the car and backed out of the spot. Damien's vehicle fell in behind us as we headed out of the parking lot. Kasiah kept her hand on her gun for the entire ten-minute ride to the hotel.

I introduced Aerona and Damien as we waited for the elevator to reach Aerona's suite on the top floor; he wasn't very excited to have been knocked out by a girl.

"Vampire?" Kasiah asked the moment we shut the suite's door.

"You need to have an open mind," I said, before turning to Damien. "Both of you."

"Vampires?" Kasiah asked again. "As in suck-your-blood vampires?"

Damien spoke for the first time: "How is it that you know about this and we don't?" he asked. "You're telling me that I'm in some cheap horror movie, and this is some big secret that only you two know about?"

"We're very good at keeping secrets," Aerona smiled, "and covering our tracks. Oh, and by the way, the first rule about vampires is don't believe anything you see in the movies."

"Let's all sit down," I suggested, seating myself at the large round table at the center of the suite. "We don't have time to debate the fact that someone is murdering innocent people by draining their blood, and now it appears that the same someone is stealing precious stones. We may never have another chance at stopping him if we waste time debating his existence."

"Are you guessing this is a vampire, or do you know it is?" Kasiah asked, pulling out a chair for herself.

"I know who I saw on that security footage," I said, still trying to make myself believe the truth. "What I don't know is what this particular vampire is trying to accomplish. His kind has spent a lifetime ensuring their existence remains a secret, and considering they've been alive for centuries, I'd say they've done a hell of a job. Your world has more evidence to prove a Sasquatch exists than vampires."

As Kasiah lowered her guard and sat at the table, I couldn't tell if she was listening or getting ready to call the cavalry. Damien stood near the suite's door; it was probably a technique taken directly out of the interrogation handbook—keep yourself between the door and the suspect.

"The nodule he stole," I continued, "is *not* from this world. Atmoro is *not* from this world."

"What do you mean *this* world?" Kasiah asked, leaning closer.

I caught Aerona's eyes, and she gave me a nod to continue. "Aerona and I are not from this world either," I said, stopping to let Kasiah comprehend what I had just told her.

"Not from this world?" Kasiah and Damien asked at the same time.

"This is going to take all night if I have to keep repeating myself," I said, looking at Aerona. "We don't have time for this. Show them."

There's only one thing Aerona loves more than music: magic. She's among the only warlocks I know with more spells memorized than me.

Aerona's lips curled into a wide smile as she pushed her chair back and stood up. She narrowed her eyes.

Warlocks don't have to incant aloud; we can simply think of the spell to trigger it. The more complex spells require greater focus and energy, and large spells can even drain us completely, leaving us vulnerable until we can regain our energy.

Aerona extended her hand out flat, as if she was handing Kasiah an invisible gift with her empty palm. A tiny flame ignited above the center of her hand, slowly growing into a small fireball. Aerona placed her other hand over the flame and squeezed water from thin air, making it rain and dousing the flame.

"I've seen the same act in Vegas," Kasiah said sarcastically.

If I've learned anything about my sister, it's not to piss her off. Aerona wasn't amused by Kasiah's comment, and Damien was about to pay the price.

"Sorry, Damien" she said, closing her eyes.

In a flash, Damien was gone. He was replaced by a twelve-inch stone statue that was an exact replica of Damien with the same confused look on its tiny, stone face.

Kasiah's chair crashed backwards as she jumped up from the table.

Aerona stretched her arm out toward Kasiah, pinching two fingers together to shut Kasiah's mouth—literally. Kasiah floated off the floor, her legs dangling as if she was being hoisted by an invisible cable harness. The balcony door burst open, and a cool breeze rushed in. Kasiah was helpless as Aerona spun her in a full circle toward the balcony.

"That's enough," I said, rising my hand to bring her back.

"But I was just warming up," Aerona said, frowning.

"Put her down," I said, "and wake Damien up now!"

Aerona lowered Kasiah within a few inches above the floor, and without warning, she dropped her. Kasiah was barely able to keep her balance. Aerona then walked over and gave Damien's tiny statue a quick kiss on its stone cheek, a life-sized Damien instantly reappeared.

"What the hell was that!" he yelled. "I could see and hear what was going on, but couldn't say or do anything!"

"Did you see that in Vegas?" Aerona smiled as she flicked her hair back as though she had just finished a show. "You may want to sit down. The immobilization spell can sometimes leave you a little disoriented."

"Let me explain," I began. "This is a lot to take in at once. If you both will open your mind to the impossible, then maybe we can stop Atmoro together from hurting anyone else."

Kasiah and Damien finally decided to listen to what we had to say, and we spent the next two hours talking about the Shadow World. Aerona and I gave them the short version with just enough information to get them on board. We explained how we are both warlocks—wizards to them—and have been hiding for nearly a century.

We also discussed the Light World. Kasiah and Damien had the same disbeliefs about angels, elves, and fairies as they had about vampires, werewolves, demons, and goblins. I reassured them that the quite impossible is possible. Aerona's little display was a big help there.

The main topic of conversation was Shadow Vampires.

"Shadow Vampires," I explained, "are normal Shadows created by the Shadow Council in the Shadow World. They're trained to be protectors of our kind. They're basically an elite police force. They're also hunters of Shadows that jump illegally to the Light World."

"So, the vampires that we see in movies and hear stories about aren't real vampires?" Damien asked.

"That's mostly true," I answered. "The origin of most vampire stories begin with a vampire that was turned in this world. The key difference between Shadow Vampires and other vampires is that the vampires here are humans from the Light World that have been transformed by a Shadow Vampire. These vampires only have a fraction of the Shadow Vampire's incredible strength and enhanced senses, but they're still a deadly weapon when trained properly."

Midnight came and passed by the time Kasiah believed our story and shared a few secrets of her own. It turned out she and Damien were not part of the Madison White Collar Crime Unit; they were part of an FBI team that received a tip informing them that my alias was visiting each crime scene.

Kasiah's FBI tip comment caught me off guard. *Who was tracking me and why?* I wondered. There was no time for more complicated twists to this case, so I focused on the task at hand—stopping Atmoro.

According to Kasiah, the American Geological Society scheduled a black-tie dinner on Friday to unveil their display at the University. The guest list was packed with college professors, city officials, and even the Mayor of Madison.

We decided Atmoro wouldn't try to retrieve the other half of the nodule until after the dinner party; that's when the display items will be transported from the convention center to the actual display location, where the FBI would concentrate their security efforts.

Kasiah and Damien were already in touch with their team back in Madison. We fed them fabricated information that Damien received an online tip about someone in a chat room claiming to be the serial killer. Tara set up a fake chat room and conversation to coincide with our story. She sent us the transcript along with several fake computer IP addresses that would help verify the tip. Then, all the fabricated information was forwarded to Kasiah's team in Madison.

We wrapped up the tactical planning by 2:00 a.m. The display pieces would be transported from the convention center to the university in a secured armored truck followed by a full police escort along one of two preplanned routes. Several unmarked chase cars would drive in unison on parallel side streets. The actual route would not be chosen until the transport leaves the convention center. A helicopter, equipped with an infrared camera, was scheduled to fly over the motorcade the entire way to the display site. The only other detail was Kasiah adding us to the guest list, so we could identify Atmoro if he showed up.

Since we were finally able to convince Kasiah and Damien we were not the killers, they headed back to Madison to assist their team with the final preparation. We were to meet them Friday evening before the dinner party.

Now, to catch a vampire.

SEVEN

Jake crouched next to the TV in the mansion-sized home Atmoro had *borrowed* for their weekend in Madison. Jake was connecting the camera to show his master the latest surveillance footage. He sensed Atmoro standing over his shoulder, expressionless as usual. Jake purposely took a few extra minutes hooking up the camera just to make Atmoro wait. The other four vampires in the room were becoming impatient.

Who does Atmoro think he is? Jake thought to himself, fantasizing what it would be like to watch Atmoro pleading for his life, begging Jake to stop inflicting pain. The only thing stopping Jake was that he needed Atmoro to lead him to the hidden gateway into the Shadow World, but after that...

The screen changed from blue to black as the video started. Two women and a man were walking quickly through a filled parking lot. Atmoro recognized the man and one of the women as the same FBI agents from Jake's previous video. His plan was working like clockwork. Two days prior, he had Jake make an anonymous phone call to the FBI about a man in a bar who was bragging about a serial killer case, and this man was using his fake FBI credentials to visit all the crime scenes.

By that point, Atmoro knew the FBI was hungry for any leads or information. They took the bait—hook, line, and sinker.

A small, blinking low-battery icon flashed in the upper corner of the screen. Atmoro glared at Jake in disapproval as the video continued with several minutes of nothing but silence as the agents were seen arguing inside their car.

The TV screen changed back to blue as the video ended.

"The battery died," Jake said quietly. "Nothing exciting happened. Her partner showed up, they made some sort of agreement, and then they all left together."

"Did you follow them?" Atmoro asked. "Or did your car run out of gas like the battery?"

"Of course I followed them!" Jake snapped. "They went to a hotel about ten minutes away."

"We have enough information to move forward," Atmoro declared, ignoring Jake's attitude. "Just as planned, the FBI has enlisted the help of a warlock. He will help us find the stone."

Atmoro turned to leave the room.

"This is pointless!" Jake shouted to Atmoro as he walked away. His fuse was getting shorter by the minute. "I can retrieve that worthless rock without help from anyone in this world, or yours!"

Atmoro stopped in the doorway. "You are young and foolish," Atmoro said calmly, not turning to meet Jake's glaring eyes. "You know nothing about vampires or my world. Warlocks are more powerful than you could imagine. They are the only creatures that vampires fear. A skilled warlock can steal the air from your lungs without uttering a single word. Yes, a vampire does not need to breathe to stay alive, but it's very painful to have your lungs empty and burning for air. That is just one of many spells they can cast in seconds before your tiny mind can even comprehend what had happened."

"YOU ARE THE FOOLISH ONE!" Jake shouted, struggling to keep his anger under control. It was time for Jake to show Atmoro who was in charge. "You are the one with your back turned to the strongest vampire in the room. Maybe it's time we elected a new leader." Anger filled Jake's veins. "ONE FROM THIS WORLD!"

Jake never saw Atmoro move from the doorway, and it all happened in an instant. Jake was airborne and tumbling straight for the far wall. The impact broke his shoulder.

Atmoro seized Jake by his throat and lifted him up several inches off the ground, slamming him against the damaged wall. Atmoro was fuming inside, but he remained calm and in control; he still needed Jake.

"Shall I remind you who is in charge?" Atmoro asked, squeezing Jake's neck.

"No." Jake whispered, trying to pry his hands from his neck.

"If you do not stop questioning me," Atmoro warned, knowing he could slaughter every vampire in the room, "you will find out just how easy it is to slay a vampire."

Jake gasped for breath as Atmoro released his grip. It would take time for his wounds to heal fully.

"That also goes for the rest of you," Atmoro said, addressing the other vampires in the room. "I created you, and I can destroy you—all of you."

No one else attempted to stop Atmoro as he left the room.

Finally, after decades of searching, Atmoro was closer than he had ever been to possessing the stone with the power to unlock the Forgotten Shadow City, which would allow him to release his long-lost love from within prison walls.

Ten years back, Atmoro had uncovered an ancient scroll with writings of a secret gateway to the Forgotten Shadow City; a gateway that was built by the Shadow Council out of fear that someday one of the council members may find themselves trapped within the walls of the inescapable prison. The key to the secret gate was encrypted in the riddle *The Blood of a Stone will release them alone.* Atmoro had spent every day of the last ten years searching for a stone that bleeds.

Atmoro's quest for the stone gained momentum when he caught an elf tracking him and his trail of dead bodies. The elf refused to give up the name of his master, but he did share a valuable piece of information just before Atmoro tasted the elf's blood; the word 'stone' was symbolic. It referred to a fallen angel created when an angel breaks a law in the Light World, then that angel is cast down to Earth to live as a mortal. According to the elf, stones were bigger myths than vampires.

The nodule was not the stone referred to in the ancient scroll, but Atmoro was betting the warlock would lead him to the blood of a fallen angel, so he could save his love, Christine. Atmoro let his mind slip back to a time that felt as if it was yesterday—a time when he was next in succession to lead the Shadow Council and write the Shadow laws, not just enforce them.

Atmoro had not always been a heartless killer. He was the last of his bloodline and one of the most naturally skilled Shadow Vampires ever known. In late eighteenth century, he was sent to the Light World to hunt a jumper: a female Shadow Vampire, Christine, who had crossed over to the Light World illegally. She was among the most feared Shadow Vampires of her time, and she wasn't known for her mercy. If a jumper was being hunted by Christine, they were as good as dead. Although, dead isn't *dead* in the Shadow World. If ever unfortunate enough to be caught by a Shadow Vampire, a jumper receives one of two fates: the jumper either has their head and limbs severed and burned (real dead), or they spend eternity imprisoned in the inescapable Forgotten Shadow City (as good as dead). The jumper's fate basically depended on the Shadow Vampire's mood and the trouble the jumper had caused. The council simply wanted their secret world to remain a secret.

No one knows why Christine had jumped. The Shadow Council summoned her for a hunting party to track several werewolves that had jumped the previous day. When she didn't respond to the order, they found her home deserted—she had vanished.

Crossing over to the Light World was difficult but not impossible. There are only two crossings to the Light World, and both are heavily guarded by werewolves. Although, where there's a will, there's always a way; and Christine found a way by simply pretending to be summoned for a hunt, which automatically granted her access to cross into the Light World. The werewolf guards never even questioned her. It wasn't every day that a Shadow Vampire jumped to the Light World—Christine was the first.

Atmoro was chosen to hunt down Christine. He was given strict instructions not to harm her; the Shadow Council wanted her back alive to use as an example. Basically, if a Shadow jumped, they made the choice to be hunted. The Shadow Council spent many lifetimes protecting the Shadow World's existence, and anyone who compromised their secret world was labeled an enemy and was eliminated.

It took Atmoro nearly two months to track down Christine. He caught up with her in Yellowstone National Park, which had only been named a year before. There were several unusual animal attacks within the new park and all indicated vampire attacks.

The day before Atmoro arrived at Yellowstone, a mountain lion was found dead with two tiny puncture wounds in its neck. Atmoro impersonated a forest ranger to gain access to the dead animal. After inspecting the wounds and considering the speed, power, and agility it would take to bring down a mountain lion in its own environment, and the nature of the wounds, he knew it was the work of a skilled vampire—Christine.

The lion was killed near what is now known as Heart Lake. Atmoro traveled by foot through the mountains to the lake, spending two nights tracking Christine. On the third evening, he was deep in the mountains when he heard a mountain lion fast on the move. It was clearly running away from something. All the other animals in the forest were dead silent—they were hiding.

The night sky was illuminated by a magnificent moon surrounded by millions of bright stars. The mountain lion raced through the forest, changing its course several times. Atmoro shifted his position from side to side until he was sure to be on collision course with the speeding cat; he could feel the lion's footsteps on the forest floor.

The mountain lion came into view and leapt up to a towering red oak. Sinking its claws into the thick bark, it climbed hard and fast. Atmoro felt a second set of vibrations in the ground, softer and quicker than the lion's. The steps slowed down as they neared, probably sensing that the mountain lion had changed course or was now in the trees. Atmoro promptly realigned himself with the new steps as they changed course once, then twice—he was hunting the hunter. When the steps were only twenty feet away, Atmoro stepped out from behind a tree, stopping Christine dead in her tracks. She knew exactly who he was and why he was in the Light World. She cursed at herself for letting him surprise her, but she was hungry; her senses had been focused on the mountain lion.

Like Christine, Atmoro was frozen in place, stunned by her incredibly beauty. Shadow Vampires were well equipped with not only strength and speed but also beauty that can hardly be described by words. Atmoro had never seen Christine face to face, only in photos. Her long, blonde hair was rarely seen on vampires. She was every inch as tall as Atmoro, and her legs were strong and fast enough to catch a mountain lion in the forest. Atmoro noticed her feet were bare to grant her more speed. Her blue eyes were wide, desperately searching for a way out.

"You will have to kill me," Christine said, surprisingly still as calm as any other Shadow Vampire. "I'm not going back."

Atmoro was equally calm. "I have instructions not to harm you unless necessary," he said, trying to reassure her safety. "The Council wants you alive. Do you know why?"

"The *Council* has no authority here," she said, emphasizing the word 'council' with venom on her tongue.

"You know who I am and why I'm here," Atmoro said. "You know you're going back, one way or another."

Christine spoke from her heart, knowing it could have been her last request. "I love the Shadow World," she explained. "It's a beautiful and magical place. It's my home, but I cannot keep taking orders from a corrupt council. Three months back, the council's newest member, Malance, imprisoned my father in the Forgotten Shadow City for speaking against him. Malance did this so his brother could have a seat on the council next to him. They labeled my father a traitor. For what? So they could continue smuggling humans into the Shadow World for their own sick pleasures. They've developed a taste for the forbidden fruit—the blood of humans. And not just humans, they've been feeding on elves and fairies. There will be a war if the Light Council ever finds out their kind are being sold to the Shadow World. This breaks every line of the treaty signed with the angels."

Atmoro digested what he had just been told. He had never perceived any of this with his own eyes, and he was about to become a council member himself. Becoming a member of the Shadow Council was something he had desired his entire life. Although, sacrificing the lives of innocent humans and other creatures of the Light World for his own pleasure was not something he was willing to do.

Atmoro was caught between a rock and a hard place. If he questioned the Shadow Council about Christine's story, there was a chance he would be locked away in the Forgotten Shadow City as a traitor for eternity. If he did nothing, he'll be part of a corrupt council that's on its way to causing a war that would bring about the end of both worlds.

"I'm free here," Christine said with tears in her eyes. "Free to find a way to save my father."

The two Shadow Vampires stared at each other for what seemed like an eternity.

Atmoro had never seen a Shadow Vampire cry.

The thought of running entered Christine's mind.

Atmoro broke the silence. "You would have to disappear," he said. "Forever. You can never return to the Shadow World. I would pay with my own life if they ever found you alive after I inform them of your death. You must accept that your father is gone. You know there is no escape from the Forgotten Shadow City."

"But you have orders to bring me back alive," Christine debated, brushing the hair away from her eyes. "Why have they requested this?"

Atmoro's heart-beat increased along with Christine's. "I do not know the answer to that question," he admitted. "The Council must want to know why a Shadow Vampire jumped to the Light World. Although, from what you've told me, it's clear they already know the answer. They'll lock you away in the Forgotten Shadow City and forget about you."

"Life here is difficult," Christine said softly. "I miss my home. I don't want to feed on humans to survive, but the forest animals only provide enough energy to last a day in this sunlight. I can never fight the council and free my father without my full strength. I need human blood."

"I will return to the Shadow World with news of your death," Atmoro said, considering his own fate. "Your father is gone. You must live your life. It's what any father would want for his beautiful daughter."

The word 'beautiful' left Atmoro's lips before he could stop it.

Christine leaned forward and kissed his lips gently. Atmoro returned the kiss. Atmoro had never been in love; nor did he believe in love at first sight. Christine was beyond beautiful. He felt a connection to her.

They spent the next two weeks falling in love—a feeling neither of them had ever felt. Christine, as hard as it was, accepted the fact that she would never see her father again. Their time together passed quickly, and it wasn't long before Atmoro had to return to the Shadow World and inform the council of Christine's "death." The council was skeptical of Atmoro's story, but after severe interrogation, they finally accepted that Christine was gone and assigned Atmoro his next hunt.

As promised, Atmoro would visit Christine whenever he was sent on hunts for jumpers. They set up a home in a small town along the coast of California, pretending to be a young married couple. Atmoro claimed to be a businessman from the big city, which explained his extensive traveling. To keep her strength up, Christine picked up a new hobby: preying on criminals in nearby towns. She didn't feel bad feeding on these humans since they were evil. Their blood gave her the strength she needed.

It wasn't long before Atmoro and Christine made a remarkable discovery—Shadow Vampires had the ability to conceive children in the Light World.

Less than a year after meeting Atmoro, Christine gave birth to twin boys. One had a head full of dark hair, and the other was blonde like Christine. The two bright-eyed smiling newborns grew at an alarming rate, requiring more blood than Christine's body could afford to give. Atmoro returned often with deer blood to feed their sons, but this diet only satisfied them for a short time. The twins would soon need to learn to hunt on their own.

Atmoro made quick work of any hunts assigned by the Shadow Council. He spent the rest of his time with his family. It was a constant struggle to keep their secret a secret, but they somehow managed to go about their way of life for the next four years as a happy, small town-family.

Life was perfect.

It's amazing how a person's life can change entirely in a single split second. Atmoro and Christine's life changed forever the day a hunting party of seven Shadow Vampires and just as many elves broke down their front door.

Atmoro and Christine were gagged and their hands were bound by specially designed cuffs forged in the Shadow World. Two Shadow Vampires held the twins, and four others restrained Atmoro and Christine as they were injected with Daylight; an illuminated liquid that looked as though sunlight was ensnared in a syringe.

The effects of the Daylight worked quickly. Atmoro's limbs weakened, his eyes drooped, and his strength deserted him. He recognized the vampire in charge of the others—the head councilman's only son, Malance.

"Atmoro and Christine," Malance said through an evil grin with entirely too much arrogance, "you are both labeled jumpers and have been sentenced to death by the Shadow Council. Do you have anything to say in your defense?"

Atmoro's gag prevented him from defending the allegation. He looked at Christine, and without a word, they conveyed how much he loved her. She nodded her head in response.

"I'll take that as a no," Malance said smiling. "Now, let's get this party started!"

Malance directed his tone toward the vampires holding Atmoro and Christine. "Do *not* let them go!" he ordered.

Atmoro struggled with his captors, but the Daylight had weakened him to the point of exhaustion.

"Don't worry, little ones," Malance said, kneeling in front of the twins, patting the dark-haired one on the head.

The twins were much stronger than Malance had anticipated. After all, no one had ever seen vampire children. All previous Shadow Vampires were turned as adults, not born. They simply didn't exist… until now.

The dark-haired twin wrestled his way out of his captor's grip, lunging toward Malance. The Daylight clearly didn't have the same effect on the twins.

The child landed on Malance's chest, sinking his teeth in his shoulder. Malance screamed out loud. He may not have known the twin's incredible speed, but their strength was no match for his own. He snatched the little one by the scruff of his neck and tossed him across the room. The twin was back on his feet in milliseconds, running right back at Malance. The boy lunged through the air, attacking again.

Atmoro was proud of his son and yet terrified at the same time.

The child never reached his intended target. His chest was pierced by an illuminated arrow shot by one of the elves and fell motionless at Malance's feet. A pool of blood formed on the floor.

Christine and Atmoro were out of control. The effect of the Daylight was wearing off, and the vampires had a difficult time restraining them. Malance ordered the guards to remove them from the room and dispose of the other twin.

Atmoro and Christine were separated. Atmoro was chained to the large ceiling beam in the bedroom.

Malance entered the room. "Your uncle is the last of your family that will serve on the council," Malance said as he raised a large knife blade. "Your bloodline ends here. It's a new world—a world without you." Malance tightened his grip on the knife. "The Shadow Council would be excited to know you were able to conceive children here in the Light World. It's a shame the evidence must be destroyed along with you. Your wife will have to live out her eternity within the walls of the Forgotten Shadow City knowing you could not protect her new family."

Malance let out a dark laugh as he plunged the knife into Atmoro's chest.

He was left hanging from the beam to die; never to see Christine or their sons again.

The hunting party set the house on fire. The wooden beams hissed and crackled in the flames. Smoke filled Atmoro's lungs. Using his free hand, he was able to break one side of the chain and pull the knife out of his chest.

Blood poured from the wound; luckily, the knife had missed his heart. The ceiling collapsed, trapping Atmoro. He heard his family's screams as he passed out from the blood loss.

When Atmoro's eyes opened again, he was completely covered in charred wood that was once his family's home. Crawling clear of the ashes, Atmoro lay on his back, staring at the stars, wishing he was dead. The pain in his chest was excruciating. He could barely take in a single breath of the night air. His muscles ached. He was in agonizing pain, and he needed blood to restore his energy.

The sound of voices intensified, getting closer. Atmoro tried to move, but the pain had sent his body into shock.

"There's a survivor!" a man cried out, waving to someone else. "Over here! Hurry! He's hurt!"

Atmoro motioned for the man to draw closer. He gathered as much strength as he could and plunged his fangs into the man's neck. Moments after the first drop trickled down his throat, Atmoro felt his strength increase. The man tried to yell for help, but nothing came out. Atmoro's strength had returned.

He searched the burnt down home for signs of his children, but he found nothing. The twins' small bodies must have perished in the fire without a trace. His heart ached.

Atmoro snapped back to reality. His hatred for the Shadow Council intensified along with a new found disgust for whoever helped them here in the Light World. Malance had taken Christine back to the Shadow Council as proof of Atmoro's betrayal. Atmoro had spent every waking moment since looking for a way to retrieve his wife from the Forgotten Shadow City. All he needed now were a few drops of a stone's blood; he'll be taking all of it though—just to be safe.

EIGHT

Sleep eluded me that night. I found it difficult to close my eyes and drift into unconsciousness while Atmoro was out there somewhere planning his next move. Instead of sleeping, Aerona and I reviewed the FBI's plan a few times, then outlined an escape route to get us out of Madison in a hurry in case our plan went sideways. We had no intentions of being trapped in a city with a pissed off Shadow Vampire.

The sunrise chased us as we drove back to Madison. It was a beautiful day to slay a vampire. Kasiah and her team weren't scheduled to meet us until the dinner at eight o'clock, so Aerona and I checked into a hotel to get cleaned up before the dinner party. Clothes shopping was our next stop. Neither of us had proper attire for a formal event, nor did we desire to stand out in the crowd. It took me all of twenty minutes to grab a sports jacket, some pants, shoes, and a black tie—it wasn't that easy for Aerona.

Aerona was rarely seen wearing anything other than an ordinary shirt—usually with some offensive or sarcastic text—and an expensive pair of jeans. She did, however, seem eager for that rare opportunity to shop for a dress. I was dragged into what seemed like every clothing store in Madison. I lost count of the stores, but I believe the final dress she tried on at Citrine on State Street was somewhere around the twentieth. She walked out of Citrine's dressing room with a shy smile on her face, her eyes looking down at the floor nervously. A unique tropical green blended into deep black brushstrokes down the dress. Thin black straps crisscrossed the back, and crystal beading was wrapped at the waist. The deep v-neckline could have used some extra, um, *padding* to fill it completely. She looked absolutely wonderful, but there was just one problem—she would definitely stand out.

"What do you think?" Aerona asked with a sparkle in her eyes. "How do I look?"

"Like a mirror image of Mother," I said. "It's absolutely perfect."

Aerona fought back her tears as she returned to the dressing room. Then, she bought the dress.

We spent the rest of the afternoon familiarizing ourselves with the surrounding streets. The city was alive with football fans, most wearing Wisconsin red and white for the game against Penn State this weekend. The fans were oblivious to the fact that the world's most dangerous predator was lurking in their own city.

Aerona and I eventually found our way back to the hotel before the sun set into the horizon over the west lake. Beautiful oranges and dark reds swirled together as if someone had painted the sky complete with a few sailboat silhouettes in the distance. I silently hoped the blood red sunset wasn't a sign of what was to come.

Once we had showered and changed, we made our way to the dinner party. Aerona pointed out that she hadn't seen a single police cruiser or any other signs of law enforcement on the way to the university. This either meant they were good at blending in or that they aren't taking the threat seriously—I hoped it wasn't the latter.

Kasiah and her younger sister, Hayley, met us a block from the convention center. Last night, Kasiah gave us a few brief details, so we were familiar with her sister. Hayley was a student at the University of Wisconsin, and she had just turned twenty-one in February. She switched majors from education to engineering and now environmental science; it sounded like she was working her way through the E-majors. Our story as friends was that we met while Hayley spent two semesters at NYU before transferring back home to Wisconsin and UW. Aerona and I were visiting for Summerfest and sightseeing. Hayley knew enough of her FBI sister to not ask too many questions; she was just happy to help.

49

"How are you enjoying your vacation to the Midwest?" Kasiah asked, winking.

"It's been fun," Aerona replied, imitating Kasiah's accent. "We even got to milk a real cow."

I don't think Kasiah found Aerona's accent humorous. They needed to have an old fashion cat-fight to get some aggression out.

"Nice to meet you, Hayley," I said quietly, shaking her hand. Aerona did the same, so no one else could hear that we had, in fact, just met.

"I love your dress, Aerona," Hayley said.

I half-expected a sarcastic remark from her, but Aerona surprised me by being polite. "Thank you," she said politely. "You both look beautiful."

Kasiah and her sister looked amazing; they could have been twins if not for their hair color. I hadn't quite noticed before, but Kasiah looked stunning out of her standard issue FBI jacket and pants. Her big, brown eyes sparkled in the city lights, and her dark chestnut hair, perfectly smooth and straight, was let down just past her shoulders. A maroon dress fit tight against her toned body, leaving little space to conceal her gun, which was probably the only accessory in her tiny purse.

Hayley wore a short, sleek black dress with an elegant necklace. Her skin was tan from what looked like natural sunlight. Her blonde hair, exactly the opposite of Kasiah's, was a little curly and longer, with subtle streaks of black throughout. She had the same cute Midwestern accent as Kasiah.

The girls led us through a large glass door into the convention center's main lobby. Two enormous, intricate glass chandeliers were suspended from the twenty-foot-high ceiling. One wall, made entirely of glass, overlooked the twilight-shimmering lake that bordered Madison's east side. Several staff members served trays of drinks, expertly weaving their way through the crowd.

Aerona's eyes were busy scanning every face in the lobby. I felt her emotion; she was tense, but in control. I'd know the moment she sensed anything out of the ordinary.

"I don't know about you two," Hayley said, "but I'm in need of a beverage. Preferably one with alcohol."

"Count me in," Aerona smiled. Her mood was calming down a bit. "Relax, little brother," she added. "I heard vampires don't like blood with a high alcohol content. The real fun doesn't begin until after dinner"

I shot her my best *little brother doesn't approve of you joking about vampires in front of Hayley* look as they disappeared into the crowd. I wasn't worried. Aerona was more than capable of handling herself.

Kasiah brushed away a few strands of hair from her face. "Your sister's right," she said. "Loosen up. My team has this under control. This is what we do."

I agreed with Kasiah, but far back in my mind, I knew that was exactly what heroes usually said before being slaughtered on the big screen. This was no Hollywood flick.

"I just hope you're right," I said, holding my arm out to escort her. "Maybe we should move to the main ballroom to see what all this fuss is about. Let's have a look at that nodule."

Kasiah smiled her beautiful smile as she looped her arm through mine. The scent of her perfume was tattooed in my memory. We stopped at the bar outside the ballroom.

"Drinking on the job?" I asked, joking as the bartender poured our drinks. "They should advertise that as an FBI perk."

Kasiah laughed and shook her head, using the tiny straw to twirl ice cubes around her glass. She leaned over and bumped my shoulder with hers. "It's a little known fact," she said, "that vodka helps you fight crime. It's actually Superman's secret weapon… well, that and his x-ray vision, of course."

I deny any allegations of me flirting back.

We made our way into the ballroom, where twenty or so round tables were set perfectly in an interlocked pattern with six formal plate settings in each. Along the furthest wall, a thick, velvet rope stretched out a few feet in front of several tall glass display cases, preventing anyone from actually touching the cases. The only security I noticed were two university police officers positioned at either end of the display and another standing right next to the nodule's case.

"Don't you think there should be more security in this room?" I asked.

"They're here," Kasiah reassured me. "You just can't see them. Trust me, if you could see them, then Atmoro could see them. Just relax."

Aerona and Hayley found their way to the display. They were laughing together like old friends. Aerona was very easy to get along with on most days. Just don't find your way to her bad side, or she'll turn you into a gnome. Kasiah shifted a little further away from me. I think she may have been little afraid that Aerona might lift her up to the ceiling for touching her *little brother*.

"Isn't it beautiful?" Hayley asked as we looked at the center piece of the display—the Shadow World nodule.

I exchanged a look of reminiscence with Aerona. Both our hearts sped up a few beats at the sight of the nodule; we hadn't been back to the Shadow World or seen a nodule like this in nearly a century. The nodule was in a case by itself, surrounded on three sides by heavily tinted glass that blocked enough light to trigger the inner cobalt crystals to glow. It was actually emitting and releasing photons of light. It resembled an everlasting magical stone light bulb.

I could feel how much Aerona missed our world, and I'm sure she felt my emotions as well.

More of the lobby's crowd made its way into the dining hall. Everyone eventually found their tables as the staff served appetizers. Our dinner conversation—which was surprisingly not awkward—moved from topic to topic as if we were old friends catching up. I kept my eyes and ears open for anything that felt out of place.

I learned that Kasiah and Hayley were born and raised 30 minutes south of Madison in Janesville. Kasiah majored in criminal justice at UW and came first in her class. Hayley, clearly proud of her older sister, told how Kasiah spent only two years in the Rock County Sheriff's department before graduating to the FBI. She excelled at the FBI to Special Agent in Charge faster than any other woman in the bureau's history. Also, at the age of twenty-six, she was one of the youngest female agents in the FBI's history.

Kasiah laughed and smiled at the compliments. I think Aerona gained a little bit of respect for Kasiah.

"My superhero sister," Hayley continued, "once saved a sixteen year old girl from a sociopath who was collecting young girls. The FBI tracked him down after three long months in pursuit. Kasiah and Damien were first on the scene, which was a farmhouse in the middle of practically nowhere. With their backup more than two hours out, Kasiah made the decision for Damien to hold the perimeter while she went in alone. We just ate, so I'll spare you the details of what she had found inside, but Kasiah ended up with a knife wound in her leg before shooting the maniac four times."

"Impressive," Aerona said. "The girl was OK?"

Hayley's smile faded as she continued to tell the story. "The young girl was found in a cage in the basement," she explained. "She was alive, but half-starved and raped more than once. After a thorough search of the property, they found fourteen other young girls' bodies buried in the garden area. It was tragic, but Kasiah put an end to his reign of terror."

"That's amazing," I said, impressed by Kasiah's courage. "Is there a cute scar to go along with this adventure?" My mouth moved quicker than my brain, and my face burned with embarrassment.

"Down, little brother," Aerona said, grinning. "Don't make me take out the fire hose."

Kasiah came to my rescue. "A private showing may be arranged later," she said, flashing a smile and sipping her drink. "Have your people call my people."

Some of my embarrassment faded, but I was sure Aerona felt my growing fondness for Kasiah. She gave me one of her famous Aerona eye rolls.

We were in the middle of a good laugh when the lights went off. I felt Aerona's adrenaline pumping as someone screamed out.

NINE

I heard shattering glass and instantly turned to see the display cases. The emergency lights turned on, then off, then on again. Atmoro, wearing the same full-length leather trench coat, stared back at me expressionless from in front of the nodule's shattered and empty display case. He was holding a security officer in front of him. The other officers were lay dead at the feet of two other vampires.

Kasiah stared in disbelief at how things had changed so rapidly.

Then, with one swift motion, almost too fast for me to see, Atmoro twisted the guard's neck, dropping his lifeless body to the floor. This certainly wasn't the first time he had snapped a neck.

I exchanged an uneasy look with Kasiah. "Get Hayley out of here," I said, taking charge.

Kasiah didn't move; she was frozen in her seat.

"GO!" I shouted.

Kasiah pulled Hayley through the screaming crowd toward the rear exit, away from the rush of people to the main ballroom. The Mayor's security team reacted without hesitation. They had her extracted to safety before the first minute could tick by.

I turned my attention back to Atmoro; he hadn't moved since killing the officer. The entire ballroom was in chaos, but Atmoro didn't flinch. He was perfectly calm and in control, staring right at me.

Suddenly, one of the other vampires started sprinting across the floor in attack right for us.

I sensed Aerona using her gift to speed up her perception of time, which slowed the vampire down in her vision, but she was too late. The vampire hit her hard, and Aerona flew backwards, crashing into a table behind us, infuriating her. She recovered quickly and was back on her feet in a flash. The makeup around her eyes had smudged, and a glass of wine had spilled on her dress. Fire flared from her finger tips—she was not happy.

The vampire that attacked Aerona was young, perhaps recently turned in the Light World. Atmoro's *so you've decided to become a vampire* speech must have left out the part about not playing with warlocks.

Somehow, Atmoro had anticipated our presence at the event. He knew exactly who and where to look in the crowd, which is why his vampire guard attacked us specifically. That left even more unanswered questions. *Why would Atmoro risk the stone's theft with over a hundred witnesses?* I thought to myself. *He can't possibly be planning to kill them all, and where is Kasiah's team?*

The vampire that attacked Aerona was holding a young woman in front of him as a human shield. The expression on the woman's face was straight out of a vampire horror movie. She looked terrified.

"Let her go, newbie," Aerona demanded, "or I'll burn you to a crisp."

The vampire laughed at Aerona, ignoring her warning. Instead, he sunk his teeth into the woman's neck. Blood spilled out from his mouth and dripping down her neck onto her elegant white dress. Everyone within eyeshot screamed out. The vampire was clumsy; he was clearly not worried about witnesses.

Atmoro, displeased with his creation's actions, was in front of us in the blink of an eye. He grabbed the vampire by the back of the neck, and then lifted him off the ground, causing him to drop the woman to the floor.

Several gun shots cracked loudly outside in the lobby. The entire place was in panic. This situation was getting less fun by the second. I closed my eyes and drew in every bit of energy I could, casting a spell I hadn't used in many decades. All the guests went silent; I had immobilized everyone… well, everyone from the Light World. When I opened my eyes, it was as if the guests had been replaced with mannequins positioned in various dramatic poses, frozen in fear.

"The blood of a stone," the vampire said, struggling to free himself from Atmoro, "will release them alone."

"You are going to a much darker place," Atmoro said, dropping the vampire, then nodding to Aerona.

Fire flared from Aerona's fingers, engulfing the vampire in flames.

Atmoro turned to look at me, his eyes narrowed. I was standing face to face with one of world's greatest predators—my mind went blank.

We had prepared for numerous scenarios, none of which included Atmoro stealing the nodule right in the middle of dinner as hundreds of witnesses watched on. This is proof that anything could happen, and it probably will. Even odder than Atmoro risking extracting the nodule during the dinner party, he didn't seem in a hurry to escape to go play with his new rock.

Damien rushed in the main doors, distracting me for no more than a second, and when I looked back, Atmoro was gone.

Aerona shut down her vampire barbeque, leaving nothing but a pile of grey, vampire ash.

"Oh my God," Damien said, noticing all the other guests were frozen in place.

"Trust me," Aerona spoke up, "God had nothing to do with this madness."

"Where's Kasiah and Hayley?" Damien asked. "Kasiah's not answering her phone, and her mic is dead."

"This way," I said, leading them. "They ran out the rear entrance."

As soon as I left through the swinging doors at the rear of the ballroom, the immobilization spell lifted, and the petrified mannequins came back to life, gasping and screaming.

The swinging door led to an access hallway used only by staff members. The left side ended only ten feet away, so we ran down the hallway to the right. Aerona followed us, fingers of fire at the ready. The immobilization spell had drained all my energy; I felt weak, like I was going to pass out any second. Adrenaline was the only thing that kept me moving. I could barely stay on my feet

We came to a screeching halt around the first corner. It was a gruesome scene. Kasiah was on her knees beside Hayley's body, a large pool of blood surrounding them both. Tears streamed down Kasiah's face. She had her hand placed gently on Hayley's forehead. Several large diagonal gashes were open on Hayley's chest, exposing her pink flesh. Her neck was almost torn out completely.

Damien continued down the hall and passed the girls to the next corner to provide cover. Aerona watched our backs in the other direction. I knelt beside Kasiah—my knees dipped in blood.

"I'm so sorry," I said softly.

Kasiah turned and buried her head in my chest, crying.

I removed my hand from Kasiah's side to brush away the tear from her cheek, and my hand was covered in blood. The side of Kasiah's dress was torn open, and the blood blended in with the color of the fabric. She was wounded badly.

"DAMIEN," I shouted. "KASIAH'S INJURED!"

Damien rushed over, already calling the paramedics on his radio.

As we waited for help, I wondered how this went so wrong so quickly.

Outside, red and blue lights flashed from atop multiple police cruisers, ambulances, and fire trucks. I had only known Hayley for a couple hours, but it was as if my own sister's corpse was being wheeled into that ambulance. I continued to hold Kasiah, letting her emotions fall on my shoulder. The paramedics placed a temporary bandage over her wound, but she needed to go to the hospital for stitches.

"What did that vampire say?" Aerona asked me. "The blood of a stone will release them alone?"

"I'm not sure," I said, wondering the same thing myself. "Atmoro knows who we are, yet he still risked stealing a worthless stone? It was almost as if he was testing our abilities."

"Or," Aerona added curiously, "showing us his."

I left Kasiah with Aerona while I went to call Tara.

"Hello," Tara answered overly excitedly. "Your friendly neighborhood hacker speaking. How may I help you?"

"Hey, Tara," I said solemnly. "I have some bad news."

I gave Tara the condensed two-minute version of the night's events.

"That saying doesn't mean anything to you?" Tara asked. "The blood of a stone will release them alone."

"I'm not sure," I said. "It's halfway tied to why Atmoro's been killing all those people with names of rare stones, but I have no idea why or how all that connects to the nodule. I can't imagine he's going to try and squeeze blood from a useless rock. Maybe we should start by trying to decipher the blood of a stone."

"I'm on it," Tara said. "I'll get back to you as soon as I pull some information from the internet. Bye."

I walked back over to where Aerona and Kasiah were leaning against the bumper of an ambulance. "I'm sorry about Hayley," I said. "This is my fault. I should have never brought you into this."

"Please don't blame yourself," Kasiah said, moving away from the ambulance. "I chose to follow you to Milwaukee. I chose to listen to your story of a magical world. I made the decision to bring Hayley into this, and now, she's gone. The nodule and Atmoro are also gone. More people are going to die."

Kasiah's heart was in pain from her loss. I could see it in her eyes.

"The monster that attacked Hayley," Kasiah continued, "he was like nothing I could have ever imagined. There was no stopping him. I shot him three times before my gun was ripped from my hand. He never even slowed down, and he moved so fast. My eyes couldn't even keep up with the… the… the monster. How can we ever fight them?"

Kasiah brought up a good point. We were under the assumption that Atmoro was working alone. We had no way of knowing how many vampires he had recruited. Even newly turned vampires can be deadly. Things just became much more difficult.

Damien made his way through the crowd of emergency personnel. "I took care of the locals," he said. "Everyone else knows that several security officers and two women were killed as a result of a botched robbery. Aerona took care of the vampire. It's just a pile of ash now."

"Thank you, Damien," I said, turning to Kasiah. "We need to get you to the hospital for stitches. Have your parents been contacted?"

"They passed away," Kasiah said, tears filling her eyes again. "It was a car accident several years ago. Hayley was the only family I had left."

My heart sank, and I could feel Aerona's sadness as well. I even contemplated using compulsion to erase Hayley's death from Kasiah and Damien's minds, but it was best to not mess with their heads too much right now. We needed them to be alert.

"How do we stop him?" Kasiah asked, raising her head as her authoritative FBI tone returned.

"This isn't your fight," I answered. "Now you see why I couldn't simply call the FBI and tell them a vampire was loose on the streets? There isn't a task force for this… at least, not one in this world."

"Then we need help from your world," Damien suggested.

"Our world?" Aerona added. "I don't think so. Erone and I are dead there. We faked our deaths to jump to this world. If we show up suddenly asking for help—to help the Light World—we'll be labeled jumpers, and then we'll be hunted ourselves. There's no way we're going back there. Besides, we couldn't get in anyway. The new Shadow Council has the gateways sealed from their side."

"Atmoro is here in this world," Kasiah said. "You two are here in this world. There must be others like you—others who didn't jump to cause trouble or hunt humans. There must be others who have a new life here in this world. Someone else must want to preserve your secret as much as you two."

"As much as I don't want to admit this," Aerona confessed, "Kasiah's right. We need as much help as we can get without including the FBI, which would quickly turn into a media frenzy. We need someone with some experience in hunting—"

"—Shadow Vampires?" I asked, finishing her sentence. "It's not like we can just post a 'help wanted' ad in Sunday's newspaper. What would it say: '*Wanted,* An immortal with incredible strength, speed, and a taste for blood. Must be willing to hunt evil supervillains, expect to work weekends,

59

holidays, and kill without mercy or hesitation. Salary based on experience?' I don't think so."

"Well, aren't you the comedian?" Aerona said jokingly. "It just so happens that I know someone who might be interested in submitting their resume for that position, and I hear they're highly qualified."

"Who?" I asked, wondering if she was kidding.

"I've heard stories of a vampire," she explained. "The stories are all the same. A vampire with strength and speed matching any Shadow Vampire. He's a loner—a ghost. He's also our only shot at stopping Atmoro. Not to mention, that Atmoro now has an evil little vampire army of his own that I hate. Let's face it, we don't stand a chance alone. It's a damn miracle that he let us live tonight."

"Sounds like a fairytale," Damien said.

Aerona gave him a quick look of disapproval; he backed off, not wanting to spend the rest of his life as a miniature statue.

"How do we find him?" Kasiah asked without looking up.

"Let me see your phone," Aerona said, stretching her hand out to Damien.

Damien handed his phone to Aerona reluctantly.

"Now you're telling me there's a hotline number for Shadow Vampires?" Damien asked.

"Hardy har har," Aerona mocked, not amused. "I'm searching the net to see when and where Kate's Mind is playing. I've heard this vampire follows that band wherever they go. He doesn't miss a show. Find the band, find the vampire."

Kasiah interweaved her hand slowly with mine. My heart skipped a beat the moment her skin touched mine.

"Hayley's gone," she said, "and there's nothing I can do to bring her back. I'm not asking if I can come with you, but you are taking me. We're going to stop this madman before anyone else loses a sister. And when we find him, the one that stole my sister's life, he's mine."

"Hah!" Aerona exclaimed. "Who's up for a road trip? What luck! Kate's Mind is playing in Erie, Pennsylvania tomorrow! I'll take this as a good sign. It's only ten hours from here."

"Does this mystery vampire have a name?" Kasiah asked.

"He certainly does," Aerona said, still scrolling through the internet, "Rain."

TEN

"Did you know that tonight is my twentieth Kate's Mind concert?" Ember asked.

"I stopped keeping track of mine after fifty," Rain replied.

"I think that makes you an official band stalker," Ember laughed. "Maybe you can get your picture posted on watchdog.com or something."

Rain squinted his eyes and smiled at Ember. The two of them became close friends after Rain had saved Ember from nearly being raped—and probably killed—by the Lucky Thirteen motorcycle club in Tulsa a couple years earlier.

Ember was quick to fly away that night in Tulsa. Her intentions were to never run into another vampire, ever. She was grateful for everything Rain had done to save her, but Ember wanted to keep as much of her blood inside her body as possible. However, fate had another plan for her.

Two months later, Ember was at an art school in Scottsdale, Arizona, when she saw a flyer for Kate's Mind. Even though her first time at the band's concert ended with the brutal murder of two motorcycle club members, it was a risk she was willing to take to see the band again. Since her last Kate's Mind concert, Ember had purchased as much of the band's music as she could get her hands on, playing it over and over on an endless loop. She was addicted to their music.

The next night, Ember stood outside the club, staring up at *Kate's Mind, Tonight only!* spelled out on the marquee. She took a deep breath, paid the cover charge, and walked in. She scanned the club for any sign of the Lucky

Thirteen club: patches, jackets, hats, or tattoos. She didn't see any. She was still on guard though, considering her powers were limited when she was in human form. As a precautionary measure, she decided to keep her fairy dust pouch safely tucked away in her bra, in case someone nabbed her purse again. She wasn't about to make the same mistake twice.

The club was buzzing with anticipation for the band to start. It felt good to be out again with normal people. She walked up to the bar and ordered a drink, and that's when a hand brushed against her butt. She had been to enough clubs to know it wasn't an accident.

"What's a beautiful girl like you doing here all alone?" said the man behind her.

Ember froze. She cursed her mother for her good looks. *Here we go again,* she thought. *I've only been here for two damn minutes.*

"Touch my girlfriend again," said another man from behind Ember, "and I'll break every bone in your body, slowly, so you can hear each one crack."

Ember immediately recognized the voice. It was etched permanently into the back of her mind—Rain. She turned around and met Rain's eyes. He was standing face to face with the creepy ass-grabber guy. Ember wasn't looking forward to getting this guy's blood on her new shirt.

Several seconds passed by before the creepy guy said anything in response; he was calculating his chances with Rain. "You can have her," he said, backing away into the crowd. "There's plenty more from where she came from."

"Somehow," Rain said, paying for Ember's drink, "I doubt there's more than one of you."

"It's becoming a full-time job," Ember smiled, breathing a sigh of relief, "you saving my life."

"Well, the pay sucks," Rain retorted, meeting her eyes, "but in this economy, I'm just happy to have a job."

Ember smiled. Her brain directed her to run like the wind, but her heart told her to stay. She leaned into Rain's ear. "I didn't know vampires were rock star groupies."

"I wasn't aware fairies had good taste in music."

They found a table and watched the concert together. Afterwards, they spent the night walking around town and talking until dawn. Ember was surprised to hear how Rain didn't know much about the Shadow World. Apparently, he couldn't remember anything about where he's from, and he kept a low profile in the Light Word, except for when he's saving fairies on the weekends. Sunlight never really bothered Rain, which surprised Ember, since that completely contradicted all vampire myths she had heard. He nevertheless preferred long sleeve shirts, pants, and dark sunglasses while anywhere near the smallest amounts of sunlight, which Ember didn't mind. She enjoyed the black of night as much as Rain.

Ember got the feeling Rain didn't want to talk about his past, so she didn't push him to. She did, however, tell Rain about how she had spent the past few decades attending the finest schools in the country, collecting a mountain of degrees along the way. Rain was surprised to learn how Ember used one of her degrees, a masters in computer science, to jump on the internet train in the early 90's. Her web-based company, the site or name of which she refused to tell Rain, kept her bank account more than full. It had been a long time since Ember had had someone to talk with, even if she did most of the talking. She had no problem carrying the conversation and continued chatting about her love for music, how her fairy dust pouch is never-ending, and that her favorite color is black.

Ever since their chance meeting in Arizona, Rain and Ember had remained close friends but not lovers. They enjoyed each other's company and appreciated discussing their unique lives with someone who understood. With Rain by her side, Ember had her own personal vampire bodyguard.

This night, on Ember's twentieth Kate's Mind concert, they were in Erie, Pennsylvania at Flagship, a club where the band was playing for the first time. Rain and Ember were out enjoying the small city for a few days after spending the last couple weeks cruising Ember's two-hundred-foot mega yacht from Florida up along the country's east coast into the Great lakes, finally docking at Port Erie. The captain and the crew were paid well enough to never ask questions, and Rain took care of any loose ends along the way.

Rain and Ember were seated at a semi-circle booth under the rear balcony of the club, partially hiding them from the rest of the club. They watched as the roadies for Kate's Mind finished testing the band's gear—it was show time!

"Your heart is racing," Rain said, noticing Ember was becoming anxious.

"They have a local chapter, you know," she said, referring to the Lucky Thirteen motorcycle club.

"Well," Rain said, grinning, "it's been a while since I had to save that cute smiling face of yours. Some action might be a nice change of…"

Rain's voice faded quickly as he fell silent. His eyes were fixed on the club's entrance. He stopped breathing.

"What is it?" Ember asked quietly, her heart pumping rapidly. She knew enough not to turn her head around to see what had caught Rain's attention.

Rain didn't respond, nor did he move a muscle. His eyes were fixed on the four people who had just walked in, clearly looking for something—or someone. The tall woman with long dark hair wore a black T-shirt with white script letters "I Don't Kiss Strippers" printed across the front.

"Four people just walked in," he said, leaning back. "They're searching the crowd for someone."

"Should we be concerned?" Ember asked, her anxiety heightening.

"No worries," Rain said, calming Ember. "I don't miss Kate's Mind for anything."

ELEVEN

The drive east from Madison through Chicago toward Erie was a nightmare. The traffic was six lanes in one direction, and all racing eighty miles per hour most of the way. It was completely out of control. Aerona insisted we were going to crash, keeping up with the traffic between toll booths. It was stress we didn't need. I asked her to busy herself by surfing the internet for hotels. She reserved four rooms at the Ramada in Erie.

I spoke to Tara twice during the drive. She came up empty-handed on decoding the "blood of a stone will release them alone" riddle. She called one last time as we were driving through Cleveland.

"Hey, Tara," I answered the phone, still frustrated with the traffic, "I'm only accepting good news right now."

"I FOUND IT," Tara shouted.

I had to hold the phone away from my ear so I wouldn't go deaf. I think Tara knocked over her chair when I answered.

"I was poking around on the Pentagon's main server," she explained, "and I tripped over some files that led me to an encrypted site created by… are you ready, Erone? Elves! Can you believe it? Real live elves!"

"As surprising at it may seem, Tara, yes, I do believe it. Please continue."

"It took me a good three hours to break the encryption," she said excitedly. "It's wild stuff. I've never seen code like this before. It's light-years beyond anything else—"

"Blood of a stone, Tara," I interjected. "Keep on track."

"Oh, yes. OK," Tara said, hammering down on her keyboard. "Well, this site isn't public by any means. It's more of a mass storage server with remote internet access. There's a couple dozen terabits of information stored on this one server alone. I found some scrolls scanned and stored digitally. Well, let me rephrase that, I found *ancient* scrolls that are almost a *thousand* years old. I also uncovered some financial information, business and real estate documents, personal records, and some unusual medical information. You name it, I found it. All their records. Real live elves!"

"Tara!" I yelled into the phone, making everyone else in the car look my way.

"Oh, yes. OK," she continued. "I did a mass search on the site for the phrase 'blood of a stone' and found this…"

There was silence on the other end. I could hear Tara typing on her keyboard.

"OK," she said. "Have you ever heard of a place called the Forgotten Shadow City?"

"Yes," I said, exchanging an uneasy look with Aerona. "Unfortunately, I have heard of the Forgotten Shadow City. Go on."

"OK. OK. OK. The Forgotten Shadow City is like totally ten times more secure than… umm… well let's say it's just easier to get to mars than to get out of this city. There's some council that sends people there for breaking certain laws and blah blah blah. The interesting part is that the elves are involved, because they helped build a secret sort of back door to the city slash prison, just in case a council member ever found themselves sentenced there. Guess what the key is?"

"The blood of a stone?" I asked.

"Yes, Erone! The elves built the door and sealed it with a spell, and it can only be broken by the blood of a stone. Hence, 'the blood of a stone will release them alone.'

"So how do we get blood from a stone?" I asked, shooting Aerona a confused look to ask her if it made any sense. She shook her head no.

"I got booted from the server," Tara continued, still banging on her keyboard. "I tried jumping back on, but they've already changed their security encryption. I'll get back in, just give me some time. Elves! Real live elves!"

"Good job, Tara. Keep me posted and be careful. Elves aren't as cute and cuddly as Hollywood makes them out to be. Let me know as soon as you find any more info. And call if you need anything."

"Will do, Erone. You guys be careful on your end as well. I'll hit you back in a few hours. Bye!"

I relayed what Tara told me to everyone else in the car. "Does this mean anything to you, Aerona?" I asked.

"No," Aerona said, thinking, "but I can make a few calls and see what I can dig up, now that we have a starting point. Damn elves. This day just keeps getting better by the minute... and by better, I mean worse."

We arrived in Erie within ten hours of leaving Madison. It was eight o'clock in the evening. We stopped at the hotel only long enough to check in and have a quick shower. I was a somewhat concerned that Kasiah and Damien would wear their FBI super suits and flash their shiny badges all over, but when we met in the lobby, I was surprised to see that wasn't the case.

Damien ditched his FBI suit for a pair of faded jeans and a blue untucked shirt. He looked good; I'm sure he could easily start a conversation with the opposite sex. He left the hotel lobby to pull the car around to the front.

Kasiah, once again, looked incredible. She pulled off the rocker chick style well. I was certain Aerona—self-proclaimed queen of rocker chicks—lent a helping hand, probably even throwing in one of her famous makeup sessions. Kasiah's hair was let down, which darkened her eyes a few shades. Her black T-shirt's low-cut, frayed V-neck was made to appear as though it had been torn open; it exposed just enough cleavage to appear sexy—very sexy. A pair of snug jeans showed off her toned figure. I confess; my eyes stole more than one look as we stood there waiting.

As for me, I had on my usual club attire, which was pretty much the same as Damien's. I threw on a black button-up shirt (untucked, with the sleeves rolled up one turn—a habit I can't seem to lose) and a pair of slightly worn-in jeans with a small tear on one knee. It would probably be a surprise that I spend more time shaping my hair into a perfect rockstar-ish mess than any other hair style I've sported.

Aerona never had to try hard. Her makeup was always flawless, and her hair was always styled to perfection. She, of course, had on one of her many sarcastic T-shirts; this one was black with white script letters "I Don't Kiss Strippers" printed across the front. I was sure it would offend at least one person at the club by the end of the night— and that's exactly what we didn't need.

"So," Aerona asked, giving a runway twirl, "what do you think of your lady escorts for the evening?"

"Beautiful," I said, catching Kasiah's eyes.

She smiled for the first time since last night. Thoughts sped through my mind, wondering how she must have felt after losing her best friend and sister. I nodded my head to the side, motioning for Aerona to give us some space. She wandered over to a large leather sofa, leaving me alone with Kasiah.

"How are you doing with all of this?" I asked hesitantly.

"I'm OK," Kasiah said, smiling but holding something back.

I had only known her for two days, but I could tell Kasiah's heart was ripped in two. Her eyes filled with tears as she touched her side where the vampire had injured her. She was trying hard not to let her emotions show.

"I miss her," she admitted, her smile fading. "I feel like a piece of me had gone missing. Hayley died right in my arms, and I was helpless. I've spent my whole life training for that very moment, and I failed her miserably."

"Don't blame yourself," I said, taking her hand. "That wasn't a situation the bureau could have possibly prepared you for. I should have anticipated Atmoro turning more vampires, and it was my mistake thinking he'd be working alone. I shouldn't have brought you in on this. I should have just compelled you and Damien to go back to your lives, wiping me from your memory. This is my fault, and I know I can't bring her back, but I will find a way to put that unbelievable smile back on your face."

"You're an amazing person," she said, wiping her tears away. "I only wish I could have met you in a different place at a different time."

I pulled Kasiah close to me and wrapped my arms around her. She rested her head against my shoulder and held me as though she would never let go.

Aerona felt my heartache. I could feel her mood change as I glanced in her direction. She wiped away a tear, pretending to watch the lobby's TV.

We headed downtown to Flagship, where Kate's Mind were to take the stage. I hoped Aerona was right about a vampire fan who never missed their show. I had been trying to think of an easy way to convince a vampire to help us—I came up with nothing.

We walked in just before ten. The club's main entrance, more of a hallway than a doorway, was guarded by a brawny bouncer checking ID's and collecting the cover charge. The bouncer strapped wrist bands on us before we entered the main club area.

The hallway opened directly into a room with a full length bar down one side. The bartenders raced back and forth, pouring drinks and making change. The club was just as dark as every other club I had been to; and despite the citywide public-area smoking ban, the air was thick with cigarette smoke. On the bright side, though, the club was fairly small; if the mystery vampire was there, we would find him.

Kasiah leaned into my ear and said, "How about you and Aerona take a quick walk-around to get a layout of this place. Damien and I will stay here by the bar and watch the door."

It was too noisy inside to answer her back without yelling. Aerona and I just nodded, turned, and started weaving through the crowd.

An old, red brick wall separated the bar from a much larger second room with an elevated stage and a spacious open floor. The concert room was packed with waiting rock fans. Aerona had seen the band once at a small club in New York City and said they're phenomenal. I secretly hoped we wouldn't find the vampire until, at least, after the first set, especially if their singer was as good live as he sounded on their albums. I had to remind myself we were there to find a vampire and not to catch a rock show.

The stage itself was big for a club of this size. It was raised at least three feet off the main floor and spanned the full width of the room. Immense sound systems were racked on both sides of the stage, and massive lights hung from above.

As we swerved through the crowd, I noticed several sets of eyes sizing up Aerona. She received smiles from the guys and evil-eye scowls from their girlfriends; they nonetheless shot Aerona a second look.

"Hey," I said, nudging her arm, "You're on your own if one of these girls claws your eyes out for winking at their man."

"I can handle myself," she smirked back. "It's not my fault these girls can't keep their men from checking out my fine body."

Aerona spoke loud enough for a girl to her right to hear. The girl shot her an angry glare, and Aerona smacked her own ass, then blew the girl a kiss with the other hand.

That's my sister, always polite with her greetings. "Let's keep moving," I said, pulling Aerona forward. "It looks like the band is almost ready to start. We don't want to be caught in this crowd when they hit the stage."

We weaved our way to the back of the club near a staircase that led up to a small, poorly lit balcony overlooking the stage. The balcony was packed with eager fans. We would have to check that later. There were a few half-hidden tables under the balcony with several people seated at each. The club was dark, and it was going to be more difficult than I had anticipated. We decided to start back toward the front entrance.

The floor was packed to the point where we were almost swimming through a sea of sweaty fans. Aerona led our way back to Kasiah and Damien, dodging right past the same evil-eyed girl.

"Don't," was all I said to Aerona.

Aerona turned and flashed me her wicked grin. "I haven't turned anyone into a toad in decades," she sneered. "I may or may not remember how to turn them back. Let's hope she behaves herself."

The girl's back was turned to us. As we passed by, Aerona couldn't resist rubbing her body against the girl and her boyfriend.

"Sorry," Aerona yelled, looking straight into the boyfriend's eyes. "Excuse my sexy body for rubbing against yours!"

We were a few feet past the two by the time the girl noticed what had happened. She shot her boyfriend a disapproving tonight-you're-sleeping-alone look. He shrugged his shoulders and held up his palms with a confused expression.

"Nice, Aerona," I said, finally getting out of the thick crowd. "We've been here ten minutes, and you've already made friends with the locals."

"Do you think she'll approve me as her friend on Facebook?" she asked excitedly.

"Like I said," shaking my head, "You're on your own."

Kasiah and Damien had lost their position by the door. Fifteen or so beefy bikers had just pushed their way into the club. I found it unusual that it was the middle of summer, and each one had on a black leather vest over a thick T-shirt. Each vest had sewn-on patches of a large green spade and the number thirteen in the center, "Lucky Thirteen" was embroidered above the spade and "Erie, PA" underneath. Oddly, a few of the guys also wore "Tulsa, OK" vests. That seemed like a long way to travel for a concert.

We let the bikers have their end of the bar. They were busy drinking beer and getting worked up about something. I didn't care what they were doing as long as they steered clear of us. On the other hand, I did recall Aerona wanting to turn someone into a toad tonight.

"So how's it look?" Damien asked.

"Busy," I replied. "It's packed in here. Even if we do find him, we won't be able to talk to him here."

"We need to find one of the band members," he suggested, "or someone else that's with the band at every show... like the tech who runs the sound or lights or maybe the band manager. Just anyone who may know what Rain looks like. If he's at every show, then someone is bound to know what he looks like."

We all scanned the crowd. Kasiah kept quiet as she sipped her drink; at least she had her game face back on.

The lights went out, and the crowd erupted in a cheer. I felt Aerona's heart begin to race as adrenaline pumped into her bloodstream.

TWELVE

Kate's Mind was five songs into their set when I decided, without a doubt, they're the best band I had ever seen; keep in mind that I've been attending rock gigs since they were invented.

The band's stage presence was unbelievable. They owned every square inch of that stage, playing to the entire club from front to back. The sound was mixed perfectly; usually the drums overpower the guitars and the vocals or vice versa, but not a single instrument sounded louder than the others. The vocals were crystal clear and the harmonies were flawless. The band had a unique way of slowing the rhythm down while their front-man, Jimmy, sang a verse almost as though he was narrating a story. The rhythm would then build back up, and they'd be jamming again. They rocked so hard, I think the building shifted two inches to the left. They weren't amateurs by any means.

The band was on their sixth song when one of the Lucky Thirteen bikers walked over and stood right in front of Kasiah and Aerona. The guy was pretty big—Ultimate Fighter big. His eyes were glossy from excessive alcohol. The front of his vest displayed two patches: one with "Erie President" embroidered, and the other "Spider."

"How about you two lovely ladies ditch these losers and come have a few drinks with us?" Spider offered, wedging his way between Kasiah and me, placing his hand on the bar. "Maybe go for a ride with us?"

"Beat it, jerk," Aerona shouted back at Spider. "We're watching the show, and I don't ride bikes with training wheels."

Aerona turned her attention back to the band.

I expected nothing less from my sister.

"Your friend's kind of a bitch," Spider said to Kasiah, looking past her to his biker buddies.

Damien and I both moved around Spider and stood in front of Kasiah. She held up her hand to let us know she could handle the situation.

"Look," Kasiah said flatly, "we're not interested. My friends and I are trying to enjoy the show. I suggest you turn around and get back to your side of the bar unless you want to explain how you got a black eye from a girl."

Spider took his hand off the bar and set his beer down in its place, which apparently was the signal for his biker buddies to come save him. Ten seconds later, we were surrounded by a dozen mean looking bikers, several with bulges under their vests—holsters.

I felt Aerona's anger flare to boiling point. I shook my head slowly once. I noticed the muscles in her face tense up in disapproval. She was pissed that her rock show was being interrupted by a couple of drunken idiots.

One of the bartenders ran over. "I've told you guys before," she said, waving to one of the bouncers, "no trouble or you're out of here."

A typical club bouncer—also moonlighting as a cage fighter—quickly made his way through the crowd, flashing hand signals to the other bouncers positioned throughout the club. This was exactly the type of attention we were trying to avoid.

Kasiah stepped away from the bar and moved to my side. I put my arm around her waist and pulled her close. I didn't want to leave the club without finding what we came for, but I wasn't going to let these guys lay a hand on any of us. Kasiah and Damien both said at the hotel that they didn't want to cause a ruckus by flashing their FBI badges; although, this scenario may be the exception. I pulled in all the energy I could find and felt Aerona do the same. This wasn't a situation we couldn't handle. We would just have to leave afterwards—in a hurry.

One of the other Lucky Thirteen members waved to Spider. "Hey man," he said, grabbing Spider's arm and spinning him around. "These jerks aren't worth it. I didn't come all the way up from Tulsa just to get kicked out of a bar for hitting on a couple of chicks. Save it for when we find Rain. You can take it out on him."

The massive bouncer from the front entrance and two others stepped into our little group to take control. "This is your last warning," he cautioned. "Next time you're out the door."

Spider relaxed. Aerona and I held our energy, just in case. The bikers retreated to their side of the club. The four of us shared a look of confusion when we heard them say they were looking for Rain.

Damien leaned in close to me. "Why do you suppose a group of bikers are looking for the same vampire as us?" he whispered.

"I don't know," I said, wondering the same. "They probably don't know he's a vampire, or they would have been a little more discreet. I'd like to be there when they find out who they're dealing with."

I removed my arm from around Kasiah's waist. I didn't want to lose sight of why we're here or how dangerous this could get. Not many people in this world would search for a vampire; most actually tend to run from them.

"This might work to our advantage," Damien whispered. "The new plan might be to watch these characters to see where they lead us."

"Good idea," I nodded. "We have no clue what Rain looks like, or if it's safe to ask about him. Let's keep an eye on those guys to see if Rain turns up."

An attractive young girl in a short, tight blue dress walked up to the bar next to Kasiah, smiled, and ordered two drinks.

"Obnoxious, aren't they?" the girl remarked, nodding her head in the bikers' direction.

"And then some," Kasiah said irritably.

The girl was tall and pretty with long, dark hair and crystal blue eyes. She had the bluest eyes I had ever seen—as clear and lustrous as sapphire.

"Otherwise enjoying the show?" she asked.

"Yes," Kasiah said, her irritation fading. "They're a great band, and this is my first time seeing them."

The bartender cut in. "Twelve dollars," she informed.

The blue-eyed girl paid for her drinks. "Enjoy the rest of the show," she said before walking away.

We spent most of the next hour keeping an eye on the bikers. They doubled in number since our first encounter and covered both sides of the bar. Rain couldn't possible evade all of these guys. Our plan stayed the same: wait for the bikers to make their move, then see where it takes us.

Kate's Mind finished their set, and the stage went dark. The house lights didn't come on, so I assumed there would be one more song.

A minute ticked by before Jimmy walked back out with his guitar. "I want to thank you for coming out to our show," he said, brushing strands of dark hair from his face. "If ya look waaaay at the back, you'll find Steph sellin' our gear. The band will be back there with her in just a minute to take pictures with you crazy rock fans. Don't be afraid to stop by and say hey." Jimmy paused for a second to brush the hair out of his face and have a quick swig of water. "Is it OK if I play one more song?"

The crowd cheered louder than they had all night, which is saying something. This was an insane crowd of rock fans.

Jimmy smiled. He clearly loved every second of being on stage. He took a few steps back and started strumming a nice clean tone from his guitar, running through a couple measures before stepping back up to the microphone. "This one's called You've Got Nothing to Prove…"

"Hayley would have loved these guys," Kasiah said, squeezing my hand. "I want to see them again when all this insanity is over."

"Count me in," Aerona said, interrupting our moment. I gave her the death look. She rolled her eyes and turned back around to hear the rest of the song.

"It's OK," Kasiah said, smiling. "She's growing on me."

"Yeah, well, you can have her."

Aerona didn't turn around to comment. Instead, she showed me her nicely manicured middle finger.

The Lucky Thirteens were on the move. Ten or so of them pushed their way through the crowd as though they owned the place. They headed straight toward the tables under the balcony, right where the blue-eyed girl went. They left a couple guys posted at the entrance and a couple more near the rear emergency exit. There were several of them for every bouncer in the club.

"Here we go," Damien warned.

All four of us were on alert. Aerona was focused on the guys at the front door. She was ready to clear us a path.

I heard a low growl that overpowered the massive sound system; seconds later, a body came crashing through the brick wall that half separated the bar area from the stage room. Red bricks and dust filled the air as screams erupted from people pushing and shoving. Jimmy stopped playing altogether as another body flew through the air, landing near the stage onto several unsuspecting fans.

The whole place had turned into a madhouse in a matter of seconds.

"I think it's safe to say we found our vampire," Kasiah said, moving next to me.

Three Lucky Thirteen members—Spider among them—came rushing through the crowd, their guns drawn, dragging the blue-eyed girl forcefully along with them. Two of the bikers fired several blind shots into the darkness under the balcony.

That was our cue. I grabbed Kasiah from behind, and Aerona pulled Damien in next to her. Aerona and I cast the same spell together, creating a massive updraft of air as a makeshift shield of air around us. The current was strong enough to deflect any stray bullets, giving us time to figure out a way out of the club. The girls' hair flew wildly as if we were in the middle of a tornado.

The bikers had taken out all the bouncers and had all the exits covered. They had practically taken over the entire bar. We only had a few minutes to get out before the police would show. If we didn't move fast, we were surely going to be caught in the line of fire.

The blue-eyed girl put up a good fight. She kicked and screamed as the bikers dragged her out the front door. "RAIN!" she shouted as the door slammed shut behind her.

Another loud growl came from the back of the bar. Two guys flew through the air, crashing into the stage.

"Let's move!" yelled Aerona.

The air around us dissipated as we released the spell. We started to make our way to the front door when one of the bikers slid across the floor on his back from under the balcony, crashing low and hard into the bar in front of us.

The guy was dazed, but he still started crawling away.

Another figure emerged from under the dark balcony, limping from a gunshot wound. His arm was bleeding badly. We watched his wounds heal in front of our eyes.

We had found Rain!

Rain moved toward the biker, effortlessly lifting him off the floor and slamming him against the bar. I gave Aerona a nervous look as the biker fought to escape Rain's iron grip. He slammed the biker's head into the bar and knocked him unconscious. The wooden bar top splintered, and glassware smashed on the floor. Rain's deadly, sharp fangs sunk into the biker's neck; the fresh human blood acted like a rush of adrenaline for him. Rain released the biker and was out the front door before his lifeless body hit the floor.

As much as I hated the thought of chasing after an angry vampire, there was only one thing we could do. "We have to go after him!" I shouted.

Kasiah looked at me with uncertainty. "Are you sure the safest place to be is right behind the vampire everyone is trying to kill?" she asked.

"If we lose him now, we'll never find him again!"

THIRTEEN

The night went from bad to worse. Outside the club, many of the bikers were backed up against the building across the street, their faces painted with looks of intense surprise. Several overturned motorcycles littered the street, and a parked car with a motorcycle through the windshield had ignited into a ball of fire. Spider held a large knife against the blue-eyed girl's neck. The whole scene looked straight out of the next big Hollywood action flick.

"What… is that?" Kasiah asked, pointing at the enormous, ugly beast on Spider's side of the street.

"A troll," I said, surveying the chaos. "I think it's safe to say Atmoro knows we're here. Those two guys over there aren't human. They're werewolves, and they're pack hunters, so watch your backs for more."

The troll was easily seven feet tall and ugly—special emphasis on the ugly part. Trolls are shapeshifters, transforming into humans or shadows or even simple objects; this is the only way they can blend into the Light World, and they have no supernatural powers when transformed into any form other than troll. They're strong—very strong; most trolls could lift a city bus, but they're dumb as rocks. This one was in its natural, ugly form, even for a troll. It wore some dirty, torn cloth covering the most unpleasant parts, and its colossal hands gripped a long broadsword, ready to strike. Fortunately, trolls aren't much of a threat if you know how to handle them.

The two werewolves were my major concern. I was impressed by Atmoro's little army; any Shadow Vampire can create more vampires here in the Light World, but it takes some convincing to get werewolves and trolls to join forces.

My earlier conversation with Tara started to make sense; Atmoro was trying to release all the Shadows from the Forgotten Shadow City. That was the only way werewolves and trolls could work together with a Shadow Vampire—they had a common goal.

Both the werewolves were also in their human form. Typically, they only transform into wolves when they need to feed or travel long distances. They have incredible strength and speed, rivaling Shadow Vampires, and they're excellent fighters, which is why the Shadow Council employs them to guard the entrances to the Shadow World. Most werewolves would make UFC fighters look like a bunch of school girls fighting over a jump rope. These two were no exception; they were tall and burl, with long greasy hair and razor-sharp claws for finger nails.

The last few minutes weighed on me like a ton of bricks. I underestimated Atmoro for the second time, and I wasn't about to let it happen again. Although, I still couldn't wrap my mind around how Atmoro was able to track us. We had left Madison as soon as we conceived the idea of driving to Erie, and there was no time to let the plan leak or be heard by anyone else. Despite how troubling the mystery was, there was no time to solve it now.

I heard sirens in the distance, maybe only a minute or two away. I looked to where Rain was—on our side of the street. He was tall, even for a vampire, and his face didn't appear a day over twenty-five. The back of his black shirt was torn open from what was probably a knife wound that had already healed. Rain was carefully calculating his next move, focusing across the street at Spider. Based on my experience, this wasn't going to end well for Spider.

"Kasiah and Damien, stay here and find cover," I ordered, taking control of this seemingly out-of-control situation. "Aerona, you're with me."

They both nodded. After what had happened in Madison, Kasiah and Damien gained respect for Shadows and our abilities; they knew this situation had already escalated beyond what they could control.

With Aerona by my side, I took a few steps toward Rain.

"Rain," I said in as non-threatening a tone as I could to avoid being beaten to death by an angry Shadow Vampire, "we need to get you out of here."

Not appearing shocked that we knew his name, Rain glanced at us for a second, then turned his attention back across the street; apparently, he didn't see us as a threat—not a bad first impression.

"I suggest," he replied, still glaring at Spider, "you head back inside and finish your martini before you get blood on that fancy shirt."

Considering his friend was being held at knife point, Rain spoke with an amazingly clear and calm voice. He was extraordinarily handsome; his facial features were sculpted perfectly to match his equally sculpted body. He could have just walked off the set of a fashion commercial. Rain had total control of his emotions, even when his friend was being held captive. His heart beat a slow and steady pace, and he did not take his eyes off Spider and his hostage.

A couple blocks up the street, two police cars drifted around the corner, driving as if filming a chase scene. Red and blue lights bounced off the glass buildings.

Without hesitation, Aerona conjured a twenty feet high wall of fire stretching across the entire street from building to building. The police cars came to a screeching halt in front of the wall of fire. Other than being eaten alive, people only fear one other thing—being burnt alive. The fire had to do for now, unless the werewolves had their way.

The inferno distracted Spider and his gang of misfits' attention away from the vampire across the street. Flanked by a werewolf on either side, the troll stepped into the street, lifting its sword above its head. He was focused on Rain.

"You're either with me or against me," Rain said firmly, his eyes still fixed on Spider.

"We're with you," I said, wondering where that decision would take us. "You get the girl. We'll handle these delinquents."

Rain made the first move, attacking the troll low and knocking it off its feet. The troll went down hard, swinging the sword recklessly at Rain. Sparks emitted as the sword clanged loudly into the pavement, missing its target.

Rain's speed was incredible. He was on the troll in an instant, severing the hideous head from its shoulders. The troll's body collapsed into a pile of dust and ashes.

There was no question; we had definitely found our vampire.

"Get the girl!" I yelled to Rain.

The werewolves, though stunned by the troll's slaughter, were confident in their own abilities. They advanced fast as I pulled my hand high behind my head, then shot it out like a rocket, sending a blast of air hurtling toward the werewolves (like an afterburner of a fighter jet). The werewolves flew back, crashing into a parked truck with enough force to lift its side off the ground. Aerona wasn't the only one that knew how to play with fire.

Despite the impact, the werewolves were back on their feet quickly. Their attention had shifted from Rain to me. My hands ignited with roaring flames, thrusting powerful bursts of blazing air down at the ground. I controlled the flames direction like two tiny flame throwers, raising one hand toward the werewolves. An explosion blazed one into a ball of fire, leaving nothing but a pile of ashes.

The other werewolf retreated around the corner—he'd be back.

"Nice work, little brother," Aerona said, beaming.

We turned back toward Spider. The blue-eyed girl's hand moved slowly up her torso, then down into the neck of her shirt.

"What the hell is she doing?" Aerona questioned.

She pulled her hand out from her shirt and raised it over her head.

"Don't move!" Spider yelled, nervously gripping the knife at her throat.

Her hand opened, releasing a sparkling shower of dust that fell down like a million tiny diamonds. She was now only six inches tall, flying just above Spider's head.

"She's a fairy!" Aerona yelled excitedly. "I love fairies!"

As if Spider hadn't seen enough, a tiny fairy now flew above his head. The look of confusion on his face could have won an award. The fairy's small hand waved goodbye.

Rain used the distraction to his advantage, closing the space between him and his prey. Two other bikers raised their guns and fired at him racing down the street. Just as the muzzles flashed, my hands flew up in front of me, curving the two bullets around Rain and careening them back into the bikers' legs. They both fell screaming in pain. I hadn't done that in decades; I actually shocked myself a little by recalling the spell so quickly and not aiming the bullets at my own head.

Spider carelessly swung his knife at Rain. I didn't necessarily want to watch, knowing how it was going to end, but Spider deserved everything he was about to receive.

Rain deftly dodged Spider's blade several times as it sliced through the air, missing every time. Rain calculated his timing carefully, and at the exact moment, he grabbed Spider's arm mid-swing and squeezed hard. I heard the bones shatter. Spider bellowed in pain as the knife fell clanking to the ground.

Rain wrapped his hand around Spider's throat, slamming him against the red brick wall, leaving a crumbling dent. Glass shattered and fell from the window above.

"We need to get out of here!" Aerona shouted. "I can't keep this fire-wall up forever!"

Through the wall of fire, I noticed more police cruisers had arrived. More were probably racing around the block from the other side.

"Rain!" I shouted across the street. "We need to leave, now!"

Rain picked up the knife from the sidewalk and slashed it across the left side of Spider's face, leaving a gaping wound extending from above his eye down his jaw. The wound was deep, and blood streamed down his face and onto the street.

What happened next was completely unexpected: Rain simply turned away and left Spider bleeding on the sidewalk. I had never known a vampire from this world resist fresh human blood. To vampires turned in the Light World, human blood is an addictive drug; they lose control at even the scent of a single drop. Shadow Vampires, on the other hand, have control over their thirst for blood, and they only feed from humans when they require the strength human blood provides. Rain walked away from a fresh kill without even tasting a drop.

That meant only one thing—Shadow Vampire.

Suddenly, one of the burning cars exploded, rattling the nearby buildings.

"Troll!" Aerona yelled, her flames weakening.

A second troll had appeared suddenly around the corner of the same building that Rain had slammed Spider into. A blow-gun, most likely dipped in poison, was pinched between its ugly, cracked lips. A dart blasted out of the tube toward Aerona. She used her ability to speed up her perception of time to promptly dodge the high-speed dart that flew right into Kasiah's shoulder.

Kasiah dropped to the ground instantly.

Rain hit the troll with the same force as he did with the last, knocking down. The troll rolled on its back and blasted a second dart. Rain, still on the attack, caught the dart midflight, jamming it into the troll's eye. It let out a horrific scream. With one quick movement, Rain removed the troll's dagger from its belt and slashed through the troll's neck; its head and body turned to the same cloud of dust and ash as the first one.

Kasiah lay motionless on the sidewalk outside the club as Damien pulled the dart from her shoulder—she wasn't breathing.

"We need an ambulance!" Damien hollered, his eyes full of fear.

"There's no time," I replied, hoping that wasn't true. "That dart was poisoned with a yaksha plant. Without the antidote, she doesn't have much time."

"Can't you heal her?" Damien asked frantically. "Can't you draw out the blood with some magic or something?"

The fairy hovered over Kasiah's forehead, assessing her condition. "Rain," she said in her tiny voice, "we need to get her to the dock!"

Rain looked at me for approval. With no other obvious options, I nodded in agreement.

"It's ten blocks down to the waterfront," the fairy quickly informed. "There's a yacht docked in the last pier. You can't miss it. Meet us there."

We didn't even have time to argue. Rain lifted Kasiah as if she were weightless, and the three of them were gone in a flash.

It was at that moment I realized how much I cared for Kasiah.

Aerona dropped her wall of fire, exposing us to the police. I closed my eyes and pulled in all the energy I could handle. Kasiah's sister flashed through my mind. The world around me went silent. Every street light and shop window went dark. All the police strobe lights went out, and their scanners and radios were silenced. When I opened my eyes, only the light of the moon lit the streets.

The police were disoriented. It was now or never. We moved quickly, staying close to the wall as we made our way to the end of the block and around the corner toward the waterfront. The spell had weakened me; I was stumbling and disoriented. Damien and Aerona had to help keep me on my feet.

"A yacht?" Aerona asked, astonished.

FOURTEEN

The dock was quiet this time of the night. The pier's lights glimmered in the tiny waves slapping against the dock. Exactly as the fairy had informed, a massive yacht was docked in the last pier. It was easily two-hundred feet long; we couldn't have missed it even if we tried. The yacht's name, Ember's Star, was painted in large, dark blue script across the yacht's stern.

The fairy, back in her human form, was waiting for us at the edge of the dock. Her eyes resembled tiny, blue lights, the same bright eyes were detailed perfectly in a goth fairy tattoo on her shoulder, complete with a trail of tiny, sparkling stars trailing behind.

"I'm Ember," she said. "Rain and Kasiah are inside. Please hurry aboard. We're about to cast off."

"How do we know you can be trusted?" I asked, suddenly not so sure this was the best idea.

"You can either get your asses on board," she said firmly, "or wave goodbye as we pull away from the dock. Either way, this yacht will be cruising through the bay in less than a minute, so please choose quickly."

At this point, we had no choice but to trust Ember; besides, it wasn't every day a fairy and a vampire invited me out for a night cruise on their multimillion dollar yacht. We boarded.

As soon as we were aboard and the ramp was raised, an exceptionally loud horn sounded as the yacht began to cast away from the dock. The vessel seemed even more massive as we followed Ember across the main deck through a large, impressive sitting area complete with white leather couches and other expensive furniture. The doorways were trimmed with lavish, deep auburn hardwood, and both sides of the room were made entirely of tinted glass, allowing a panoramic view of the water.

We followed Ember downstairs one level to the lower deck along a narrow hallway with doors on either side. The layout looked a lot like a typical hotel. Ember stopped at the last room and opened the door. Inside, Kasiah was seated on the bed, her eyes open and alert.

"I thought we had lost you," Damien said, breathing a sigh of relief.

"I think you did," Kasiah said softly.

She placed a hand on her temple. "My head is throbbing, but other than that I'm fine. I don't remember anything after seeing the second troll."

"You were struck by a poisoned dart," I explained, hoping my voice didn't show how amazed I was that she was, in fact, still breathing. "You have no idea how lucky you are to be alive."

"You must be Erone," Ember said, pouring Kasiah a glass of water from the bedside table. "Kasiah woke up on the way to the yacht, gasping for breath and calling your name."

"Yes," was all I said. I didn't feel comfortable giving any more information than that.

"We'll have time for proper introductions later," Ember added, walking to the door. "Welcome aboard Ember's Star. There's a room for each of you down the hall. Take a few minutes and get cleaned up before we meet on the main deck to discuss the night's events."

"Where are we headed?" I asked, not sure if I wanted to know the answer.

"I've instructed the captain to sail us into Canadian waters as soon as possible. The Great Lakes are big enough for even this yacht to hide. Don't worry, you're safe with us."

"Is Rain on board?" I asked, again unsure if I wanted the answer.

"Yes," she nodded, "and he's very interested in knowing who you are and why you were at the club tonight. For now, please make yourselves at home. I'll see you on the main deck shortly."

Ember left the room.

I turned to Kasiah. "You know you should be dead, right?" I said, bluntly.

"Funny," she replied. "That's exactly what Ember told me. I remember seeing the troll, then blackness, then waking up being carried by a vampire. For lack of a better phrase, I freaked out. Ember calmed me down and gave me the short version of what had happened. She told me you were on your way. Honestly, I didn't know whether to believe them or not, and it didn't seem like I had a choice in the matter."

"I've never seen anyone survive a yaksha dart without the antidote," I said. "Even with the antidote, there's no guarantee. I think maybe Hayley was looking after you on this one."

I instantly regretted bringing Kasiah's sister into the conversation. A tear rolled down her cheek, and she hung her head low.

"We're just glad you're safe," I said, trying to redeem myself. "You gave us quite a scare. Maybe you should work on your dart dodging skill?"

My humor was a poor attempt at trying to make Kasiah smile, but it still worked. She lifted her head and sniffled a little. Her beautiful smile returned.

"I have to admit," Aerona interjected, cracking a smile. "I was a little upset that you were dead." Aerona pinched her finger and thumb close together. "Only a little."

Kasiah returned Aerona's smile.

"Let's get cleaned up and find Rain," Damien suggested.

"I second that," Aerona added.

Damien and Aerona left the room.

I walked over to the edge of Kasiah's bed, unsure what I could do to comfort her. She scooted over to the edge and pulled me close, burying her head in my chest—as she broke down crying.

After several minutes, Kasiah let go and asked if I could stay in her room while she took a quick shower; she didn't feel comfortable being alone.

I collapsed in a chair next to the king-size bed, closed my eyes, and listened to the shower stream playing a rhythmic tune against Kasiah's body on the other side of the bathroom door. I was going to sleep for a month once this nightmare was over.

I forced my eyes open and sat up in the chair when the shower shut off and the bathroom door opened. Wet strands of dark hair hung in Kasiah's face as she walked out wearing a fluffy white towel, the top neatly tucked in. She looked so innocent and beautiful.

"Thank you so much for staying," she said, brushing a few wet strands of hair from her face. "Something about being on a yacht in the middle of nowhere with a vampire just doesn't make a shower relaxing."

"It was my pleasure," I said, as though I was a total idiot.

A knock at the door saved me from further embarrassment. Kasiah retreated behind me, still in nothing more than a towel.

"Who is it?" I asked loudly, knowing it was Aerona. I felt her walk up to the door seconds before the knock. I knew she must have felt me as well, or maybe she thought I was in the next room over.

"It's me," Aerona replied. "I was thinking maybe Kasiah could use some company. Sorry, I'll come back."

"It's OK," I said. "Come in."

Aerona slowly opened the door, covering her eyes as she walked in.

"Aren't you the comedian," I said sarcastically.

Aerona was quick on her feet. "Well, the last thing I want to see is my brother naked," she said wryly.

"Well," I continued, showing Aerona my best I'm-not-amused expression, "now that I'm completely embarrassed, I'll go find a room to get a quick shower."

"Make it a cold shower," Aerona smiled.

I sought out a room and a shower—my face burning with embarrassment. The spray of hot water relaxed me more than I thought was possible. Unfortunately, it was over too soon. The bed looked entirely too inviting as I stood drying my hair; I dared not try it on for size. I dressed and headed upstairs to meet everyone else.

Kasiah stood alone at the top of the stairs to the main deck, her eyes lost overlooking the moonlight glistening in the waves.

"Beautiful, isn't it?" I remarked.

"Incomparable," she whispered.

The yacht was moving fast for a vessel of this size. I could no longer see the city lights, and I'm not going to lie, it bothered me. The moon was bright and full, and twinkling stars filled the clear night sky. The crests of the small waves reflected the moon's glow, creating a never-ending light show. The only sounds were a slight hum from the yacht's engines along with the rhythmic splashes as the bow cut through the waves. It was actually very peaceful out here in the middle of nowhere. We stood there for several minutes, enjoying the view.

The lower deck door opened, and Aerona and Damien joined us.

"Everyone should have one of these yachts," Aerona said excitedly, leaning over the railing.

"Let's not forget why we're here," I reminded her.

"To be tasty vampire appetizers?" she teased.

"Not funny," Damien said, his voice sober. "Last week, I would have laughed, but now that I've seen an actual vampire rip a troll's head clean off, and I've been turned to stone, vampire appetizer jokes are no longer amusing."

We found Ember and Rain in the large glass-walled room in the main deck. Rain was seated on one of the several plush white couches. He kept his back toward us as he stood up, staring out the glass wall into the black of the night. He had traded in his tattered, bloodstained shirt for a black zip-up hoodie.

"Welcome," Ember greeted us. "Please have a seat and make yourselves at home."

Kasiah and I sat on one of the couches across from Ember, and Aerona and Damien sat on the one next to us. The couches were as comfortable as they were expensive.

Rain turned around from the window to study his new guests.

"Such an eventful evening," Ember started. "You must be hungry. We have a fully stocked kitchen and a fantastic chef ready to prepare anything you desire, and I do mean anything—he's wonderful."

"You have an extraordinary yacht," I said, breaking the tension, "and we can't thank you enough for getting us out of the city so swiftly, but I think we're all fine for the moment."

Ember sipped from her glass of wine. "It was my pleasure," she said. "After all, you came to my rescue without even knowing who you were rescuing. I'm the one who owes you a thank you."

"Let's call it even," I replied.

Rain wasted no time in getting right to the point. His eyes moved from me to Aerona and back. "So," he began, "I've seen enough to know you two aren't from this world."

FIFTEEN

I felt no reason to lie or bend the truth with a Shadow Vampire in the room. They're typically not very forgiving creatures. "My name is Erone," I said. "I'm a warlock from the Shadow World. This is my sister, Aerona, also a warlock. Kasiah and Damien are both with the FBI."

Kasiah and Damien traded glances of confusion, as if I had just blown their cover.

"What were you doing at the club tonight?" Rain asked.

I met his eyes. "Looking for you," I told him.

"Do you care to elaborate?" he asked, studying me closely.

"Have you been watching the news?" Damien questioned.

"As little as possible," Ember responded. "It's too negative, and they only tell you what they want you to hear to promote their own narrative and please their advertisers."

I felt the yacht make a slight right turn. It was a smooth turn, but we definitely changed course.

"Very true, Ember," I said. "Well, the one thing they have reported accurately is a serial killer has been leaving a trail of bodies from the east coast to the west, and we believe it's a Shadow Vampire like Rain."

Rain tensed, his eyes narrowed.

"*Like* Rain," I stressed again, "Not Rain. We're here for your help in tracking down the killer. We need to fight fire with fire, and you're it: a Shadow Vampire."

Rain looked confused. "Shadow Vampire?" he asked.

"That's what you are, aren't you?" I asked hesitantly.

Now I was the confused one.

"I am a vampire," Rain said. "My thirst for blood tells me I am. But I've never heard of a Shadow Vampire."

I exchanged a confused look with Aerona.

Ember detected our confusion. "You should know," she said, interjecting, "Rain doesn't exactly remember his past. All he knows about the Shadow World is from what I've told him, and I know very little, being a fairy. We were forbidden to even say '*Shadow.*'"

"But your strength and speed as you instinctively attacked those trolls," I said, redirecting my attention back to Rain, "combined with the ability to ignore fresh human blood, you're more advanced than any vampire created in this world. You're a Shadow Vampire."

"Created in *this* world?" he asked.

"Yes," I nodded. "Vampires created in this world have certain weaknesses. For example, they don't have control over their thirst. A single drop of human blood can send them into a feeding frenzy, similar to a great white shark. They literally can't help themselves. You didn't even think twice before walking away from Spider."

"I've tasted biker blood before," Rain said, grinning. "It's like a bad beer. You only drink it if there's nothing else."

"Speaking of the bikers," Kasiah joined in, "why were they after you?"

"The short version of the story is," Ember replied, "a few years ago, some of their biker buddies caught me in human form without my dust. They were ten seconds away from raping me when Rain came to my rescue. Unfortunately, as you may have noticed, Rain has a way of saving people that sometimes results in a few broken arms, crushed necks, and a dozen crashed motorcycles."

Aerona jumped in. "I'm thinking they don't let something like that go easily."

Ember took another sip of her wine. "Apparently not," she said.

"There really was no avoiding them at the club tonight," Rain explained, "and we just had no idea they were friends with werewolves and trolls."

"Well," I said, "I think we may have had something to do with that. The werewolves and the two trolls may have been sent by the other Shadow Vampire we spoke of—the one we're tracking. He had probably heard the bikers were searching for you, then paid them to let a few of his own henchmen tag along to make sure we didn't meet. Based on the bikers' surprised expressions, they had no idea they were traveling with trolls and werewolves.

"So why is this other Shadow Vampire after you?" Ember asked. "Shouldn't he be out on his killing spree?"

"We crossed paths with him in Madison," I explained, trying to tell the next part delicately. "A situation ensued, and we lost Kasiah's sister, Hayley."

Kasiah leaned back into the sofa, fighting back her tears.

"His name is Atmoro," I continued, "and he is definitely not working alone. In Madison, he had several other vampires working with him, ones turned in this world. Also, we don't believe this is a random killing spree. He's searching for something—the blood of a stone."

Ember shifted uncomfortably in her chair. "The blood of a stone?" she asked.

"Does that mean something to you?" I asked eagerly.

Ember was quiet for several seconds, debating whether to tell us what she knew. "Perhaps," she began cautiously, "it has something to do with a story I was told many years ago as a child. By definition, a stone is an angel who has been cast down to Earth to live with mortals, which doesn't happen often. Actually, from what I've been told, it hasn't happened in well over a century. See, being cast down to Earth is considered the worst form of punishment for an angel. They start growing old, but not as fast as typical humans. It takes a long time for an angel to lose all their power. It may even take a few decades for their power to drain. Eventually, their powers dwindle, they grow old, and die. That's when their soul is given a second chance."

"Atmoro wants the blood of an angel?" Kasiah asked, more to herself than anyone else.

"What is he planning to do with it?" Damien asked. "Does that make some kind of super vampire or something?"

Ember's additional insight into the mystery was an interesting discovery. I just wasn't sure where it would take us next. We needed to figure out how the blood of an angel would open the Forgotten Shadow City—and why.

"I have a friend," I said, thinking Tara might provide the help we needed. "A hacker who's been helping us try and piece together this little riddle. Let's see what she can find with this new piece of information. I don't want to jump to any conclusions right now, but it sounds like Atmoro intends to use the blood of an angel to open the Forgotten Shadow City."

"And that's bad," Rain commented, "right?"

"Bad isn't exactly the word I would use," I said, reminding myself of the type of criminals locked away in the prison. "I think catastrophic may be a better description or maybe the end of life as we know it. If the lock spell to the Forgotten Shadow City is broken, it could release all the Forgotten Shadows who have been imprisoned there for hundreds of years. This scenario is definitely filed under disaster."

That's when it struck me.

Aerona sensed my mood change. "What is it?" she asked.

I paused, knowing Atmoro would stop at nothing to get what he wanted. "I think I know what Atmoro is after," I said, wondering if it was possible.

"A cure for insanity?" Aerona kidded.

"No," I said, shaking my head. "He intends to break his wife out of the Forgotten Shadow City, and unfortunately, the only way is to release all the Forgotten Shadows."

Aerona recalled the same story from long ago when word of Atmoro's death spread throughout the Shadow World. "Christine!" she exclaimed. "Atmoro knows his wife was sentenced to the prison for jumping to the Light World."

"That's the only thing that makes sense," I said, running my hand through my hair. "That kind of motivation will push Atmoro to do whatever it takes to find a stone that bleeds. He's looking for the blood of a fallen angel."

"We know what Atmoro wants," Kasiah reasoned, drawing from her FBI experience, "and what he plans to do when he gets it. So, who in the room knows how to find an angel? There can't be very many *stones* wandering around. If we can find one, then maybe we can calculate Atmoro's next move."

Ember sipped her wine. "The only thing harder than finding an angel," she started, pausing to take another sip, "is finding a stone. Angels may lose their powers, but they have the greatest minds any world has ever known. Stones are ashamed of their punishment, and they've had centuries of experience hiding their true identity. They're so good at hiding themselves, even the FBI has never heard of them."

"Well, my brother and I," Aerona added, "know a few things about keeping secrets and hiding in the Light World."

"And even you two," Ember insisted, "had never heard of stones until today."

"True," I said, wondering how it was possible that I had never heard of stones. "Even so, we have more resources now. We have two warlocks, two federal agents, a fairy with knowledge of the Light World, and a Shadow Vampire. If anyone has a chance of stopping Atmoro, it's us. I, for one, like my life the way it is, and I don't want Atmoro to destroy it. We have fought too hard for too long to keep our existence a secret."

Aerona leaned back in the couch. "Atmoro and his crew of misfits," she said, "have caused enough commotion in the Light World. By now, news of a rogue vampire on a killing spree has certainly reached the Shadow Council. They may not know it's Atmoro and have no reason to suspect it, but they'll dispatch a hunting party to stop the vampire soon enough."

"That's a good point, Aerona," I said, considering her comment and wondering how we could use that to our advantage without leading the hunting party to ourselves. "We'll have to keep an eye out for a hunting party. We don't want to cross their path."

I felt the yacht change course for a second time, ever so slightly.

"The council you keep talking about," Damien suggested, "why don't we just let them take care of this problem?"

Damien was hoping we could all just wake up tomorrow and pretend as though nothing had ever happened.

"We have to assume the council doesn't know they're dealing with Atmoro," I said. "As far as the Shadow Council is concerned, Atmoro is dead. It's likely they believe it's a vampire created in this world that doesn't have any self-control over its thirst for human blood. The council had probably assigned a single Shadow Vampire to the hunt, not realizing Atmoro is behind all this chaos. For all we know, Atmoro has an entire army of vampires, werewolves, trolls, and probably even more. I'm sure he's anticipated the Shadow Council's involvement, and he may even be counting on it."

"Why don't you two contact this Shadow Council and tell them exactly that?" Damien continued. "Inform them that Atmoro is trying to break into their prison. We could get the FBI involved. You and Aerona could show them your unique abilities."

"Aerona and I have spent the last hundred years pretending to be dead," I explained, disagreeing with Damien's suggestion, "so we could protect our own identity. If we tip off the council, there's a possibility we would be found out and labeled jumpers. We'd end up in the Forgotten Shadow City for violating Shadow law."

"The only upside to that," Aerona said, always the optimistic one, "is then we'd both be rooting for Atmoro to succeed, so we could escape the Forgotten Shadow City. I think we've already shown that the FBI doesn't have the skills to deal with an army of Shadows. It would take far too long to convince the U.S. government that they have a war of worlds on their hands. They'd probably lock us up. Those idiots would spend millions of tax payer dollars dissecting us and trying to figure out how to market my beautiful flaming hands to China."

Aerona smiled her best evil smile as she held up both hands, palms up, with a baseball-sized rotating fireball hovering in each.

Ember's eyes widened. "No fire on the yacht!" she exclaimed.

Aerona extinguished the fire.

"Erone's right," Kasiah added. "The FBI doesn't have the resources to deal with something like this."

One of the yacht's crew members entered the room. She walked directly to Ember, whispered something in her ear, and then left the room as quickly as she had appeared.

Ember sat quietly for a few seconds before she stood up. "There's another vessel following us," she said. "It's about three miles behind, but it's been on our radar for the last twenty minutes. The captain has changed course twice, and the other vessel changed its course to follow. Right now, they've slowed down to match our speed, and they're still trailing us."

"Please tell me," Damien started, "you have some kind of actual defenses on this floating building."

"We have him," Ember said, pointing to Rain.

Aerona laughed out. "I had no idea vampires could swim."

Ember didn't seem amused with Aerona's comic relief—most people aren't.

"My crew has extensive defense training," she said, reassuring us that her vessel can protect itself. "And we have a well-stocked armory. We sail this yacht around the globe, and believe it or not, pirates are still a large threat on more than one ocean. In about ten minutes, we'll be in Canadian waters. If it's the U.S. Coast Guard, sometimes they escort large vessels to the edge of U.S. waters. If it's anyone else, we'll slow down and launch the small boat. Rain will slip back. He can see in the pitch black of night better than we can on a sunny day.

"You have a boat on your yacht?" Damien asked, surprised.

"Yes," Ember nodded, assuming everyone had million-dollar toys. "We have a twenty foot, 260 horsepower ski boat and two jet skis. They all launch from the stern. We use the boat for water skiing, parasailing, and going to the shore for supplies whenever shallower waters make it unsafe to dock the yacht at port. The jet skis are just for fun. The boat can be launched in just a few minutes."

"I'm clearly in the wrong profession." Damien said, shaking his head. He'd be lucky to afford the smaller jet boat on his FBI salary, let alone a ten million dollar yacht.

"It's not a good idea for Rain to go alone," I protested, "considering what was waiting for us outside the club tonight."

"I can handle myself," Rain stated.

I almost forgot I was talking to a Shadow Vampire that could kill everyone in this room.

"I'm just saying if you would like help," I reasoned, easing the tension, "count me in. I may be able to shut the vessels electronics without even boarding, which means their radar won't work, and we could leave them safely in our wake without any more bloodshed."

"My crew is monitoring the other vessel on radar," Ember added. "They'll report any changes to me immediately. If we need to take defensive action, we'll make the decision then."

"Atmoro is somehow able to track our movements," I said, still confused how he is tracking us. "Our cell phones may have been compromised. What other communications do we have with land?"

"We have a satellite phone," Ember explained. "It has a secure link to a fairy satellite. You are more than welcome to use it."

"Fairies have their own satellites?" Damien asked, surprised again.

Ember smiled. "I'm beginning to think you could fill an entire warehouse with all the things the FBI doesn't know."

Except Damien, we all laughed out.

"I need to contact Tara and give her this new information," I said. "Maybe she can piece the rest of the puzzle together and help us find a stone."

SIXTEEN

"I just uploaded the video," Jake said, holding the phone between his chin and shoulder. He pressed a few more keys on his laptop. "You should be able to access it now."

Atmoro, more than a thousand miles away, logged on to the secure website set up by his hacker/tech. He clicked the play button on the latest video from Jake, and the screen came alive.

"I can see it now. I'll call you back when I'm through," Atmoro said before hanging up.

The video bounced back and forth and up and down as Jake ran while filming. He stopped at the corner of a brick building to steady the camera and focus across the street. The image panned slowly left, then right, showing a typical downtown street lined with storefronts, a few park benches, and several large, evenly spaced maple trees lit by equally spaced street lights.

The image then stopped, zooming and focusing on one of the club entrances. A group of men exited the club, dragging along a young girl wearing a short, tight blue dress. She put up quite the struggle. The men all wore the same leather vests, appearing more as a group of motorcycle club bikers than typical club bouncers. They watched the club entrance, waiting anxiously for someone else to exit.

The club's door swung open, nearly ripping from its hinges. One man stood motionless, staring directly at the girl; he didn't look happy with the bikers. Atmoro assumed the girl was bait, and this guy was their chosen prey.

The video zoomed out to show more of the street. Atmoro was pleased with Jake's filming skills; he was improving.

The lone man moved unlike what Atmoro had ever seen, faster than even Atmoro himself. It was clear the man wasn't from the Light World. In a single second, the camera barely caught his movements as he grabbed the closest biker and flung him into the air. He crash landed through one of the storefront windows. Two other bikers, knives in hand, circled the man; he didn't seem fazed by them.

Both bikers attacked at the same time, anticipating their target couldn't fight them both at once—they were wrong.

Almost as if it was a well-choreographed fight scene, the two men lunged together. The lone man stepped forward, spun around, and grabbed each of their wrists below the knives, bending it in a way that made both men scream out. As if on cue, the two bikers fell to their knees, and each one received the other's sharp blade deep into their shoulders.

All of this happened in a split second, and it wasn't over yet. The bikers fell to the ground, clutching their shoulders with their unbroken hands. The lone man grabbed the closest injured biker and yanked the knife from his shoulder. He then forcefully held the biker's other hand against a nearby tree trunk and speared the blade through his hand—pinning him to the tree. The second biker, frozen with fear, received the same fate.

Several gun shots rang out, startling Jake as he filmed; the camera jumped. More shots popped through Atmoro's speakers. The lone man grabbed the closet motorcycle, lifted it up as if it was only a toy, and tossed it toward the gunman, who attempted to stop it with his face. A second motorcycle flew gracefully through the air, landing less gracefully on the windshield of a parked car. The gas tank exploded, and the car erupted into gasoline-fueled inferno.

Atmoro was impressed with this mystery man. His strength and speed were astonishing; it was that of a vampire. It troubled Atmoro that this vampire had such control over his thirst for human blood—he was a Shadow Vampire. Atmoro's crew had not trained to deal with a Shadow Vampire.

The bikers, losing confidence in their attack, retreated across the street, still holding the struggling girl. A troll and two large men, clearly werewolves based on their size and movements, appeared from an alley. It was getting interesting.

Four more people emerged from the club. Atmoro recognized them immediately as the two FBI agents and the two warlocks from Madison. The vampire seemed to be on the warlocks' side of the madness, only because he didn't nail them to a tree in the first three seconds. Two warlocks and a Shadow Vampire working together—that was checkmate for the werewolves and the troll.

Police sirens filled the speakers, and their red and blue lights danced on the glass buildings. Without hesitation, the female warlock created a wall of flames, blocking the police cars. The fire's intensity was too bright for the camera to handle; it took several seconds for the camera to focus correctly.

Jake's voice could be heard through the speakers as he was filming. "Holy shit!" he yelled.

Atmoro had seen warlocks perform this same illusion before, though not of this scale. The top of the flames reached the roofs of the buildings.

Unfazed by the fire, the troll was the first to attack. It stepped into the street, earning the attention of the vampire.

Atmoro's experience with trolls was minimal. Besides their ugliness— and this one *was* ugly—Atmoro also knew trolls were powerful creatures, and they could easily crush a vampire, assuming they managed to get their enormous hands on one. He was curious to see how this vampire dealt with something of that size.

The vampire took the offensive approach, attacking the troll down low. The troll crashed down, frantically swinging a giant broadsword, which the vampire easily dodged. The sword cracked the pavement, spraying about a shower of sparks.

The vampire was fast—extraordinarily fast. He leapt into the air, landing on the troll's back as it tried to stand, and forced it back to the pavement. Leaning closer to the small screen, Atmoro watched as the vampire latched onto the troll's head, ripping it clean off. The troll's head and body turned to ash and fell to the street.

"Damn!" yelled Jake from behind the camera. "This is award-winning footage!"

The two werewolves weren't discouraged by the troll's headless fate; they advanced together. The other warlock wasted no time, and directed his full energy toward the werewolves, knocking them back twenty feet into a parked truck; the impact lifted the left side off the ground, pushing it back.

Although stunned by the blow, the werewolves were back on their feet in seconds. This warlock apparently also knew how to play with fire. He shot powerful flames down the pavement, which resembled water spraying from a large, angry hose. The warlock extended his hands in front of him, combining the fire to form one concentrated stream. He had incredible control over his powers and was too fast for the werewolves to react. The fire met the first werewolf in the middle of the street, knocking him to the ground and burning him to ash. The other werewolf retreated to avoid the same doom.

Amazed, Atmoro continued to watch as the vampire and warlocks made the task of werewolf-and-troll slaying appear easy. Near the edge of the screen, a bright flash of light caught Atmoro's eye. The camera zoomed in to the struggling girl, who had transformed into a tiny fairy, only a few pixels on the screen.

Very interesting, thought Atmoro. *Why is a vampire so interested in saving a fairy?*

The fairy's transformation left the bikers vulnerable; they no longer had a hostage to use as a body shield. The vampire attacked the bikers, targeting the one who held the struggling girl.

Gun shots cracked through the speakers. The two bikers had just shot each other. The warlocks weren't in view, but one of them must have curved the bullets around the vampire and into the bikers. Atmoro leaned back in his chair. "Impressive," he remarked.

What happened next took Atmoro completely by surprise. With a deadly knife, the biker slashed wildly at the vampire. The surprising part wasn't that the vampire was able to easily dodge the blade, or that he grabbed the biker's arm in mid swing, broke it, and then slammed it into the brick wall behind; it was surprising to him that this vampire used the knife to make a long gash in the biker's face and then simply walked away from the fresh human blood.

The camera zoomed out suddenly to show a second troll appear from nowhere. Jake zoomed in to the far side of the street; the female FBI agent had collapsed. Atmoro watched intently as her partner removed something from her shoulder. Jake zoomed in. It was a dart. Atmoro knew from experience that the FBI agent didn't have long to live. Not even warlocks have the power to save someone from a poisoned troll dart.

When the camera zoomed back out, Atmoro noticed that the second troll had met the same fate as the first. It had turned to ash at the foot of the vampire, just as the camera came into focus.

The vampire raced to the agent struck by the dart. He had a brief conversation, one that Atmoro wished he could have heard. Seconds later, the vampire lifted the unconscious FBI agent and was gone. The wall of fire was dropped, and a moment later, every city street light, build light, police cruiser, and anything else electric—including the video camera—went out. The screen turned black.

Atmoro dialed Jake's cell phone.

Jake's phone came to life; the screen lit up and the ringer sounded. Atmoro's name flashed across the tiny screen. Jake let the phone ring several times before answering it. He enjoyed making Atmoro wait.

"Hello," Jake answered cheerfully.

"What happened to the video?" asked Atmoro.

"I'm not sure," Jake said. "Everything electrical just shut down for several minutes, and then just as suddenly, turned right back on."

"Did you follow them?" Atmoro asked.

"No," Jake said, lying. "I started in the same direction, but ran into an empty pier down at the lake. I'm pretty sure they're on the water somewhere."

Atmoro paused for several seconds. "OK," he said. "It's probably for the better. Their new friend is a Shadow Vampire. You're not ready to deal with a vampire of that level."

"I saw his capabilities," Jake said, frustrated with Atmoro's lack of confidence in him, "and there's nothing to worry about."

Atmoro's voice wasn't so pleasant as he spoke again. "No," he said angrily, "you will not pursue this vampire any further. You did not see even a fraction of his capabilities. A vampire with his strength, speed, and control would make short work of a newborn such as you."

Jake fought hard to keep his rage under control. "I think *you*," he said, the anger lurching inside him, "underestimate *my* capabilities, Atmoro. Do you think because a vampire took down a few drunken bikers and some sluggish trolls, that… that he's a super hero? This is absurd! I don't want to be hiding in the shadows filming videos. It's time I got into the action and got my hands a little dirty!"

Atmoro squeezed his cell phone, cracking the screen in several places. "You are talking from inexperience," he said, insulting Jake. "This vampire would run over you as if you weren't even there. You are not to pursue them any further. I have someone closer who will take it from here. This is the end of the discussion."

Jake's anger flared up. "Someone closer!" he yelled. "How many more secrets do you have, *master*?"

"You forget," Atmoro replied, growing impatient with Jake's defiance, "what I had told you from the beginning: I require your assistance for a short time, and if you disobey me, I would end your time as a vampire as quickly as it had begun. Now, you will obey me, or you will suffer the consequences."

Jake took a few seconds to calm down. He didn't need Atmoro second-guessing him. Truthfully, he didn't even know Atmoro's location, and he didn't want to be looking over his shoulder for the next decade, wondering if Atmoro was there waiting to kill him.

"I'm sorry, Atmoro," Jake said, attempting an apology. "I'm just a little anxious. I understand you have many more years of experience than me. I'm upset with myself for losing them at the dock. I trust your judgment, and I will wait for further instructions."

"It is understandable," Atmoro said, calming himself. "Do not let this happen again. I will be in touch soon. We are getting close. I can sense it."

Jake heard the line go dead. "Nice talking to you too," he said, shutting the laptop and sliding it back into his bag. He focused back on the water. The yacht was approximately two miles ahead, but Jake could still see its lights directly off the bow of the boat he had borrowed from the dock.

Jake figured he didn't know where Atmoro was, so why should Atmoro know where he was? Reluctantly, Jake agreed with Atmoro when he said this Shadow Vampire may be more than what Jake could handle right now, at least, out here on open water. Jake needed to regroup and rethink his plan. He pressed a few buttons on the GPS to set the dock location he had saved before heading out to follow the yacht. He turned the steering wheel and pushed the throttle down hard, lifting the bow out of the water as the engine roared as he headed back to shore.

SEVENTEEN

The phone rang several times before going to Tara's voice mail. "The number you are dialing has either been disconnected or is currently out of service. Please hang up and try again."

I was using Ember's satellite phone to call Tara from the bow of the yacht. Tara's heart was almost certainly pounding as an unrecognizable number popped up on her phone. Her misleading phone message was just to give the illusion that the number didn't exist. I let the message play through, then waited for a full thirty seconds of dead air before hearing the beep indicating I could leave a message.

"Tara, pick up," I said. "It's Erone."

I heard the phone line click on.

"Hey," Tara answered. "You're not calling from jail, are you? You better not be calling my land-line from a jail phone."

"No," I reassured her. "I'm on a secure satellite phone. I think maybe my phone has been tapped or compromised some way. Atmoro has been tracking us, and I need you to run some checks on our phones."

"I already did that a few hours ago," she said. "If Atmoro's tracking you, he's not doing it through your cell phones."

"Thanks, Tara," I said, considering the other ways through which Atmoro could be tracking us. "I'm not sure if that makes me feel better or not. Somehow, he knew we'd be in Erie right down to the exact address, where he had trolls and werewolves waiting for us."

"Trolls and werewolves?" she asked. "This keeps getting more exciting."

"You wouldn't be saying that if you were there. I actually called you with some more pieces of the puzzle that I'm hoping you can help decode."

"Let me just swing around here to my computer. OK, the last time we spoke, I got booted from that elf site. Let me tell you, those little creatures have kept up with technology. I seriously can't get back into that site. I've tried cloning my machine and sneaking in from a few backdoors I found the first time. They were all closed up. Water tight. No way in. I even went down to this little cyber café to use a dummy machine, and unfortunately, it didn't nearly have the security I needed. That machine is down for the count. I didn't even get to the second firewall when the elves fried the hard drive. I don't think I'll be allowed back to that particular café."

"Is there any good news?" I asked

"Not on my end," she said, sadly. "You?"

"I have what may be the missing piece of the puzzle," I explained. "Our new fairy friend had some very interesting information."

"Holy shit!" Tara said excitedly. "Now you're teamed up with vampires *and* fairies? We are so selling this story to some rich Hollywood film producer."

"We?" I asked jokingly. "Let's just get through this alive before discussing a movie deal."

"I wonder who they'll have play me," Tara said, fantasizing her nonexistent movie career. "Maybe…"

"Tara!" I exclaimed, cutting her off. "You'll just have to play yourself. No one else could possibly have enough energy to portray your character on the big screen. Now, pay attention!"

"Gotcha. Go."

I repeated what Ember had told us about stones.

"That certainly explains a lot," Tara remarked. "It takes our search in a whole new direction."

"True," I agreed. "Our new goal is to find a fallen angel, preferably before Atmoro does."

"Erone, I love how you make it sound as if it's an everyday task, like you need to find the closest coffee shop to your hotel or something. Can't your new fairy friend help?"

"She's trying," I said. "But we don't want to draw much attention from the fairies. She has family members on the Light Council, but if she starts asking questions about fallen angels, they're going to know something is up. The last thing we need is the Light Council thinking the Shadows are planning an attack."

Images of a war between the Light World and the Shadow World flashed through my mind. The casualties of such a war would be astronomical.

"Let's focus on finding a stone," I suggested, still disturbed by the images. "The only good news is that Atmoro may not be able to find a stone on his own. For all we know, he's interpreting 'the blood of a stone' as literally squeezing blood from a rock, which would explain why he risked so much to steal the nodule. Although, he must be rethinking his plan, since he's also been killing people with names linked to precious stones."

I tried to convince myself that Atmoro wasn't two steps ahead of us.

"How is Kasiah doing with the loss of her sister?" Tara asked.

"Well, despite almost losing her own life tonight," I said, "she's holding up."

"She's fortunate to have you by her side."

"I'll keep her safe," I responded, hoping it wasn't a lie.

"So what's the next step once we find a stone?"

"I'm not sure," I said, looking at my watch—it was 2:00 am. "We're getting together shortly to put a plan together. It'll probably be pretty straight forward: find the stone and keep him or her out of Atmoro's hands."

"Any idea how many stones are out there?"

"According to Ember," I explained, "it's very unlikely there is more than one stone, if any at all. Fallen angels are few and far between. Atmoro has been searching for who knows how long, and he's come up empty handed. And from what we've seen, he'll stop at nothing to get his hands on the blood of an angel."

I paused, letting my next thought sink in before saying it aloud.

"It's possible," I continued, letting the realism of the situation sink in, "that we may have to sacrifice the stone ourselves to keep the blood out of Atmoro's hands."

"Wow, that's heavy."

"It is," I agreed. "I'll make sure that's the last resort. I have a few tricks up my sleeve that would amaze God himself."

"Hah!" Tara laughed. "Well, if you turn any water into wine, save some for me. Knowing stone implies a person, and assuming blood is a literal translation, I can focus on finding that stone."

"Sounds logical. Let me know the moment you find anything."

"Will do, Erone. I'm all over it."

"Oh, and Tara…"

"Yes?"

"Watch your back over there. This is a dangerous game we're playing. People are dying, and the end is far from over."

Tara was silent for a few seconds.

"Are you still there?" I asked.

"Yes," she said quietly. "Don't worry about me. I also have a few tricks up my sleeve."

"I bet you do," I smiled. "I don't know how close or how far away you are from all of this, and I don't want you to ever tell me where you are, but please do watch your back. Keep covering your tracks and contact me if you need anything. You're a special person. I'm here if you ever need anything, and I mean that. Don't hesitate if you think something is out of place."

"OK, Erone. You watch your back too. Don't worry about the stone. I'm on it."

"Thanks, Tara. Hope to hear from you soon."

I hung up the satellite phone. The night breeze was blowing softly off the lake's surface up to the bow of the yacht. I thought I'd be out if I closed my eyes.

I walked back along the deck to meet everyone else.

"Erone," Ember said as I walked in. "The boat that was trailing us has suddenly turned around and headed right back to port."

"Coast guard?" I asked.

"We're not sure," Ember said. "The crew will be on double watch tonight. No need to worry."

"That's good news," I said, feeling safer. "Where exactly are we?"

Ember looked out the wall of glass into the night sky. "We're anchored approximately five miles south of the Canadian peninsula, Long Point. We can get to a number of ports in a hurry if need be."

I repeated most of my conversation with Tara, leaving out the sentimental part at the end.

"Just keep this information as quiet as we can for now," I warned. "We don't want it falling into the wrong hands. We'll give Tara a few hours."

"We should get some rest while we wait for more information," Kasiah suggested.

"I have a few questions for Erone," Rain said. "Maybe tomorrow we can talk about Shadow Vampires. I'd like to learn as much as I can. Anything that may help me remember who I am and where I came from."

"Definitely," I said, jumping at the chance to learn more about Rain's unknown past. "Any information I have about vampires is yours. You're a truly unique creature, even for your kind. I would be honored to help you."

"Get some rest," Rain suggested. "We can talk tomorrow. I'll head up to the bridge and take the late watch so the crew can get some rest. It may be a long day tomorrow."

Rain walked toward the door, stopping long enough just to whisper something in Ember's ear. Then, he gave her the warmest embrace I had ever seen. I've been watching them, and I don't think they're a couple. I feel he loves her as a sister, and he would do anything for her.

Rain disappeared through the doorway.

Aerona and Damien said their goodnights, then left to find their cabins for some much needed rest.

"Thank you so much for your hospitality," I said to Ember.

"And thank you for coming to my rescue," she replied. "Atmoro is a problem for all of us and our way of life. If he succeeds in releasing the

Forgotten Shadows, it could destroy my world as well as yours. Fate has brought us together. We're in this with you."

"Please don't hesitate to wake us if you need anything," I said, grateful for her support, "especially if that other vessel returns."

"Good night to the both of you," Ember said. "It was a pleasure meeting you both."

"The pleasure is ours," Kasiah smiled.

Ember smiled and followed Rain out.

"Well," said Kasiah. "I suppose we should get some rest, assuming I can relax enough to close my eyes."

"I know what you mean," I said, staring out into the darkness. "I have so many thoughts running through my head right now. I think the only way I'll get some rest is if I can convince you to strike me over the head with a large, blunt object."

Kasiah looked around the room. "I'm afraid everything in this room is far too expensive to be broken over your head," she joked, her lips forming a beautiful smile. "We may have to resort to beating it against the wall."

We both broke out in a laugh. Kasiah's humor turned out to be just as attractive as the rest of her.

"I miss her," Kasiah said, her smile changing into a frown.

I knew she was talking about Hayley, but I didn't know what to say. I don't think I could handle losing Aerona the same way Kasiah had lost her sister. My sister has been my best friend for as long as I can remember. Just the thought of anything happening to her sends a chill down my spine. I can't imagine what Kasiah was feeling knowing that she put Hayley into the situation that took her life in such a horrible way.

I don't think words were what Kasiah was looking for. I reached out and pulled her close, and she placed her head on my shirt to hide her newly formed tears.

"We're going to stop him," I assured her, holding her tight. "We found Rain and Ember for a reason. Together, we have a pretty good chance at stopping Atmoro."

Kasiah drew in a breath. "I should have listened to you," she wept. "I should have taken you more seriously. I overestimated my own ability as an agent. I failed Hayley. She's always thought so highly of me, as if I was some kind of a superhero. I failed her when it mattered most."

I pulled her in even closer. "I know there's nothing I can say that will bring her back or make you feel any better," I said, fighting back my own tears. "Time is the only thing that will heal that wound, but I do know Hayley would want you to take all your courage, all your strength, and every piece of your soul to stop this from happening to anyone else. Somewhere out there, an angel is being hunted by a vampire who intends to draw out and use its blood as a key to open a door that shouldn't even exist. We're the only ones who can stop this from happening. I don't think Hayley has ever been more proud of her big sister than this very moment as she watches from the sky above."

Kasiah raised her head; her eyes had gone red from the tears. "You're one of a kind, Erone. I wish I could have met you at a different time, a different place. Let's go get some rest."

I nodded in agreement.

We left the massive main room and followed a spiral staircase down to the lower level into the cabins. The lights were dimmed for the night, giving off just enough light to navigate the hallway.

"I think this is your room," I said, approaching the room Kasiah was in when we boarded the yacht.

Kasiah stopped by the door, and without a word, she turned and pressed her lips to mine.

113

EIGHTEEN

My pulse reached warp speed as our lips parted. Kasiah's beautiful, brown eyes met mine, and without even thinking about it, I kissed her back, passionately.

We were startled by a door slamming down the hall, causing us to separate again.

"Good night," Kasiah said, smiling devilishly as she walked into her room.

The door swung slowly closed behind her, leaving me alone in the hallway.

"Good night," I said, my voice barely a whisper.

I started toward my room, feeling more confused than I had ever been before. I didn't have time to fall in love with an FBI agent; we were supposed to be saving the world. Yet, I couldn't shake Kasiah's kiss from my mind. It was the single most amazing kiss of my life, and I've been around for a long time. Her lips were unbelievably soft—softer than the smoothest silk. I could have stayed in that moment for eternity.

Several minutes later, I found myself back at Kasiah's door, knocking quietly while secretly hoping she wouldn't answer. "Erone, you're an idiot!" I said to myself.

The door cracked open.

"Took you long enough," Kasiah said, opening the door wide enough for me to enter. "I actually thought I was going to have to sleep alone tonight."

The room was dimly lit by the moonlight shining through the port window. My heart was racing.

Kasiah opened the minibar and took out a bottle of wine. "I'm sorry I caught you off guard," she said, handing me the bottle and a corkscrew.

My cheeks flushed. "Maybe I was a little surprised," I admitted.

"I surprised myself a little too," Kasiah replied, taking two glasses.

The bottle opened with a *pop*, startling us both. I poured two glasses of wine and handed one to Kasiah.

She took a sip from her glass. "Well," she continued, turning her gaze out the window, "one of us had to make the first move, and I asked myself, 'when is the next time I'll be on a multimillion-dollar yacht with a cute warlock from another world?'"

I walked up behind her and placed my hands lightly on her shoulders, and as if it was scripted, she leaned back against me.

"It's such a beautiful night," she remarked, tilting her head back.

"As are you," I said, letting my hands slide down to find her hips.

She turned and pressed her mouth to mine; her lips were soft and gentle.

"That's true," she said, kissing me again. "When you look at me, I feel… I feel you are seeing something no one else can see."

Another kiss.

"I see you, Kasiah," I said, running the back of my hand along her cheek. "I see your unique personality, and your contagious smile that cuts through the darkest sadness."

She kissed me again, harder this time. I tasted the wine's sweetness on her lips. I could feel the rapid beat of her heart against my chest, racing faster to keep pace with mine. She let out a slight sigh as our lips separated.

"You're not a bad kisser," she observed, running her hands through my already messy hair.

"Lucky for you," I said, trying to be charming. "I usually charge an arm and a leg for these up-close-and-personal lessons."

"Where do you get your charm, Erone?"

I smiled. "That's part of my mystery."

"I like you," she said, laughing with me.

We talked as we finished the bottle of wine. It was easy to be with Kasiah. I hadn't felt those feelings in a long, long time. Forgetting about the mad world outside, we focused on each other instead.

Kasiah kicked off her shoes and set down her empty glass. Before I knew it, she was standing in nothing more than a light blue bra and intricate lacy panties. A bright white bandage covered the wound on her side. She kissed me again, more aggressively this time. My hands explored her back, eventually finding her bra clasp. I spun her around and cupped her firm, warm breasts from behind. Her breath increased with my touch as her hands loosened my belt.

"You have the gentlest touch," she whispered, leaning back into me.

I told her how incredibly sexy and soft her body was as we moved backwards toward the bed, falling onto the covers, she landing on top of me.

Kasiah continued to kiss me with intense passion, squeezing her legs around me as I went inside her. We moved together to the center of the bed, kissing harder, faster. Her fingernails scratched down my chest; the pain releasing a dose of adrenaline into my blood.

She screamed out—so did I.

Afterward, with her naked legs wrapped around me, we lay under the silk sheets holding each other, wishing time could freeze.

"If this is a dream," Kasiah said, rolling halfway over so her back was against me, "please don't wake me, okay?"

I squeezed her gently.

We laid still, tangled in each other, lost in the moment. I felt Kasiah's breathing slow down as she fell asleep. If vampires weren't trying to kill us, it would have been a perfect evening.

I waited until Kasiah was long off in dreamland before slipping out from under the sheets. I paused at the bathroom door to look at Kasiah, naked and stretched out elegantly along the bed, her head nestled comfortably on a pillow. She looked so strong and beautiful. I walked silently back to the bed and covered her with the white silk sheet.

Our clothes were scattered throughout the floor and I didn't bother trying to collect them. I had a quick shower and wrapped my waist with one of those fluffy towels. I was careful not to turn on the lights as I stepped back to the room. I didn't want to risk waking Kasiah; she needed her rest. We both did.

NINETEEN

Jake slammed his fist against the desk, knocking over the lamp. "Dammit, kid!" he yelled into the phone. "I swear I'll make an unscheduled stop in Boston and break your skinny, little neck if you don't crack this encryption!"

Ian, a twenty-two year-old graduate student at MIT, was typing as fast as his fingers would allow him. He didn't usually mind working for Atmoro, but this new guy had some serious anger issues. Normally, Ian would have been able to get through the code easily if there wasn't a maniac screaming at him on the other end of the phone.

"If you will just listen!" Ian yelled back at Jake. "Whoever wrote this code is a damn genius. I don't know what you want me to do. I'm working as fast as I can. And stop calling me kid. It's Skywalker!"

"What I want you to do, kid," Jake reiterated, "is figure out who's been searching the internet for blood of a stone. That is what you're getting paid for, isn't it? And for the record, I am not calling you Skywalker... KID!"

Ian was beyond irritated with this impatient simpleminded asshole. Less than a month back, Ian hacked into a bank server that had a Yakashi 6100 security system, supposedly the most advanced bank security software in the world. It took him less than three hours to do the job. As usual, he didn't particularly care why his client wanted the job done, especially since his own bank account was now a hundred thousand dollars heavier as payment. Besides, he may or may not have spent an extra few minutes building in a backdoor to the Yakashi so he could go back in later.

And now, here he sat, arguing with this screaming idiot, attempting to hack this one little computer—without success.

Ian was on his last nerve. "What do you think I'm doing here, Jake?" he screamed, losing his temper. "I'm certainly not tuning my fucking piano! The signal keeps jumping around. First it was in Colorado, then Mexico, and now it's bouncing around Japan. I'm chasing it as fast as my PC will let me. So back off!" Ian calmed down a bit "I thought Atmoro was tough. You have some serious anger issues. You're lucky your boss pays me so well, because you're a real dick to work with."

In his hotel room in Erie, Jake kicked the desk chair to the wall. He was still fuming that his plan to eliminate the warlocks went so horribly wrong. He needed to find out who was helping them, and then take them out of the game—with or without Atmoro's permission.

Jake was thirsty; he needed some blood to calm his nerves. He turned his attention back to the phone. "Listen here, you little hacker bastard..." he began.

Ian put the phone down next to his laptop. He could still hear Jake yelling into the phone. Ian was not easily impressed, but whoever set this security system up had ingenious skill. Ian's been breaking through one firewall after the next, and he still kept getting shut down. Five minutes before, he was almost in; then he got completely booted out and had to start all again. He would like nothing more than to finish the job and get Jake off his phone.

Finally, he made some headway. The system he was hacking must have been a home system. He guessed there was wireless link from a smart TV to the network router. Most people don't realize if their TV has a wireless internet connection for downloading movies, which is typically a connection that has minimal security and is vulnerable for cyber-attacks. Ian only needed to piggyback whatever show was streaming, and he was in!

He quickly cloned his second laptop as a decoy. He had looped that one to continue knocking on the firewall to keep the user's attention as he slipped in through the TV's wireless connection with his main machine.

Piece of cake, he thought to himself.

It worked; Ian was in. He picked up the phone and said, "I got an IP address. Give me a few minutes to backtrack it, and I'll get you the home address, you impatient prick!"

"You're on my list kid!" Jake shouted, still thirsty. "Better lock your window tonight!"

"I'm terrified," Ian joked. "Are you going to have your mommy drive you over here?"

Ian didn't really care about pissing Jake off. Truthfully, he didn't even really know who was on the other end of the phone. He didn't care either. All Ian knew was that Jake worked for Atmoro, and Atmoro paid on time. Ian didn't have anything to worry about. He wasn't a student at MIT or even Boston—he's never even been to Boston. Jake only knew him as Skywalker, the name he used when dealing with Atmoro. Ian's not dumb enough to take the types of jobs he takes and give out his real name. Whenever a job was done, he destroyed his laptops, phones, and everything else. He vanished without a trace. After this job, he was close to being done with Atmoro. The whole thing was getting a bit weird, and it was time to get out before it's too late.

Ian heard crashing sounds over the phone, and he thought he heard another phone ringing on Jake's end. He knew he was getting on Jake's nerves.

"I've got your info," Ian explained. "I was only in for a few seconds before the user noticed and booted me, but it was long enough. I'm sending it to your email now."

"Don't forget to lock your window tonight," Jake warned before ending the call abruptly.

Jake's hotel room phone was ringing off the hook. All he needed now was for the hotel manager to come banging on the door. "Hello," Jake answered.

"This is the hotel manager. We've had several noise complaints for your room. You need to keep it down in there, or we'll be forced to call the police."

"Great," Jake responded in anger.

"Excuse me, sir?"

"I said *wait*, don't get carried away. We're in bed now, and there shouldn't be any more issues."

"No more noise," the manager warned and hung up.

Jake slammed down the receiver. He was still pissed off at that hacker kid and his cocky attitude. Didn't he know he was dealing with a criminal mastermind? To top it off, one of his hotel neighbors was making a stink about a little noise.

Jake grabbed a quarter off the nightstand and flipped it in the air. "Heads, right room. Tails, left."

The quarter flipped swiftly into the air. Jake caught it with his right hand and slapped it onto the back of his left; Washington's face stared back at him. The couple in the room to his right were about to have a very unpleasant wake up call.

"I'll give you a noise complaint," Jake grumbled, poking a few buttons in his cell phone to access Skywalker's email. "*Tara Whitefield, 3246 East Washington Ave. Chicago, IL*"

TWENTY

I was wakened by my cell phone vibrating on the nightstand. It took me a few seconds to get my bearings and open my eyes. I was in what appeared to be a hotel room; a room with a port window? I reached across Kasiah's naked body to grab my phone, knocking over an empty bottle of wine from the nightstand. Kasiah didn't stir. She was still sleeping peacefully.

"Hello?" I answered, barely awake.

"I found her!" Tara yelled.

"Found who?" I asked quietly, trying not to wake Kasiah.

"THE STONE!" she shouted. "I found a fallen angel!"

I sat up immediately as images of the past few days flashed through my mind. It all came rushing back.

"Tara, did you just say you found a fallen angel?"

"That, my friend… is correct."

"What do you have?" I asked, swinging my legs off the bed.

I heard Tara typing rapidly in the background. She was a master multitasker.

"Well," she continued, still typing, "I started by searching for fallen angels, stones, and a few variations and I came up with the same old dead ends. I tried poking around a few times at that elf site, hitting the same walls as before. I was getting nowhere fast. So, I started asking myself 'how do you start searching for something that supposedly doesn't even exist?' And that's when it hit me like a freight train. I should be looking for something that doesn't exist! I don't know why I didn't think of this before—"

"Something that doesn't exist?" I interrupted.

"Sorry," she said. "To make a long story short, I started checking birth records against social security numbers and death certificates. I guessed fallen angels must have *existed* at one time or another. They were real people before they were angels, right?"

"That sounds like logical reasoning," I said, nodding my head as if Tara could see me.

"I know, right?" Tara said excitedly. "So anyways, if they were real people, then they'd have birth certificates for when they were born and death certificates for when they… umm… passed over? Is that right? Passed over?"

"Yes, Tara. That'll work for this story. Go on."

"OK. OK. OK," she said. "Umm where was I? Oh, so I searched for active social security numbers with birth information that would have made the person, well, made them old, very old, maybe too old. I was looking for numbers where the person, if still alive, would have to be the oldest person on the planet. My whole theory was that fallen angels were people born many years ago. They died and went to heaven, became an angel, and then sent back as fallen angels for one reason or another. I figured that they might have used the same names as their previous lives. I was thinking maybe they'd wanted to make things right or whatever. That's what I would do."

Tara paused. I heard more typing.

"Sorry," she continued. "The past couple hours I've had some attacks on my firewall. Don't worry, I've got it under control."

While Tara was ranting about hackers, I climbed out of bed and found my clothes. Kasiah stirred, rolled over, and replaced me with a large, fluffy pillow. The morning sun reflected off her hips. Her bandage was still nice and white, meaning her wound didn't reopen through the night.

"Erone, you there?" Tara asked.

"Yes, go on," I said, shaking Kasiah's body from my mind.

"Well," Tara continued, "I weeded out all illegal immigrants who bought or stole deceased social security numbers. Oh, and for your information, there's a lot. You wouldn't believe how many fake or reactivated social security numbers exist. It's rather ridiculous. Hold on…"

Tara was typing furiously. I almost felt bad for her keyboard. I pictured her at a desk with monitors all around, playing the role of an evil supervillain. In reality, she was probably sitting in a college dorm room with nothing better to do.

"This little bastard is persistent," Tara scoffed. "Just wait until I give this jackass my full attention. I'll cook their machine like a marshmallow over a backyard fire on a nice cool fall night."

If she wasn't an evil supervillain now, she would be someday.

"OK, Erone, I'm back. Argh! So, I narrowed my list down to just a few hundred—"

"A few hundred!" I cried out.

"Yes," she replied, "there are seven hundred and twenty-four to be exact. An hour ago, I narrowed the list down to just two names: Richard and Tamitha Dunham. Two people who perished in a house fire twenty years ago."

I was still lost. "How does that help us?" I asked.

"Patience, Erone. Patience," Tara insisted. "Mr. and Mrs. Dunham were only thirty-five at that time, and yet, they were both born in 1828 and were married in 1844. Tamitha's maiden name was Jenson, and they were in their early forties when their original death certificates were issued. The cause of death was never recorded."

"Interesting," I mumbled, more to myself than to Tara.

"Interesting!" Tara exclaimed. "This is the smoking gun, my friend!"

"Tara, didn't you just say they both died in a house fire?"

"Yes, but I didn't tell you the best part," Tara said, pausing dramatically. "They had a daughter 21 years ago. If they were dead, how did they conceive a child? Only if they weren't, and if I'm right, this is the first true-blood angel… EVER! See, angels are created in heaven, but this one was *born* here on earth. She's the daughter of two fallen angels—two *stones*. Doesn't that also make her a stone? She's like a super stone."

"Do you have any information on the daughter?" I asked, knowing she would have everything.

"I have everything."

More keyboard clicking.

"OK, here it is," she continued. "Her name is Jade Dunham. She turned twenty-one last month, and she's currently a student at the University of Montana. Did you know it's considered the most scenic university in the country? I didn't know that, but then I thought it does have mountain views full of rich dark forests and—"

"Tara!" I exclaimed, keeping her on track.

Kasiah rolled over to her other side, taking the covers and leaving one of her legs exposed. I saw a tiny, multicolored butterfly tattoo on her ankle. *Interesting.*

"Sorry," Tara said, calming down. "Richard and Tamitha Dunham perished in a house fire, but their one year old daughter, Jade Dunham, survived. Their neighbors, Mr. and Mrs. Harper, adopted Jade. Later that week, they changed their surnames to Dunham. That's strange, right? Changing names? Well, other than that, Jade has grown up like a typical young woman. This is her third year at Montana, and she has a dual major, Microbiology and Chemistry."

"What about her social life?" I asked. "Friends, job, or hobbies?"

"That's the weird part. Her social life is slim to almost non-existent. I couldn't find any social network pages or even an e-mail address other than her school email. She also doesn't belong to any local athletic clubs, the library, or the video rental store."

"Great job, Tara. This wasn't an easy task by any means, and like you said, you were searching for something that wasn't even supposed to exist."

"Thanks, Erone. It means a lot coming from you."

"You're welcome, Tara. I'm going to wake everyone else and fill them in. I'm not sure of our travel plans yet, but I'm sure we'll start as soon as possible."

"I'm so glad I was able to help," Tara said, breathing a sigh of relief. "I love a good challenge, but this one takes the cake. Let me know if you need anything else. I have to get going and take care of this annoying hacker wannabe messing with my network. Be safe."

I ended my call with Tara and dialed Aerona's number. The phone only rang once before she picked up.

"Little brother," Aerona answered, "if you're calling to tell me how you scored with Kasiah last night, save it. It was torture being within range of your emotions. I tried everything to turn it off, and none of it worked. You owe me big for this one."

I felt my cheeks heat up from embarrassment. "Sorry," I said, "I didn't think of that. It must have been awkward."

Aerona's voice wasn't as comical as it was before. "Awkward!" she cried. "Awkward isn't the right word. I had to lie awake in bed while my brother's dirty thoughts ran through my head. You know you're a pervert, don't you? At least, for Kasiah's sake, you lasted more than five minutes your first time."

"Nice, Aerona, real nice," I said, embarrassed. "Let's keep this between us. I don't want the rest of the team thinking our heads aren't in the game."

"*Our little secret*," she mocked. "I kind of like having something to hang over your head anyway."

Aerona sounded entirely too excited. I wasn't looking forward to her future blackmailing. "Well," I said, changing the subject, "we have some good news from Tara. She found a fallen angel, possibly the only one on earth."

"She did what?" Aerona shrieked. "Wow! When do we leave?"

"As soon as we can. Can you round up Damien, Ember, and Rain? We'll meet upstairs in thirty minutes. I'll fill everyone in so we can make a plan."

"Copy that," she agreed. "I'm ready to go, and I bet Damien is already up, chomping at the bit. We'll see you in thirty."

"Thanks, Aerona."

"No problem. Oh, and one more thing…"

"Yes?" I asked, not really wanting to know.

"Don't forget to smack Kasiah's cute little ass while you're in the shower!"

"You're so mature," I sneered.

I heard Aerona laughing as she ended the call

I sat back down next to Kasiah. I hated having to wake her up; she looked so peaceful. I kissed her cheek. Her breathing paced up. I ran my hand from her thigh up to her hip, and as she rolled over onto her back, I let my hand fall away.

"Good morning," she said, smiling and rubbing her eyes. "I was wondering if you'd still be here when I woke up."

"Nothing from this world," I said, "or mine, could have stopped me from holding you all night. You're an amazing woman."

"And you are an amazing man. Thank you for staying."

"It was all my pleasure," I said foolishly. "I wish we could lay here as though we were on a wonderful world cruise, but Tara called me. She found a stone."

Kasiah's eyes popped open. They were a nice, light chocolate color in the morning.

"Her name is Jade," I explained, "and she's in Montana. I'll give you all the details later. We need to get moving. We have no idea how long it'll be before Atmoro retrieves the same information. He may already be on his way."

Kasiah pulled the silk sheet over her body and sat up, resting her back against the headboard. "What makes you think he'd already have this information?" she asked.

"I'm not sure how Atmoro's been tracking us," I said, wishing I did, "but somehow he was aware of every move we made. If we have the stone's location, he's sure to be right behind us."

"Have you told anyone else?" Kasiah asked.

"I just got off the phone with Aerona. She's gathering everyone else, and we're to meet them upstairs in thirty minutes."

"Do I have time for a quick shower?" she asked, holding the sheet around her as she got out of bed.

"Yes. I'm going to run to my room and do the same. I'll be back to get you in twenty."

"See you in twenty," she said, letting the sheet fall away as she walked into the bathroom.

127

TWENTY-ONE

As I finished with my shower, I was surprised to find my backpack on the bed. Everything had happened so quickly after we were attacked at the club, we never had a chance to go back to the hotel and collect our belongings. Ember certainly had something to do with this; it's amazing what you can accomplish with a bottomless bag of money.

I dressed in a fresh pair of jeans and a vintage T-shirt that purposely appeared much older than it was, then shoved my cell phone in my pocket and grabbed my watch. It was a nice feeling wearing clean clothes again. Unsure of what to do with my dirty clothes, I folded them and kept them at the end of the bed; who knows, maybe someone would wash them and leave a mint on my pillow. I headed to Kasiah's room.

"Hello, handsome," Kasiah said, answering her door.

Her fashion tastes were similar to mine: a stylish pair of jeans enhanced by a black leather belt embedded with miniature metal stars fit her curves perfectly. Her black T-shirt had a white star pattern that started at her shoulder, then spiraled down to the opposite side, becoming smaller as it disappeared around her back. The shirt's neck and edges had the same tiny tears as my own, giving it that same worn-in, vintage look.

"Come in," Kasiah said, tying back her long hair.

She ran her hand through my hair several times, giving it a natural messy style. Then, she stood back and formed both of her hands into two Ls, like a movie director.

"Much better," she remarked, peering at me through the frame.

"Thanks," I said. "I never had an FBI stylist before."

"Wait until you see the bill," she smiled.

"I hope you accept fake credit cards," I said, sitting on the edge of her bed, "since I never carry cash."

"We accept several forms of payment," she added, building up the punch line. "One of which you prepaid with last night."

"Well, if that's true," I continued, "then I'll take two cases of whatever you're selling. You can expect payment later today."

"So, you're a morning person?" she asked, sitting beside me to put her shoes on.

"I am when I wake up next to a beautiful woman," I said, shoving my foot directly into my mouth.

"Does that occur often?" she asked, questioning me like an FBI agent questions a suspect. "The beautiful woman part, I mean."

I'm smart enough to know a trap question when I hear one, and that was a trap. This is the same as when a girl asks if her jeans make her look fat—Kasiah's definitely did not.

I looked at my watch as a way out. "We need to get moving," I said, grinning. "Everyone else is probably waiting for us."

Kasiah gazed at me for a long moment. "Nice save," she said. "Well played."

The morning sun welcomed us on the main deck at the bow of the yacht. I couldn't see any other vessels on the horizon. The lake itself was incredibly quiet, and there was no wind, not even a breeze, which made the surface of the lake appear as smooth as a sheet of glass. The sky was scattered with a few puffy, white clouds, and the sun rays cut their way through a thin fog. It was very peaceful. I could get used to mornings like this.

A fairly large swimming pool, especially for one on the deck of a boat, was surrounded by several round tables with woven grass umbrellas perched on bamboo poles through the center of each table. Ember and Rain were seated at one of the tables. Rain, motionless like a statue, had on dark sunglasses and a long-sleeve black hoodie—hood up. Thin wires dangled from earbuds down to his phone. I found it interesting that he was able to be out in the morning sun; even a strong Shadow Vampire would have issues with today's sun. Yet, Rain didn't seem affected at all.

Ember's khaki shorts and bright blue bikini top enhanced her eyes and the dark blue dress on her fairy tattoo. She was relaxed, sipping a cup of coffee across from Damien, who looked very nautical in his shorts, sandals, and white button up shirt.

Aerona discreetly flashed me her middle finger as we joined everyone on the deck. She wore a shirt with "Nerd Tossing Champion 1996" stenciled in faded lettering around a humorous logo across the front.

"Wasn't it a violation of contest rules to toss yourself?" I asked Aerona.

Aerona's quick wit was second to none. "You're just upset because you didn't place that year," she shot back.

My sister's playful sarcasm showed me she wasn't still upset with the flood of emotions from my night with Kasiah; if she didn't respond at all, then I'd be in trouble.

"Ember," I started, "thank you for retrieving our bags from the hotel. I hope you didn't risk too much in doing so."

"Actually it was Rain," she explained. "He took the small boat back to Erie and returned before sunrise."

"Thank you, Rain," I said, not knowing if he heard me with his earbuds in. "It's nice to wear a fresh set of clothes."

"You're welcome," he replied without looking up. "The city is swarming with police and pissed off bikers."

"Any sign of vampires?" Kasiah asked.

Rain took one of his earbuds out. "I didn't have time to do any scouting," he continued. "I went straight to the hotel and back. After seeing the police presence, I'd say we shouldn't go back to Erie for a while."

"We won't have to," I said. "We may be headed to Montana."

Ember put down her coffee cup. "Montana?"

Kasiah and I sat down at the table with everyone else. A member of the crew, dressed in white shorts and a white polo shirt with "Ember's Star" embroidered in elegant script over the pocket, rushed up to the table and placed menus in front of us. The menus looked like they belonged in a five-star restaurant. Each had a picture of the yacht and the same Ember's Star logo on the cover.

"My name is Andrea," she said, pouring us glasses of orange juice. "Our chef's special this morning is a 10 oz. hickory-smoked bone-in ham steak served with two eggs, hash browns, and fluffy, buttermilk pancakes. We also have a wide variety of fruits available, including fresh strawberries, pineapple, black-berries, mangos, and orange slices, all topped with freshly whipped cream. I'll give you a few minutes to decide."

Andrea backed away from the table, folding her arms behind her. "Ember," she said, "the rest of your guests' orders will be ready in a few more minutes. Is there anything else I can get you?"

"Thank you, Andrea," Ember said. "We're fine for now."

Andrea disappeared just as fast as she had arrived.

"So why are we going to Montana?" Ember asked.

I took a sip of my orange juice. "I got a call from Tara. She believes she found a stone. Her name is Jade Dunham, and she's a student at the University of Montana."

Rain took out the other earbud. "It's that simple?" he asked.

"Actually, it might be," I said. "There's a good possibility Jade doesn't even know she's a stone."

I gave them the condensed version of the conversation I had with Tara earlier.

"Jade's parents died twice over a hundred years apart?" Ember asked, as I did when Tara first told me. "How did no one else notice this?"

"I asked myself the same question," I said. "I suppose the U.S. government handles death records like they handle everything else—poorly. I guess when someone is born, there's no reason to search archived records to make sure that same someone hadn't been born before, right?"

Ember nodded and took a sip of her coffee. "Very true," she said, taking another sip.

"Based on the information we have," I continued, "I think we should, at least, follow up the lead by locating Jade and verifying our information. She could be in a lot of danger in the very near future. We're about to take the next step in an extremely dangerous game."

"How do we play a game," Rain asked, sitting up in his chair, "when we don't even know the rules?"

"I don't believe Atmoro plays with rules," I replied. "That's what makes it so dangerous, especially with such a valuable prize."

"I think I know someone who may be able to help," Ember added, "someone that's used to quick-changing rules."

Rain shook his head. "Not Whisper."

"Yes," she nodded, "and you two need to kiss and make up."

"Who's Whisper?" I asked.

"Whisper is unique," Ember continued. "His vast knowledge of the Light World will surely be helpful, and he has a few special skills that will prove invaluable"

Rain shook his head a few more times. "Whisper is unique alright," he remarked sarcastically, air quoting as he said unique.

"What's the story between these two?" asked Aerona, always wanting to spark a fire.

"There is no story," Rain murmured.

"The story," explained Ember, "is that Whisper and Rain are like two alpha male lions trying to lay claim to the same piece of land. They're just too much alike for their own good. Typical men who don't realize that together they're stronger."

"He cheats, and you know it," Rain said in his defense.

"Whisper owes me a few favors," Ember said, ignoring Rain. "This may be a good time to cash in on one or two."

"Can he be trusted?" I asked.

"Yes, "she nodded. "I'll vouch for Whisper. He has many skills that may come in handy over the next few days."

Andrea and two other crew members walked out on the deck again, each carrying a large serving tray. They placed full plates of food in front of Rain, Damien, and Aerona. It looked like they ordered the chef's special.

Most people would be surprised to see a Shadow Vampire eating like everyone else. It's a myth that they only crave human blood. Blood contains all the nutrition they need to survive, and it is the key to their abilities, but they enjoy a good breakfast just as much as anyone else with taste buds.

"And for you, miss?" Andrea asked Kasiah.

"I'll just have a cup of mixed fresh fruit and a lightly toasted bagel with cream cheese," she said, handing the menu to Andrea.

"And you, sir?" Andrea asked me.

What Kasiah ordered actually sounded quite appetizing. "I'll have the same," I said.

"How was your breakfast this morning, Ember?" Andrea asked.

"It was perfect, Andrea. Please give Carlos my compliments. Also, please instruct the captain that we'll be sailing to Put-in-Bay near Cleveland. We'd like to hoist anchor and make way as soon as possible."

"Yes, ma'am. Anything else?"

Ember looked at me and then to Kasiah. "Should I call Whisper?" she asked.

I looked at Kasiah. She nodded.

"From what I've seen of Atmoro," Kasiah said, "we're going to need all the help we can get."

"Very good," said Ember, turning toward Andrea. "We'll need to get in touch with Whisper. Tell him there's blood in the wind. He'll understand. Also, call Candice's cell and ask her to ready the jet. I'll call her directly within the hour to brief her with flight and destination instructions. Let her know she'll be meeting us at Hopkins International this evening. We'd like the jet fueled and ready for departure by eight."

Andrea nodded and hurried off.

"You have your own jet?" asked Damien. "Notice I wasn't as surprised this time, like when you said you have a boat on your yacht."

"You haven't seen anything yet," Ember smiled, standing up.

Ember walked to the edge of the pool, shed her shorts to reveal the rest of her blue bikini, and dove into the water.

TWENTY-TWO

By the time Kasiah and I finished our breakfast, the fog had lifted, and the sun was shining brightly as we cruised through Lake Erie. The sunrays bouncing off the surface of the water were more intense than the actual sunlight.

After finishing her early-morning swim, Ember joined us back at the table. "How was breakfast, everyone?" she asked, wrapping a towel around her waist.

Everyone praised their meals and thanked Ember.

"Wonderful," Ember continued. "I'm going to talk with the captain about our docking plans and then contact my pilot with instructions for our flight. I won't provide her with our final destination until we're in the air. Hopefully, that'll help keep the info out of Atmoro's hands and keep us ahead in the game."

"That sounds like a good idea," Damien agreed. "Will you dock the yacht in Cleveland? It's hard to miss this massive vessel. Your crew may not be safe in port."

"That's a good point," Ember said, considering Damien's opinion. "I'll instruct the captain to refuel and restock the vessel. They can sail through the Great Lakes toward Thunder Bay, Ontario, in Lake Superior. Better to keep them close in case we need to get out in a hurry."

"Good idea, Damien," Kasiah said, realizing that since Hayley's death, she had abandoned her responsibilities as special agent for the FBI and practically forgotten her partner existed. "I know you've sacrificed a lot being here with me. The bureau won't be too happy with us for going dark like we did. We'll have some explaining to do when we get back."

"Nothing we can't handle," Damien smiled. "I kind of like being away from the office. We spent the night on yacht, and soon we'll be flying in a private jet. Actually, Ember, maybe there's something I can do to help with travel plans. I have extensive training with diverting tactics. The bureau has researched hundreds of thousands of criminals and their methods of diverting attention away from their actual strategies."

"Definitely," Ember said, appreciating his expertise. "Would you like to accompany me to the bridge to talk with the captain?"

"No problem," Damien replied, excited to see the bridge.

"Aerona," Ember said, "you are more than welcome to join us for our strategy session. We could certainly use your input."

"I'm in," Aerona answered quickly.

I wondered how long it would take for Tara to compile Jade's profile. "Ember," I asked, checking my watch, "do you have internet access on board? I need to receive some information from Tara."

"Yes," she said, "Rain can show you to the library. There's a computer and printer that you're more than welcome to use."

Rain nodded once. It was the most I've seen him move since breakfast.

"A library," Damien said, surprised. "Shocking!"

"How long before we reach port?" Kasiah asked.

"We should dock in just a few hours," Ember replied. "If the weather holds up, we'll be able to cruise at full speed, twenty-two knots or about twenty-five miles per hour. Although, we'll be taking a less direct route to ensure no one follows. You've been through a lot over the past couple days, Kasiah. If you'd like to take a few laps in the pool and clear your thoughts, I have a new, black swimsuit that you're welcome to use."

Kasiah's expression brightened. "That would be wonderful," she smiled. "I was going to ask, but didn't want to intrude. The pool looks relaxing. A swim would be perfect."

"It's no problem at all," Ember said. "I'll have Andrea bring it to your room."

Ember, Damien, and Aerona left the main deck and headed up to the bridge to make travel plans for Montana.

"I'm going to change and test out that pool," Kasiah said, pushing her chair away from the table. "I'll see you two later."

I watched as she walked away, leaving me on the deck… with a Shadow Vampire.

"What are you listening to?" I asked Rain, attempting to start a conversation with a lethal weapon.

"Pop Evil," he said, still not moving. "Have you heard of them?"

"Absolutely," I said, surprised that a Shadow Vampire had such good taste in music. "Their song 'Monster You Made Me' was stuck in my head for weeks after it was released."

"Mine too," he said, rolling up the earbuds. "I like how they pick up the tempo and dirty up the guitar riffs a bit as the song progresses. They have a cool sound."

"They're on tour now," I said. "In fact, they were just finishing up their set at Summerfest when I went to look for Aerona. I didn't get to see any of the show except the tail end."

"That's a bummer," Rain added. "I've heard they have a pretty killer show."

I decided to dive right into the conversation. "Yesterday," I started, "you mentioned about asking some questions concerning Shadow Vampires, possibly trying to piece together your past."

Rain sat motionless for almost a minute. "I don't know where to start," he finally said, shifting in his chair. "Everything I know about the Shadow World, I've learned from Ember. I've always thought of that world as a fictitious, far-off place. It's frustrating for me to know I'm a vampire, and yet, I have no idea how or why I was created. I've been trying my entire life… of what I can remember… to forget I'm a vampire."

Rain lowered his sunglasses. His eyes were dark, and his stare was hard as stone. He was very serious when he spoke again.

"And now," he said, looking me straight in the eyes, "since I met you, I can't seem to get vampires out of my head."

I didn't know what to think or how to react to what he had just told me, and I definitely didn't want to upset a Shadow Vampire out here in the middle of nowhere. I could easily find myself at the bottom of the lake if I did.

"I'm sorry you feel that way," I said, hoping to find a way to reroute the conversation from me to him. "Where I come from, being a Shadow Vampire is a great honor. My world is full of vampires, werewolves, warlocks, and practically every other mythical creature you can imagine. There are even dark corners of the Shadow World, where creatures like trolls and demons inhabit. Out of all the creatures in that world and this one, Shadow Vampires are the most respected. They are our protectors and our police. They protect our royalty, and they hunt down jumpers who threaten to expose our way of life."

"If it's such an honor to be a Shadow Vampire," Rain said, "then why are you trying to kill the only other one you know?"

"That's a solid argument," I said, "but if Atmoro opens the Forgotten Shadow City and releases the Forgotten Shadows, then they'll jump to the Light World. Our worlds will collide like never before, and the ensuing war will cause unimaginable destruction. Life as we've come to know it will end."

"Not good," Rain said bluntly.

"Let me back up a bit," I said. "I guess I should start by explaining why jumping is considered such a crime. Over the years, there have been many instances where a Shadow jumped to the Light World illegally, and by doing so, they compromised the existence of our secret world. The Shadow Council believes—and they may be right—that if the wrong group of humans were to discover the Shadow World, they wouldn't hesitate to destroy it, not any differently than they have so many other things. It seems to be human nature. An example is what occurred in North America when Columbus arrived. Following his quote unquote *discovery,* more and more people flocked to this newly discovered land. They took what they wanted from the natives, and eventually, they kicked the natives off of their own land."

Andrea appeared suddenly from what seemed like nowhere.

"Would either of you like anything else?" she asked.

"Thank you, Andrea," Rain said, smiling. "We're fine."

"Very well," she said politely. "Don't hesitate to call if you need anything."

Andrea left as quickly as she had arrived. I wondered if she was a fairy like Ember.

"As I was saying,' I continued, "the Shadow Council was at its peak when Columbus landed. Back then, Shadows could come and go into the Light World as they pleased. The natives knew to stay clear of any creatures of the night, and likewise, the Shadows did not disturb them. At that time, there weren't many more natives than there were Shadows…"

Something on deck caught Rain's attention. He lowered his sunglasses to the tip of his nose and looked to the far side of the pool. I turned around in my chair and noticed Kasiah wearing a black bikini top and a white towel wrapped around her waist. She was dipping her toes into the water to test the temperature, pretending not to see us as she pulled her hair back into a pony tail. Then, as if auditioning for a swimsuit advertisement, she dropped the towel and dove into the pool.

The moment Kasiah surfaced, she swam gracefully through the water, turning her head to take a breath every few strokes. Her rhythm was perfect. The water glistened off her back as she swam. I guessed this is how she kept in shape back in Wisconsin.

Rain pushed his sunglasses back into position. "You were saying?" he asked.

"Yes," I said, momentarily lost in Kasiah's beauty. I had to force my eyes away from the distraction in the pool. "The Shadow Council witnessed firsthand the destruction these new humans from across the ocean had caused. It wasn't long before the council started enforcing more and more rules, until finally, a law was passed to prohibit anyone from entering the Light World without permission from the council. If any Shadow did enter the Light World without permission, they were labeled a jumper and hunted as a criminal. Nine times out of ten, they were condemned to the Forgotten Shadow City for eternity. As you can imagine, Shadows didn't approve of the new laws that prevented them from exploring the Light World. The

Europeans, essentially, took the land from the natives and the Shadows. The Shadow Council feared the same fate for their own world if it were ever exposed."

"Why didn't the Shadows fight back?" Rain asked.

"The council seats are held primarily by Shadow Vampires, and it's a known fact that anyone who disagrees with them is dealt with harshly."

"Why is it such a bad thing for a Shadow to be in the Light World?"

"The Shadow Council has worked for many lifetimes to keep their secret world a secret. There are mineral deposits of gold and diamonds ten times the size of anything ever found here in this world. There are strong rivers that flow from mountain peaks to the valley floors. The landscape is full of natural beauty. I would say the lack of sunlight is the most unique difference."

"It's always dark there?"

"Not exactly," I explained. "There's no sunlight because there's no sun, but there is light. Thick forests of sapphire trees emit a brilliant sapphire glow, and the sky always appears painted as if a warm, blue sun had just set. Picture the most perfect sunset you've ever seen, then replace the oranges and reds with blues and purples. There are also other small plants that emit different, colorful photons. It's a beautiful place and is worth protecting from the destructive nature of humans."

"If the Shadow World is such a magical place," Rain said, "then why are you and your sister here? Don't you two risk being locked up in the same prison that Atmoro is trying to unlock?"

"Aerona and I jumped after our parents were killed in a fire," I explained, recalling the horrific night, "which was no accident. Our parents believed that the Shadow Council was corrupt and guilty of breaking many of their own laws. My father alleged that certain members of the council were sneaking humans into the Shadow World, using them to feed their own blood cravings and sexual desires."

"A corrupt government," Rain said jokingly, "I've never heard of such a thing. If vampires weren't permitted to hunt humans, how else did they get blood?"

"In the Shadow World, vampires don't require human blood to survive. There's something about the sun in this world that drains a vampire's power. They feed on human blood to enhance their powers and regain their strength. That's why you're tired if you don't feed."

"I've seen vampires here that are driven mad by their thirst."

"That is true," I replied. "Those were vampires created in this world. They're a copy of the original vampire who turned them. They have all of their weaknesses, yet, they have only some of their enhanced skills. Vampires turned here in the Light World have an instant thirst for blood. It's like a drug to them. They'll die without it."

Rain was catching on fast. "So the Shadow Council became addicted to human blood?" he asked.

"Yes, several members," I confirmed. "One, in particular, was Malance. He was one of the youngest members, and like I said, human blood is like a drug to Shadow Vampires. It can become very addictive if they don't have enough self-control. My parents held secret meetings with a small group of Shadows to collect information against Malance and several others. They were planning to present the information to the council elders, and that's when Malance burnt our home to the ground. My parents never made it out of the house."

I paused, remembering the night my parents were murdered, which ultimately forced me to make a decision to jump to the Light World. And here I am, trying to save the world I vowed never to return to.

"Are you OK?" Rain asked.

"Yes, sorry," I said, shaking the memories from my head. "Aerona and I feared the same fate for ourselves and we decided it wasn't safe for us in the Shadow World. We jumped here, and I think we've done a good job of keeping our true identities a secret, which wasn't always easy. Along the way, we've had to dispose of several careless jumpers who risked compromising our secret."

"Like Atmoro?"

"Definitely not like Atmoro," I said. "Most jumpers are simple-minded demons or young, reckless werewolves. They're easy to track and easy to dispose of quietly. Atmoro is much different. He's stronger, faster, and smarter. Atmoro has a goal that, from the looks of things, he'll do anything to achieve."

I could feel the gears spinning in Rain's mind.

"I understand why the council prohibited unauthorized visits to the Light World," he said. "They wanted to protect their world. But tell me why Atmoro jumped when he knew the consequences of his actions could expose the world he vowed to protect, and his actions could potentially lead to his imprisonment to the Forgotten Shadow City."

"What motivates a madman?" I asked rhetorically. "Knowing the answer might make hunting him a lot easier. Atmoro's jump to the Light World was a shock. See, long ago, Atmoro was one of the most skilled Shadow Vampires the council had ever seen—maybe even their most trusted. The council didn't take his betrayal lightly and dispatched a massive hunting party to find him."

"No one knows why he jumped?"

"The council keeps a lot of secrets. Maybe you'll get a chance to ask Atmoro yourself. Well, has any of this helped? Do you remember anything about your past?"

Rain sat motionless. I wasn't even sure if he was breathing.

"Is your name the only thing you remember from your past?" I asked.

"No," he said, pausing, "I gave this name to myself. My earliest memory is me waking up in a forest. I was young, maybe five, lying on my back, staring up at a dark sky. The gentle sound of rain dripping through the thick forest foliage was the only thing I heard. I lay there for what seemed like eternity as rain poured down from above."

Rain paused again. I couldn't see his eyes behind his sunglasses, but I got the impression he was staring off into space, taking his mind back to that moment in time.

"Eventually," he continued, "I stood up and started walking. I was lost in the forest for days. It rained the entire time. I was hungry and weak and only a few small animals filled my stomach. I hungered for something more. It was only when I came across a small village that my hunger was satisfied. I don't think I need to explain what happened there."

"I think I get it," I nodded, feeling sorry for Rain. He had no one to explain what or who he was. He discovered everything on his own. It must have been a terrible experience.

"In time," Rain continued, "I realized that this wicked, blood-craving curse had benefits. My strength was beyond that of any other human. I could outrun any animal in the forest. My body healed itself moments after being injured and my vision was clear even on the darkest nights. In the end, I grew into a man's body and learned to deal with the cravings. I hunted only when necessary, and I learned to blend in with everyone else. For the most part, I tried to forget the monster that lived inside me. Every now and again, I would run into another vampire. They were usually much more aggressive than me, so I tried to steer clear of them when I could. I disposed of any that caused trouble where I was living at the time. Luckily, a few years ago, I met Ember. She's the only friend I've ever had."

Rain cocked his head to look past me.

Kasiah was climbing out of the pool. She patted herself dry and wrapped the towel back around her waist, waving quickly as she disappeared back inside the yacht.

Rain pushed his chair away from the table. "The sun seems to drain the life right out of me sometimes. It's way too bright out here. Let's go inside. I'll show you the way to the library so you can access the internet."

"That'd be great," I said. "Thank you for sharing your story. I wish I could be of more help."

"It's just nice to know someone else who can understand my twisted past."

Rain's past was truly a mystery, and I may have the ability to penetrate Rain's mind to release some of his repressed memories. Although, I decided to keep that ability to myself… for now.

TWENTY-THREE

I glanced at my watch. 6:00 p.m. We had just passed Cedar Point Amusement Park on our way to the small island of Put-in-Bay about three miles off Ohio's coast. Some of the roller coasters' lift hills extended above the trees, and I wondered what the yacht looked like from the riders' perspective. The closer we got to the bay, the busier the waters became. Numerous small boats were cruising the lake, mostly full of families out enjoying the nice sunny day. A few boats pulled inflatable tubes full of screaming children. The tubes bounced behind the boats, skipping over the wakes.

Ember's Star was easily the largest yacht on the water. Damien was right about the yacht's size; it stuck out like a sore thumb. We towered above the largest boats in the bay. Several smaller thirty-foot cruisers, which on a normal day were the biggest boats in the bay, circled us a few times, taking pictures as we slowly navigated our way to the slip Ember had reserved earlier in the day.

I was fascinated at how incredibly agile the yacht was for such a large vessel. Underwater thrusters navigated the yacht parallel to the dock, and as soon as the yacht was positioned perfectly, the crew tossed and tied the dock lines, dropped the tiny walkway down, and sounded a loud horn. Our brief voyage came to an end.

The crew was on double watch now that that yacht was docked and more vulnerable to an attack. Ember gave strict instructions to the crew not to allow unauthorized persons on the dock or anywhere near the yacht.

I met everyone in the yacht's formal cabin on the main deck. Damien was explaining our travel route to the airport; he had everything detailed in a small pocket notebook.

"It's a quick ten-minute ferry ride to the mainland," Damien explained. "From there, it's an hour's drive to the airport in Cleveland. We won't have to worry about airport security, since it's a private flight. The jet is currently in the air and will be touching down in Cleveland within the hour."

"What about Whisper?" Ember asked. "I haven't heard back from him."

"Whisper is on board," Damien said, reassuring Ember. "The jet picked him up from Maine this afternoon. He said he had a present for Rain."

"Perfect," Rain muttered.

"It should only take an hour to have the jet refueled and get us on board," Damien continued. "We're scheduled to be in the air and on our way to Montana no later than 8:00 p.m. As a precautionary measure, and to try and throw Atmoro off our scent, we've given a false destination to Cleveland's ground control. We'll initially head south toward Orlando, Florida, and continue flying that route until we're off Cleveland's radar. Then we'll change flight plans and proceed to our actual destination, Missoula International airport in Montana. The overall flight time will be approximately four and a half hours, depending on the weather."

Damien did a great job presenting the information. This obviously wasn't his first time prepping a team with a tactical plan.

"There's a two hour time difference between Cleveland and Missoula," Damien continued. "That puts us on the ground in Missoula at 10:30 p.m. We've arranged for ground transportation from the airport to the hotel. Once we're checked in and settled, our main objective will be to locate Jade, verify she's a stone, and extract her from the city quickly and safely."

"How exactly do we verify she's a stone?" Kasiah asked.

"Erone can take that one," Damien said, flipping the page of his notebook.

"Earlier this afternoon," I explained, "Ember and I had a lengthy discussion on this topic. Other than witnessing some supernatural display of actual angel powers, there's no real way of knowing she's a stone. Right now, we're basing everything we know on the information Tara had provided, which all indicates Jade's parents may have been fallen angels a.k.a. stones. If we're right, we'll know soon."

"And if we're wrong?" Kasiah questioned.

"We'll cross that bridge when we get there," I replied. "There are far too many variables in the equation for us to be absolutely sure Jade is a stone."

Damien continued his briefing. "By the time we get situated in the hotel, it'll most likely be too late to make contact with Jade. Erone and Rain, you two will locate Jade's place of residence. She rents a one bedroom apartment off campus. You are to observe only. What we don't want to do is barge into the city and snatch Jade up, or cause any scene that may attract attention. We don't know who else is watching her or what kind of personal security she may have. Jade was very young when her parents passed away, and there's a good possibility she doesn't even know she's the offspring of two angels. That may make it a lot easier."

"In my experience," Aerona added, "most of the time when something is perceived as easy is precisely when it goes horribly wrong."

"That's true," Damien agreed. "We'll want to approach Jade with caution. When the extraction takes place, we don't want any of her friends or family calling the police because she's missing. It would be better if she left town on her own terms, and then sometime later, notified people that she'll be out of town because her grandma is sick or something. From what Ember had told me, young stones can be very powerful, which makes them extremely dangerous. We'll need to handle Jade with care. If she runs, we may never see her again. This may be our only chance."

Damien grabbed a stack of photographs from the glass coffee table, handing each of us two photographs of Jade. They were fairly simple photos of her in her freshman year at Montana University. The first was from the shoulders up, and the other was photographed from further away to capture more of the scene. They were taken outside with Jade sitting on neatly mowed, green grass with her back against a large tree trunk. A brightly colored flower garden could be seen in the background, which mostly had various purple flowers. She was dressed as any other college freshmen would have been—a pair of jeans and a casual tight blue tank top. The angle of the photos made it difficult to make out the necklace around her neck.

Everyone was in awe over the photographs. To say Jade was stunning would be an understatement—she was beyond beautiful. Her unique deep dark green eyes left no doubt of her name's origin. They reflect the sunlight as if they were made from rare gemstones. Her long, blonde hair—the color you might expect an angel to have—was perfectly straight. Her skin looked like it had a natural tan, not fake-baked on by a tanning bed. Her brilliant white smile shined with as much beauty as her green eyes, and based on her expression, I got the sense she loved every breath of air that entered her lungs. She was more content in that single moment than most people could wish for in a lifetime. Gorgeous is the only word that even came close to describing Jade, a girl's life we were about to turn upside down.

Aerona tossed the pictures onto the glass coffee table. "I'll just come out and say what everyone is thinking," she started. "This girl is hot as hell. Damien, please tell me you enhanced these photos with some airbrushing or some type of rendering."

Damien was still in his professional FBI mode. "Jade's a beautiful girl," he replied, "and it's our job to keep her that way."

Rain was seated next to Aerona, studying his own set of photos. "I suddenly have a new found enthusiasm for this adventure," he remarked.

Aerona shot Rain a dirty look.

"What's the plan for first contact?" Kasiah asked, finally back in FBI mode.

"We discussed that briefly," Damien said. "We feel it makes most sense for you and me to make the initial face to face. We know little to nothing about stones, and they may even be able to sense someone not from this world. We're essentially going in blind, and we still haven't figured an easy way of explaining the situation to her, well, not without freaking her out, especially if she doesn't even know her history. It may be difficult getting her on the same page. We'll play the FBI card to get our foot in the door, then improvise from there."

"Plan B?" asked Kasiah.

"Plan B," Damien continued, "is the old fashion snatch-n-grab. We don't want to spook her, and on the other hand, we want to be out of town as soon as possible. We have forty-eight hours, but after that, we go with plan B. If things don't go as planned—and as Aerona pointed out they usually don't—we still need to accomplish the objective of extracting Jade and keeping her safe."

"Exit strategy?" was Kasiah's next question.

"The jet will be refueled and waiting for us at the airport. Are there any other questions before we move on?"

We all shook our heads no.

Damien flipped a page in his notebook. "The school is on summer break," he continued, "which means we won't be able to shadow Jade in class. We're also not sure if she has a summer job, and unfortunately, we don't have any details of her daily schedule. Tara came up empty with a search of the city's social hot-spots. Jade doesn't have a gym membership, nor does she belong to any other local organizations. All we have is a name and an address."

Aerona turned to Rain. "These pictures are totally touched up," she said, obviously jealous. "You know that, right?"

"There's only one way to find out," he said, standing up and putting on his sunglasses.

Damien checked his watch. "6:20 p.m." he said, "We need to be packed and ready to leave the yacht in thirty minutes. If there aren't any more questions, I suggest we get moving, so we can get off this old decrepit poor excuse of a boat."

Ember laughed out as we all started to leave. "I'll remember that when I send out the invitations for my next world cruise," she said.

By the time we met at the bottom of the dock ramp, the sun had already made its way down to the horizon. The bay was still busy with boats coming in from the lake after a day of fun, as people headed out to watch the sunset.

Several of the yacht's crew members loaded our bags into one of two black SUVs that were parked at the end of the dock. They were the same as the one Kasiah and Damien had back in Wisconsin. Damien, Aerona, and Ember rode in the first SUV. I rode with Kasiah and Rain in the second one.

"We'll see you guys at the airport!" Aerona yelled as she stepped into her SUV. "Don't get any speeding tickets!"

"Your sister has quite the personality," Rain remarked, climbing into the front passenger seat.

"She grows on you," I said, sitting next to Kasiah in the backseat.

The interior of the SUV was exactly as I had pictured it. It had black leather seats, a power sunroof, dark tinted, one-way security windows, and a chauffeur complete with a freshly pressed suit and driver's hat.

The SUVs pulled away from the dock, and I suddenly felt exposed after leaving the safety that the yacht had provided.

"Ember sure knows how to travel in style," Kasiah said.

"You should see her garage back home," Rain responded.

"Where exactly is home?" I asked.

"Curiosity killed the cat," Rain answered, playing with the stereo's buttons. "There's a killer—no pun intended—radio station out of Cleveland that I can never find."

The digital display stopped at 100.7.

"…listening to Cleveland's rock station!" the station DJ announced, finishing an advertisement. "Home of the non-stop rock block!"

The speakers exploded with growling guitar riffs. Rain, satisfied with his station selection, turned up the volume until the chauffeur raised his hand to tell him enough. He settled back in his seat.

I never thought I'd see a chauffeur-driven vampire. Now, I've seen it all.

The drive to the ferry took less than five minutes, exactly as Damien had planned. We followed the first SUV onto the car ferry and parked behind them. We waited several minutes as the ferry filled with vehicles.

Kasiah stared out the SUV's window, sliding her hand underneath mine and interlacing our fingers. I squeezed her hand lightly, and she squeezed back. We hadn't really discussed our sexual exploration. I think we both understood that we needed to place our personal feelings on hold until we stopped Atmoro. Neither of us wanted to cloud our judgment with Cupid's arrow during an already dangerous game of chase-the-vampire.

The ferry sailed off and docked in the mainland in less than five minutes. We were right on schedule.

Just as Damien had estimated, the drive to the airport was a little less than an hour. We entered the airport through a side gate secured by two armed guards. The first SUV stopped to talk to the guards, and I saw one of them hand a clipboard through the passenger side window. Moments later, Ember handed it back; I assumed she had to sign some type of authorization form. The guards waved both vehicles through the gate. I was surprised how easy it was to enter a U.S. airport with two unmarked black SUV's full of fairies, warlocks, and vampires.

We drove past several rows of small aircraft hangers similar to those self-storage buildings you see outside any city. Only these had airplane-size doors. We turned right at the end of the row, then sped up to at least sixty mph as we drove down one of the taxiways. A very large commercial jet roared past us on the next runway; its engines' thrust rocked our SUV as its nose inched off the ground.

The SUV made a wide U-turn as we finally came to a stop on the opposite end of the airport. The chauffeur turned the radio down as Rain opened his door and stepped out.

Without warning or a single word, Kasiah pulled me close and kissed my lips softly, and just as suddenly, she released my hand and was out the door.

The chauffeur was watching me in the mirror. "Don't look at me," he said. "Go get her."

"I wish it was that simple," I responded, exiting the SUV.

I had never been on a private jet before, and I didn't know what to expect; of course, after getting off one of the most amazing vessels on water, I was excited to see what the jet had in store for us.

Rain was standing next to me as I looked over the jet. "She's an impressive aircraft," he said.

The setting sun glistened off the cockpit's windshield. Two powerful jet engines sandwiched the vertical stabilizer of the tail section. The front part of the fuselage was pure white, fading midway back to a glossy black that covered the entire rear section and the top of the wings. The transition from white to black was painted in a way that made it appear as though the black paint was peeling off from the intense speed. The name of the jet stood out more than anything else; "Ember's Star II" was painted on the tail with the same large script letters as on the yacht.

"Not a very inconspicuous paint job," I said.

"Actually," said Rain, "the paint is blended with Ember's dust. We only see it like this because she wants us to. Once we're on board, she'll change it back to a typical plain white."

"Fascinating," I remarked.

"Remember what I told you about curiosity?" Rain asked.

"It killed the cat," I nodded, knowing I wasn't going to get an answer if I asked how Ember was able to make the paint change color. I've seen stranger things in my time.

"It's not easy for us to travel using commercial air," Rain said as we approached the plane. "People have changed. Neither one of us can be around so many idiots in such a small space. I always have this uncontrollable feeling and want to take over the plane and break everyone's neck. People bug me."

Aerona walked up as Rain finished. "I hear that, Rain," she said, pointing to the jet. "This is the only way to fly."

Ember stuck her head out of the main cabin door. "Come on in and get comfortable," she yelled as the engines started to wind up.

I heard the sound of screeching tires on the runway as another commercial airliner landed in the background, touching down with a puff of smoke trailing behind its wheels.

We all climbed the stairs into the main cabin of Ember's Star II. The interior was unlike any commercial airliner I had ever seen. Ember was seated in the cockpit next to a blonde, female pilot, who was busy checking and rechecking instruments and jotting notes in a logbook.

The rest of the jet was luxurious. A small kitchen area, complete with a small refrigerator, oven, and even a slim dishwasher was just outside the cockpit; the counter tops looked like real granite, which I'm sure were artificial for weight reduction. The main cabin extended for nearly the full length of the fuselage. Two sets of dark stained wooden tables, each with four white luxurious leather chairs, were on either side of the cabin in front of a wet bar made of the same dark wood and artificial black marble tabletop. Several expensive bottles of liquor were securely fastened behind the bar. Beyond the bar was a sofa-style seat and a small glass coffee table, similar to the one on the yacht. Four more white leather, luxury airliner seats were at the rear of the main cabin. Considering the overall length of the aircraft, the main cabin seemed to end short. I assumed the door at the rear of the main cabin led to Ember's private cabin.

"Feel free to take any seat," Ember said, shutting the cockpit door and joining us in the main cabin. "We'll be ready for takeoff in just a few minutes."

I decided on one of the seats at the table to the right, making sure I was facing forward; I don't mind flying, though I just didn't think I would like flying backwards.

Kasiah sat across from me with Ember. Rain, Aerona, and Damien sat at the other table.

I looked at Kasiah and said, "You do realize you'll be flying backwards?"

"For someone from a world full of mythical creatures," Kasiah said jokingly, "you sure are afraid of some weird things."

To my surprise, Andrea appeared from what seemed like nowhere—again. She was wearing a crew member uniform as she did on the yacht, except this one was more flight attendant style.

"Would any of you like something to drink?" Andrea asked. "We have a full bar and a variety of sodas available."

"I'd take a beer if you have one," said Aerona excitedly, "and a slice of orange please."

"I second that beer," said Damien, "minus the orange."

Rain just nodded once to Andrea. She nodded back. I guessed that meant we wanted the usual.

Using her cute Midwestern accent, Kasiah asked for two waters for us.

"I'll be right back with those," Andrea said, darting away to the bar.

Aerona looked across the table at Rain. "So," she started, "where's your boyfriend, Whisper?"

Rain took off his sunglasses and gave Aerona a look that could have stopped a city bus.

"Aerona," I cut in, praying Rain wouldn't explode, "I'm not so sure pissing off a Shadow Vampire at thirty thousand feet is necessarily a good idea."

"Don't worry," came an unfamiliar voice, "Rain is all bark and no bite."

We all looked toward the main cabin door. I was amazed to see a young, dark-haired boy carrying an old-style leather satchel, its strap running down over one shoulder across his chest. The kid didn't look a day over sixteen.

"I'm Whisper," he said.

TWENTY-FOUR

Tara, startled by a loud knock on her front door, tiptoed from her kitchen to the front room to peer out the door's peephole. A man in a blue Speed Demon Cable uniform and hat was standing outside on the porch staring down at an electronic clipboard. "Steve" was embroidered on his nametag.

Tara stepped to the side and pressed her back against the wall, silently hoping the man would just go away. She covered her mouth when the doorbell rang; her head was right next to the ringer.

"Tara Whitefield," Steve called out, "I'm with Speed Demon Cable. We've had some issues with DVR service in your area, and we'd like to check your box."

Tara tried to recall if she had any issues with her cable. Her heartbeat raced like a rabbit running from a fox. She glanced at her watch; it was 7:00 p.m., which seemed like an odd time for a cable guy to be out on a service call. Tara remained pressed against the wall as she slid over to her large front window. She parted the curtain just enough to see a white van parked in her driveway. "Speed Demon" was painted on its side in large blue letters.

Steve knocked on the door again. "Miss Whitefield," he called loudly, "if you don't answer the door, we'll have to fix the problem remotely. Your service may be down for several days."

Tara snuck back over to the front door and looked through the peephole one more time. She didn't like the thought of letting a stranger in, but she also didn't like the thought of missing her favorite shows because her DVR wasn't working correctly.

"Just a minute!" she yelled, intentionally directing her voice toward the back of the room.

Tara tiptoed over to her laptop and typed several quick commands, activating the internal security cameras hidden throughout the house. Unlike the cameras outside that run 24/7, the internal ones only recorded when the alarm was set. She then walked casually to the door and undid several locks, leaving the security chain latched as she cracked the door open.

"Can I help you?" she asked.

"Miss Whitefield?"

"Yes, can I help you?"

"My name is Steve, and I'm with Speed Demon Cable. We've had multiple complaints with DVR equipment in your area. It appears that the XL250 boxes have been infected with a virus. I'm going to need to check your box. If it's infected, it may need to be replaced."

Tara was hesitant, but Steve seemed legitimate. She unlatched the security chain and let him in.

"Thank you, Miss Whitefield," Steve said. "You're my last stop of a very long day. This should only take a few minutes."

Tara showed Steve to the living room, pointing out the DVR. "The DVR is right under the television."

Steve set his clipboard down next to the TV. "You have some nice furniture," he said. "I like the dark stain over the oak. It gives the room a nice vintage look."

Tara found it odd that a cable guy was commenting on her furniture, but it's probably his way of making the long day go by.

"Thanks," Tara replied, glancing at Steve's clipboard. The screen was black. "So, what exactly is the problem?"

Steve opened the console cabinet door. "Something to do with the communication signal," he explained, turning the unit on. "It's between our server and the home units."

Tara slowly backed away, desperately trying not to look terrified; Steve had just turned on her Blu-ray player instead of the DVR.

"OK," Tara said, trying to remain calm. "I'll just let you get to work. I'm going to get back to my computer. You can holler when you're done or if you need anything."

Steve removed a small screw driver from his pocket. "OK, will do," he said, removing the screws from the cover of the Blu-ray player.

Tara backed away, keeping her eyes on Steve until she was in the next room. Then, as soon as she was out of sight, she hastily closed her laptop and shoved it into her bag with her small purse and cell phone.

"How's it going in there?" she asked, taking a deep breath, struggling to control her anxiety.

"You're in luck," Steve answered, his voice echoing off the walls. "This unit hasn't been infected. I'll button it up, and you'll just need to sign a job form."

Tara didn't waste another second. She swung on the bag, tiptoed through the kitchen, and went straight out the back door.

Jake, a.k.a. Steve the cable guy, heard a door shut behind him. "Fuck!" he yelled, furious that he did not just grab the girl as soon as she let him in. He did, however, kind of enjoy pretending to be Steve the cable guy for a day; it gave him the sense of being normal again. He dropped the Blu-ray player and ran into the next room. "Son of a bitch!" he shouted, racing out the open kitchen door.

Jake looked from side to side, trying to determine the direction Tara had taken. A gate to the side yard swung shut, triggering the latch to fall into place and lock the gate. He hurtled himself over the fence and into the side yard, running full speed to the front of the house. The next thing he saw was the hood of a small, copper SUV slamming into him. His head ricocheted off the SUV's windshield, cracking the glass in several places. Jake felt as though he was flying backwards in slow motion over the roof of the car, face first, down to the lawn. He opened his eyes just in time to receive a face full of dirt and grass from the rear tires of an SUV as it drove over the curb out onto the street. The SUV's tires screeched loudly as Tara drove away.

Blood dripped down Jake's face and onto his lips. He was hurt, badly. His head pounded from the impact, blurring his vision. The pain of several broken bones fueled his rage. Overcoming the pain, he forced himself to stand up and limp to the Speed Demon van.

Nothing was going to stop Jake from catching Tara and proving to Atmoro he didn't need the warlocks. He pulled himself into the van and turned the key. The engine roared to life. He jammed the gear shift into reverse and pressed the accelerator to the floor. The van lurched out of the driveway, crashing into a car parked across the street. Jake slammed the gear shift into drive and pressed the accelerator back down to the floor.

"That bitch is dead!" he yelled, sideswiping another parked car.

Jake had no idea where Tara was headed, and he had already lost sight of her SUV, but he knew there was a main highway just a few blocks over. He took a risk and decided that was her best escape route.

Rushing through a stop sign without slowing down, Jake swerved to miss a car already halfway through the intersection. Blood would hurry the healing process of his wounds. He reached his arm behind the front seat and grabbed real Steve's lifeless body, pulling it between the front seats. He lifted Steve's arm to his mouth, and sunk his fangs into his wrist.

Tara screeched to a halt at a red light, with every intention of running past until she saw a motorcycle light approaching from the crossroad. The rider passed through the intersection only inches from her hood. Tara's eyes searched the rear-view mirror for anyone following. She couldn't see the van but noticed her long red hair was an absolute disaster. She shut her eyes and took a couple deep breaths, letting her head rest back on her seat. Her heart was ready to burst through her chest. The gruesome image of Steve's face cracking her windshield flashed through her mind. There were blood streaks on the windshield where his head had impacted.

"There's no way he got up from that," she said, shaking the image away.

A horn blasted behind Tara, forcing her back to reality. Her eyes opened wide, and her head snapped around to face the blowing horn. The driver in the car behind her had his hands up, shaking them in the air. The horn blew again.

Tara steadied her breathing and turned right towards the on-ramp to the highway, spraying washer fluid to try and clean the blood off the windshield.

The wipers flipped back and forth, smearing thick red streaks across the windshield before it finally flowed off with the rest of the fluid. The blast of another horn caught Tara's attention. Her eyes shot back to the rear view mirror just in time to notice the Speed Demon van forcing the car behind her off the ramp.

Tara couldn't believe her eyes "How is that possible?" she screamed, recklessly turning onto the highway. She swerved into the next lane to avoid hitting a truck in front of her. Her free hand frantically searched the bottom of her bag for her cell phone. "Where is the damn thing!" she yelled as she swerved back into the other lane, barely missing a car.

Finally, her hand passed over the hard plastic of her cell phone. She yanked it out from her bag and searched her contacts for Erone, trying to keep her eyes on the road as she swerved lanes again. The Speed Demon van smashed into her rear bumper, throwing the phone out of her hands and into the back seat. Her head bounced off the headrest, causing her to momentarily lose sight of the road. The van slammed into the bumper a second time, and Tara's foot slipped off the accelerator. She fumbled to regain control of her vehicle, losing speed.

The car next to Tara honked its horn several times as the van crashed wildly into its side, pushing it off the road. She heard the faint sound of a police siren as the van smashed into her passenger side, causing the side window to implode. She was now halfway off the road, driving on the gravel shoulder. Instinctively, she yanked the steering wheel toward the van. Tara had the position advantage this time, connecting with the van at its rear wheel. The tire shredded and ripped off as sparks sprayed from the tireless rim. The van struggled to keep speed next to her. Now was her chance. The engine's RPM revved high as she pressed hard on the accelerator, pulling ahead of the van.

Red and blue flashing lights in the rear view mirror caught Tara's attention. The sound of police sirens had never sounded so sweet, but when her eyes finally found the road again, she saw the brake lights of a tractor trailer in both lanes. Tara pressed the brake pedal with both her feet, turning the wheel sharply toward the left shoulder. The SUV skidded sideways on the loose gravel, losing control in a cloud of dust and gavel.

The vehicle finally came to rest sideways in the grassy median. Tara's side window was faced directly back toward the highway. Her eyes widened with fear at the sight of the Speed Demon van approaching rapidly. Everything happened so quickly, she didn't have time to react. The van collided right behind the driver's side door.

The sound of the collision was defining as metal hit metal and glass shattered all around Tara. The seatbelt dug into her shoulder, and several airbags exploded around her, protecting her head and side. The Speed Demon van pushed the SUV backwards until the passenger side wheels caught a drainage ditch, causing the SUV to roll several times before finally coming to rest on its roof.

Stunned, Tara opened her eyes. It took her a few seconds to realize she was upside down, hanging from her seat belt. She couldn't hear anything— not a single sound. She tried to yell, but nothing came out. She couldn't hear her own voice. She closed her eyes and wished it was all part of a bad dream. Her left arm was in extreme pain; it was probably broken. She spat out a mouthful of blood. Car horns and police sirens gradually became louder as Tara's hearing returned. Two loud gun shots cracked outside the window, thrusting her back into reality. A police officer fell to the ground in front of the windshield.

Tara heard herself scream this time.

The mangled door of the SUV was torn from its hinges. A man's hand reached inside and grabbed Tara's seatbelt, ripping the buckle from its latch. Tara fell to the roof of the SUV, and her world faded to black as she passed out.

It took every ounce of self-control Jake had to overcome his thirst for Tara's blood. He was about to go mad as he yanked her out of the overturned SUV.

TWENTY-FIVE

When Ember suggested she knew someone who could help us, I did not recall her mentioning Whisper was a teenager enjoying a relaxing summer beach vacation. His messy brown hair gave the impression that he had just rolled out of bed to catch the next big Pacific wave. A brown leather satchel was looped over his shoulder across a white T-shirt with an old-school, faded Batman symbol. The satchel's leather looked aged and appeared much older than Whisper. It was something Indiana Jones would have carried.

Rain noticed my confused expression. "Not what you were expecting, Erone?" he asked.

Whisper didn't miss a beat. "Ignore Rain," he said. "He's just jealous of my boyish good looks."

"Don't let Whisper's size fool you," Ember cut in. "He's been on this planet for well over three hundred years, and as you know, Erone, physical strength is not the only way to defend yourself."

Whisper laughed. "Now, Ember, that's not fair. You can't give away all my secrets in the first five minutes."

"There's plenty more from where that came," she smiled.

By the time my eyes shifted from Whisper to Ember and back to Whisper, he had vanished. His voice now came from behind me at the bar.

"When does this bird fly?" Whisper asked as he watched Andrea make him a Bloody Mary.

"Teleportation," Aerona remarked. "Now that's a useful trick."

Teleportation was one of many spells I wish my parents had allowed me to master before their untimely death. I was sure this skill had kept Whisper out of harm's way over the past few centuries.

"How far can you travel?" Aerona asked.

"My exact distance is a closely guarded secret," Whisper answered. "Though, for the purpose of this flight, from there to here is my limit."

Rain answered before anyone could actually ask a question. "Yes," he said, "he's like this all the time."

Andrea arranged two green olives on a plastic novelty toothpick, dropped it in the drink, and handed it to Whisper. He took a long drink from the glass.

"Thank you, Andrea," Whisper smiled. "It's perfect."

Andrea picked up a tray of drinks and replied, "You're very welcome, Whisper."

Whisper sat on the sofa seat next to Rain, which I found was an awfully brave move. He handed Rain what seemed to be a small wooden box with intricate carvings on every surface. Rain looked it over curiously but didn't open the tiny box.

"Thanks, Whisper," said Rain. "Where did you find it?"

"I'll tell you later," he replied as he stood up. "It's somewhat of an adventure story. It's good to see you again, Rain."

Rain stuffed the tiny box into the pocket of his hoodie. I was puzzled.

Whisper paused in the aisle in front of Aerona. "How far?" he asked her.

Aerona gave him a puzzled look. "How far to what?" she asked hesitantly.

"How far did you have to toss the nerd to win that shirt?" he teased Aerona about her nerd tossing champion T-shirt.

Aerona narrowed her eyes. She didn't know what to make of Whisper.

"Careful, Whisper," I warned, attempting to save Whisper's life. "She bites."

"The exact distance of my nerd tossing ability," Aerona answered, mocking Whisper's response to her teleportation question, "is a carefully guarded secret. Although, for the purpose of this flight, from here to there is my limit," she said, pointing outside the plane's window.

"Hah! I like you," Whisper grinned. "What's your name?"

"I'm Sarah," Aerona said. "It's nice to meet you."

None of us corrected Aerona on her name joke.

Whisper flashed Aerona a curious smile. "Nice to meet you too, Sarah. What's your favorite flower?" he asked.

"Well, on a day like today," she replied, hoping to fool Whisper, "a girl can't go wrong with a few lavender lisianthus."

Whisper opened the flap of his leather satchel. "You have unique taste in flowers, Sarah."

For the second time in less than five minutes, I was completely amazed. Whisper pulled out a bouquet of purple flowers, complete with several lavender lisianthus, a pair of white lilies, and a few other lavender colored flowers accented by tiny baby's breath.

Whisper handed the bouquet to Aerona. "It's all I could do with such short notice."

Rain shook his head. "Show off," he muttered.

Aerona accepted the bouquet of flowers from Whisper, and as soon as her fingers touched the bouquet, all the purple flowers changed to a deep, burnt orange. Aerona smiled her wicked smile. "You're not the only one with a few tricks up your sleeve," she said, sniffing the newly colored orange flowers before changing them from orange to crimson and then back to their original lavender.

A grin stretched across Rain's face. He clearly enjoyed Aerona's twist to Whisper's pull-a-rabbit-out-of-a-hat trick.

"I'll remember to keep my eye on you, Sarah," Whisper said, reaching out to shake Damien's hand.

"Nice to meet you, Whisper. I'm Damien. No flowers for me please."

"Nice to meet you too, Damien," he said, slipping his hand back into his satchel. He pulled out two white roses, handing one to Kasiah and the other to Ember.

"Thank you, Whisper," Kasiah said. "It's lovely. I'm Kasiah. It's a pleasure to meet you."

"You're very welcome, Kasiah. Such a beautiful name for a beautiful woman," Whisper said, stretching his hand out for me.

"Erone," I said, shaking his hand. "No flowers for me either."

Whisper had a firm grip for a tenth grader. "It's nice to meet you, Erone."

"Ember," Whisper said, kissing the back of her hand, "it's so nice to see you again. It's been far too long."

"Well, aren't you the charmer this evening," she responded.

Whisper claimed the empty seat next to me. "I bumped my head a few weeks back," he said. "I haven't been right since."

A woman's voice came through the cabin's intercom system. "Welcome aboard Ember's Star," she announced in a professional tone. "My name is Candice, and I'll be your captain this evening. Please be sure to fasten your seatbelts and remain seated until we're in the air and the seatbelt light located above the main cabin door is turned off. As we taxi to the runway, Andrea will review a few safety procedures with you. Our scheduled flight time to Orlando is just under three hours from wheels up to wheels down. The weather looks clear from here to Orlando, and it should be a smooth flight throughout. Andrea, you may secure the main cabin door at this time. We'll be taxiing onto the runway momentarily. Enjoy your flight."

Andrea darted to the front of the cabin to close the main door. The rest of us buckled our seat belts. I could hear the hydraulics shutting the cargo door. The engines roared as Candice performed her throttle test.

"If I could have everyone's attention," Andrea began from the front of the cabin. "I'll review several safety precautions as we taxi to the runway. Please feel free to stop me if you have any questions."

The engines whined down to a low hum, and the jet began to roll forward. It was surprisingly quiet inside the cabin. The only sound was the slight hum of the engines. Candice navigated the labyrinth of taxiways like a stock car driver. I guessed the plane was traveling at least thirty miles per hour across the airport, which looked a lot faster from inside the jet. I could feel the *bump bump bump* as we passed over each divide in the concrete.

Two minutes later, we turned a sharp ninety degrees and came to a sudden stop. Candice's voice sounded through the intercom again. "We're currently second in line for takeoff," she announced. "Andrea, please be seated at this time."

Andrea sat quickly in the seat next to the kitchen area and buckled her seatbelt.

I looked out the window and saw a large plane move forward onto the runway to our right. Its engines went to full power as the jet launched down the runway.

We were next.

The engine RPM wound up again, inching the jet forward. Typically, this was when the pilot would stop the aircraft and perform a triple check of all instruments before actually taking to the sky. Candice, though, never even slowed down. She turned the jet sharply to the right and lined us up with the runway perfectly; the engines roared to life as we rushed down the runway like a bullet, which thrust me back against my seat. The jet's nose lifted from the runway, and a few seconds later, the rear wheels were off the ground—we were flying.

The jet climbed rapidly, making a sharp left turn from the airport. For the next several minutes, we continued to climb until finally leveling off after two more turns. In one of the turns, my window pointed straight down toward the ground, and another pointed it straight up at the sky. The sun crept lower into the horizon, lighting the sky with dark reds and oranges as though it were on fire.

"We have reached our cruising altitude," came Candice's announcement. "Twenty-seven thousand feet. I've turned off the seatbelt sign. Feel free to move about the cabin."

Everyone unbuckled their seatbelts.

"She's a good pilot," I remarked to Ember.

"Candice is the best," she replied. "She was the pilot the manufacturer used for the initial test flight of this model, and only a few minutes after signing the purchase agreement, I made a generous offer she couldn't refuse. She's been my pilot ever since."

"I bet the manufacturer loved that."

The corner of Ember's mouth curled into a smile. "They were less than excited that I snatched their best pilot," she admitted.

"What kind of range does this amazing machine have?"

"The maximum range is around 7,100 miles at a cruising speed of 500 miles per hour."

"Impressive," said Damien. "That beats rush hour traffic any day."

Andrea approached Ember and whispered in her ear. My heart skipped a beat when Ember asked me to accompany her to the cockpit.

"Is there a problem?" I asked, not wanting to know the answer.

Ember started toward the cockpit. "I have to go inform Candice of our change in flight plans," she said, "and I thought you may want to see the cockpit. You seemed interested in the aircraft."

"Absolutely," I said excitedly. "Let's go."

Ember shut the door behind us as we entered the cockpit. I had never been in the cockpit of an airplane. Several LCD screens full of numeric information were scattered throughout the main console, and dozens of buttons and switches surrounded the screens. The view out of the cockpit windows was absolutely spectacular. The windows wrapped around the entire nose of the aircraft. We weren't flying into the sunset, but I had a good view of it out the side window. *Where's a camera when you need one?* I thought to myself.

Candice was seated to the left. Ember pointed for me to occupy the empty seat to the right, introducing me to Candice as an FBI consultant.

"It's nice to meet you, Erone," Candice said, smiling politely. "Are you enjoying the flight?"

"Yes," I said, still taking in the complexity of the console. "Ember tells me you're an excellent pilot."

"Ember tends to exaggerate," she smiled, "I'm a decent pilot on my best day."

"What was so urgent?" Ember asked.

Candice looked at me, then to Ember for approval.

"He's cleared," Ember said.

"OK," Candice began. "As we taxied to the runway, I noticed three unmarked cars racing down the taxiway. I didn't think much of it until I was contacted by Cleveland Air Traffic Control. Their supervisor-in-charge instructed me to abort the flight. I didn't respond to the tower until we were in the air, blaming radio interference for the delayed response. The tower informed me that the FBI had instructed our aircraft to abort our flight plans and return to the airport immediately."

"That's interesting," Ember said, surprisingly calm "Have you been in contact with the tower since?"

"No," Candice replied, flipping a couple switches in front of her, "I've been on radio silence since their last transmission."

"Are we still on Cleveland's radar?" Ember asked.

Candice made a slight adjustment to several dials. "Typically," she continued, "air traffic control only has control over a few nautical miles from their tower. Their radar may reach a radius of up to fifty miles past that, but we're well out of range by now."

"OK good," Ember said, handing Candice a small piece of paper. "Change course to the Missoula airport in Montana and please make minor course corrections several times for the remainder of the flight."

"Yes, ma'am," Candice agreed. "Is there anything else?"

"Not now," Ember said. "But once we're on the ground, please make the appropriate arrangements for refueling. I'll need you and Andrea to stay with the plane and be ready to fly at moment's notice."

"Yes, ma'am," Candice said, already entering numbers into a keypad.

Ember put her hand on Candice's shoulder. "And don't hesitate to contact me for any reason," she assured her. "You did a great job back at the airport."

"It was nice to meet you, Candice," I said, standing up to leave the cockpit.

"Enjoy the rest of your flight," Candice smiled.

Ember and I returned to the main cabin and sat back down at our table.

"We may have a problem," I said.

"Problem?" Aerona questioned, "As in we're out of ice for our drinks problem, or we're going to crash somewhere in Kentucky problem?"

"Problem," I continued, "as in the FBI was chasing us down the runway in Cleveland. They ordered us to abort our flight and return to the airport." I paused to look at Kasiah. "Is there any reason why they'd be looking for you two?" I asked.

Kasiah and Damien both looked confused. "The FBI?" they asked in unison.

"Yes," I said. "Just minutes before we took off, Candice was contacted by Cleveland's ATC with instructions from the FBI to abort the flight. Once we were in the air, they contacted her again with the same instructions. Do you two have any idea why the FBI is on our tail?"

Damien looked puzzled. I could sense the gears spinning in his head, trying to piece this together.

"Neither of us have been in contact with the field office since the incident in Madison," Damien said. "I'd have to believe this is something else."

"It's possible the FBI was brought in by the local Erie police," Kasiah suggested. "A forty foot wall of fire and a blackout that shut down four city blocks has a tendency to scream terrorist attack."

"That's a good possibility," I said. "Homeland security would have the resources to pull satellite feed from the dock in Erie, and they could have tracked the yacht to Cleveland. Although, I don't see how they caught up with us at the airport. We were in the air less than an hour after we got off the yacht."

"I don't see the U.S. government moving that fast," Rain remarked.

"I second that," nodded Whisper. "They still haven't figured out where I am."

"Rain's right," Damien said, the gears still spinning. "Since 9/11, there's a lot of red tape to jump through. One would think the system would have been streamlined to reduce response time, but the exact opposite has happened. Considering they took into account that the suspected terrorists may flee by aircraft, the Cleveland field office may have dispatched their tactical team without Homeland Security's authorization."

"Do you think Damien and I should risk checking in with the Madison field office?" Kasiah asked.

I thought about it for a minute. "I don't think so," I reasoned. "If the FBI is looking for you, we don't want to risk them tracing your call. They have the same faulty information we provided Cleveland's ground control."

"I'll contact Ember's Star," Ember added, "and find out what they know about the situation. I can direct them to put the small boat in the water to see if they're being tailed."

I liked how our newly formed team was thinking and acting as one.

Ember turned to Andrea. "Please contact Ember's Star," she instructed, "and let me know when you get them on the phone. I'll need to speak to the captain directly."

"Yes, ma'am. Right away," Andrea nodded before hurrying away.

Rain relocated from the sofa style seat to the chair across from Aerona.

"The FBI couldn't shut down the plane in Cleveland," Rain said. "What's their next tactical move?"

Damien flipped out his tiny notepad and began writing notes as he talked. "Their first priority after losing an aircraft would be to determine its final destination."

"Which they believe is Orlando?" Rain asked.

"No," Damien shook his head, "They'll certainly think Orlando is a decoy, especially if they believe the aircraft is piloted by terrorists."

"What are the chances they discover where we are intending to land?" I asked.

"I've dealt with this type of situation before," Damien continued. "According to government databases, there are roughly 14,950 airports in the U.S. of those, only about 5,000 have paved runways, where this jet could land safely. Only about 360 of those 5,000 have regular airport service, which terrorists would most likely avoid after being instructed to abort their flight plans by a federal branch of the U.S. government. The bottom line—it's going to be difficult for the FBI to establish which airport we're headed to, if any. This jet has a range of over 7,000 miles. We could very well be landing outside this country."

"So their next move is…" Rain urged him on.

"Their next move would be to get the Air Force in the sky after us. Luckily for us, searching the U.S. skies will prove much harder than finding a needle in a haystack. At any given time, there's an average of 4,000 planes over 3.8 million square miles of U.S. airspace.

"If the FAA knows how many planes are in the sky," Whisper reasoned, "doesn't that mean they track every plane? Aren't they tracking us right now?"

"Not exactly," Ember said, smiling slyly. "Let's just say I know someone who has the capability to disable the onboard transponder. We turn it on before we enter an airport's airspace and switch it off once we're clear of their radar. We also have the ability to clone our transmitted flight number to match any approaching or departing flight. This plane is essentially invisible to the FAA, unless someone gets close enough to the aircraft for a positive ID"

"And," Damien added, continuing Ember's thought. "We've already scheduled a false flight number for landing in Missoula."

"Question," Aerona cut in. "What happens if the FBI is waiting for us when we land?"

"She brings up a good point," I said, agreeing with Aerona. "Do we still feel confident enough to land in Missoula?"

Damien closed his notebook. "I believe there is a risk in continuing with our current flight plan," he said, "though, statistically the risk factor is the same no matter which airport we choose."

"He's right," Kasiah nodded. "The worst thing we could do right now is change plans. We've researched Missoula. We know the layout. If the FBI is aware of our plans, then Atmoro will find out soon enough. We need to stay focused and extract Jade swiftly."

Whisper leaned back in his chair, cupping his hands behind his head and said comically, "Well, I hope everyone brought their vampire hunting shoes."

TWENTY-SIX

Candice, speaking through the Jet's intercom system, woke me from my dream. "…upright and locked positions," she announced. "Andrea, as we prepare for landing, please collect all loose objects, such as glasses and any other items, throughout the cabin. The weather in Missoula is currently seventy-two with rain and strong winds from the northwest. We'll be on the ground in about ten minutes."

I leaned my head back against the seat and closed my eyes, trying to remember my dream that would perhaps be better described as a nightmare. My thoughts were fuzzy, and my memory was blurry; I could only recall pieces.

I dreamt of when I was a child in the Shadow World. Aerona and I, maybe thirteen at the time, were hiding in the hallway of our home, eavesdropping on our parents' conversation. They had just returned from one of their secret alliance meetings, and my mother was expressing her concern for our safety.

"This is getting far too dangerous," my mother said. "Malance has taken over the Council, and if he discovers we've been investigating him or have this information… I don't… I don't know what he'll do."

"This is for the good of all Shadows," my father said quietly, almost too low for me to hear. "Malance will be appointed as the new Head Councilman. If we don't stand up to him now, no one will. He'll rule the Shadow World, and we both know if that happens, every Shadow will be in danger, especially once the Light Council learns how Malance has been exploiting humans."

169

My mother began to weep. "We have the twins to think about," she said. "They're not old enough to defend themselves if something were to…," she lowered her voice, "…happen to us."

My father reached out and wrapped his arms around her. He held her tight and kissed her forehead. "Nothing is going to happen," he assured her. "The evidence against Malance is too strong for even his uncle not to listen. There are enough of us who know the truth, who believe. We'll protect each other. The decision has been made. We'll present the evidence to the elders in two nights at the next council meeting."

Suddenly, both my parents were frozen in place. They had literally become blocks of ice wrapped in each other's arms. Their skin turned cold blue, and their expressions were frozen in time. An army of Shadow Vampires burst through the kitchen door. Malance was always the last to enter—the coward.

My mouth dropped open when Noshimo, one of the warlocks from my father's secret alliance, walked in behind Malance. He had been a friend of my family long before I was born. I found it hard to believe he had associated himself with Malance, but it explained the frozen spell.

Before Aerona could scream out, I threw my hand over her mouth. I felt her emotions erupt into a fiery ball of anger over Noshimo's obvious betrayal. I struggled to drag her backwards down the hall to my room as Malance barked orders to the Shadow Vampires.

"Check the house!" Malance yelled. "The children must be here somewhere! Go find them!"

I spun Aerona around. "Aerona," I said, looking into her eyes, "we have to focus. They're coming for us. Concentrate. We need to make ourselves invisible."

Aerona shut her eyes and steadied her breathing. She always had incredible control over her emotions when she put her mind to it. Invisibility was a spell we had only learned recently and were nowhere near mastering the technique, but it was do or die. We pulled in as much energy as we could and created an electromagnetic field that bent the light around us. Our bodies no longer reflected light—we disappeared.

My bedroom door flew open, and a Shadow Vampire rushed in. Aerona and I were motionless against the far wall. I had never seen this particular Shadow Vampire before today. He looked young and moved unsteadily, as though he was a new vampire. Malance had probably created him for his own private, evil army.

The Shadow Vampire was careless. He searched the room like a common criminal looking for valuables. He rummaged through the closet, peered under the bed, and checked the locked window. He never stopped to rely on his other senses. We were there, he just couldn't see us.

The Shadow Vampire left the room to continue the search. Aerona and I immediately released the spell to save our energy.

"We need to get out of here," I whispered.

"What about Mother and Father?" she whispered back. "And why is Noshimo here?"

"I don't know what Noshimo is doing here," I said, wondering the same thing myself. "He may be one of Malance's rats."

"That's impossible!" she said in denial.

I put my finger to my lips to shush her. "Aerona, if you have learned anything, I hope you have learned that impossible is simply a word. Do not cloud your vision of reality with thoughts of the past. Noshimo is a close family friend, which is true, and now we know why."

My dream jumped from an image of my parents frozen in blocks of ice to Shadow Vampires ripping our home apart, searching for my father's safe. My memory floated back down the hallway to my old room, where teenage Erone and Aerona were making a choice that would impact the rest of their lives.

"Aerona," I said, "Father always told us a day may come for us to make a decision we didn't want to make. He warned us that someday we could be left with a choice that would put life against death. That day is today. If we try to save them, we'll end up in a prison cell, or worse, a grave next to them."

A tear rolled down Aerona's eye as she comprehended what I had just said.

"Survive," I said, "is what Mother and Father would want us to do."

Aerona nodded her head. "You must retrieve Father's spell book. Do you know where he keeps it?"

"Yes," I replied, "but there is no time to retrieve it now. They're in his safe under the large sapphire tree behind the house. We can come back. Malance will never find it tonight. If by chance he does, it's locked with a spell that even Noshimo could never break."

We heard noises from our parents' room. It sounded like wood breaking as furniture was turned over. Malance was desperate to find my father's evidence.

I snuck over to my bedroom window and peered outside. There were no signs of guards outside the house. I unlatched the window and boosted Aerona up. She leapt down, then helped me out behind her. We ran as hard as we could through the thick sapphire forest—away from the smell of our burning home.

My eyes popped opened, and I was thrust into reality. Damien and Aerona were staring out the jet's windows. Rain, with his head resting against his seat, was busy ignoring Whisper. I didn't see Ember; she must have been in the cockpit with Candice.

"How was your nap?" Kasiah asked. "Any exciting dreams full of beautiful women?"

"Unfortunately, no," I replied. "How long was I out?"

"A little over an hour," Aerona cut in from across the aisle, "and yes, you snored."

Kasiah slid her hand underneath mine. "We're flying through a storm. Candice warned we may experience some turbulence as we descend."

Tiny raindrops streaked across my window. There didn't seem to be much of a storm outside. I was unsure of our altitude, but I could see two rows of red and white lights sparkling below. If I had my bearings right, the lights were from vehicles traveling along I90; the countries longest coast to coast interstate highway, the same highway we traveled on from Madison to Erie.

The traffic lights vanished completely as we flew into a low cloud. The jet's floodlights cut through the darkness. I heard the hydraulics lowering the landing gear; we must have been closing in on the runway. The jet dropped several feet unexpectedly, rocking the plane from side to side as it recovered. The drizzle turned to rain, and the turbulence became worse as the jet descended through the clouds. We flew out of one dark cloud and went right into another. Heavy rain pounded against the jet. The engines powered up, then down, struggling to maintain a consistent speed. The jet dropped several more feet as we descended below the clouds.

I have always wanted to pilot a plane, but I did not envy Candice at that very moment. She had her hands full, landing a multimillion dollar jet in a storm at an airport surrounded by towering mountains.

Andrea stumbled past us through the cabin toward her seat.

I felt Aerona's fear as the jet lost altitude again.

Kasiah squeezed my hand tight.

A bright streak of lightning flashed outside the window, illuminating the cabin briefly. Booming thunder echoed a second later. It was difficult to see much of anything through the rain. All the city lights were blurred, but I could tell we weren't flying straight. The jet was definitely flying at an odd angle against the strong wind. When the long, parallel airport light patterns finally came into view, I could see them from my window—out the side of the jet!

Only during landing do passengers get a sense of an aircraft's true speed. We approached the runway lights rapidly, sideways, hovering a few inches above the runway for what felt like an eternity until we finally touched down. The rear wheels of the jet contacted the pavement, forcefully aligning the jet to the runway. If we weren't wearing seatbelts, we would have all been tossed to one side of the cabin.

Candice used reverse thrust, redirecting the engine's power to slow down, producing a horrendous sound. It was almost as if she had pushed them forward to full throttle in an attempt to abort the landing.

The good news was that we were slowing down.

"Welcome to Missoula International," Candice announced over the intercom. "The local time is ten forty-five. I apologize for the bumpy ride. If you're conscious and alive, please remain seated until we come to a full stop.

The ground traffic at the airport is reasonably inactive right now, so it should only be another minute or two until we reach the hangar."

"That was intense," Kasiah said, releasing my hand.

"I second that," said Aerona. "I'm surprised Whisper didn't teleport himself onto the runway."

"Honestly," Whisper added, "I would have, but the accuracy of my teleportation is greatly affected by an aircraft being tossed around in a storm."

Candice navigated the jet through the complex taxiways to a reserved hangar on the northern end of the airport. It was the only hangar with its door still open and the lights on. As soon as the tail section was clear and inside the hangar, a gigantic overhead door began shutting behind. The winding down of the jet engines reverberated off the walls as the jet finally came to a stop.

The cockpit door opened and Ember and Candice joined us in the main cabin.

"Did everyone live to tell the tale?" Ember asked.

"That beats any roller coaster," Whisper joked. "If we have time, I wouldn't mind doing it again."

"Whisper," Ember smiled, "with a little bit of luck, we will never have to do that again."

"Great job, Candice," I said, genuinely impressed. "You were entirely too modest earlier when you said you were a decent pilot at best."

"Another day at the office," Candice smiled, playing down the difficult landing. "I guess it wasn't bad for having my eyes closed the entire time."

We all laughed out at her joke.

Ember turned to Damien. "How's our time schedule?" she asked.

"We're right on target," Damien responded. "Has our ground transportation arrived?"

"Yes," Ember said, opening the main cabin door. "We're ready to move."

Two empty black SUV's were ready and waiting for us as we stepped off the jet; apparently, black SUV's are the preferred mode of transportation for FBI agents and fairies.

Rain bolted outside the hanger to check the perimeter. He returned with nothing to report, except wet hair and clothes.

"Let's get to the hotel and regroup," Damien suggested. "There are no threats right now, but that's not to say the FBI wasn't delayed due to the storm."

We all agreed and loaded our bags into the vehicles.

"Want to throw to see who drives?" Whisper asked Rain.

Rain just looked at Whisper and nodded his head.

"Not this again," Ember said, shaking her head. "Just get your asses in the vehicle."

I don't know where Whisper found his courage, but he was fearless in the face of a Shadow Vampire.

"Come on, sissy," Whisper snorted, provoking Rain. "Best two out of three?"

Luckily for us, throwing turned out to be a game of rock-paper-scissors. Rain won by throwing rock two times in a row. Whisper was unable to read Rain's poker face as he switched from paper to rock in midflight on the third game. I wondered how long these two have been playing this game. For the first time since I had met Whisper, he was without a smile, while Rain proudly shined the largest smile I had seen on him.

"You can drive, but the stereo's mine," Whisper mumbled, climbing into the passenger seat.

"Children," Ember declared, closing her door.

As if we couldn't avoid it, we ended up driving on I90 to the hotel. The storm started to let up, and the traffic thinned as we exited the highway onto the city streets. The city appeared to be deserted this time of night, which we found odd, since it was a college town.

Rows of trees lined practically every street. I felt I was driving through a forest. Breaking through the clouds, the moonlight cast just enough light to outline the mountain tops behind the city skyline. From what Tara had told us, the mountains are covered with thick, dark forests, prefect for hiding Atmoro and who knows who or what else.

"The storm must be keeping people inside," Whisper remarked.

"Ghostly," added Kasiah.

I focused out the window for anything out of the ordinary. "Sure is," I said. "How's our rearview, Rain?"

"Clear," he said. "No tail."

The hotel was only another two or three minutes down the road. The rain picked back up as we pulled into the packed parking lot. We found two parking spots all the way in the rear.

"Great," Rain said, opening his door into the storm.

Whisper laughed. "Don't worry, Rain, you're not sweet enough to melt."

Rain shot a glare at Whisper.

I looked around to see if anyone was outside. Satisfied no one was watching, I closed my eyes and pulled in enough energy to form a shield over the SUV. When I opened my eyes, I saw the rain rolling off the invisible bubble, as if a big plastic dome had been placed over our vehicle.

"I can't keep this up forever," I said, opening the door. "Let's go."

"Now that's a neat trick," Whisper remarked, sticking his hand outside the invisible bubble. He turned his palm over and watched the rain dance on it.

Fast-paced footsteps splashed in the water behind us. Instinct compelled me to turn and press my back to the SUV, ready for anything. The footsteps turned out to be Damien running past us toward the hotel entrance; his bag was raised over his head as a makeshift umbrella. Aerona and Ember were walking side by side, dry as the desert sand. Aerona had created her own invisible dome over their heads. The rain poured over the clear dome, running straight down to the ground around them. They waved comically as they walked by.

"Showoff!" I yelled.

TWENTY-SEVEN

During our flight in, Ember had reserved the entire top floor of the hotel—sixteen rooms. To accommodate her request, the hotel clerk had to relocate several guests to other floors. She seemed puzzled when we walked in with only six people.

As I said before, it is amazing what one can do with an endless bag of money.

After checking in, we gathered in Ember's room. I did a double take when Rain walked in through the door. He had traded in his hoodie and torn jeans for a tight black T-shirt over a long-sleeved white shirt and black leather pants with silver zippers on every pocket. His belt had a rather large, intricately carved metal Celtic knot buckle; the silver metal had a dull finish that appeared very old—probably because it was. A thin layer of dark eyeliner made his dark eyes stand out even more than usual. His hair was the same old Rain—messy and out of place.

I caught Aerona's eyes giving Rain a detailed scan from head to toe. I secretly hoped she didn't have a thing for Rain. Aerona had had enough trouble with her other Shadow Vampire boyfriends to last a lifetime. Although, I was in no position to offer advice to anyone else. I was falling head over heels for a human FBI agent who had the cutest Midwestern accent of all time.

Aerona, Kasiah, and Ember had all changed for a night of mingling at the local clubs to search for Jade. They would all blend in nicely without drawing too much attention. To my surprise, Aerona had changed in her usual witty

177

shirts for a low-cut white, casual button-up shirt. She wore our mother's necklace, which I hadn't seen her wear in years. The necklace was much more than a simple chain and pendant. It expanded into an intricate, almost vine-like woven pattern of white Shadow gold. The center stone was a large amethyst, believed to attract love and calm fears. I wondered which of the two feelings inspired Aerona to wear the necklace tonight.

"You three look ready for a night of clubbing," I commented.

Kasiah smiled her beautiful smile. "Don't mind us," she said, "we're just three innocent girls out for a night of fun after a hard workday."

"This weather may play to our advantage," Damien said, buckling his shoulder holster. "The storm will most likely keep everyone inside. Anyone you see out tonight may have the same objective as us, so be aware of your surroundings."

Whisper reached into his satchel and pulled out a small, high-tech looking aluminum case the size of a small book. It made a slight suction sound as he opened the lid, as if it was held closed by vacuum pressure. Inside, there were two rows of small, glass-like pieces on a black velvet liner. They resembled the shape of kidney beans.

Whisper walked around the room and handed one of the glass beans to each of us.

"These are state of the art communication devices," he said, placing one in my hand. "I've been developing them for the U.S. military. They're code named ECHO."

I turned the tiny earpiece over in my hand, studying it carefully. From a distance, it appeared to have a glossy finish; up close, it was soft with a strange rubbery texture. There was something embedded in the center—an electronic device.

"Echo?" I asked.

"It's an acronym," Whisper explained. "Electronically Controlled Hearing Organism. ECHO."

"Organism?" Aerona asked, confused.

"Yes, organism," he repeated. "Due to its top secret clearance, and somewhat confusing science, I can't tell you everything about ECHO, but the short version involves a classified microchip placed into a mold. Then we introduce several clusters of a newly developed microorganism that multiplies at an incredible rate around the chip, eventually filling the shape of the mold. It takes about two minutes for the organism to fill the mold and crystallize. After that, it's basically in a state of hibernation, which is what you see now.

I like to think I had kept up with modern technology. Apparently I had not.

"The microorganism serves two purposes," Whisper continued. "The first is a cloaking device, which makes the unit invisible. Once it's inserted in your ear, it activates and automatically adjusts its shape to fit the contour of your ear, but don't worry, it won't increase in size. The exterior of the microorganisms reflect light in a way that makes the unit invisible to the naked eye. The second purpose of the microorganism is power supply. The microorganisms emit short electrical pulses that supply power to the microchip, which is the brain of the unit. The microchip receives signals from other units, then decodes them into audible sounds for the user. In reverse, it codes your voice before sending the signal out to other users on the same network."

Aerona held the earpiece in her hand carefully, as though it was a deadly spider. "I'm not putting this thing in my ear!" she exclaimed.

Whisper laughed at how Aerona was holding the earpiece. "Sarah," he continued, "Trust me, ECHO has been through extensive testing. It's a hundred percent safe. There's nothing to worry about."

"I'm not putting this bug in my ear," she repeated sternly. "And I guess the Sarah game is over. My name is Aerona."

"ECHO's not a bug, *Aerona*," Whisper added defensively. "It's a complex piece of technology that is going to give us the advantage of hearing each other as if we were in the same room, even when we're miles apart."

I gave Aerona my best *I'm going to kick your ass if you don't shut up* look. "She'll be fine." I said. "What's their range?"

Whisper appreciated my interest in his creation. "The signal bounces off any one of multiple military satellites. The range is anywhere in the world.

Oh, and don't worry, the signal is coded as random noise, so if anyone monitors the satellite, they won't know we're hitching a ride. To activate ECHO, gently press it into whichever ear you feel comfortable. They're soft and will form to your ear in just a few seconds. The unit's volume adjusts based on the ambient noise, which means you never have to worry about adjusting it yourself. The microphones are very sensitive, so there's no need to raise your voice when you talk. They'll pick up the slightest whisper, no pun intended."

The rest of us, except for Aerona, inserted our ECHO devices. It immediately began reshaping itself to fit my ear, an odd sensation that lasted only a few seconds. After the transformation was complete, I could barely tell ECHO was even there.

"I don't hear anything," Damien said.

"That's normal," Whisper explained. "The units are receiving data as we talk to each other, but they know we're within hearing distance for the current levels." He lowered his voice. "If I talk like this, you should be able to hear it, because the unit now knows we're in a hushed state, and it will transmit the sound."

I could hear Whisper's hushed voice clearly in my ear.

"Can we turn them off?" I asked.

Whisper put on a thin, black leather jacket, leaving the Batman symbol exposed through the front. "Yes," he said, "and we'll actually turn them off until they're needed. That way, you don't have six voices running around in your head all night. ECHO recognizes voice commands from the user, and it's already imprinted your unique voices. Simply say, 'ECHO off.'"

"ECHO off," I said, sounding like I was ordering a dog off the sofa. The unit beeped once in my ear and switched off.

"What's the point of having these earpieces if they're all turned off?" Kasiah asked.

"ECHO is on a network," he added. "Say 'ECHO 911' to activate the other units on your team's network."

"ECHO on," Damien said, turning his unit back on. "Kasiah, these are perfect for our tactical teams. We need to invest in a few dozen when we get back."

"ECHO off," said Kasiah. "I'm not so sure these are in our price range. What do they cost, Whisper?"

"They're a steal. Just under fifteen thousand a pair."

"Well," Damien considered, loading a full magazine into his 9mm, "scratch that off my Christmas list."

"ECHO off," Aerona said.

We all looked at Aerona, surprised she gave it a chance.

"What?" she asked. "The peer pressure got to me. It's not so bad. It better not try to eat my brain or something."

I laughed. "Well, if its main source of nutrition is brains, then the poor thing is going to go hungry."

Aerona gave me one of her angry, death stares she had perfected over the years.

I ignored her and looked at my watch. "It's almost midnight," I continued. "We should still be able to move around the city unnoticed until the bars close. After that, we'll want to either be in a stakeout position or back here at the hotel."

Our plan hadn't changed; Rain and I would take one SUV to locate Jade's residence and check for signs of her or Atmoro. Meanwhile, Kasiah, Ember, and Aerona would catch a cab downtown to mingle at the local nightclubs to see if Jade was out for the night. Damien and Whisper would take the other SUV to monitor the perimeter of the city.

Damien grabbed his jacket off the desk. "Does anyone have any other questions?" he asked.

"Just remember," Ember added. "We all have special areas of expertise and skills, but we know practically nothing about stones or their powers. Keep in mind that Jade is the child of two powerful angels. She may or may not know her capabilities, but we need to approach her as if she knows everything."

181

TWENTY-EIGHT

Tara woke up to excruciating pain in her left arm. She tried to lift it, but even the slightest movement shocked her with intense pain. She was in complete darkness. It took several seconds for her pupils to widen and adjust. The sound of raindrops hitting a pane of glass drew her eyes to the dark outline of a draped window. She was in what appeared to be a small, empty room. It felt cold and damp, and it smelled like an old, forgotten farmhouse. She tried not to think of the spiders hanging from the ceiling or crawling up her leg.

Tara's mind was clouded and dizzy. *Where am I?* she thought. *What happened?* She attempted to move her right arm but it didn't budge—it was stuck. She yanked harder, releasing a dose of adrenaline into her bloodstream. The realization of being trapped took hold of her. She tried to move her legs, but they too were trapped. She tried to scream for help, but her mouth wouldn't open either. She focused on a thick silver line around her wrists, and that's when reality punched her in the stomach—she was duct-taped to a chair.

Memories engulfed in dizziness flooded Tara's confused mind. She recalled a knock at her door and a cable repair man. The images jumped through time, too fast to catch more than bits and pieces. The next image Tara could recall clearly was a cable repair man's head crashing into the windshield of her SUV as Tara drove through her lawn. The final two memories were of a van on a collision course with her driver's side door and a dead police officer falling to the ground as Tara hung upside down from her seatbelt.

182

Panic squeezed the air out of Tara's chest. Her eyes opened wide as the flood of memories raced through her mind. Being unable to move her limbs or open her mouth terrified her. She struggled to gain control of her breathing.

A bolt of lightning flashed outside the window, momentarily filling the damp dark room with white bright light. The room in front of her was bare, except for an empty chair in one corner opposite the door. As light filled the room, Tara quickly looked down and inspected her wrists. The duct tape held her firmly to an old wooden chair. Her hands and arms were filthy. Her jeans, just as dirty as her arms, were ripped in numerous places. Several streaks of dried blood stained the front of her white shirt. She turned her head from side to side, desperately trying to see what was behind her.

A loud boom of thunder rattled the window. Her mind began working on the complex problem of first getting out of the chair, then out of the room, although she had no idea what was on the other side of the door.

Suddenly, a man's voice echoed behind Tara, causing her heart to jump and her muscles to spasm.

"You're stronger than I first thought," the man said.

She recognized the man's voice. It was Steve, the cable guy, who was forever embedded deep in her brain.

"Before we begin," he continued, "I think maybe it's time for proper introductions. My name is Jake."

Tara froze in her place as Jake stepped in front of her. She stopped struggling with the tape on her wrists and ankles, knowing she would need the energy later. Her eyes followed Jake's outline as he moved in the dark.

Jake sat in the empty chair across the room. "I'm going to make this short and sweet," he added. "You have been researching a topic that has sparked my interest—the blood of a stone."

Jake waited for Tara's reaction to his allegation. She didn't react. She was terrified.

"This is a very simple game," he continued. "You answer my questions, and your pain goes away. The alternative is if you don't answer, then I'll give you more pain than one human body can withstand over an entire lifetime."

Another bolt of lightning lit the room, allowing Tara to see Jake for no more than a second. It was long enough. He looked like an average, everyday man. He was younger than she could remember from his Steve-the-cable-guy masquerade, maybe only a year or two out of college. His face was calm and in control. His eyes seemed kind as he stared at Tara from across the room. Jake was dressed like an average twenties guy: casual khaki pants and a dark, untucked button-up shirt. At first glance, Tara never would have guessed this man to be a killer, which is exactly what is said about most serial killers.

"We'll start with a few yes or no questions," he said. "Do you work for a vampire named Atmoro?"

Tara shook her head, trying not to look terrified by the name of the same vampire Erone had warned her about. She wondered if Jake was a vampire himself, already knowing the answer to the question, considering Jake was standing after being run over by an SUV and shot by a cop.

"Question two," Jake continued. "Have you found what you were looking for?"

Again, Tara shook her head no. She never thought she'd be in a situation where she'd face being tortured for information. She wondered how much pain she could handle before Jade's name would escaped from her lips. Tara pushed the name far back in her mind, trying to lose it.

"Is the information you seek for yourself or someone else?"

Tara looked confused. She couldn't answer that question by shaking her head.

"Let me rephrase that," Jake added. "Do you work for someone else?"

Tara nodded slowly. A tear rolled down her cheek. She closed her eyes and forced herself to gain control. She had to remain focused to get through this nightmare. There's a solution to every problem, even when one wakes up to find themselves taped to a chair while being interrogated by a thirsty vampire.

Another flash of light filled the room, much brighter than last. Tara's pupils closed to compensate for the burst of intense light, temporarily blinding her. The room went dark, and her pupils switched gears from tiny to wide-open. The window pane shook from the clap of thunder that followed the lightning. When Tara's eyes finally focused back, she found the chair across the room was empty.

"Boo!" Jake shouted, now right next to Tara's ear.

His laughter was chilling. A surge of fear ran through Tara's body. Her left arm tensed up, sending pain shooting up her shoulder.

Jake reached his hand out toward Tara's face.

She closed her eyes, holding her breath.

"I'm going to remove the tape from your mouth," Jake said. "This isn't a movie, so I'm not going to tell you not to scream. Actually, feel free to scream. No one will hear you."

Jake grabbed the end of the tape and yanked it from her face.

"SERIOUSLY!" Tara cried out. Her sarcasm filter wasn't something she could manage at a time like that. "Your bedside manner could use some work! That hurt, psycho!"

Jake taped back over her mouth. "Rule number one," he said calmly, "I'm in charge. Rule number two... I'M IN FUCKING CHARGE!"

The room was so dark that Tara never even saw Jake's hand hurtling through the air until it collided with her cheek. Her head snapped back from the impact.

Jake was losing his patience, and he was running out of time. He desperately needed to get this girl talking, so he could get ahead of Atmoro in his little game of cat and mouse. He ripped the tape from her mouth a second time. "Now let's try this again" he suggested, "preferably without your sarcasm."

The throbbing in Tara's left arm intensified as she tensed her muscles to cope with the pain from the tape ripping across her lips. She could taste blood from Jake's powerful slap to the face.

"Now, where were we?" he continued calmly, as though reading a bedtime story. "Oh yes, the blood of a stone." He placed his hands on the arms of the chair, looking her straight in the eyes and inches from her nose. "You need to spill your guts before I spill them for you."

Tara forced herself to calm down. She put her head back, took a deep breath, and exhaled. "I don't know what you're talking about," she said in a weak voice.

Jake slapped her again, even harder this time. "LIAR!" he roared. "Fine! Let's do this the hard way! You want to play the little redheaded hero, then I'll play the evil psychotic villain!"

Tara thought that sounded about right.

Jake leaned in close. "Do you know why it takes law enforcement so long to get information from a suspect?" he asked. "It's because they have rules of interrogation. They have proper protocols to follow, so the evidence obtained during the interrogation can be admissible in court. It's unfortunate for you that I don't abide by that same set of rules and guidelines."

Jake pulled a switchblade from his pocket, flipped it open, and plunged the knife through Tara's left hand—pinning her to the arm of the chair.

A deafening scream erupted from her lungs. The pain of the knife through her hand competed for worst pain ever with the pain of her broken arm. She tried not to look at the knife sticking out the back of her hand, but she failed. A dark stream of blood instantly formed around the blade, pouring down to the floor.

Tara couldn't see Jake's eyes in the darkness as they changed color from a soft blue to a dark brown, though she did notice his breathing increased. Tara looked back at her hand, at the blood that was about to make Jake lose his mind.

Jake fought to gain control of his thirst; he knew blood was among his only weaknesses. He shut off his sense of smell and turned his eyes away from the blood to Tara's frightened face.

"Let's try this again. Did you… Tara… find what you… Tara…. were looking for?"

"Go… to… hell," Tara said through clinched teeth in the same tone that Jake asked the question.

Jake was amazed at how much fight the little redhead had in her. He knew he couldn't kill her until he got what he needed, but it was taking every ounce of self-control he had not to break her tiny neck to satisfy his thirst. Jake decided to try a different strategy, switching roles to good cop. He retreated to the opposite side of the room, away from the blood, away from the temptation. "Look," he said in the best good cop voice he could manage, "I just want to know where I can find the stone. Tell me where it is, and you'll be out of here in time to catch the eleven o'clock news."

It took everything Tara had in her not to scream out from the throbbing pain in her hand and arm, although she still had enough sense to know Jake was full of it. "As if," she added weakly, "you're just going to let me walk out that door after I tell you where this rock is hidden."

Tara used the word *rock* intentionally, to see if Jake even knew what he was looking for or why.

"Scout's honor," Jake said, saluting Tara. "You tell me where the rock is, and we're done here."

Tara's bait had worked; he didn't know he's looking for a fallen angel.

"Were you smart enough to grab my laptop bag?" she asked.

"You're awfully mouthy," Jake remarked, growing more irritated. "You're lucky to be breathing, and yet you sit here making jokes."

Tara took in a breath. "I'm just saying," she continued, "if you want your stupid rock, then you better have grabbed my bag."

"Well, don't go anywhere," Jake said, laughing. "I'll be right back."

Jake slammed the door behind him as he left the room.

TWENTY-NINE

From outside the house, after having heard Tara screaming in pain, Ian was about to dial 911. His heart thumped rapidly as he shifted his hiding position behind a large oak tree at the edge of the overgrown lawn. "I should have never followed this damn idiot," Ian whispered to himself. "This is the worst idea ever!"

The night before, after Ian got off the phone with Jake, his conscience kept telling him what Jake might do to Tara. He felt horrible for giving away the name and address, which turned out was only a 45-minute drive from his own apartment in Chicago. Ian finally decided that maybe he could warn her or something. He couldn't just sit there and do nothing, knowing Jake was about to do something dreadful.

It was late afternoon by the time Ian turned up on Tara's street. He decided to merely watch her house first, to see if she was home. He parked down the street and waited for at least two hours. Nothing happened. He couldn't wait forever, so he decided to call Tara and warn her that she may be in danger. Just as Ian picked up his phone to dial her number, a Speed Demon cable repair van pulled into Tara's driveway. A uniformed man hopped out of the van and checked his clipboard before walking up to the front door.

It took several minutes of the cable guy knocking and ringing the bell for someone to open the front door. Ian couldn't see who answered, but it meant someone was home. He looked as his watch and thought seven o'clock was an odd time for a cable repair man to be making a house call.

Less than five minutes after the cable guy entered the house, a red-haired girl sprinted out from the back of the house. It looked like she left in a hurry, and she wasn't looking back. She tossed a backpack into a small copper SUV and practically threw herself into the driver's side. She didn't waste time trying to maneuver around the cable van blocking her driveway; instead, she took the SUV on the path less traveled, cutting a trail right through her front lawn.

What happened next was a scene straight off the big screen. A moment before the vehicle turned the corner of the house, a man shot around from the side yard like a bullet. He was moving so fast, his movement was only a blur until he ran straight into the hood of the fleeing SUV. The man's head bounced off the windshield, sending his body into a slow motion somersault over the roof. Unlike cats, people don't always land on their feet. This guy actually used his face to cushion the landing. Ian cringed and looked away.

The sound of tires screeching on pavement made Ian look up. The man was on his feet and limping back to the van. If this was Jake, then he was some kind of supervillain. His wounds healed right before Ian's eyes.

The van backed out of the driveway at full speed, crashing into the parked car across the street. Ian didn't exactly know what made him start his own car, but he was now in pursuit of the van, racing after the SUV.

Ian lost sight of the van around the second corner. He had to swerve into oncoming traffic and speed through a red light to catch back up. He was only three cars behind the van as it rushed up the on-ramp to the highway, running a soccer mom's minivan over the shoulder. Sparks flew from the side of the minivan as it scrapped along the guard rail.

They continued down the highway for several miles before Ian caught sight of the copper SUV in front of the cable van. The sound of police sirens made Ian check the rearview and notice the red and blue flashing lights of a police cruiser. Police presence was Ian's cue to back off. Yes, he felt horrible for not calling the girl five minutes earlier, although he had no intentions of being caught up in a police investigation of any kind. He took his foot off the accelerator and let the cruiser pass by.

Unable to turn around, Ian had no choice but to continue down the highway in search of the next exit. A few miles and two curves later, Ian slowed to a stop at the crest of a large hill. Smoke spiraled into the air from an accident halfway into the grassy median at the bottom. The copper SUV was overturned and the van only a few yards away. Smoke spiraled up from the crumpled hood of the van. With its lights still flashing and the driver's side door open, the police cruiser was parked just off the road on the gravel shoulder.

Ian heard the unmistakable sound of gunshots echoing through the air. His eyes focused on two men near the front of the overturned SUV. The girl was nowhere to be seen. A tiny flash of light sparked in front of who Ian thought was the police officer. A moment later, Ian heard another echo of gunfire. The officer was definitely shooting. Ian couldn't believe his eyes when Jake jumped through the air like a wild animal, landing behind the policeman. Ian squinted to make his vision clearer, but it looked like Jake was biting the officer's neck.

What the hell just happened? Ian thought to himself. He was in shock. He couldn't move, he couldn't think. He could just watch the horrific scene playing out. The officer fell to the ground motionless. Jake ripped the overturned SUV's crumpled door right off its hinges, then reached inside and pulled Tara's unconscious body from the wreckage, tossing her to the ground. Jake took several steps away from the SUV, slamming his fists into the side door. He knelt by the officer's body and bit him again.

Ian hoped Tara wasn't dead, but it didn't look good. *This is my fault,* Ian thought to himself. *I killed her. She's dead and it's my fault.*

Jake carried Tara up the hill, then tossed her in the back seat of the police cruiser. He climbed into the driver's seat and slammed the door shut. The rear wheels of the cruiser created an enormous cloud of dust and gravel as it sped back onto the highway and out of sight.

Ian's conscience kicked him again, forcing him to inch his car toward the accident scene. Several other motorists had also stopped. One woman came running up the grassy hill. "He's dead!" she yelled. "The cop's dead! Call 911!"

The scene had become cluttered with onlookers, and Ian could hear more sirens in the distance. He needed to get the hell out of there, fast. He ran down the hill to the overturned SUV, faltering more than once, sliding most of the way down the hill. He forced his eyes away from the dead cop's body and observed the SUV. He didn't know what he was looking for, but his gut told him to keep searching.

On his second time around the SUV, a piece of pink plastic caught Ian's eye. He reached through the broken window and came out with a pink cell phone. The screen lit up. It was still working. Ian was in too much of a hurry to properly search the vehicle and didn't waste any more time. He shoved the pink cell phone in his jacket pocket and climbed back up the grassy hillside to his car.

Ian checked his rearview mirror as he pulled away from the accident site. Several police cruisers crested the same hill Ian had been watching from only a few minutes prior. He pushed the accelerator down hard as he sped away. Once he was off the highway, he hacked into the state police's main server and tracked the stolen cruiser's GPS locator. The signal went dead ten minutes later, but Ian had enough information to catch up to them on an interstate heading south of the accident. He then followed the police cruiser for a little over an hour to an abandoned farmhouse far outside the city.

Ian's mind returned to Tara screaming from inside the abandoned farmhouse. The front door flew open with a bang, and Ian froze in place, holding his breath. He had been watching the farmhouse for almost three hours. The sun had long since set, and the forest around him was eerie quiet. He watched as Jake raced from the porch to the police cruiser. His speed was amazing. Jake opened the door and pulled out a backpack. Ian assumed it was Tara's, possibly her laptop bag.

Jake slammed the cruiser door shut and headed back to the house, stopping abruptly to stare directly at Ian's hiding spot. Ian didn't move a muscle; he didn't even breathe. After a few seconds, his eyes started to burn. He needed to blink, and when he finally did, Jake was gone.

THIRTY

"In two hundred feet, turn left," the GPS announced, in its typical, over-demanding tone.

Rain tightened his grip on the steering wheel. "Once we find Jade's place, can we toss that GPS out the window?" he asked.

"We may need it to find our way back," I replied, "but I'd rather be lost out here all night than take anymore lip from this thing. Jade's apartment should be just around the next corner."

"Continue three hundred feet to your destination on the left," the GPS commanded.

The storm had begun to let up, and the rain slowed to a drizzle. The outlines of mountaintop silhouettes could be seen in the distance over small businesses, most of which were closed for the night. The lights of a few bars and dance clubs were scattered here and there. The streets were mostly empty, with the exception of a stumbling college kid or two on their way home from or to the next club.

Rain kept a steady pace as our GPS tour guide led the way.

"Arriving at destination on the left."

The lower level of the large white building to our left looked like some sort of a storefront closed for the night. Several of the lights on the second floor were dimly lit, probably apartments. Rain drove past the building.

"Recalculating!" the GPS announced, sounding as agitated as a computer could get.

I turned the GPS off before it turned on the killing machine in Rain.

We parked in a small, empty bank parking lot a block beyond Jade's building. A crisp, cool breeze greeted us as we exited the SUV. The street lights shimmered off the wet pavement.

Rain joined me on my side of the SUV. "I noticed a few doors next to the business entrances," I said. "They probably lead to the upstairs apartments. Hopefully, there will be names on the mailboxes we can use to ID Jade."

We started up the sidewalk towards Jade's building. A black pickup truck crept past us, almost idling by. The dark tinted windows hid the driver well; they looked almost as if they were painted black.

"An F150 Raptor," Rain said, admiring the truck. "Those are mean looking trucks. That deep black paint is wicked."

The truck revved its engine and picked up speed down the street.

"I've read about those trucks," I said. "They basically designed a factory-made off-road monster with the beauty and grace of a sports car."

"A monster," Rain repeated, walking backwards down the sidewalk, continuing to admire the truck as it disappeared around the corner, "with a heart pumping enough horsepower to make most modern-day sports cars cry. Add that muscle to a 4-wheel drive and suspension system specially designed to tackle any terrain, and you have the vehicle you want to see in your driveway when zombies take over this world."

"Zombies?" I questioned comically. "You know those don't exist, right?"

Rain turned around and fell in step beside me. "Technically speaking," he added, "I don't exist, and just a few days ago, I had never heard of fallen angels, stones, or warlocks. So, better safe than sorry."

"Very true," I nodded, agreeing with Rain's logic. "You should add that to the next letter you send to the North Pole."

"Santa Claus?" Rain asked. "You know he doesn't exist, right?"

I couldn't tell if he was mocking me or not.

We stopped at a metal door built between two shops, but the door didn't appear to lead to either one. A small overhead light illuminated an intercom panel with four little red buttons. The nametag next to the third button down the list was "J. Dunham."

"That's our girl," Rain remarked.

The metal door was locked with a numeric keypad.

I bent down for a closer look. "I don't suppose you know the code?"

Rain walked over and punched in a few numbers. A loud *beep* sounded twice. The door didn't open.

"Apparently not," he muttered, stepping back.

I motioned for him to follow me up the sidewalk. "Let's keep moving. We don't want to have to answer why we're here if anyone stops."

"ECHO 911," I said, turning on my ear piece to transmit to the rest of the team. "This is Erone and Rain. We've located Jade's residence."

Kasiah was the first to respond—her accent was unmistakable. The ECHO device functioned well. It sounded as though Kasiah was standing right next to me.

"Good job," Kasiah responded. "Are there any signs of Jade?"

I heard loud club music in the background as Kasiah spoke, so of course I did the cliché—yell into the phone as I answered her. "Negative!" I said loudly. "There's a door to an upstairs apartment with J. Dunham on the intercom. Rain and I are walking the perimeter now."

Rain smacked my arm and put his finger to his lips.

"Sorry," I said, lowering my voice and looking around to make sure no one else was within earshot.

Damien's voice echoed in my ear. "No need to yell, Erone," he said. "Keep us informed. Whisper and I are driving the perimeter of the city. No signs of any surveillance so far."

"Actually," Whisper said, "there are no signs of anyone. It's a little weird."

"That's because everyone is downtown," Aerona joined in. "It's a madhouse down here at Club Raven."

Ember picked up where Aerona left off. "Jade could be standing ten feet away from us, and we'd never know. It's a typical night out in a college town."

"I'm so relocating to Missoula," Aerona added excitedly.

"I'll help you pack," I joked.

Rain and I reached the end of the block and followed the sidewalk around the corner.

Damien's voice cracked through the ECHO. "Whisper and I are out. Keep us posted."

"We're out too," said Kasiah. "Everyone be safe."

I heard everyone say "ECHO off."

"Well," Rain said, kicking an empty soda can down the sidewalk, "sounds like we got the raw end of the deal."

"No kidding," I agreed. "We're stuck walking in circles out here, while the girls are partying like rock stars." I took Rain's joking as a good opportunity to ask a question and figure out what two immortals might exchange as gifts. "So, Rain, what was in the small box Whisper gave you earlier?"

Rain contemplated for a minute before answering, probably wondering if it was any of my business or not.

"It's an 1857 U.S. one-cent piece," he said. "It rounds out one of my many coin collections. 1857 was the last year the penny was produced entirely made of copper."

Even though I found it odd that a vampire had a rare coin collection hobby, I was careful not to make light of it. "You have one U.S. penny of every year they were minted?"

"I do now," Rain replied. "Well, except 1793. That's the first year pennies were minted in the U.S. There are only four known to exist, all stored in museums."

Something metallic reflected the streetlight back into our eyes.

"Did you see that?" I asked Rain.

"Sure did," he whispered, not making it obvious.

I thought my eyes were playing tricks on me, but Rain noticed it too. Just as we turned the next corner, the black Raptor was passing through the far intersection.

"Looks like we might have an admirer," Rain remarked. "Give him one more time, and we'll get an up close and personal look at that monster machine."

The Raptor distracted both of us, and when our eyes found their way back to the sidewalk, we noticed the outline of two men walking our way. It was too late to take a different path without being suspicious.

"Keep moving," Rain whispered.

We saw the two men clearly as they walked under a street light maybe twenty feet away. They were both dark skinned and built like football players. They made it a point to intentionally stop just beyond the reach of the street light. One of them yelled to us as they approached.

"Hey man, you got a light?" the taller of the two asked, punching his buddy in the arm. "Dickhead lost his lighter back at the bar."

We stopped a few steps from the two guys. "Sorry, man," I said, "we don't smoke."

Dickhead, the guy who lost his lighter, looked nervously around as the taller one did the talking. "I didn't ask if you smoke," he said rudely. "I asked you if you had a light."

Rain and I glanced at each other and sighed, knowing what was about to happen next.

"Trust me guys," I said in a poor attempt to save their lives, "you don't want to do this."

The tall guy's tone turned from humorous to aggressive. "Well, I don't think you're in a position to tell us what to do," he said, looking around before flashing a large knife from under his jacket. The blade reflected the street light from behind them.

Rain lowered his head. "Tell me these two idiots didn't just pull a knife on us."

"Shut up, you two!" the taller guy shouted. "I don't have time for this shit! Wallets, now!"

This isn't exactly how I had envisioned the night would play out. I bet the girls weren't having near as much fun.

The other guy became increasingly nervous. "Come on, Mike," he said, "I don't think this is such a good idea anymore."

"Shut the fuck up, *Dan*!" Mike yelled at him. "Thanks for using my name!"

The two wannabe muggers took their eyes off us for a single second, but that was all Rain needed. When they turned their attention back toward us, Rain had vanished. Mike's face was painted with confusion. He aimed the tip of the blade toward me.

"Hey!" he shouted. "Where'd that other guy go?"

Rain kicked Mike's knees from behind, and as if on command, he fell to the ground as the knife clanged to the sidewalk.

Dan let out a slight whimper.

"Run," I suggested to Dan. "Now."

There was clearly no loyalty between the two. Dan took off running full speed.

Rain had his foot on Mike's back, pinning him to the ground as he struggled to get free. It was pointless for him.

"We don't need this," I said to Rain. "Just let him go."

I knelt down so Mike could see my face. "If we let you go," I asked, "will you go home to mommy and climb straight into bed like a good little girl?"

Mike began crying. "Yes, man! I swear! We were just goofing!"

"Let him go," I said. "Karma will catch him sooner or later."

Rain had an unusually evil grin on his face, kind of like when the Grinch decided to steal Christmas from Whoville.

"What?" I asked, not wanting to know the answer.

Two minutes later, Mike was sprinting down the street in nothing but his shoes, which Rain so generously let him keep. I had to hand it to Mike; he moved pretty fast, considering his hands were busy covering his private parts, leaving everything else exposed to the chilly night air.

"Run home to mommy!" Rain yelled town the street after Mike. "Same time tomorrow night?"

Mike never looked back as he stumbled over the curb and around the corner.

Rain opened up the dumpster in the ally. "Well," he said, tossing Mike's clothes in, "I don't think our new friend there will be telling anyone about us anytime soon."

"Rain, you have an unusually effective way of dealing with the world's little problems."

He swung the dumpster lid down, shutting it with a loud bang. "Those two," he grinned, "will never know how close they came to taking their last breath."

My brain gave me a good kick in the ass to remind me I was playing stakeout with a Shadow Vampire. I needed to keep my senses sharp and my eyes on Rain.

My ECHO device turned on in my ear. "… has been spotted."

It sounded like Ember, but the transmission was cut short.

"Repeat," Damien requested.

"Jade has been spotted," Ember said.

"Excellent," I responded. "Are you confident it's her?"

"If this isn't the girl from the picture," Ember continued, "then it's her clone. Aerona made first contact, in the restroom of all places, and now they're having a drink at the bar to celebrate Aerona saving Jade from being hit on by an obnoxious guy old enough to be her father."

"What's our move?" I asked.

"If Aerona is successful making friends with Jade," Kasiah suggested, "then we may be able to move up the time frame. We're going to wait for Aerona to report back with Jade's after bar plans. Surprisingly, it looks like Jade is here alone. Although, every guy in the bar is trying to make sure she doesn't leave like that. I'm warning you guys right now, those pictures do not do her justice. This girl is stunning."

"Kasiah," Whisper said, "why can't we hear what Aerona and Jade are saying?"

"Because Aerona's ECHO is in her pocket. She said it would make her nervous if she had little voices in her ear."

"That's the only flaw in my design," Whisper retorted, clearly not impressed with Aerona's decision to disable ECHO. "It has to be in place and turned on to work."

"Don't worry, Whisper," Ember said, "Aerona's more than capable of handling this situation. Kasiah and I have our eyes on Jade. She's not going anywhere we don't want her to go."

Whisper grumbled something about working with warlocks and wasted technology.

"Hold on," Kasiah said, "here comes Aerona."

Rain and I turned the corner and headed back towards our SUV.

"Hey guys," Kasiah whispered, "we're coming your way. Jade told Aerona she's done for the night and heading home. We'll give her a few minutes to get out the door. We'll be right behind her."

"OK, Kasiah," I said. "Rain and I are parked a block down the street from Jade's place, at a Copper Bank parking lot. We'll be on the lookout for her."

"Copy that," Damien confirmed. "Whisper and I have a few more routes to check, then we're headed back in. We'll meet everyone at the bank parking lot."

"ECHO off."

With ECHO off, it was dead silent, except for the now familiar purr of a Raptor's engine. The truck wasn't moving this time. It was sitting idle somewhere close.

Rain answered before I could even ask the question. "It's behind us on the next block over."

"Echo—" I started.

"Wait," Rain said, cutting me off. "Let's see who this is before we go alarming everyone over nothing."

"Jade is headed this way right now," I argued. "We don't have time to debate this."

"I agree," Rain said. "No arguing. Are you coming, or are you going to sit here and suck your thumb until your sister gets here to hold your hand?"

"Lead the way," I sighed.

Rain grinned. "We go up."

"Up?" I asked, confused.

Rain pointed to an old rusty fire escape bolted to the side of the building next to the bank. There was just one problem, the retracted ladder was at least twenty feet off the ground.

"I didn't know Shadow Vampires could fly," I said sarcastically.

Rain crouched down as if he was about to tie his lace, then jumped straight up and grabbed the lowest rung of the fire escape, unlatching the locking mechanism. The ladder came sliding down, sounding like a freight train barreling down the tracks. A spray of sparks chased the ladder all the way to the ground, clanging loudly as it hit the stops.

"That was subtle," I said. "Are you trying to wake the dead?"

Rain started climbing the ladder. "I'm already wide awake."

I shook my head and followed Rain up the ladder. With every rung I grabbed, the more concerned I became that the rusty bolts would give away, and I'd be forced to remember my levitation spell in a hurry.

To my surprise, we reached the top alive. The roof was empty and flat, except for a large air conditioning unit in the center. The view from the rooftop was amazing. The moonlight painted a dim halo over the distant mountain peaks. The cool breeze from down the sidewalk turned into a chilly gust of wind at the rooftop.

We slowly moved to the edge of the roof and peered over. Just as Rain had predicted, the Raptor was sitting idle with its lights off on the opposite side of the building. The engine was growling ever so softly, just waiting to be unleashed.

"What do you think," I asked.

Rain looked curiously at the truck. "I doubt that's a yellow cab waiting for the next fare. What do you figure he's waiting on?"

I looked back and forth down the block both ways. "Us."

"Well, do you think we should go down there and introduce ourselves? They might be lost and may need directions. We could offer to let them use our annoying GPS."

The nice, soft tone of a woman's voice startled us from behind. She sounded young, maybe in her mid-twenties. My heart actually skipped a beat when she spoke, not because of her smooth, eloquent English accent, but because she had used my name—my Shadow name.

"Erone of Stonegate," she stated, "by authority of the Shadow Council and the Shadow law, you are being placed under arrest and transferred back to the Shadow World, where you will be tried as a jumper."

THIRTY-ONE

Erone of Stonegate. I hadn't heard that name spoken out loud in many decades, and I admit, it frightened me. The only thought that ran through my head was the fact that our rooftop visitor knew my real name, which meant she was a Shadow Vampire.

Our uninvited guest was a lot to take in at one time. She was as beautiful as I'm sure she was deadly. Her hair was long, straight, and black as the night sky. She was slim and every inch as tall as Rain. The moonlight shimmered off her eyes, enhancing their electric blue to a fierce fire-like stare; I had seen the same fierce look in Rain's eyes after the bikers grabbed Ember. It surprised me when Rain didn't hear her approach us, which was more proof of her skills as a Shadow Vampire—a Shadow Vampire who had just tracked her next target to a rooftop in Missoula.

Believe it or not, this was the first woman I had ever seen dressed head-to-toe in skin-tight black leather and latex, complete with black leather boots. I wondered how many comic books she had had to research to perfect her hunting suit style. Two silver buckles strapped the suit's collar high on her neck, making it appear sexy and long. A thin, full-length custom leather trench coat hung open loosely, revealing an intricate embroidered black leather corset that complimented her sculpted Shadow Vampire body.

I couldn't help but think how Kasiah would have looked in the same tight clothing. I forced the image to the back of my mind; it would be foolish to risk being preoccupied while a Shadow Vampire was standing less than ten feet away.

202

The Shadow Vampire didn't move a muscle. She stood as still as a century-old statue. Her eyes never left mine as the seconds ticked by. It didn't look like she had even noticed Rain, which meant she had no idea who or *what* he was. I was counting on that to get us out of the situation. She may have tracked me down, but she apparently had no idea I had my very own Shadow Vampire.

"Your name is Stonegate?" Rain asked, also ignoring the only other Shadow Vampire on the roof.

"Rain," I said, trying to remain calm, "now is not the time to discuss my surname."

"Erone is correct," she said in a soft yet commanding tone, nicely complimenting her slight English accent. "This does not concern you, boy, and if you're smart, then you will leave while you still can."

Rain, just like any other Shadow Vampire, didn't like to be told what to do.

"Who died and made you queen of the rooftop?" Rain questioned. "Boy? Who the hell does this chick think she is?"

"I am not the queen of anything," she said. "My name is Ashes. You will not have a second chance to leave on your own."

"By what authority do you claim your jumper?" I asked, hoping to hold Rain off from starting a rooftop war in the middle of us extracting Jade and saving the world.

"By order of high council member Malance," she said, "I have strict instructions to deliver you and your sister back to the Shadow World."

Malance's name sliced painfully through the memory of my parents' death. The only reason he would want us alive would be to torture any useful information out of us himself.

Slowly, Rain moved one step to the left.

Ashes, with her eyes still glued to mine, shifted her arms back slightly, opening her jacket to expose a black leather belt strapped around her waist. The butts of two glimmering handguns and several full magazines were visible on the belt.

Reasoning with a Shadow Vampire is never a good idea; reasoning with an armed Shadow Vampire is just plain stupid. Somehow, I needed to buy us a few moments to get us off this roof. I may not have been able to move faster than Ashes, but if Rain could somehow manage to draw her attention for even a second, then we had a chance.

"You don't understand," I pleaded. "Malance is corrupting the council. The only reason he would want us back alive would be so he can destroy us himself. Everything you think the council stands for is a lie."

"You are the lie," Ashes declared, "and you're not the first jumper to try and talk your way out of the laws you have broken. Your fate is not for me to decide. I have strict orders to return you and Aerona to the council. Malance will decide your fate."

Rain took a second step. The three of us were now spaced out equally on the rooftop, although Rain and I were at a disadvantage with our backs to the roof's edge.

"Do not move again," Ashes commanded, still not taking her eyes off me, "You have made your decision to stay. A foolish choice."

"You know something, Ash?" Rain started, shifting his weight to take another step. "You and I have something in common, neither of us like being told what to do."

Anticipating Rain's movement, Ashes lunged towards him; the length of her trench coat trailing behind her. For the first time since our unplanned meeting, her blue eyes left mine. Rain avoided Ashes's grasp easily. She appeared surprised to find he had the same superhuman speed as her. The two had essentially switched spots. Ashes back was now at the roof's edge. She had made a vital mistake underestimating her opponent, but she recovered quickly. In a move too fast for even my eyes to catch, Ashes drew out both her handguns; one found its sights pointed at Rain, and I was staring down the barrel of the other.

Contrary to my own self-proclaimed warlock greatness, if shot in a specific spot deep within my brain, the bullet will kill me, and unfortunately, it appeared Ashes knew the exact location.

A grin spread across Rain's face. He had probably been shot before, and he knew it would hurt, but he would recover quickly. Honestly, sparring with another Shadow Vampire would be good for him, assuming Ashes doesn't tear his head off.

Ashes stole a quick glance over the roof's edge, calculating her odds. "Erone," she continued, "I was unaware you had a pet vampire. He moves with unusual speed for a vampire in this world. You have trained him well."

"You're no snail yourself," Rain jeered, admiring Ashes's abilities. He had never come in contact with anyone with the ability to match his rare gifts.

"You can either leave with me or I can take you," Ashes said, wasting no time redirecting the conversation. "The choice is yours to make. I advise you to choose quickly, before your friend here does something to end his life."

I was always more of a visual kind of guy, so I preferred to show Ashes my decision instead of plainly telling her. Rain must have read my mind, or he had just been around me and my sister long enough to know we enjoyed solving tough situations with fire. He bolted toward the fire escape, which was a fitting escape route for what was about to happen. Exactly as I had hoped, Ashes trained both guns in Rain's direction, and bright orange flashes exploded from the muzzles as she fired two simultaneous shots.

I had to act quickly. Two more shots rang out, chasing Rain as he disappeared over the roof's edge. Ashes wouldn't be distracted for long. I drew in every ounce of energy I could find, and that's when she made her second mistake of the night—taking her eyes off the warlock.

Realizing her mistake, Ashes stopped firing and slowly turned her electric blue eyes back toward me. My hands controlled a growing sphere of intense blue flames, perfectly matching the beautiful color of her eyes. I lowered my head and extended my arms out in front of me, sending a gigantic wave of electric blue flames racing across the rooftop.

When the flames extinguished, Ashes had vanished along with them. I doubted she was incinerated by the intense flames. Although, hopefully, it made her retreat long enough for us to get off the rooftop.

My ECHO turned on with Kasiah's voice in my ear. "Did you guys hear gunfire?" she asked.

Rain responded first. "Sounded like firecrackers to me," he said, grinning.

"All clear here," I said, reaching for the fire escape.

There was no need for the team to take their focus off Jade. Ashes had lost the element of surprise. She wouldn't make another appearance until she regrouped. Hopefully, we could get Jade out of Montana before that happened.

"We're all clear out here," Damien said, checking in. "We're about ten miles outside the city limits."

Kasiah wasn't buying the firecracker story. She had heard gunfire numerous times before that night. "That was no party popper," she said. "It was faint but definitely the echo of several gun shots. They were elevated, maybe on a rooftop. Eyes open everyone. Jade has left the club and is headed home. She'll be there in approximately five minutes."

I didn't like the fact that a Shadow Vampire was lurking around town. Although if Ashes had any idea why we were actually here, she wouldn't have tried to arrest me on the rooftop. She would have waited until Jade was in sight. I was confident she didn't know about Jade.

I finally made it down the old rusty fire escape to meet Rain. He had two holes in the front of his blood-soaked shirt—exit wounds. His flesh had already healed.

"Are you OK?" I asked.

"I owe her two to the back," he said, inspecting his shirt.

"Be thankful you're alive," I pointed out. "We haven't seen the last of Ashes. She has spent her entire life training to be a hunter, a killer. She'll be back. I'd bet on it. Let's get back to the SUV."

Rain and I double timed it to the SUV parked at the bank, keeping our eyes peeled for Ashes. We arrived to find glass scattered under the driver's side window.

"Ashes?" Rain asked.

I scanned the parking lot, looking for other signs. "I would guess not," I said. "Shadow Vampires are more tactful than breaking random windows that would draw unwanted attention. I'm beginning to think the crime rate in this city is higher than what's reported."

Rain cleared the broken glass from the driver's seat, and we both climbed in and shut the doors.

"Dammit!" Rain cursed. "The thieves stole our GPS!"

We both looked at each other and started laughing uncontrollably. It felt good—just the thing we needed.

"I hope that crazy GPS drives the thieves off a cliff," Rain laughed.

I've never seen this side of Rain. Laughter was an unusual quality to find in a Shadow Vampire. However, over the past few days, I've learned Rain is anything but your ordinary Shadow Vampire.

The girls appeared around the corner of the bank. They looked like three sexy young women on their way home from the clubs.

"You two monkeys could be heard a mile away," Aerona said, climbing into the back seat with Ember and Kasiah. "What's so damn funny? And why did you break the window?"

Rain and I both answered her at the same time. "What window?"

"Well, it's good to see you've bonded," Ember said.

Kasiah powered down the back window. "Jade should be just another minute around that corner over there," she said, "And why did you break the window?"

"Well," Rain started, pointing to the empty slot in the dashboard, "someone broke the window and stole the GPS while we were out getting mugged by the locals."

"Sounds like a story to me," Ember smiled, shaking her head.

"Hey, there's our girl." Rain said, pointing in the distance.

Jade walked slowly with her hands in her pockets. She didn't have a care in the world. Her bright blonde hair was blown back slightly as the night's cool breeze picked up. I couldn't help but notice the carefree smile painted on her face. She *was* an angel.

"How on earth did God let that girl fall from heaven?" Rain whispered.

"Oh please," Aerona said sarcastically. "First of all, she's the accidental child of two cast-out angels who did who knows what to who knows who to get sent down to this wasteland. Second, she's just a girl. Give me five minutes with any trailer-trash bimbo, and I could make her look twice as hot as her."

We all ignored Aerona's rant, which only fueled her jealousy. Jade paused for a brief second to punch in the security code at the front door to the apartments upstairs. She disappeared through the door.

Kasiah stuck her head between us in the front seat. "Now we see which lights turn on," she said curiously.

I shifted over so she could get a better look out the windshield. "This stalking stuff is surprisingly easy," I remarked.

A cute smile crossed Kasiah's lips. "The FBI prefers the term 'stakeout' over stalking," she corrected me.

"Stakeout probably does sound better in court," Ember commented from the backseat.

A light switched on in an upper window on the far-right corner of the building. Unfortunately, like every good angel, Jade had the window shades drawn.

"So, what's the FBI's protocol when the shades are drawn?" I asked.

"According to section C-22 of the handbook," Kasiah explained, as though instructing a training session, "when confronted by a window shade, the next step is to kick in the door with guns blazing, shoot everything in sight, and take no prisoners."

"That sounds about right," I smiled, matching her enthusiastic instructor voice.

"In reality," Kasiah said, sitting back in her seat, "we need to make a decision if we go knocking on her door now or in the morning."

I looked at Rain, and he nodded.

"We should probably talk about Ashes," I said hesitantly.

"Who's Ashes?" the girls asked in unison.

THIRTY-TWO

Ian pushed his legs to run faster into the darkness. His heart practically beat out of his chest. The pitch-black forest made it nearly impossible for him to see anything more than the blurry outline of trees passing by just inches from his head. He grabbed one of the trees, spinning him around to the backside as he fell to the wet ground, fighting to catch his breath.

"HOLY SHIT!" he shouted, taking deep breaths as dripping sweat burned his eyes. "This is insane!" He let his head fall back against the tree. "I need to work out more. Buy an elliptical or something."

Ian shut his eyes and held his breath, listening for sounds of anyone chasing after him. The only thing he could hear was the typical deep, dark creepy forest sounds of leaves rustling in the wind.

The wind felt good on Ian's face. After a minute, his breathing finally slowed, and his heart rate steadied. He opened his eyes and peered around the tree trunk carefully, seeing nothing other than the silhouettes of even more trees in every direction. His pupils were fully dilated to absorb each tiny photon of light, desperately trying to make out the shadows of the night. Still, Ian couldn't see more than a few feet from his resting spot.

His fear returned and started to take over Ian's mind. He realized he had no idea of the direction he had been running. His original path was straight back to his car. Unfortunately, after two stumbles and a smack in the face by an unseen branch, he had lost his sense of direction.

"Good job, jackass," Ian said, closing his eyes again. "Lost in the woods while trying to save some chick you don't even know. That'll look great on your tombstone, assuming anyone ever finds the body pieces."

Ian's options were simple: he could sit and wait for Jake to find him, or he could get up and get moving again. His major dilemma was choosing the direction to run. He couldn't determine if he would be running away from Jake and the abandoned house or right back to it.

Ian held his breath again, listening out for anything out of the ordinary. Thirty long seconds ticked by before something off to the right caught his senses. *Was that a car horn?* he thought to himself. It was distant, maybe a mile or two. He wondered if his ears were playing tricks on him, deceiving him into thinking there was hope when all that was out there was certain death.

He heard the sound again—it was definitely a horn. It sounded strong, maybe a big rig driver blowing his horn at a car for cutting him off. The highway was Ian's only chance, particularly since he had no idea now which direction his own car was in. If he could find the highway, he could flag down a passing driver to call the police and let the professionals handle Jake.

Every muscle in Ian's body told him not to move. He was going to ache from head to toe in the morning, assuming he would live to see the sunrise; but somehow, Ian managed to convince his muscles to find that last bit of energy and get him up on his feet. He had only taken two steps in the direction of the highway when a loud *crack* of a branch broke from behind the tree. He spun toward the sound instinctively, frantically searching in every direction for what had broken the branch. He stepped backwards, straining to hear or see anything.

The ground wasn't where it should have been. Ian tumbled backwards down a ravine, grasping anything to break his fall. He rolled head-over-heels, crashing through everything in his path. Finally, after bouncing off a large tree, he came to an abrupt stop at the bottom, splashing into cold water. He lay motionless in the middle of a shallow, fast-moving creek at the base of the ravine.

"REALLY!" Ian hollered, staring up at the night sky.

The cool, gushing water gave Ian a second wind. He slammed his fists at the bottom of the creek bed, struggling to stand in the shallow water. He slipped and fell several times on the wet rocks before making it to the bank on the opposite side. It took every ounce of strength Ian had to pull himself up with the help of a few roots that stuck out like ladder rungs. The muddy bank made the climb nearly impossible.

After what seemed like forever, Ian collapsed at the top of the ravine, out of energy. He strained to see across the creek. Two deer, frozen in place, stared back from the opposite side. The deer had implemented their never failing *if I don't move then he can't see me* camouflage technique.

Ian started laughing. "You two scared me half to death!" he yelled, as though the deer could understand him. "Hunting season's only a few months away. I'll be back for you two."

The larger of the two deer trained its ears straight towards Ian, then back again to the sides. Its eyes darted back and forth, searching the darkness. The deer looked more terrified than Ian. It obviously knew something Ian did not.

"BOO!" Ian shouted at the deer.

The reaction from the deer was not what Ian had expected. They drew back on their hind legs and leapt high up in the air, not away from Ian, but toward him. Both the deer cleared the creek in two jumps, digging their hooves to climb the muddy ravine wall. Ian covered his head with his arms, expecting a painful impact. Unexpectedly, the deer raced right past him on either side. They were gone with a flash of their white tails.

Ian slowly lowered his arms, stunned at what just happened. "That's right!" Ian's shout followed the deer. "You better run!"

After falling down the ravine, Ian had again lost the bearings to the highway. He had no choice but to climb back up the other side and start over. As he brushed the mud off his jeans, he had a sudden feeling of being watched. He slowly lifted his head and looked across the creek—Jake!

Ian lunged forward through the trees. He was by now a professional forest runner, leaping over fallen trees and dodging branches left and right as though he was aiming for a gold medal in a new Olympic sport. Less than a minute had passed since he noticed Jake from across the creek. *Don't look back! Keep moving!* he thought to himself.

Several minutes and a few dozen trees later, Ian found a new wave of hope. In the distance, he saw red and white lights. The highway wasn't far now. He stumbled forward, pushing himself to run as fast as he could, running chest first right into Jake.

Ian landed on his back, hard, which knocked the air from his lungs.

Jake's smiling face was the last thing Ian saw before he blacked out.

When Ian regained consciousness, his chest was throbbing with pain from his several broken ribs. His face was flat on the floor, covered with a thick layer of dirt. A dry musty smell filled his nostrils. He forced out several coughs, blowing a large cloud of dust around him, causing him to cough some more. Pain compressed his chest as he tried rolling to his back. His wrists were attached to something metal above his head, preventing him from turning completely over or sitting up. He yanked hard, letting out a shriek from the ache in his chest and now his wrists.

"There's no use struggling," Tara said from across the room.

Ian was startled. He couldn't see who was speaking to him. "Who are you?" Ian managed to ask in between coughs. He had given up rolling over and somehow managed to get to his knees to see what was holding his wrists—handcuffs.

"Why am I handcuffed?" Ian demanded.

"Why is water wet?" Tara replied cynically. "Why is the sky blue? Why am I duct taped to this chair? All these questions may never be answered."

Still on his knees, Ian scooted himself closer to his bound wrists, relieving the tension from the tight handcuffs. At closer inspection, he saw the handcuffs were looped around a copper pipe connected to an old sink in the corner. Ian hung his head down. "This is crazy," he muttered.

"Crazy is one way of explaining our current situation," Tara explained. "Although I would have gone with insane... or maybe fucked. This is fucked. Yes, that sounds much better. That phrase definitely suits our current situation better than simply saying it's crazy."

"You're crazy!" Ian hollered. Another round of pain shot through his chest. He forced his head to turn far enough to notice Tara, and to his surprise, he found that she was most definitely duct taped to a chair on the opposite side of the room. She looked like hell; her clothes were filthy and torn, a thin streak of blood trailed down from her nose, and her red hair was tangled like a wild animal.

"Is that a *knife* through your hand?" he asked, tilting his head and squinting to see more clearly.

"Now, there's something you don't hear every day," Tara replied irritably. "Look, who are you? You look like you've been rolling around in the mud and fighting with a tree."

Ian looked down at his clothes. He was even more of a mess than Tara. His shirt and jeans were covered in mud and ripped in several places. His jacket was tossed out of reach on the other side of the room. Images of running through the forest raced through his mind. The creek, the mud, the deer, and Jake came crashing back all at one time. He looked around the room anxiously. "Where is he!" Ian hollered. "Where's Jake?"

Tara ignored Ian's hysteria. "It's nice to meet you. I'm Tara. Tell me someone knows you're here, and that same someone is bringing a small army to save you."

The intense pain in Ian's chest intensified with every breath. "My name is Ian, and well, actually, I'm here to rescue you."

"Well, Ian," Tara continued, "this must be the worst rescue in the long sad history of bad rescues. Did you happen to notice you are handcuffed to a pipe for the sole reason of keeping you fresh for Jake, the super-uptight-no-sense-of-humor vampire? You know that, right?"

Ian only heard one word of what Tara had said. "Vampire?" he asked quietly, more of a question to himself than to Tara.

"Oh my God," Tara said, rolling her eyes and talking to herself. "How on earth did I get stuck with this guy as my designated hero?"

"You know," Ian said, repositioning himself, "you're not very nice. Maybe I should rethink my rescue strategy and leave your sarcastic ass here in this... where are we?"

"Strategy?" Tara asked angrily. "Was ending up captured with me a part of your little so-called strategy? Do I know you or something?"

"Or something," Ian said, ignoring the rest of the question. There was no way Ian would confess he was the one who had led Jake right to her front door. "What do you mean vampire?" he asked.

"Vampire. As in break every bone in your body and suck your blood vampire."

"There's no such thing as vampires," Ian replied, trying to convince himself more than Tara.

"Well," she continued, looking at the ceiling and laughing, "then you're in for a rude awakening. Oh, and by the way, you never answered my question. How did you end up here to rescue me?"

Ian did the only thing he was good at without a computer—he lied through his teeth. "I live up the road," he said, "and we don't see many cops out here in the middle of nowhere. I was a little curious when I saw a cop car drive by, especially since the only thing at the end of this road is old man Snyder's place, and he's been dead for two years now. I followed the cop car here, and that's when I saw you get carried into the house. I got scared and started to run home. Somehow, I got turned around in the woods. Then Jake found me, and I'm here with you. End of story."

Tara stared at Ian, taking in his story. "And let me get this straight. When exactly did Jake introduce himself? Was it before or after he knocked you out, dragged you through the mud, or beat you against a tree?" Tara's patience was wearing thin. "How do you know Jake's name, and what are you doing here?"

Ian never would have made it as an undercover agent; he had always been lost without his computer to hide behind. He didn't have an answer to Tara's question.

Tara knew that Jake could return any minute, and she was not looking forward to another knife in the hand or watching Jake kill Ian. "OK, Ian," she sighed, "I don't care why or how you got here. Just tell me you're *not* the only one who knows you're here. Do you have a cell phone? Give me something. Anything!"

Ian looked down the front pocket of his jeans where he kept his cell phone. His kneeling position stretched the wet, muddy denim tightly around his leg. The pocket was empty. He hung his head down. His arms were practically numb. "My cell is gone," he said halfheartedly. "Jake must have taken it. Not that I could reach it if he hadn't."

Until Jake had carried Ian through the door and tossed him in the corner, Tara had lost all hope of escape. *Everything happens for a reason,* she told herself. *Why did Ian end up handcuffed to a pipe here in the same room? Jake could have just killed him outside or left him in another room.* That got her mind spinning again. Fate had put Ian there for a reason. Before Tara could finish her thought, Jake burst through the door.

"I know, Atmoro!" Jake shouted into his phone. "I'm not a mindless idiot! I won't lose them again! Yes, sorry. Just keep me posted on their position in Montana. I'll be at the airport soon. If you find that little prick Skywalker, tell him to get a hold of me. I have a damaged laptop that I need to pull some information off. It could help us find the stone."

Jake slammed his finger on the phone's screen, ending the call.

Ian swallowed hard at the sound of Atmoro's name. He also wondered what Jake might do if he knew his hacker, Skywalker, was handcuffed to a pipe less than ten feet to his left.

Ian couldn't get his mind wrapped around Jake being a vampire, even though it did explain how he was able to get up after Tara had struck him with her SUV, his incredible speed, and how the cop's bullets didn't stop him. Ian was always so careful in selecting his clients. He always performed proper background checks and research before committing to a job. He should have listened to his gut and dropped Atmoro just one day earlier.

Jake ignored Ian in the corner and went straight to Tara, yanking the knife out of her hand. She cried out in pain but was quickly silenced when Jake held the blade to her throat.

"Your laptop screen is smashed and unusable," Jake said through clinched teeth. "You have one more chance to tell me where the stone is, or I'll just leave you here for the rats."

"Everything I know is on that laptop," Tara replied. "Maybe you should have thought about that before running me off the road."

Jake was beyond frustrated at this point. The blood on the blade was triggering his thirst. He had to leave this house or risk accidentally killing Tara. He needed her alive in case this new Atmoro lead didn't pan out. He thought about satisfying his craving with Ian in the corner but shook the idea from his head. He knew he wouldn't be able to stop once he got started. Jake couldn't risk turning his fangs to Tara once he was done with Ian.

"You've made your decision," Jake declared, removing the knife from Tara's throat. "Maybe two days without food and water will change your mind. That is if the rats don't take care of you before I get back. Maybe they'll start with your roommate over there as you watch. You'll be singing a different song when I return."

Without looking, Jake hurled the knife in Ian's direction, and the blade stuck in the wall a few inches above his head. Another cloud of dust rained down on Ian from the old dirty wall. He tensed all his muscles to prevent another coughing fit. His ribs were burning with pain.

Jake slammed the door behind him, cursing as he left the room. The pressure in the house changed when the front door was slammed shut. The police cruiser's tires spun wildly out of control in the gravel driveway, spraying stones at the front porch. Tara and Ian listened closely to the car as it faded away down the abandoned road.

The vampire was gone.

"Now," Tara said, breaking the silence, "would be a good time to resume your poor excuse of a rescue attempt."

Ian relaxed his muscles and let out a few heavy coughs. The pain was overwhelming. He couldn't help but yank on his handcuffs again. His wrists were bruised and bleeding. "This," Ian replied, interrupted by another cough, "is what's referred to as an impossible situation."

This is not the way Tara had envisioned how life would end. Not that she often thought of how her life might end, but this scenario had never crossed her mind, where she's left bleeding and taped to a chair in an abandoned house with a strange man handcuffed to a pipe in the corner.

216

Tara turned her head toward Ian and listened carefully. "Did you hear that?" she asked.

"Hear what?" Ian questioned, coughing again, "the sound of me dying or the angry vampire returning to put us out of our misery?"

"No, listen," Tara said, shushing Ian. "It sounded almost like… there! Do you hear that?"

Ian held his breath for a brief second, straining to hear whatever strange sound Tara thought she had heard. He didn't believe it at first, but it was the unmistakable buzzing sound of a cell phone vibrating.

"I thought Jake took your phone!" Tara cried. "It's coming from behind you! It must be in your jacket on the floor!"

Ian twisted his neck as far to the right as he could, struggling to see the jacket out the corner of his eye. The buzzing sound was definitely coming from his jacket pocket. Ian's mouth dropped open with amazement once he understood what it was.

"That's not my cell phone vibrating," he said, looking right at Tara. "It's yours."

THIRTY-THREE

The phone rang several times before being forwarded to Tara's misleading voicemail. I didn't leave a message.

Kasiah, from the backseat of the SUV, placed her hand on my shoulder. "No answer?" she asked.

"No," I replied, stuffing the phone back into my pocket. "It's odd. Tara always answers. I'll try again after we make contact with Jade. If anyone can help us track Atmoro's movements through cyberspace, Tara can."

I turned around and looked past Kasiah to the third row seat where Aerona had been unusually quiet ever since Rain and I filled in the team on our encounter with Ashes. Aerona's eyes were lost out the side window into the emptiness beyond the glass, searching for an answer that would never come. I knew my sister better than anyone; and I can count on one hand the times something had left her speechless. Aerona and I were both aware that a Shadow Vampire would not simply stop and go home because she got spooked on the rooftop by a flashy fire show. Neither of us would ever return to the Shadow World without a fight—a fight that Aerona was preparing her heart and mind to handle. Not only did we have to keep one eye open for Atmoro, now we had to keep the other eye open for Ashes. I could have easily gone cross-eyed.

Time was racing away from us; it was two thirty in the morning, and Jade had been home for little more than fifteen minutes. Her apartment lights were still on. She appeared to be somewhat of a night owl. Ashes's presence had forced our team to make the decision of contacting Jade before morning. We had no idea what or who the sunrise would bring, and we had no intentions of waiting around to find out. For all we knew, Ashes was out recruiting reinforcements.

A quick flash of blue light shimmered off our windshield; if I wasn't paying attention, I would have missed it altogether. Ember opened the door and climbed in the backseat of the SUV, softly shutting the door behind her. She leaned between the front seats and checked her hair in the rearview mirror.

"Everything's clear from the sky," Ember said, sitting back. "I covered a three block radius and didn't see a single other person, dead or alive. It's quiet."

Kasiah flipped open her FBI credentials, exposing the badge as she tucked it into the front of her belt. "Are you sure we don't have time to return to the hotel and change?" she asked. "I'd feel more comfortable knocking on her door in something a little more FBI-ish. My gun barely fits in this ridiculously small purse."

Kasiah struggled to zip the purse around the gun.

"There's definitely no time," Ember responded. "There's no telling what the morning may bring."

Aerona broke her silence. "The sunrise will bring darkness," she said. "I can feel it inside. We must move now or never."

We could all feel the negative energy in the air. It was like the calm before the storm.

I looked into Aerona's eyes. "We're going to be OK," I reassured her. "Mother and Father will be with us every second of the way."

Aerona's eyes welled up. She fought hard to keep her tears from rolling down her face. Bringing up our parents was cruel on my part, but I needed Aerona at her best, and my reminding her why we do what we do was a necessary evil. My twin is both physically and mentally stronger than she appeared on the outside. We were lucky to have her on the team.

"Let's go, Kasiah," I said, opening the door.

The dome light illuminated the interior of the SUV. Rain's arm swung past my face like a ninety mile an hour fast ball as he quickly switched it off.

219

"Sorry," I whispered.

We all piled out of the SUV. There was no need for additional conversation. We all knew the parts we were to play. Rain and Aerona were going to watch the entrance to Jade's apartment, keeping their eyes peeled for any signs of Ashes. Kasiah and I would make first contact with Jade. My fake FBI credentials may not have fooled Kasiah and Damien, but I doubt Jade has taken a class in spotting a fake ID.

A flash of light from the corner of my eye signaled Ember was off to be our eye in the sky. I was a little apprehensive of having her be the only one going solo, but the benefit of having an aerial view outweighed the danger.

As soon as Kasiah and I reached the storefront next to the door that led upstairs to the apartments above, we heard something crash loudly down the alley. It sounded a lot like someone had just knocked over a pile of empty cans. I was impressed at how fast Kasiah drew out her gun from the tiny black purse. I pressed her up against the brick wall of the storefront beside us; we didn't exactly blend in with the brick. The seconds ticked by as we waited, holding our breath, to see what had caused the racket.

We both released our breath when a little, shaggy dog walked slowly out from the alley. It stopped and turned its brown shaggy head to look right at us, dropping the empty soda can it had been carrying in its mouth.

"Tell me that's not a werewolf," Kasiah whispered.

I released my protective grip around Kasiah. "That's definitely not any werewolf I've ever seen."

The dirty dog raised its nose in the air and sniffed several times in our direction, and then, as if we didn't exist, it lowered its head and picked up the soda can to continue its lonely nighttime stroll down the sidewalk.

"That…" I said as the dog disappeared around the corner.

"…was weird," Kasiah said, finishing my sentence.

I looked back to see if Aerona and Rain had witnessed our minor scare. They were nowhere to be seen. Kasiah motioned with her hand for me to follow.

"So," I said as we reached the apartment entranceway, "tell me you know some FBI trick for cracking a numeric keypad lock."

220

Kasiah studied the keypad. "We find it easiest to have the correct code."

"Sounds logical," I nodded. "And if you aren't fortunate enough to have been provided with the code?"

"Improvise," Kasiah stated, reaching her hand out to press the next button down from Jade's name.

No one answered the intercom's beep. I wasn't surprised, considering the time of night. Kasiah pushed the next button on the list, and then the next. She was just about to press the last button on the list when the door buzzed, and we heard a small click. The lock mechanism was deactivated.

"Someone is always expecting someone else," Kasiah explained. "Maybe that certain someone is known to forget their keys, or maybe it's just a late night booty call. Either way, people are just too unwary these days. You'd be surprised at the number of break-ins that happen without any sign of forced entry. This is exactly how criminals gain access."

I opened the door for Kasiah before the lock could reengage. "At this point," I said, "nothing surprises me. How confident are we that Jade will answer the door when we knock?"

"Slim to none," Kasiah remarked, entering the stairwell.

The door shut behind us. A set of steep, poorly lit wooden stairs creaked with every step as we inched our way up. Kasiah led the way, her gun drawn. She clicked on a small LED flashlight and held it parallel to the barrel of her gun, illuminating the hallway at the top of the stairs. The hallway was short with only two doors on either side before turning a corner to the left. Assuming we kept our sense of direction as we entered the building, Jade's apartment was the last door on the right before the corner.

Kasiah clicked the flashlight off and placed the gun back in her tiny purse. "Ready?" she asked without making eye contact.

"Ready," I whispered.

We stopped in front of the empty door. It was plain except for a peephole. A thin beam of light shined from the crack under the door. There was no turning back now.

Kasiah looked at me for approval.

I nodded my head yes.

Kasiah softly knocked on Jade's door.

There was no response from the inside, so Kasiah knocked again, more forcefully this time. My heart skipped a beat on the second knock.

"Jade Dunham, this is Special agent Kasiah Johnson of the FBI."

A shadow appeared and vanished in the light under the door as Jade darted past the door without stopping to check the peephole.

"FBI?" Jade asked hesitantly.

"Yes, Ma'am," Kasiah responded. "We're sorry for the inconvenient time, but we would like to ask you a few questions."

"It's two-thirty in the morning," she said, implying we had no idea of the time, "and who's the second person with you?"

I shot Kasiah a surprised look. I hadn't moved a muscle since the first knock. Jade could sense my presence.

"Special agent Wesley," I announced, using my best FBI voice. "It's imperative that we talk to you concerning your parents."

"My parents?" Jade asked cautiously. "What do they have to do with the FBI?"

"Jade," Kasiah continued, "this is not something that should be discussed through a door, neither can it wait till the morning. Your life is in danger. Please, look through your peephole to view our identification."

We both held up our identification while Kasiah lit them with her flashlight.

Jade's shadow appeared under the door. The wooden floor planks creaked under her as she lifted herself high enough to peer through the peephole. She was silent for several seconds as she studied our IDs.

"You don't look like any FBI agent I've ever seen," Jade said. "I'm calling the police!"

Her shadow disappeared.

"Perfect," I murmured, looking back down the hallway, half expecting to find Ashes.

"I told you we needed to change our clothes," Kasiah said, smirking.

We listened closely for the sound of Jade dialing a phone. The only sound we could hear was of our own breathing. Jade remained motionless on the other side of the door.

"Jade," Kasiah started, "you are more than welcome to call the local police. They'll show up with their lights flashing, sirens blaring and guns drawn. They'll probably wake up your neighbors, and you'll spend the rest of the night filling out paperwork, but in the morning, you'll still need to answer our questions."

The floor squeaked again as Jade shifted her position. She was still close to the door.

"Jade," I added, looking at Kasiah. "If we aren't who we say we are, then this thin wooden door isn't going to stop us from breaching this apartment before the cops get here. Save your locks and let us in to talk."

Kasiah's eyes opened wide. She mouthed the words, "What are you doing?"

Like a child caught with his hands in the cookie jar, I held my hands up. "What?"

The distinct *thud* of a deadbolt unlocking drew our attention back toward the door. It cracked open just enough to allow a small stream of light into the hallway.

"IDs again," Jade insisted, studying us through the opening. A heavy security chain hung in front of her face. Her eyes sparkled as if they were made of rare green crystal. A faint line of brown circled each pupil.

We both held our ID's up for Jade's inspection. She studied them carefully, then closed the door. I heard the security chain slide across the locking channel. The door opened wide.

"Come in," Jade said reluctantly, backing away from the doorway.

I closed the door behind us as we entered, relocking the deadbolt and security chain, not that they would keep anything out that was hunting Jade.

Jade leaned against a large windowsill across the room, the same window we could see from the SUV. "What is this about," she asked.

Kasiah took a step toward Jade. "Please stay away from the window," she said. "It's not safe."

Jade shifted her green eyes from me to Kasiah, then to the window before finally moving away.

Jade's apartment was like any other college student's apartment. A small countertop divided the living room from the tiny kitchen. An old brown sofa and a loveseat were set up in an L-shape around a cheap beat-up coffee table. In the corner, there was a fairly new TV set up on an equally beat-up TV console with two small glass doors. The apartment walls were mostly bare— probably a stipulation of the apartment lease to reduce the numerous nail holes that eventually turn apartment walls into Swiss cheese. Several framed pictures of various sizes were neatly arranged next to the TV and along the end table between the couch and the loveseat.

The only other door in the apartment was open, revealing piles of dirty clothes guarding the entrance to her bedroom. Jade noticed us giving her place a once over and quickly kicked the dirty clothes into the room before closing the door.

"So, you better start talking," Jade said, grabbing a few loose shirts off the back of the loveseat. "I swear I'm calling the cops if you don't get…" She paused, giving Kasiah a closer look. "Hey, didn't I see you out tonight? Have you been following me?"

"Yes," Kasiah confessed. "My team was observing you from a distance to make a positive identification."

"Hey!" Jade yelled at me. "Put that down!"

I set the frame back next to the TV where I found it. The photograph was of Jade at her high school graduation. She was dressed in a dark maroon cap and gown. As with all the other photographs, Jade's eyes practically jumped out of the scene. An older man and woman were on either side of Jade. They must be the neighbors who took in Jade after her biological parents perished in the fire.

"How much do you know about your parents?" Kasiah asked.

Jade brushed a few strands of her bright blonde hair from in front of her eyes. "My parents are good people," she said. "I don't think they've ever done anything to bring the FBI knocking at my door at two-thirty in the morning."

Kasiah sat on the opposite end of the couch from where Jade was leaning. "So, do you know where your parents are right now?"

"Yes," she said harshly. "They're sleeping in their bed like normal people. You're crazy if you think I'm giving away their address."

I sat down in the loveseat, sinking deep into the cushion. The furniture may have been as old as me. Jade spoke of her parents in the present tense, as though they were still alive. I saw no signs of her lying or searching for a story to try and throw us off. She knew nothing of her past or who her parents were.

Kasiah threw the next question into the room like a grenade. "Jade, how much do know about your *biological* parents, Richard and Tamitha Dunham?"

The question caught Jade off guard. She repeated the question. "My biological parents?"

A door slammed in the hallway. Our eyes shifted immediately toward the apartment door, expecting it to shatter into a pile of splinters as an army of vampires, werewolves, and trolls came crashing through.

"Look, Jade," Kasiah continued, her eyes still on the doorway. "We don't have time to explain everything to you right now. I'm going to get right to the point, and I apologize for being so direct."

Kasiah paused. I'm sure in her line of work, she has had to deliver many next-of-kin notifications. This, however, was probably her first time telling a young girl that the people she believes to be her loving caring parents—the parents who have raised her and given her every memory she's ever known—were not actually her real parents. Hayley's death had stolen more than just sleep from Kasiah. She forced herself to gain control of her emotions. Closing her eyes and looking down at the floor, she took in a deep breath. Her heart was broken in a way that could never be healed, but if she ever wanted to find the monster that brutally stole her sister's life, she would desperately need to find the strength to keep going.

Kasiah exhaled and looked at Jade. "Your biological parents died when you were very young. Your neighbors took you in, changed their names to match yours, and raised you as their own."

225

Jade didn't say a word. She stared at Kasiah as though she was looking right through her. Her mind was searching all its files to try and make sense of Kasiah's accusation.

After two full minutes of silence, Jade stood up from the couch. "I want you to leave," she said. "Now."

Kasiah and I looked at each other. We were losing her.

"Jade—" I started to say.

"Right now!" Jade insisted. "This conversation is over, and I want you to leave! I'm calling the police!"

Jade grabbed her purse off the kitchen counter. She started digging through it in search of her cell phone. "You people are insane," she said, tossing things out of her purse. "Dammit! Where is my phone?"

My ECHO came alive with Damien's voice, catching me off guard. "...a major problem!" he said.

"Damien, this is Erone, we only caught the end of that. Please repeat."

"We have a major problem here!" Damien screamed. It sounded like he was out of breath from running. "Take Jade and get out of town. Do it NOW!"

"Found it!" Jade yelled from the kitchen. "I'm dialing!"

Kasiah put her finger to her lip, shushing Jade. "Damien, what are you talking about?" she asked. "What's the situation?"

"Who's Damien?" Jade asked, holding her phone to her ear. "You guys are out of your minds."

I pinched my fingers together, shutting Jade's mouth, then threw my hand toward the wall, making Jade's phone fly through the air and disappear somewhere behind the couch.

The ECHO fell silent.

"Damien, are you there?" I asked.

The ECHO came back to life with Damien's out of breath voice. "Whisper and I are approximately ten miles south of Missoula, off highway ninety-three. We took a side road up to a scenic overlook to scout further south when we saw a convoy headed your way."

"Convoy?" Aerona asked through ECHO.

226

I could tell Aerona was running too.

"Yes, a convoy," Damien said, trying to catch his breath. "Everything was quiet. We were standing at the edge of the lookout with binoculars looking north. There wasn't a vehicle in sight in either direction. Then, suddenly, a pack of four cars—black unmarked sedans—traveling at high speed, appeared from around the furthest corner south."

"Four cars do not make a convoy," Rain pointed out.

Whisper took over as Damien collected himself. "You are correct, my nocturnal friend," he said. "Which is why we did not refer to them as a convoy until we saw the four sedans, an armored SWAT vehicle, two unmarked black SUVs, and a semi with cargo covered by thick canvas tarps. From what I can tell, there's a helicopter under that canvas."

"Damien," Kasiah said, "can you confirm what Whisper has seen?"

"Confirmed," Damien replied. "We double timed it back to our vehicle and are moving northeast on a side road toward the city, trying to avoid the convoy."

Kasiah looked to me for answers. I had none, but I faked it well. "Aerona and Rain," I said, taking charge, "get back to the SUV and meet us in front of Jade's building. We're on our way out with Jade."

They responded in unison. "Be there in five."

"Ember?" I asked.

"Yes," she responded, "I'm here."

"You should contact Candice," I suggested, "Tell her to get that jet in the air as quickly as possible and fly north. We may have another ten minutes until that convoy stops to get the helicopter airborne."

"You're sending the jet away?" Kasiah asked, confused.

"We'll never make it back to the airport," I explained. "Besides, they obviously know we're here, which means they're aware of how we have arrived. The airport will be the first place they would look. We can't risk grounding the jet. We'll catch up with it once we get out of the city."

"Erone," Damien said, "where do you want us?"

I released my hold on Jade's lips, giving her a stern look to keep quiet. "Damien and Whisper, you two should hold position outside the city limits, just in case we end up on foot."

"Copy that," Whisper said. "The ECHO units may have been compromised. Radio silence unless it's an emergency."

"ECHO off," I instructed, turning my unit off so I could focus on Jade.

"Hey!" Jade yelled from across the room. "Will someone please explain what the hell is going on?"

I grabbed a backpack from the floor next to the loveseat and tossed it to Jade. "You're coming with us," I declared.

"Says who?" she asked, catching the pack.

I moved to the side of the front window and opened the drapes just enough to look outside. "Jade," I added, looking up and down the street, "it wasn't a question. You're coming with us, either conscious or unconscious. The choice is yours. I would suggest choosing conscious, since I'm not looking forward to carrying you down those old wooden stairs."

From what I could see out the window, it looked quiet outside the apartment. I didn't see any signs of a SWAT team moving into position, or a pack of werewolves gathering for a hunt. I knew all too well of the dangers the darkness could hide.

I released the drape and turned back to Jade. "Those stairs are a hazard," I said. "You should file a complaint with your landlord."

"Forget the landlord," Kasiah joined in. "You have five minutes to pack anything of importance to you in this apartment. You won't be coming back."

I pulled my cell phone out from my pocket. "I'm going to try Tara again. We're out of here in five minutes."

THIRTY-FOUR

The phone rang several times before going to voicemail again. "Tara, this is Erone. We're in a bad situation up here in Montana. Something big is about to go down—FBI convoy and helicopter big. I need you to call me back as soon as you get this message. I hope everything is OK. It's not like you to miss a phone call. Call me."

"Still no answer from Tara?" Kasiah inquired from the front window. Kasiah's been on the lookout as Jade tried to fit her entire life into a backpack in less than five minutes.

"No," I replied. "She has me worried. This is not like her at all. I just hope whoever is tracing us hasn't tracked us straight to Tara. What's it look like outside?"

Kasiah let the drapes fall. "Quiet. We need to get out of here. There's no doubt in my mind they've tracked us right to this very building. It just doesn't make any sense."

"How do you suppose they're tracking us?" I asked.

"How well do you know Tara?" Kasiah probed, insinuating Tara may have been involved with Atmoro.

"Tara is solid," I reassured her. "What about Damien?"

"I personally vouch for Damien," she said, understandably defensive. "Hayley was like a little sister to him. There's no way Damien is feeding information to Atmoro."

"I don't understand," Jade interrupted, removing the back from the same framed picture she had scolded me for touching earlier. "You guys say you're

229

with the FBI... you're special agent so and so, and if that's true, why are you so scared of this person chasing you? Can't you call reinforcements or whatever?"

"He's not chasing us," I corrected her. "He's chasing you."

Jade carefully removed the photograph from the frame and placed it between the pages of a leather-wrapped bible. "And this one man is enough to send the entire FBI into panic mode?" she asked, shoving the bible into her overstuffed backpack. "Can you, at least, tell me why he's after me, or why I have to pack everything I own and run screaming out of my own home?"

Kasiah left the window and joined me by the apartment door. "If I were you," she advised, "I'd save the running and screaming for later. You may need it."

I reached out and offered to carry Jade's backpack. "His name is Atmoro."

"Thanks, but I've got it," she said, swinging the bag over her shoulders. "Atmoro? That sounds so... what's the word I'm looking for? Oh yes, lame."

"Are you always this much fun?" Kasiah asked, clearly not amused by Jade's sense of humor.

"Are you always this intense?" Jade asked, mocking Kasiah

Kasiah squinted out the peephole into the hallway. "You're about to find out."

I leaned in close to Kasiah, letting her perfume suffuse my nose. I shut my eyes for a brief moment, recalling the night we had on Ember's Star and the touch of her silky-smooth-skin against mine.

"How's it look?" I asked.

Kasiah grabbed the door handle. "Game on!"

I put out the apartment lights and closed the door quietly behind us. Kasiah led the way to the stairs, her gun drawn. The first step creaked.

"Erone of Stonegate."

Kasiah spun around and dropped to one knee, her gun stretched straight before her. Jade flattened against the wall at the sight of her gun.

"Ashes," I acknowledged without turning around. "I didn't think we'd be seeing you again so soon."

"I'm not afraid of a little fire," she retorted. "Tell your friend to drop her gun."

"Not going to happen," Kasiah spat back, keeping her gun aimed at Ashes.

I turned and faced Ashes. She was still dressed from head to toe in her black hunting suit and trench coat, holding her two guns. "You don't understand," I tried to explain. "This is bigger than us. This is bigger than Malance and his corrupt council. We need to get this girl out of the city, and we need to do it now."

I felt no need to hold anything back from Ashes. The convoy was not her doing or her style; it was Atmoro's. I was out of options at that point, and we needed Jade out of there.

"The girl's life is in danger," I explained, "Atmoro wants to use her blood to open the Forgotten Shadow City and release all captive Shadows."

Ashes's eyes switched from me to Jade and back. "Her blood?" she asked, considering my accusation. "Atmoro has been dead for many decades. Your lips are weaving a lie. I told you you're not the only jumper to try and talk their way out of returning to the Shadow World."

"Erone!" Kasiah shouted, still on one knee and her gun trained on Ashes. "We need to move!"

I didn't dare take my eyes off Ashes. "Get Jade out of here, Kasiah."

She didn't move. "I'm not leaving without you! You can't fight this fight alone!"

"Jade is more important than I am," I argued. "Get her to Rain and keep her safe."

I could feel Aerona's presence even before I saw her step around the hallway corner behind Ashes. It was as if Aerona was gliding in slow motion, floating as though we were in a music video. All she needed was a hard rock song booming in the background, something with heavy guitar riffs. The amethyst center stone on Aerona's necklace was glowing, and her long dark hair flowed behind as she moved.

"Nice boots," Aerona teased, stopping behind Ashes, catching her off guard. "You must tell me where you got them."

At least now it was a fair fight.

Ashes threw her back flat against the wall, cracking the cheap plaster in several places. She turned one gun from me to Aerona. "This must be the twin. I have to say, I expected more style than a plain white shirt and jeans," she taunted.

Aerona was prepared for this moment. She was in total control of herself and the energy around her. "Rain is at the bottom of the stairs," Aerona said calmly. "Kasiah, take Jade and get her out of here. Erone and I will take care of our friend here."

I looked at Kasiah. I could feel the dilemma in her eyes and I nodded to her.

Kasiah grabbed Jade's arm. "Move!" she ordered. "Now!"

Jade didn't hesitate a second. She stepped quickly down the stairs with Kasiah, keeping her back to the wall. Kasiah gave me one last look before turning to follow Jade and vanished down the stairwell.

Jade's neighbor opened his door. A man stood in the doorway rubbing his eyes. "Do you assholes know what time it is?" he growled.

He stole one glance at Ashes and slammed the door shut, probably to call the police.

Aerona smiled. "Looks like we have a bit of a dilemma here."

Ashes, though, was calm. "There is no dilemma. You and your brother are jumpers and will be returned to the Shadow World, where you will be sentenced accordingly."

I looked past Ashes and locked eyes with Aerona. I could see she understood. Her lips curled into a clever smirk. Ashes's eyes moved back and forth quickly between me and Aerona, trying to calculate the odds of taking us alive or determining the one Malance would prefer dead.

"This girl is worth your lives?" Ashes asked.

"She's worth all our lives," I told her, looking straight into her eyes. "Atmoro is alive, and whether you choose to take that as truth or not is up to you. He is alive and unimaginably vexed with the Shadow Council for imprisoning his wife in the Forgotten Shadow City. He's determined to free her from the prison, and by doing so, he will release all Forgotten Shadows.

If he succeeds, there will be a war of worlds, and thousands of Shadows would flood the Light World."

Ashes remained focused on her mission. "This is something Malance will surely want to hear," she said. "He will protect the girl and secure the prison."

Unfortunately, that was not the answer I sought from Ashes. She was steadfast in following the orders of a corrupt council. Aerona pieced together the same conclusion. We both drew in the energy around us. Ashes saw what was about to happen and fired two shots simultaneously at Aerona. She used her gift of time manipulation to easily dodge both bullets.

Ashes had miscalculated which warlock to turn her back on. I extended both my arms in front of me, immediately throwing them toward the wall opposite Jade's apartment. Ashes, caught in the energy, slammed against the wall with incredible force. She crashed into the wall on her back, causing a piece of the old ceiling to collapse. The impact knocked both guns out of her hands. She growled fiercely; she didn't like being held down. To my surprise, she started to move away from the wall. I used every ounce of energy I could pull in to try and keep Ashes pinned in place.

"Aerona!" I shouted, knowing I couldn't do this alone.

Aerona threw her arms in front of her, slamming Ashes back to the wall. Ashes shut her eyes and lowered her head, taking several deep breaths. She stopped struggling for a short-lived five seconds, then her eyes flipped wide open, like two bright blue flames.

"Erone, I think we pissed her off!" Aerona warned.

Ashes somehow found the strength to push away from the wall. Aerona and I were weakening, our minds failing to keep control. Ashes had extraordinary strength, even for a Shadow Vampire. She managed to push completely away from the wall and step into the center of the hallway, her body tilted forward slightly, as if fighting hurricane speed winds.

Aerona fell to her knees, her arms stretched out and her hands smoldering. She looked at me with pain in her eyes; she was losing control. If Ashes broke free, she would go after Aerona first.

That's when it came to me. This is exactly like when you play tug-of-war as a child. What do you do when you're losing? You let go. Let the other team fall on their asses.

"AERONA! NOW!"

I didn't have to tell Aerona twice. She let her mind go blank and her arms fell to her sides, as did mine. Ashes rocketed across the hallway and passed right through the wall. A cloud of dust and splinters filled the hallway. I ran to Aerona.

"We need to go," I insisted. "Can you walk?"

Aerona coughed. "Go, Erone," she gasped. "Keep Jade safe."

"You've given yourself brain damage," I said, not willing to leave Aerona behind. "If I'm going anywhere, it's with you. Now quit being such a sissy and get your ass off the floor!"

Aerona lifted her head and looked into my eyes, shaking her head with a slight grin. She slammed her fist into the floor and found the strength to rise to her feet.

We stumbled past the Shadow Vampire-sized hole, where pieces of the wall were still collapsing. Our feet hit the stairs, just as Jade's door blew off its hinges, crashing into the hallway. Ashes pulled off an action movie stunt, rolling out of Jade's apartment and scooping up her two silver guns along the way. She began firing and found her feet, all in one swift move.

Shots peppered the wall all around us. I shoved Aerona down the stairs, dropping down so that my head could be below the hallway floor. Aerona tumbled to the bottom of the stairwell, hitting the steel door hard. She was going to hate me for that one.

Ashes stopped firing to switch magazines. I turned over onto my stomach, grasping the carpet runner that extended the full length of the hallway. I got to me knees and yanked the runner with everything I had, falling backward in the process. The last thing I saw as I fell was Ashes getting the rug pulled out from under her feet.

I hit the bottom of the stairwell, landing next to Aerona hard enough to break bones. We both gasped for a breath of air with our backs against the steel door. What a mess we were in.

Without warning, the door swung open behind us, and Aerona and I fell halfway out the door. We were now staring up at street lights and Rain's face. He grabbed us both and pulled us free from the stairwell, slamming the door shut and ramming himself against it.

Several more shots could be heard inside, ricocheting off the door; we heard the dull thuds of bullets hitting steel. Ashes struck the door hard, pushing Rain back several inches. He recovered quickly and forced the door shut. Ashes pounded the door again, but this time, Rain held his ground.

Kasiah and Jade helped us on our feet. I glanced in both directions; the street was deserted.

"Where's the SUV?" I asked.

Rain twisted around with his back to the door, getting a better grip on the pavement with his boots. "The SUV isn't going anywhere," he informed me. "Someone ripped every hose, wire, and whatever else they could grab out of the engine."

Rain lost his footing for a split second. He tried to reposition, but it was too late. The door burst open from Ashes's powerful blow.

Kasiah fired six shots into the dark stairwell, but Ashes had moved outside. Rain swung a metal park bench through the air, hitting Ashes square in her chest. He swung the bench a second time, knocking Ashes back into the stairwell. Rain threw the bench in behind Ashes and kicked the door shut.

"This girl is persistent!" Rain remarked, thrusting his body against the door. "I like her!"

Police sirens could be heard in the distance.

"Déjà vu anyone?" Aerona joked, her strength returning.

The pounding on the inside stopped.

"Think she knocked herself out?" Rain asked, not willing to release the door just yet.

"Let's not wait and see," I said, turning to leave. "We need to get Jade out of here."

What happened next was completely unexpected. Glass shattered from overhead. I looked up just in time to see Ashes descending from the third story window like an expertly choreographed stunt. She floated down to the

235

ground with her arms spread wide and her jacket dancing wildly behind. She hit the ground, bending at the knees, cracking the pavement. She wasted no time as she barreled toward Rain.

I grabbed Jade by her arm and moved her behind me. We needed transportation; that convoy was within city limits by now.

Rain blocked every blow that Ashes hurled at him, working him backward to the storefront. Rain blasted a fist on her chest, knocking her to one knee and pushing her back three of four feet. Ashes threw her head up, flipping her long, black hair away from her face. The street lights glistened off her razor-sharp fangs as she hissed in frustration. She pulled a long polished silver blade from her belt and attacked. Her movements were smooth and precise; she had trained well. The wicked steel blade caught Rain in the shoulder, and his shirt sleeve darkened with blood.

The wound didn't slow him down. In fact, it infuriated him. He dodged two more strikes, ducking on the third attempt, allowing her to move in close. Rain grabbed her around the waist and lifted her off the ground. Ashes sunk the blade deep into Rain's back. He let out a powerful growl as he threw Ashes down. The pavement cracked and caved in around her.

The police sirens grew louder, closer.

Rain fell to his knees, reaching back to pull out the knife. The blade gleamed red with blood. I shivered, just thinking of the pain he must have felt as the wounds healed.

"Let's get the hell out of here!" I yelled to Rain, not wanting to wait for Ashes to heal.

Rain stood up and rolled his head in a small half circle, cracking his neck. Then, reaching down, he grabbed Ashes by one leg, pulling her toward himself and twisting his body at the same time, tossing her away. Ashes flew through the air, crashing through a plate-glass storefront. Her body disappeared within a pile of glass shards and broken shelves.

We needed to get out of the city, but first we had to get off that street. Ashes may be down, but she was not out of the game.

THIRTY-FIVE

Rain slammed his forearm into a steel door, breaking in to a small bakery about half a block from Jade's apartment. The door swung inward. Sirens and red and blue flashing lights filled Jade's street as we shut the broken door behind us. The air inside filled my nostrils with the scents of sticky sweet cupcakes and cookies, crispy croissants, and the distinct aroma of breakfast pastries. My stomach rumbled.

The large storefront window left us exposed to the police cruisers outside. The red and blue lights filled the bakery's small showroom, dancing off the display cases. We quickly moved through a set of swinging doors into the kitchen.

In a flash too quick for even my eyes to catch, Rain checked the back door and returned in seconds. "We could get out through the back," he suggested.

"Why do I feel there's a but coming?" asked Aerona.

"But," Rain continued, looking at Aerona, "there's a maze of alleyways back there. We'll be lost, and the cops will be on us in minutes."

"Wow," Jade exclaimed, peeking through the crack of the kitchen's swinging doors. "I had no idea the Missoula police department had such an amazing response time. Does that say SWAT on the side of that enormous tank-looking thing?"

We gathered around Jade to peer outside.

"Not good," Aerona expressed, scanning the street.

Getting Jade out of the city was proving more difficult than anticipated. Several men in suits and ties stepped out of the unmarked FBI cars. They wasted no time finding out who was in charge of the local police on the scene. Two of the FBI suits had a short conversation with two uniformed Missoula officers. The local police officers hurried back to their cars and drove off, leaving us with the FBI convoy. The rear doors of the SWAT vehicle opened, and a dozen SWAT team members with flak jackets and assault rifles poured out into the street. The FBI agents turned their attention away from Jade's apartment and towards our hiding spot in the bakery.

"Seriously!" Aerona exclaimed irritably. "Does someone want to explain to me how these idiots keep tracking us with pin point precision?"

Kasiah took a step back. I saw it in her eyes before she spoke a single word. I had a feeling the night's events were about to take a hard right turn.

"I'm going out there," Kasiah said, not meeting my eyes.

"The hell you are!" I disputed, like a father stopping his daughter from going out with the guy who smokes and rides a motorcycle.

"Hold on," she countered. "They're not going to hurt me. I'm FBI. Let me talk to them. It'll give you the time you need to get Jade out of here."

"I have to admit," Rain said, agreeing with Kasiah. "This makes sense. If anyone else goes out there, we're criminals. They'll shoot first and ask questions later. Kasiah, at least, has a chance."

"They'll play it by the book and verify my identity," Kasiah said, handing her weapon to Aerona. "I'll stall them as they question my involvement with the so-called terrorist group."

"Those aren't cops out there," I protested. "They're on Atmoro's payroll. You guys are out of your minds if you think we're serving Kasiah up to them on a silver platter."

Kasiah stepped close to me and placed her hand on my chest. "Erone, please understand, Hayley would want me to do whatever I can to keep Jade out of harm's way. This is what I can do. They're not going to hurt me, and if they are working for Atmoro, there's a chance they'll take me to see him, where I can get some much-needed revenge."

"Revenge!" I yelled, my voice growing louder with every word. "I hope you like nightmares! Because that's what you're going to have if they put you in a room with Atmoro! Nightmares!"

238

"We don't have time for this," Aerona warned, attempting to calm me. "Anger is unhealthy and unproductive. Kasiah's right. Someone has to go out there, or they're coming in here. She can give us a five minute head start while they question her."

My heart pained with the slightest thought of what Atmoro will surely do to Kasiah if given the chance. Unfortunately, Kasiah was right. Jade was our priority. As I turned to continue protesting Kasiah's insane plan, her lips touched mine before I could say a word. I breathed in heavily, closing my eyes. Her perfume mixed perfectly with the bakery air, lacing the smell of cookies with a hint of jasmine. I kissed her back softly, wrapping my arms around her.

"Gross," Aerona cringed, pretending to gag.

Our lips parted, and Kasiah turned and walked out of the bakery without another word. I didn't try to stop her.

I watched Kasiah's progress through the crack in the swinging doors. She held up her badge and called out her identity as an FBI agent. The same two FBI agents who had instructed the local police to vacate the scene, stepped forward with their guns drawn. They didn't greet Kasiah as a friend or coworker; instead, they ripped the ID from her hands, forcing her down to her knees. One of the agents grabbed Kasiah by her arm, spinning her around to hold her in handcuffs.

Kasiah shot a frightened glance in my direction as the agents dragged her to a second armored SWAT vehicle, which looked more like a modified UPS van painted black. Kasiah disappeared inside, and the doors shut.

To say this didn't go as planned would be a dramatic understatement.

I turned to Aerona. My sister knew me better than I knew myself.

"I know, I know," Aerona said, lowering her head. "You're going with her." Her eyes filled with tears. "I love you," she said quietly, knowing she may never see me again.

"I love you too," I said, hugging her. "Keep Jade safe."

Rain wasn't about to try and stop me. We didn't have time for another argument, and my hands were already alive with fire. I ignited the wooden storage shelves, aiming the fire at the ceiling tiles.

"Get Jade out of here, Rain!" I shouted, aiming the fire to the front of the store.

It's not in my nature to surrender; that word isn't part of my vocabulary. Although, as I've come to realize, it's amazing what a man will do for a sexy brunette with a cute Midwestern accent. *She better be worth it,* I thought to myself.

I left the once sweet-smelling bakery with my hands on my head. I didn't notice the helicopter hovering above until I was outside. Its intense white spotlight illuminated me from above. The wind from its rotor blades spun up a tornado of debris along the sidewalk, and the rush of air fueled the bakery fire.

The SWAT team worked like a machine. Four men in flak jackets were on me in an instant, their rifles leveled to my head and heart. They ordered me to my knees, then one of them forcefully cuffed my hands behind my back, kicking me down to the pavement from behind. Someone pressed their boot into my back and pinned me in place. It took everything I had not to unleash hell onto that very street; the helicopter was my only concern.

I had to keep calm for Kasiah's sake.

The pressure from the boot on my back relaxed as one of the men shouted a command. "Put him in with the other one!"

Two men hauled me up to my feet. I glanced back at the bakery. The SWAT team brought the firepower, but they weren't prepared to fight a real, blazing fire. Several men were attempting to douse the flames with small extinguishers from their vehicles—it was pointless. The front window shattered, further feeding the flames. Smoke rolled out from the bakery as the blaze quickly devoured the storefront, pushing the SWAT team back.

I landed on the metal floor inside the SWAT van, my face to the floor. The doors banged shut behind me. Someone yanked me up to a metal bench, roughly switching my handcuffs from my back to my front. It took a moment for my eyes to adjust to the dimly lit vehicle. Three armed men, their faces covered with black ski masks, sat across from me. I could taste blood in my mouth, and I felt a warm trickle run down my chin to my neck.

The only good news was that these guys obviously weren't vampires created in this world, or the blood would be driving them mad with thirst.

Kasiah was seated beside me. Her voice was soothing, yet I sensed a bit of anger. "Tell me, Erone, exactly which part of the plan didn't you understand?"

"Possibly the part where I wasn't supposed to save you," I said, half smiling.

I could see Kasiah holding back her smile. She shook her head and sighed.

One of our captors reached out and forcefully grabbed my arm. "Be quiet!" he ordered. "Shackle his ankles and chain him to the floor!"

I wasn't concerned about the chains. They appeared to be made of nothing more than plain carbon steel. I scanned the interior of the van quickly. The only window was the one between us and the driver's compartment. It didn't look large enough to crawl through and was probably bulletproof glass. The driver wouldn't be able to hear these men scream.

The rear doors swung open, and two more men climbed in, their faces masked like the others. Both carried pump shotguns. These guys aren't messing around. The rear doors were slammed shut and locked from outside. The engine started and the van started to roll forward. I heard multiple vehicles fall in line behind us, including the loud monstrous diesel engine of the armored SWAT vehicle. The helicopter's spotlight followed us as we moved, partially illuminating the interior through the small bulletproof window.

"Where are you taking us?" I asked.

The van turned left and sped up.

The man directly across from me stood up and clipped my lower jaw with the butt of his shotgun. "Quiet!" he ordered.

My head flew back and hit the metal wall, dazing me.

Kasiah instinctively lifted her cuffed hands to comfort me.

The same man who hit me, slapped Kasiah across her face with the back of his hand. Her head bounced off the metal wall, and blood trickled down from her nose.

The man sat back down with a smile on his face. "You two aren't so tough," he insisted, elbowing the guy next to him. "This will be the easiest ten grand I ever made."

I leaned forward until my restraints tightened, then looked at the man right in the eye, pushing energy through the small space between us. His smile turned to a fearful frown, his eyes opened wide, and his lower lip began to quiver. The shot gun fell from his now limp hands, hitting the metal floor and startling the rest of the SWAT team.

The rest of the SWAT team moved uncomfortably, exchanging worried glances with each other as though this was something they were warned about. One of them stood up and aimed the barrel of his shotgun at me. "What the hell are you doing to him!" he hollered.

I steadied my breathing, continuing my mental torture on the guy across the van. A thick stream of drool and foam oozed from his quivering lip as his eyes rolled back in his head.

The shotgun man moved the gun's barrel closer to me, aiming only inches from my chest. "Stop it!" he cried. "You're killing him!"

I slowly turned my head and met his eyes, giving him a small dose of what his partner was getting. He dropped his gun and fell to his knees sobbing.

"Anyone else?" I asked.

No one else said a word. They didn't even look in my direction. They directed their stares to the corners of the van. They must have had orders to take us alive. Either way, they were probably rethinking that ten thousand dollar payment.

"My hero," Kasiah whispered.

"Oh, *now* you're happy to see me?" I asked jokily.

Kasiah smiled.

Suddenly, I heard a tiny female voice in my ear. For a brief moment, I thought maybe I had burned my own mind.

"Don't freak out," said the tiny voice.

I jumped sideways, bumping into Kasiah, jerking my head in the direction of the voice. I looked across the van at the SWAT team. They were too busy trying to imagine themselves anywhere but in that van.

The voice was now speaking to me in my other ear.

"It's me, Ember, and by the way, I said *don't* freak out."

Kasiah looked at me as if I had lost my mind. "Are you OK?" she asked.

"You didn't hear that?" I responded, looking confused.

"Hear what?"

"*Ember*," I whispered.

Kasiah opened her mouth to answer, but quickly shut it again at the sight of the tiny fairy on my shoulder.

"I'm a stowaway," Ember whispered excitedly. "You guys alright?"

"How?" I asked her, confused.

"It's easy when no one notices you," Ember said, laughing her tiny, fairy laugh. "Let's get out of here. We can tell the story around a campfire some other time."

The SWAT team looked even more alarmed than before. Now, their prisoners were talking to thin air.

The searchlight from the chopper flew ahead of the SWAT van, searching back and forth. The sound of the rotor blades faded along with the big diesel engine of the other SWAT vehicle. I assumed they were scouting the route ahead.

I felt Ember's tiny feet tiptoe across my shoulder blades.

"Can you break through that glass?" she asked.

"Yes," I said, thinking. "Maybe."

"Well," Kasiah asked, "which is it, yes or maybe?"

"Yes," I said, hoping it was true.

"OK," said Ember. "If you can break the glass, then I can fit through the window."

"What about them?" Kasiah asked, nodding towards the SWAT team. "They look—"

Without warning, the SWAT van screeched to a stop, throwing us forward. The unmistakable sound of gunfire erupted outside. The SWAT team was frozen with fear. Bullets riddled the side of the van, forming a pattern of dents on the thin sheet metal. Blood spattered on the bulletproof window between us and the driver.

"The chains!" Kasiah screamed.

I closed my eyes and drew in a breath, focusing on the chains and handcuffs. I raised my hands as far as the restraints would allow, then slammed them into the side of the bench as hard as I could. The chains and handcuffs exploded into a million shards of broken glass.

I did the same to the shackles around my legs.

I turned to Kasiah, drawing in another breath. "It's going to happen fast!" I warned. "It might hurt!"

"Just do it!" Kasiah yelled, turning her head away and closing her eyes.

I raised Kasiah's hands and her handcuffs to the side of the bench, and the steel exploded into thousands of tiny fragments.

Kasiah rubbed her wrists. "You're a very interesting person," she remarked.

We turned around to find the entire SWAT team pressed against the far corner of the van, quivering in fear.

More gunfire erupted outside, further away this time. The shooters were being pushed back. Something heavy hit the van doors, rocking the van. A second, harder thud broke the doors open. I wasn't surprised to see Rain on the other side. The scene behind him was a typical Rain rescue mission: a car on its side, a fire hydrant shooting a forty foot geyser into the night sky, and bursts of gunfire to set the mood.

"You guys waiting for an invitation," Rain asked casually, just as two bullets struck the door a couple inches from his head. "Hey, what's with the SWAT guys? They look like they've seen a ghost."

"Long story," I said, jumping to the ground and turning to help Kasiah down.

We crouched and ran behind an overturned FBI cruiser that was flipped up on its side. Bullets rattled into the roof of the car, our shield.

Ember flew low behind us, keeping next to Rain.

"Tell me this isn't where your plan ends," I asked Rain.

"I don't recall mentioning anything about a plan." Rain replied, ripping the gas tank from the underside of the car.

Kasiah moved around me, next to Rain. "Where's Aerona and Jade?" she asked, covering her head.

"Safe," Rain replied, casually tossing the gas tank over the car as if it was weightless.

The gunfire intensified.

"Your idea of safe…" Kasiah yelled over the gunfire, "or mine?"

A bright flash of fire filled the night sky as the gas tank exploded above the street.

Rain slammed his shoulder into the underside of the car, gripping the frame. "Trust me," he insisted, "they're in the safest place in this city."

He started dragging the car to the side of the street. Rain's brute strength was astonishing. Gunfire continued to pelt the car as Rain pushed, only stopping when the bumper hit the curb.

"Now what!" Kasiah shouted.

We all heard the monstrous armored SWAT vehicle at the same time. It turned the corner two blocks behind us, and it was moving fast. The driver maneuvered wide, smashing through a bus stop as the bright light from the helicopter rounded the same building.

As though on cue, the black Raptor truck from earlier in the night blasted through the alley, sliding sideways to a stop only a few feet from our faces. Several bullets dented the truck's bed, leaving silver bullet marks in the black paint. Two rounds hit the tinted side window. The glass crumpled around the bullets, absorbing the impact, but leaving the glass intact—it was bulletproof.

The helicopter hovered above us, shining light on our position.

The Raptor's driver-side front and rear doors swung open together. Loud rock music belted out of the truck. Nothing compliments gunfire better than heavy guitar riffs and heart-thumping drum beats.

Ashes emerged from the Raptor. "Move!" she yelled, firing an automatic rifle over the truck's roof as cover before turning to fire at the helicopter, forcing it to retreat.

Rain and I looked at each other, shocked.

"Now *that's* sexy!" Rain grinned.

We all sprinted to the truck. Rain launched himself into the truck's bed, and Kasiah jumped face first into the back seat. Ember flew in behind her. I dove into the front seat, sliding across to the passenger's side. Ashes shoved in the smoking gun beside me, then floored the accelerator. The Raptor roared to life, forcing the driver's door shut.

The Raptor's engine growled like a grizzly bear. The rear wheels dug into the pavement, rocketing us forward like a dragster, throwing me back into the seat. I put my head above the dashboard just in time to see Ashes steering with her knee while loading a full magazine into the rifle. She jammed the magazine into position and cocked the first round into the chamber.

I looked back to check up on Kasiah and Ember. "You guys good?" I asked, turning down the stereo.

Ashes gave me a disapproving look for touching her truck.

"We're fine," Kasiah replied. "No bullet holes here. You?"

I gave myself a quick inspection. "No blood."

Ashes turned the truck sharply to the right. The tires screeched on the pavement as we slid around the corner. I thought for sure we were going to roll over. Ashes pinned the accelerator down to the floor, redlining the RPMs. She looked perfectly calm and in control behind the wheel of the 600-horsepower beast.

Rain hammered on the cab's rear window.

Ashes slid open the power window.

"We've got company!" he yelled.

Ashes checked the rearview mirror. "Wonderful," she said, swerving past a parked car. "We're getting out of this city. Where's the blonde girl you are so ready to die for?"

Rain passed his cell phone through the back window. "I marked her location on my phone," he said, pointing to a small flashing red dot. "Hand me that M-4."

Kasiah grabbed the rifle off the seat next to her and handed it through to Rain.

I grabbed Rain's phone and zoomed in on the map. "Take the next left," I directed.

"Hold on back there!" Kasiah shouted to Rain. "We're hanging a left!"

Ashes hardly slowed down at the corner. The back end of the truck swung out wide. Ashes compensated by cranking the wheel to the right. The Raptor's engine let out a thunderous roar as Ashes muscled it around the corner.

I looked back at the vehicles chasing us. The helicopter's light shined brightly as one of the cars spun out at the corner, hitting a light post. A shower of sparks sprayed down in the street, slowing the other car and armored SWAT vehicle as they maneuvered around the crashed car.

In the truck bed, Rain crouched to one knee and wrapped the rifle's shoulder strap around one arm to tighten his grip and steady the weapon. He fired a quick, three-round burst at the second car around the corner. The bullets found the center of the car's windshield. The car's driver veered from left to right. That rifle could never stop the car without hitting a vital engine component, but Rain's shots discouraged the driver from advancing. He fired several more quick bursts at the car and a few at the helicopter to keep the pilot in check.

I wasn't surprised that Rain was good with a firearm; it was in his blood.

"Right in two blocks," I instructed Ashes. "We need to lose these guys. We're leading them right to Jade."

Ashes swung the steering wheel and drifted the truck through the right turn. "Tell Rain to stop firing," she said, "Let these guys get close to us. I'll take care of them."

Kasiah relayed the message to Rain, and he lay down flat on his back.

Ashes slowed down, intentionally allowing the car and armored SWAT vehicle to catch up. They split side by side and were on our bumper.

I leaned back in my seat. "I hope you know what you're doing."

"Seatbelts," Ashes insisted. "This could go one of two ways."

"I don't like the sound of that," Kasiah added, clicking her seatbelt in place.

An intense flash of light filled the interior of the truck. By the time I recovered and looked to the back seat, Ember had transformed into her full human size.

"Seatbelts don't work well with a one-inch waist-line," Ember said, clicking her shoulder strap in place.

My passenger side mirror shined brightly from the car on the right. Ashes drove with the tires inches from the curb, so the SWAT vehicle behind us couldn't see what was in front of us. Then, she veered hard to the left, barely missing a line of parked cars. The SWAT vehicle didn't have time to react. The driver tried to avoid hitting the parked cars but failed miserably. I saw a ball of fire exploding in my mirror, rolling the SWAT vehicle.

The helicopter flew high and wide to avoid the fireball.

"One down," Ashes said calmly, as though she was playing a video game.

The car to our left didn't slow down at the sight of its partner's accident. They attacked the left rear side of the truck, rocking it sideways. Several gunshots hit the back bulletproof window, leaving quarter-sized circular fractures.

"They're trying to pit us!" Kasiah shouted from the back seat. "Don't let them get alongside us or we're done!"

The car struck us again, causing the truck to fishtail. Ashes quickly regained control and sped up.

"Pit?" I asked.

"Precision Immobilization Technique," Kasiah clarified. "PIT. It's typically not effective on larger trucks, but these guys are out of ideas. They're going to try aligning themselves with the rear wheels."

The car caught back up, desperately trying to get alongside us.

Kasiah sat up and looked through the back window. "They'll make contact with the back of the truck," she explained, "then steer sharply into us. If done correctly, it will cause the rear tires to lose traction and start to skid. Then, they'll push the nose of their car into us, forcing the truck into a spin, most likely stalling the engine."

Ashes reached the dash and pressed the four-wheel drive button. It emitted a bright orange light. "I'm not used to being the one chased," she suggested.

That gave me an idea. "We need to get behind them," I said.

Ashes looked at me with her blue eyes as if I had lost my mind.

"Slow down," I said, checking the side mirror, "and let them position for the PIT."

Ashes looked at me from the corner of her eye. "And then?" she asked.

I hesitated, piecing the scenario together in my head. "Hit the brakes hard and let them pass you," I said, momentarily uncertain of my half-baked plan.

"That's just crazy enough to work," Kasiah said.

Ashes grinned, slowing down just enough to let the car think it was catching up. She moved the truck into the left lane to feign blocking their attack.

The car shifted to the right, edging its nose alongside the rear of our truck.

"Hold it," I said, gauging the car's distance, suddenly not so sure of this idea.

"NOW!" Kasiah yelled.

Ashes hit the brakes, and the truck's nose dove down hard as the FBI car shot past us. She pressed the accelerator, and the truck growled back to life, once again throwing us back into our seats. I heard Rain's boots hit the tailgate. I hoped the bed didn't have one of those coarse bed-liners.

Ashes didn't give the car any time to recover from our surprise move. She effortlessly maneuvered the front of the truck to the left of the car. They knew what was coming, and even tried to reposition, but it was too late.

Ashes smashed the truck into the rear of the car, causing it to lose traction and skid sideways. She pushed the accelerator to the floor, burying the front of the truck into the driver's side of the car. The grill crashed against the driver's door as it began spinning sideways.

The driver fought frantically to stop the car from skidding, but it was useless. Ashes used the Raptor's incredible power to push the car for at least half a block, until the car's right side hit a manhole cover, lifting the driver's side and flipping the entire car. Ashes slammed the brakes and let the car roll to a stop.

We left the overturned car and turned down the next street. Ashes skid the truck to a stop.

"What are you doing?" I yelled.

The helicopter's spotlight illuminated the entire street.

Ashes opened her door and jumped out.

"She left us!" Kasiah exclaimed.

A red streak of light shot into the sky, followed by a trail of fiery sparks. Ashes shot a flare at the helicopter, hitting the rear rotor. The spinning blades spread the flare's fuel over the entire tail of the helicopter. We watched as the pilot struggled to keep the injured helicopter under control as it spun out of view behind a building.

Ashes jumped back into the driver's seat.

"Women drivers," Rain commented, climbing into the back seat with Ember and Kasiah.

Ashes ignored Rain. "Let's go get your little princess and get out of this insane city."

THIRTY-SIX

"You have arrived at your destination" scrolled across the screen of Rain's phone. I stared blankly out the window at the illuminated sign at the front of the building: Missoula Police Department.

"Safest place in town?" Kasiah muttered. "Did you lock them in a cell?"

Rain turned toward me and Kasiah. "You two didn't exactly give me much time to plan a proper rescue when you got yourselves captured and thrown into a SWAT van."

"Good point," I said, stepping out of the truck. "So, where are Aerona and Jade?"

"That's a good question," Rain said, walking towards the front of the police station. "The place was deserted when we ran passed it. I guessed the officers were all out, chasing after… well, us. It seemed like the best idea at the time."

A young uniformed female officer ran out of the revolving glass door to the police station.

"Stop right there!" she demanded, removing her gun from her hip holster.

The gun shook in her hands as if it was set in vibrate mode. I was sure she had never fired her weapon in the line of duty.

"Our reputation precedes us," I said to Rain.

"You two don't move!" the officer ordered, holding the radio to her lips. "This is 125 requesting backup at headquarters. Two suspects in custody. Require immediate assistance."

251

The dispatcher responded, "Confirmed 125. Units in route. Hold for assistance."

A bright white spark ignited at the officer's neck, and the smell of ozone filled the air. She began shaking violently, causing her to finger to pull the gun's trigger and fire a single shot wildly into the air. The officer fell convulsing to the ground.

Aerona, with a police issue stun gun in hand, stood over the stunned officer, blowing the stun gun's electrode tips off as if it were a smoking gun.

"That was kind of fun," she smiled.

I shot her a look of disapproval.

"What?" Aerona asked innocently. "Like I was supposed to know it would make her pull the trigger."

"Aerona," I said, kneeling to check the officer's pulse, "it's a stun gun. It stuns people with an electric shock. You didn't think sending an electric current through an armed woman's body might be a bad idea?"

"That's why they have training classes," Rain pointed out.

Aerona put a hand on her hip. "Well, yeah, but—"

"Well, yeah, but what?" I asked, cutting her short. "I thought I told you to get Jade out of the city, to keep her safe. You're lucky this cop is still alive."

"You're welcome," Aerona scoffed, storming passed me. "That's the last time I save you. Let's get out of here before her friends show up."

"Men," Jade said, storming passed us, following Aerona.

"Great," I grumbled, turning to Rain. "We left Jade alone with Aerona for ten minutes, and she's already corrupted the poor girl's mind."

"Nice ride, little brother!" Aerona yelled back at us, opening the door to the Raptor. She jumped back immediately, shoving Jade to the side when she saw Ashes in the driver's seat.

I reached past Aerona and grabbed Jade's bag. "Don't worry," I assured Aerona, tossing Jade's bag into the back seat. "Ashes is with us."

"What do you mean *with us*?" Erone asked, peeking around me into the truck. "Am I in some kind of alternate reality where up is down? Isn't she the same Shadow Vampire who attempted to arrest us less than thirty minutes ago?"

"Yes," I replied, "and no, you're still in the same screwed up reality you've been stuck in for the past hundred years. Now get your ass in the truck. I'll explain on the way out of the city."

Police sirens could be heard echoing in the background.

"Please?" I begged Aerona, not wanting to deal with her right now.

"Oh!" she snapped, "Well, if you put it that way, then no! I'm not getting in there with *her*!"

Jade stood uncomfortably next to Aerona. "I'm with her," she said. "That scary girl wrecked my apartment."

I put both hands on the truck's hood and hung my head between them, muttering to myself. "This is nuts."

Ashes revved the engine to get our attention. "Thirty seconds and I'm leaving with or without you," she warned.

Aerona looked at Ashes, then back to me. "OK," she finally relented, "but we're in the backseat behind the vamp." Aerona triggered a bright spark across the electrodes of the stun gun. "Be advised, I think I kind of like shocking people with my new toy."

Ashes shot Aerona an unconcerned look that basically meant *bring it on*.

"Great," I said, "now that we're all friends, get in!"

Once safely outside the city limits, we joined up with Damien and Whisper, stopping just long enough to let Rain and Ember switch vehicles. We raced east towards the mountains, keeping off the highways. Tall evergreen trees lined either side of the road, which made it feel like we were driving through a never ending evergreen tunnel.

"So what made you change your mind?" I asked Ashes.

"Change my mind about what?" she asked as she fiddled with the radio.

I checked my side mirror to make sure the SUV was still following. "About taking Aerona and me back to the Shadow World."

"What makes you think I changed my mind? You are both in my custody."

I looked crossways to the backseat at Aerona. "You raise a good point," I said uneasily.

Aerona held up her new stun gun toy and happily pointed at the trigger.

I shook my head.

"Good choice," Ashes agreed, not taking her eyes off the road. "That situation had rapidly deteriorated. Interference by law enforcement units threatened to compromise my objective and forced me to improvise. At the end of the day, my intentions remain the same."

Jade spoke for the first time since we got in the truck. "How exactly do I fit into this twisted game of alternate reality?"

"Maybe you should get some sleep," I suggested to Jade. "There will be plenty of time to explain in the morning."

"I… I don't sleep," Jade said hesitantly.

"You mean you can't sleep," Aerona said, correcting her.

"No," Jade replied, hesitating. "I mean… I literally don't sleep."

Jade's comment was the first real indication that she was a stone. It actually made sense that angels didn't sleep; they had no need for rest. According to Ember, angels have an unlimited supply of energy. Ember did, however, say that fallen angels—stones—would weaken over time, slowly losing their magic here on earth. However, Jade was *born* an angel, making her a true-blood angel. She had her parent's strengths but none of their weaknesses.

I had felt an incredible amount of energy in the hallway at Jade's apartment, which I originally contributed to Aerona's presence. In fact, the energy source was Jade.

"How long has it been since you've slept?" I asked, not giving away my suspicions.

"I've never slept," Jade explained, hanging her head down as if she was embarrassed. "I… I've never told anyone this before. I thought, maybe since you all seem to have special abilities, you may know what's wrong with me."

"Didn't your parents notice you were not sleeping?" Aerona asked.

"Even as a small child, I always pretended to sleep until my parents left the room," she continued. "I didn't want them to know I was different. I spent most nights reading and staring up at the stars, dreaming in my own way. Then, before morning, I would climb back in bed and let my mother wake me."

Aerona placed her hand on Jade's shoulder. "We're all different," she said. "And trust me when I say this, it's good to be different."

"You guys seem to know something about me that you're not telling me," Jade complained. "I just wanted you to know that I know something is wrong with me. Is it like some kind of fatal disease or something? Am I contagious?"

Aerona broke out in a laugh. "Contagious? Jade, you're unique. That's why we're all here to protect you."

"Protect me? Protect me from what?"

Aerona caught my eyes, not wanting to be the one to tell her that life as she knows will never be the same. Oh, and by the way, a Shadow Vampire wants to drain every drop of precious angel blood from her body in a ritualistic manner to break a thousand-year-old mythical lock on a door built by elves.

"Everything's going to be fine," I said, attempting to reassure Jade. "You're not sick. Let's focus on getting you safely away from the city. We'll need Ember to help us explain everything else."

My phone rang. It was Damien. "Tell your chauffeur up there she has a lead foot."

I checked the passenger side mirror. The SUV's headlights were nowhere to be seen. I glanced over at the Raptor's speedometer. It was racing at 95 mph.

"We've been driving for almost two hours," I said, responding to Damien. "We should probably get off this road before the sun comes up. We need to regroup."

Ashes slowed down the truck. "We passed what looked like an old logging road two miles back," she said, "It'll be on their left."

"Damien, keep your eyes peeled for an old dirt logging road on your left. We're turning around and heading back your way."

"Copy that," Damien confirmed, "We just passed it. We'll flip around and meet you there."

I ended the call and dialed Tara's number.

The call was immediately forwarded to her voicemail again.

I shut my phone off and gently moved my left arm to wake Kasiah. She had fallen asleep on my shoulder only less than an hour ago. I felt bad for waking her. She wiggled further into my shoulder.

I could feel Aerona's emotions doing summersaults in the back seat. She didn't like the idea of riding with Ashes.

Ashes slowed down and turned the Raptor off the main road onto what was an old access road of some kind. The dirt road, barely one lane wide, narrowed to a little more than an overgrown trail with weeds and fallen trees. It looked to be rarely used, if ever. A cloud of dust encapsulated the SUV as we drove passed it without stopping.

"Where are we?" Kasiah asked, yawning as she woke up.

Ashes swerved the truck to miss a downed tree blocking half the trail, forcing Kasiah's body against mine.

I struggled to keep the armrest from digging into my side. "We needed to get off the main road and stop somewhere."

The Raptor was built for roads like this. The rugged tires stomped the gravel beneath them as they clawed their way deep into the mountains, giving the off-road suspension a workout as we sprinted through a shallow, rocky creek. The SUV headlights bounced up and down, struggling to keep pace down the trail that seemed to wind on forever.

Maybe five miles past the creek, the trail opened up through a grassy clearing bordering a small, natural pond. Ashes slowed the truck to a stop, switching off the headlights and the engine. The SUV came to a stop behind us.

Ashes stared straight ahead. "There's a cabin just beyond that tree line," she said, her eyes searching.

I have excellent night vision, yet I didn't see anything in the darkness besides more darkness.

"I don't see anything," I said, squinting.

Ashes looked at me. "It's there," she said, checking her two pistols strapped to her belt.

I looked into the back seat. "Aerona, stay here with Jade. We'll be right back."

"Yeah right," Aerona retorted. "Only if she leaves the keys. No way am I staying here while she goes off and abandons us in BFE."

Ashes tossed the truck's keys into the backseat, slamming the door behind her. She was gone in a flash, the tail of her jacket trailing behind.

"You know, Aerona," I said, helping Kasiah out of the truck, "you might want to, at least, try being nice to the Shadow Vampire."

"You know, little brother, you might want to kiss my—"

I closed the door before Aerona could finish.

Kasiah and I walked back to the SUV.

"What's the plan?" Damien asked, opening the driver's side door.

I pointed toward the tree line. "There's a cabin just beyond the tree line. Ashes went to make sure it's safe."

Whisper squinted out the windshield and said, "I don't see anything."

"It's there," Rain stated, stepping out of the SUV. "Here she comes."

A light breeze blew past us as Ashes stopped next to the SUV. "All clear," she said, running her fingers through her hair. "The cabin hasn't been used lately, and there's a barn we can fit both vehicles inside."

We parked the vehicles in the damp barn, securing the large wooden doors behind us, spooking several sleeping birds in the process. We approached the cabin cautiously. Ashes had already cleared the perimeter, and strangely, I trust her; but we were still cautious.

The cabin appeared to be hand-built with logs. It was nestled among the trees, as if it was a part of the forest. The angled roof was in good shape for the age of the cabin. A small bent chimney meant there was either a fireplace or a small stove. The cabin door wasn't open, but it wasn't fully closed either. Further inspection showed that it was forced open at some point—vandals. The inside of the cabin was bare except for a small wooden table and chairs, and the air smelled old and unused. The only other door in the cabin led to a single small bedroom with a pair of bunk beds. The cabin was most likely only used during hunting season.

Whisper volunteered to take the first watch near the pond outside, in case anyone followed us up the trail. Damien and Kasiah, the only mortals in the room, each took a bunk to catch up on some sleep. The rest of us could do without sleep for several days.

"Vampires don't exist," Jade debated after I told her about Atmoro.

"Trust me sweetie," Aerona joined in, opening the cabin window to let a sliver of the morning sun through, "vampires exist. You're in a room with two of them right now."

Jade looked from Rain to Ashes. "You drink blood?" she asked, her eyes open wide.

"Well, not out of a glass with ice," Rain responded. "But yes, we have cravings for blood. The sunlight drains our energy, and human blood replenishes it."

"Let's not scare Jade," I cautioned. "Don't worry, Ashes and Rain are Shadow Vampires. They're from another world where vampires are guardians of royalty and protectors of our kind. They aren't your stereotypical movie monster vampires."

Ashes removed her long leather trench coat and draped it over the back of chair. Her tight leather hunting suit fit her figure as if it was painted on over her perfectly toned curves.

"Rain's a Shadow Vampire?" Ashes questioned as she removed both handguns and placed them on the table. Her hands worked fast at unbuckling the polished clasps on her belt. She removed the belt and placed it next to the guns. "It's not possible," she declared. "I have had detailed training on the history of the Shadow World. I know of every Shadow Vampire the council has ever created, and Rain is not one of them."

"Well," Rain said, "if I don't exist, then who slammed you to the ground earlier tonight?"

"You are a unique creature," Ashes said, disassembling one of the guns. "You have incredible strength and speed, exceptional control over your thirst, and your wounds heal quickly. All these features do indicate you are a Shadow Vampire. Your past seems to be somewhat of a mystery."

"If you ever figure it out," Rain said, wishing he could remember his past, "be sure to let me know."

"Erone," Jade interjected, "you said *your kind*. What did you mean by that?"

"My sister and I are warlocks," I explained. "We're also from the Shadow World. In fact, Ashes is here to take us back there."

Aerona joined us at the table. "Over my dead body," she seethed. ·

Ashes began disassembling the second gun. "That can be arranged," she threatened, not looking up at Aerona.

Rain stood up. "Over *my* dead body," he said, walking to the window to shut the small, wooden window doors to block the sunlight.

"Erone," Ashes said, changing the subject, "what is the meaning behind the phrase you quoted in the apartment building, 'the blood of a stone will release them alone?'"

"The blood of a stone," I explained, "is what Atmoro is after. He believes it will open the Forgotten Shadow City and release his wife."

Ashes was confused. She stopped cleaning the guns. It's not often her targets have more information about the Shadow World than her.

"How did you obtain this knowledge?" she asked curiously.

Rain commented from across the room. "Sounds to me like the little, Shadow Vampire warrior schools need to update their course materials."

I jumped in before Ashes could give Rain a few lessons from Killing a Vampire 101. "Two days ago," I continued, "we discovered an ancient elf scroll that indicated someone high in the ranks of the Shadow Council— possibly Malance's father—had commissioned a back door to the Forgotten Shadow City to be built by elves. The door was constructed in secret, and its sole purpose was giving the Shadow Council a way to escape if they ever found themselves behind the walls of their own prison, from which there is supposedly no escape. There's only one way in and no way out."

"Where is this secret door?" Ashes inquired.

"We don't know. The door was constructed by elves. I'm assuming it's hidden here in the Light World. Although, we think Atmoro must know its location, since he's after the blood to unlock the spell."

Ashes understood where our logic was leading and caught on quickly. "The location of the door does Atmoro no good without the blood."

"If the scroll is correct," I said, wondering if it was, "and the blood of a stone is the only key, then yes."

"Never mind that," Jade cut in. "Where do I fit in?"

"The last line of the elf scroll," Ember said excitedly, "is 'the blood of a stone will release them alone.'"

"You've deciphered the riddle?" asked Ashes.

"The riddle isn't a riddle at all," Ember explained. "It's actually quite a literal phrase or an instruction. We believe the blood of a stone will actually break the elf spell and open the secret door, releasing the Forgotten Shadows."

"Not even I can squeeze blood from a stone," Ashes said.

"That's the literal part," Ember continued. "A stone does not refer to a million year old piece of granite. In the Light World, the elves world, a stone is moniker for a fallen angel."

Ashes looked at Jade peculiarly. "She's a fallen angel?"

"I am?" Jade asked, confused.

"Not exactly," I said. "But your parents were."

Jade went quiet. She still hadn't completely grasped what Kasiah had told her earlier about her parents not being her biological parents.

Ashes inserted a full magazine into the butt of each cleaned and reassembled gun. "You're saying Jade was born an angel?" she asked, chambering a round in each gun. "That makes her a true-blood. Is that even possible?"

"When angels are cast down to Earth," Ember continued, "they slowly lose their magical energy. They become more and more human. By the time they accept the fact that they will grow old and die as a human, it's too late to pass on their powers to an offspring. In Jade's case, both her parents were stones who were cast down together as husband and wife, already in love.

With angel energy still flowing through their veins, they conceived a child as soon as their human bodies changed enough to allow it."

"Let me get this straight," Jade interjected. "I'm a rock, and Atmoro is some crazy vampire who wants to use my blood to free his wife from prison? Why don't we just give him a few drops to save his wife, then everyone can live happily ever after?"

"You're a stone," Ember corrected. "You may be the only true-blood angel ever created. Your blood is the key that Atmoro is searching for, the key that will open the Forgotten Shadow City and release his wife from the prison."

"Atmoro isn't looking for a few drops of your precious blood," I added, trying not to scare her, though she needed to know. "He's not going to risk getting this wrong, especially since he may never find another stone. Atmoro will use every drop of your blood. Also, he isn't simply releasing his wife, he'll be opening a door to thousands of angry Forgotten Shadows who have been imprisoned for centuries. If they escape the Forgotten Shadow City, it'll be a chaos this world has never seen."

"Assuming Atmoro, is in fact, alive..." Ashes commented, strapping her belt back to her waist.

"Trust me," Kasiah remarked from the bedroom door, "Atmoro is alive and kicking."

"Couldn't sleep?" I asked, offering my chair to her.

"Rest will come when I've avenged Hayley's death," she replied. "Damien's out like a light."

"As far as the Shadow Council knows," Ashes continued, sliding her arms into her trench coat, "Atmoro perished in a fire when the hunting party tried to arrest him. The council will never see this coming."

"That's why Jade must be kept out of Atmoro's grasp," Ember said, "at all costs."

"Are you with us?" I asked Ashes.

Ashes thought about her response. Her eyes shifted from me to Jade, and then to Rain. "If what you say is true," she finally said, "and I am not yet convinced it is, then I am with you. Although you must understand, I have loyalty to the Shadow Council, and once the girl is safe and Atmoro is dealt with, I am delivering you and your sister to Malance."

"We're not negotiating here," Aerona countered defensively.

Ashes opened the cabin door, letting the sunlight in. "Negotiation is not necessary," she stated, walking out the door, closing it behind her.

"Not now," I said, cutting Aerona off. "I need to get hold of Tara."

THIRTY-SEVEN

For the first time since Tara and Ian found their worlds spinning out of control in what seemed like a low budget horror film, the dark room was illuminated by a sliver of morning sun through a small, dirty window. A wicked summer storm with deafening thunder and wind had rocked the old house all through the night. The early morning sun provided them with some much-needed positivity.

Ian's wrists were raw and bloodied from the cold, steel handcuffs. It had been two hours since they last heard Tara's phone vibrate in the pocket of Ian's jacket.

He strained his neck to look the jacket. "Do you think the battery is dead?" Ian asked. "It's been forever since we've heard it vibrate—maybe a few hours."

"I remember unplugging the phone from the charger when I left the house," Tara said, adjusting herself as much as the duct tape would allow. "I think it was fully charged, but the vibration might have drained the battery."

The knife wound in Tara's hand had stopped bleeding, although whenever she moved her hand, a sharp stabbing pain raced up her arm. She lost count of the times she tugged on her wrists, trying to break free from the chair. The tape had taken its toll on her skin.

Ian found the strength to stand up. The pipe he was handcuffed to was plumbed from floor to ceiling with two on/off connections running to an old sink in the corner. He worked the handcuffs up the pipe to chest level, then lifted one foot up, pressing it against the wall. It took him a minute to find the balance; and once he was confident with his position, he jumped into the air and quickly shoved his other foot against the wall. Throughout the night, Ian's attempts at breaking free off the pipe had amused Tara. He crashed to the floor more times than catching his feet on the wall.

"You're going to dislocate your shoulder," Tara cautioned.

Ian grunted as he pulled with all his might, leaning backwards, jerking hard on the pipe several times. "Right now," he said, "I'm close to chewing off my own arm to get out of here."

Ian gave one final tug on the pipe, then jumped back to the floor. "I think I loosened it that time," he said, breathing heavily, shaking the pipe pack and forth.

Tara laughed. "I think you've loosened your brain."

Ian gave Tara a disapproving look. "You're more a glass-is-half-empty kind of girl. Sarcasm is not getting us out of this room." Ian stopped and strained his neck toward the jacket. "Shhh! The phone is vibrating!"

Tara heard the phone too. They had to get that phone before the battery could drain. It was their only chance out of the old farmhouse; otherwise Jake would return to continue his twisted game of torture. Tara started to rock her chair from side to side. Maybe if she could overturn the old, wooden chair, it would crack or break. She could then get free from its sticky duct tape clutches.

At first, the chair didn't move much. Being duct taped in place made it difficult for Tara to shift her weight. The work she did throughout the night to loosen her wrists was paying off. A little extra movement was all that she needed. The left chair leg lifted off the floor a half an inch to the right. The progress excited her, causing her to lose her rhythm. The chair dropped down to a sudden stop.

"Come on, Tara!" Ian yelled. "You can do it! Try again!"

Tara began again, rocking the chair from side to side. Her increased blood pressure triggered the wound to start bleeding again. She used the pain in her hand as fuel to rock the chair more and more. The chair lifted, but this time, Tara was ready. She let her body float with the chair as it hung weightless for several seconds; then she followed the momentum back down, and at the perfect moment, as soon as all four legs touched the floor, she flung her body to the right. The chair lifted higher—it was going over.

Ian cringed, knowing Tara and the chair were about to crash to the floor.

As the chair hurtled toward the floor, Tara instinctively tried to break her fall, but her duct taped hands didn't budge. The chair hit the floor, and her head bounced off the surface.

Tara didn't scream. She lay motionless, not breathing.

Ian watched helplessly, unable to do anything as her red hair hit the floor. "Tara!" he cried, furiously tugging on his handcuffs. After a full minute of wrenching on the pipe and shouting every curse word he could remember, Ian, fighting back his tears, gave up and slumped down on his knees. His rant burned up his last bit of energy, and a wave of sadness swept over him. The phone had, once again, stopped vibrating.

Suddenly, Tara gasped for a breath, filling her lungs with air.

"Tara!" Ian shouted, blinking away the tears. "You're alive!"

She coughed several times, sucking in deep breaths. When she finally spoke, her voice sounded weak. "For some reason," she said, coughing again, "that was not how I saw it play out in my head."

"Well, it's good to know that fall didn't crush your sense of humor," Ian joked. "You scared the hell out of me."

Tara lifted her head slightly. "Now I know why they have stunt doubles," she said, tilting her head down to inspect the chair for damage.

"How does it look?" Ian asked eagerly.

Tara tried to move her arms. The duct tape held firm, and the arms of the chair were solid. Her legs were also still firmly held in place. Panic and frustration pushed Tara to the limit. She flexed her leg muscles back and forth as she let out a few choice curse words. The front right leg of the chair cracked loudly, and Tara's leg shot away from the chair with most of the chair leg still attached.

"HA!" Ian hollered from across the room. "You're my new hero!"

"Not yet I'm not," she protested. "We're far from free."

"Baby steps, Tara. Baby steps. Can you free your other leg?"

Tara fought with the chair some more. She even tried kicking it with her free leg. It was useless; the lower cross braces were too sturdy. She would only end up hurting her free leg.

"It's no use," she sighed, letting her head hang at an awkward angle on the floor.

"Can you get your foot flat on the floor?"

Without lifting her head, Tara repositioned her free leg. When the bottom of her shoe found the floor, she pushed hard, moving the chair an inch or two closer to Ian's jacket in the corner.

"That's it!" Ian cheered.

It took all of her energy to inch the chair across the floor. She dug her heel in as she pushed.

"A little more toward the left," Ian instructed, guiding her to the corner.

Tara stopped pushing. "I'm lying on my right side," she said. "My left is toward the ceiling."

"Sorry," Ian apologized, shaking his head to get his mind straight. "You're doing well. Can you see the door yet?"

Tara stretched her head back as far as she could manage. "Barely."

"Good, just keep yourself angled, so you're facing the door."

Tara pushed a few more times. "My leg is on fire," she said, sounding defeated, letting her leg fall free.

"You're doing great, Tara. You're almost there."

Tara stretched her leg. "I can't keep going on like this."

"Do you think maybe you could push yourself over to flip the chair on its back?

She repositioned her leg and pressed her foot back on the floor at an uncomfortable, odd angle. She closed her eyes and pushed with all her strength. The right side of the chair lifted slightly, but fell back down immediately.

"I can't do it! I'm not strong enough!"

"You can do it, Tara. It's mind over matter."

"Well, then you better get your mind wrapped around the fact that the angry vampire only kept you alive so he can have something fresh to quench his thirst when he gets back. You better get to work on that arm-chewing plan of yours. It's mind over matter, Ian."

"Don't think I won't do it," Ian urged, wondering what he could really do to free himself. He needed to find something to motivate Tara. She needed a fresh dose of adrenaline pumping through her system.

"Tara," Ian said, suddenly reconsidering his plan.

"Yes, Ian, my would-be rescuer. How can I help you?"

There was no other way; Ian dove in head first. "I'm the one who hacked your computer and relayed your personal information to Jake. He found your house because I helped him find it."

Tara lay in disbelief, her anger building.

"I didn't get your phone from the driveway outside. I got it from your crashed SUV."

"You were there!" she snapped, slamming her foot into the floor. "You've been lying to me this whole time!"

"Yes. I live in Chicago, and I'm a freelance hacker. Jake paid me to track you down and hijack your info."

"You asshole!" she cursed, lifting the right side of the chair off the floor, then dropping it back down. "Who does that!"

Ian didn't want Tara to lose track. He wanted her to focus her anger into flipping the chair onto its back. "I did it because Jake works for one of my clients… Atmoro."

That was all it took. Atmoro's name infuriated Tara. "You work for ATMORO!" she roared. "Are you a vampire? You scumbag!"

Tara shut her eyes and screamed as she pushed the chair up as far as she could. Then, as the chair reached its apex, it flipped onto its back, slamming Tara's head into the floor again.

Tara continued shouting at Ian. "You better pray you get out of here before I get my hands on you! Jake will be the least of your problems!"

"You did it!" Ian said excitedly.

"Did what?" she hollered.

"You flipped the chair! I knew you could. You just needed the right motivation."

Tara stopped shouting and looked up at the ceiling, trying to piece together Ian's story. The timeline added up. Her system was hacked, then Jake showed up at her front door. Ian practically put her in this situation. Her eyes flooded with tears, and she allowed her emotions to show.

Ian let her cry for a few minutes before getting her back on track. "I'm sorry," he admitted. "That's all I can say. My conscience kicked in too late. I came to your house to warn you, but I was too late."

Tara sniffled loud, blinking the burning tears from her eyes. "Too little, too late," she said flatly. "You're the kind of hacker who gives the rest of us a bad name."

"I said I was sorry, Tara."

"Well, I didn't hear you because you don't exist to me, Ian, if that's your name."

Ian hung his head down. "Ian is my name. My cyber name is Skywalker."

"The same Skywalker who Jake told Atmoro to find?"

"The one and only."

"When Jake finds out, you're a dead man."

Ian lifted his head, upset with himself for putting Tara in this situation. "I had no idea monsters like that existed. Atmoro was always very professional. He paid in advance… but Jake, well, he is a whole other story. He's a maniac, and I had no idea that I was leading him to kill such a beautiful redhead."

Salty tears burned Tara's eyes. "Maniac is an understatement, and flattery will earn you exactly zero points with me right now. Jake is a blood thirsty, heartless vampire, and right now, he's probably on his way back here to kill us both."

"Well then, we better focus on getting out of here."

"Yes, we better focus," Tara said sarcastically, "so you can hurry back to your evil hacking empire."

"So, my *thanks for rescuing me* kiss is out of the question?"

"Ian, let's just say if we get out of this, and there were a million other guys in line for a rescue kiss, you'd be at the end of the queue."

"One in a million is still a chance," he smiled.

Tara burst out laughing. "If I didn't know any better, Ian, I'd say you're an OK guy."

"You're delirious and suffering from multiple concussions," he joked. "Let's get the hell out of here."

The chair slid a great deal easier on its back, plus Tara was in a much better position to use all her leg muscles to push.

"One more push, and you're there, Tara."

Tara's head lightly bumped off the wall. She pressed her foot up against the opposite wall to turn the chair toward the jacket and pushed hard to flip back over to her side. It took a few attempts at repositioning, but she finally snagged Ian's jacket with her right index finger.

"I've got the jacket," she said, working the jacket with her fingers to search for the phone.

The tape restraining Tara's wrist was tight, making the search slow and difficult. She repositioned the chair several times, dropping the jacket. She had to start from the beginning. The first pocket she reached was empty, and just as she worked her way to the other side, the jacket slipped from her fingers for a second time—she burst out cursing.

Tara was blocking Ian's view. He couldn't see what was going on. "What's wrong?" he asked eagerly. "Is the phone dead?"

"No," Tara grunted in frustration. "I dropped the damn jacket again. Give me a minute. I have to get back over to the other pocket." Tara's fingers brushed against a hard plastic inside a pocket. "Got it!"

Tara clamped the phone between two fingers, and then carefully removed it from the pocket. Several beads of sweat rolled down to her eyes, irritating them and blurring her vision. As soon as the phone was free, she gripped it tightly with her whole hand, nearly crushing the plastic. She closed her eyes and let her head fall to the floor, wishing for a nice hot bubble bath with candles and an unlimited supply of chocolate.

After a minute of rest, Tara slid her finger across the screen to wake her phone up. "MISSED CALLS" flashed in big bold letters across the bright screen. The battery indicator was down to one bar and blinking red. She didn't have much time before the battery would die completely.

"The battery is running on fumes," Tara relayed to Ian. "There isn't enough juice to check the voicemail. We should send a text instead of calling. That will use less battery power."

"Sounds like a good plan. What are you sending?"

Tara's mind was blank from exhaustion. "I don't even know where we are, but we need to hurry."

Ian thought about it. He wasn't exactly sure where they were either. "Atmoro, Jake, vampires, Chicago, HELP," Ian said, hoping that was enough description for Tara's friends to decipher. "Be sure to capitalize help and add a few exclamation points for good measure."

Tara quickly typed in the text message, hoping it would make sense to Erone, and clicked the send button. The screen displayed "SENDING" before going blank.

"The battery's dead," she said sadly.

THIRTY-EIGHT

My phone started vibrating in my pocket. "I'm not sure, Jade," I said, pulling the phone out and motioning for Ember to take over explaining Jade's complicated new life. "I don't know enough about angels to know if you have superpowers or not."

I stood up from the table and walked to the kitchen counter to check my phone. It was a text message from Tara. *It's about time,* I thought to myself.

"Atmoro Jake vampires Chicago HELP!!!!"

My heart skipped a beat. I had to read the message again to be certain my eyes weren't playing tricks on me.

"Get Ashes!" I shouted.

Rain bolted from the cabin to retrieve Ashes from her watch post by the pond.

My hands shook as I called Tara.

"What's going on?" Kasiah asked.

Aerona stood in the cabin's doorway with a blank stare on her face. She felt my emotions taking a turn for the worse. "Tara is in trouble," she said, answering for me.

The call was forwarded straight to voicemail, which, by now, was sure to be full. I contemplated sending a text back, in case Atmoro was monitoring Tara's phone.

"What kind of trouble?" Kasiah probed.

"The Atmoro vampire kind," I said, tossing my phone on the counter.

"What's going on?" Ashes asked, bursting through the door with Rain.

271

"We need to get to Chicago," I said, "and we need to go now."

Aerona grabbed my cell phone off the counter and read the message. "Atmoro has Tara," she said half-heartedly. "Who's Jake?"

"I'd have to guess he's part of Atmoro's crew," I expressed, handing Jade her bag. "Probably another vampire."

"Atmoro?" Jade asked, looking horrified. "I thought that's who we were trying to avoid?"

"He is," Kasiah confirmed. "We are *not* going to Chicago."

"We are," I protested. "Tara knows everything about Jade. We got Tara in this mess, and now she needs our help. We led Atmoro right to her front door. We're not leaving her to deal with this on her own."

"So, we're going to take Jade right to Atmoro," she argued, "and then what, hand her over to the very monster we're trying to protect her from?"

"We can't exactly leave Jade here by herself," I countered. "If Atmoro does get hold of Tara, then it's going to take all of us to get her back. Besides, Atmoro is never going to stop looking for a stone. We need to stop him while we have his attention."

Kasiah threw her hands up. "We don't even know where Tara is for sure, or even if she's the one who sent that message. Chicago's not exactly a small town. Are we just going to drive around and ask if anyone knows where to find a Shadow Vampire's secret hideout?"

I turned to Whisper. "Can you track a cell phone through a text message?"

Whisper shook his head. "Not from here with zero equipment or even a starting point. I left everything on the jet."

Aerona pointed to his satchel. "What about your little magic purse?"

"It's not magic," Whisper said defensively, "and I can't produce complex machinery or electronics from thin air."

"Where's Candice with the jet?" I asked Ember.

"I spoke with her less than an hour ago," she replied, activating her phone. "She's several hundred miles south."

"That won't do," I said, pondering. "Can we get the jet to meet up somewhere with Whisper?"

"Whatever you need," Ember said. "I'll get Candice on the phone right now."

Whisper reached into his leather satchel and pulled out a map of the United States. He spread the map out on the table and started looking for nearby airports. "Here," he said, pointing to the map. "Candice can land in Casper, Wyoming. I can make it there in an hour or so."

"Perfect. You should take Damien with you. The rest of us can fit into the Raptor."

"You plan on driving to Chicago," Aerona questioned.

Ashes studied Whisper's map. "I can get us to Chicago in less than sixteen hours."

"Chicago is fifteen hundred miles from here!" Aerona exclaimed. "There's no way can we make it there that fast. We should just hop a ride on the jet."

"Atmoro has been anticipating our every move," I reminded. "We don't have time to wait for the jet to get back here, land, refuel, then fly to Chicago, not knowing who will be waiting for us on the ground. Even if we don't have trouble when we land, we'd have to pick up a vehicle and drive out of the city, hoping Atmoro wouldn't beat us to the punch again."

"Sixteen hours? No way!" Aerona objected.

"There's only one way to find out," Ashes said, smiling at Aerona. "Let's move."

THIRTY-NINE

Driving from sunrise to sunset, Ashes pushed the Raptor's engine hard; the speedometer only fell below 100 to stop for fuel three times. It was well into the night by the time we crossed into Illinois. The night sky was clear, and the moon, surrounded by a sea of stars, was full and high in the sky. Aerona sulked in the backseat as we passed through Rockford, Illinois at the fifteen-hour mark. We'd make it to the west side of Chicago with time to spare on Ashes's sixteen-hour estimate.

Whisper and Damien had stayed behind to meet up with the jet in Wyoming. Two hours back, we got a call from Candice; they had touched down in Chicago without incident. Whisper had yet to triangulate the origin of Tara's text message. The cell phone wasn't giving off a useable signal, which meant it was off or that the battery was dead. Whisper was tapping into a military satellite to try and track the phone's embedded GPS chip. According to Whisper, a cell phone sends out its last known position just before the battery dies.

My cell phone rang loudly through the Raptor's hands-free synchronization software that Ashes had set up when we started. "Hello," I greeted Whisper. "You're on speaker. Tell me you have good news."

Whisper's voice echoed through the truck's stereo speakers. "I'm downloading Tara's location to the Raptor's onboard GPS unit. The signal is twenty miles southwest of Chicago. The satellite image shows an old, rundown farmhouse at the end of a dead-end. There's not another building for miles in either direction."

"Good work, Whisper. Were you and Damien able to secure transportation from the airport?"

"Yes, Candice used one of her aliases to rent us a suitable vehicle. We're an equal distance from the target location. Damien will meet you there. I'm staying here to secure the jet for our departure."

"Thanks for all your help, Whisper. Tell Damien we'll see him within an hour.

Forty minutes later, we pulled up behind a small, white compact rental car. We were a mile and a half down the main road from the turnoff to the farmhouse.

Damien was leaning against the trunk of the car. "Don't say anything," he warned Aerona as she stepped out of the Raptor.

Aerona, wearing a bright pink T-shirt with *On Medication* stenciled in bold, black script letters, threw her hands up in defense. "Who, me? I like your little white car. I think it's cute."

"Let's focus here," I said, shooting Aerona a save-it-for-later look.

Ember immediately took flight, vanishing into the night sky to check the area around the farmhouse. My eyes followed the streak of sparkling dust trailing Ember.

"What do we know so far?" Ashes asked, buckling the silver clasps on her belt.

Damien spread a map on the hood of the little white car. "The house is two miles down this dirt road," he said, pointing to the location on the map. "When I stopped at the turnoff, I didn't see signs of fresh tire tracks coming or going."

"If Atmoro's here," I said, walking several steps away from the vehicles, staring down the road into the darkness, "he'll know we're coming before we get there."

Kasiah stepped in beside me. "Erone, you still haven't had positive contact with Tara?"

I touched the cell phone in my pocket. "Just that one text message."

"You could be walking into an ambush," Kasiah cautioned. "There's no way of telling who really sent that message."

"If Atmoro sent the message," I said, hoping he did not, "then he'll keep her alive until he lures us in."

A bright light flashed behind us. Ember had returned from her surveillance flight.

"Did you find the house?" I asked, walking back to the vehicles with Kasiah.

"Yes," she said, running her fingers through her wind ruffled hair, "I didn't want to risk being spotted, so I stayed above the trees. The place is pretty secluded. It appears to be abandoned. There's no sign of guards, and there are no lights on inside or outside the house. Everything is quiet."

"Good work. We'll need you in the sky watching our backs when we take the house."

Damien folded the map and tossed it through the open window of his car, then pulled out a small leather drawstring pouch, handing it to me. "Erone, Whisper asked me to give this to you."

"What is it?" I asked, studying the pouch carefully in Damien's hand.

"I'm not sure. He said Ember would know."

I opened the drawstring, pouring the contents into my hand. A tiny, bright white sphere of light hovered above my palm. The marble-sized light appeared to be spinning at a very high rate of rotation. Looking closer, I noticed the ball of light appeared as though millions of microscopic lightning bolts were creating an electrical storm.

"What is it?" I asked Ember.

"It's a grimlight," she explained. "It's a defense mechanism."

Rain bent down to get a closer look. "It looks more like a miniature thunder storm."

"I've seen a grimlight," Ashes said, stepping back. "You should put that back in the pouch before it gets away from you."

"She's right," Ember nodded. "That's to be used only as a last resort. Toss that into the sky, and it will light the night like a bright and sunny Sunday afternoon. It'll knock any vampire right to their knees and send werewolves yelping home. I've seen them burn demons to nothing but a pile of dust."

276

Ember looked at Rain and Ashes. "I'm not sure what it'll do to you, so if it's used, take cover."

Rain took a step back. "Good to know."

I slid the grimlight carefully back into the pouch, then pulled the drawstring.

Ashes checked the magazines of both her handguns. "Time to go," she said, strapping the guns into their holsters.

Kasiah and Damien stayed behind with Aerona to watch over Jade. If all went well, we'd be back at the truck in ten minutes.

I hugged Kasiah tight. "Keep Jade safe."

She squeezed me back. "Keep you safe."

I turned to Aerona. "Don't hesitate to get these guys out of here if you sense things going wrong."

Aerona, as usual, played big sister. "You take care of yourself, little brother. Get Tara and get back here, so we can go have a margarita on Ember's yacht."

"Sounds like good a plan to me," I said.

We left Kasiah, Damien, and Aerona with Jade in the Raptor. Aerona cast a transparency spell on the truck as we walked away. When I looked back, the truck had vanished. It was still sitting right where we left it, but Aerona's spell was bending the available light around the truck. They'd be safe until we returned.

The sky looked as though it was made of black velvet with millions of pinholes from the burning stars. The light of the moon, mostly hidden behind the tall trees, illuminated the gravel road as we made our way to the farmhouse. The three of us stopped at the last turn before reaching the house, and exactly as Ember had described, we saw a two-story farmhouse just off the road. The windows were dark. The white paint on the porch has mostly peeled off, leaving the old wood exposed to the elements. A broken porch swing hung at a sharp angle; one of the rusty chains must have broken long ago. The lawn had not been cared for in years. Tall weeds and saplings had taken over. I noticed a rusty old tractor through the rubble of the small barn that lay collapsed to the left of the house.

I looked at Ashes. Her eyes glowed brightly in the darkness.

"There are two human hearts beating inside," she said, not taking her eyes off the house.

"What about Atmoro?" I asked. "Can you sense him or anyone else?"

"I can hear the two hearts beating in rhythm. One of them is tired and injured. I can tell by their labored breathing. If Atmoro is here, listening to your heartbeat, he will be still and silent."

I hadn't realized it until then, but my heart was running a marathon. I took a second to get myself under control, breathing slow and evenly.

The dirty windows of the house made it impossible to see inside, leaving us only one choice—we had to enter the house blind.

Ashes switched to stealth mode. She pointed to herself, then to her left, and then she pointed for me to move right with Rain. We nodded in agreement.

Ashes disappeared into the darkness.

Rain and I inched our way along the tree line. I stayed close behind as he led the way, stopping several times to listen. Each time, Rain stood as still as a bronze sculpture, holding his breath and listening intently. An owl hooted somewhere deep in the forest behind us. We continued to make our way to the back of the house. There was still no sign of movement from within.

Abruptly, Rain stopped and crouched behind an old, forgotten woodpile stacked just inside the tree line.

"What is it?" I asked quietly, bending down next to him.

Rain shifted his position to get a better view over the chopped wood. "I hear voices," he said, listening intently. "There are two of them… one male and one female."

I struggled to hear the voices. "What are they saying?"

"I can't make out the words," he said. "They're whispering."

The distinct sound of metal clanging on metal echoed from inside the house, breaking the silence. It sounded like someone was grunting in frustration as they thrashed violently at a pipe with a small chain. The clanging and grunting went on for nearly a minute before stopping.

"What the hell was that?" I asked.

I jolted when Ashes, with her English accent, answered from behind us. "They are in the room to the far right."

Rain didn't flinch at the sound of her voice. The look on his face showed he didn't like the fact that Ashes was able to sneak up on him without a sound.

"There," she said, pointing to the corner of the house. "They're in that room."

I looked at the dark window on the far right corner of the house. I didn't see any signs indicating someone was in the house.

Ashes opened her trench coat and crouched down next to us. "A vampire was here. It was a male. His scent tracked through the front door and back out. The trail leads into the woods behind us and returns several yards east." She tilted her head towards the house. "The vampire came out of the woods with a human."

"You're sure the vampire is gone now?" I asked.

"Yes," she reassured me. "The scent stops at the driveway. He left in a vehicle a day or so ago."

"There's blood inside the house," Rain added, speaking for the first time since he was startled by Ashes. "It's human. The blood isn't freshly spilled, but it's there."

Ashes looked at Rain in a peculiar fashion, wondering how he was able to pick up the scent of blood when she could not.

"What do you think?" I asked Ashes.

Ashes peered down the dark dirt road. "I think we need to take the house before the vampire returns with whatever he went to retrieve."

As we moved through the high weeds of the lawn, the owl hooted again from somewhere deep in the forest. Ashes walked backwards, her guns drawn, scanning the dirt road. I noticed the front door wasn't fully closed as we climbed the three steps up to the porch. It looked like someone had slammed it shut too hard, then it sprung back open.

I turned back to check with Ashes.

She nodded her head to enter.

I knew I shouldn't trust a Shadow Vampire with a mission to drag me back to the Shadow World for jumping, but I trusted her.

The house was definitely abandoned; the air was dry and dirty, and the furniture had a thick layer of dust and cobwebs. We moved through the main room to the rear of the house from where Rain and Ashes had heard the two voices.

Rain tried the door handle. It squeaked as it turned open.

"Who's there?" a woman's voice echoed from inside the room.

Rain looked at me for confirmation. I knew without a doubt this was Tara. I nodded once for Rain to open the door.

The door swung open slowly. Rain stepped in first, ready for anything on the other side. The room was empty, except for a young, terrified man handcuffed to a pipe in the far corner, and a red-haired girl duct taped to a fallen chair on the opposite side of the room. The chair was on its side, and the girl's back was turned toward the door. She couldn't see us as we entered.

I ran to the girl's side and knelt beside the chair. "Tara?"

"Erone!" she cried. "I knew you'd find me!"

Tara was injured. Her hand was bleeding, and her face looked like she had gone a few rounds in a cage match. Her clothes were torn and stained with blood, and her tangled red hair hung loosely on her face. Tears streamed from her eyes.

Ashes flipped her wrist to produce a glistening steel blade, then cut Tara free from the chair.

"Are you alright?" I asked, helping Tara up from the chair.

Tara rubbed her wrists and stretched her neck. "I am now."

Ashes flipped the knife shut and tucked it back into her coat. "We need to leave," she insisted.

"What about him?" Rain asked, standing over the guy in the corner.

"That's Ian," Tara said. "He's with me."

Rain grabbed Ian's wrists and snapped the chain between the handcuffs that held him to the pipe.

Ian was amazed at how easily Rain was able to free him. "How did you—"

280

Rain ignored Ian's question as Ember flew into the room, crash landing on Rain's shoulder. She was completely out of breath.

Rain cupped Ember's tiny fairy body in his hands.

Ember drew in a deep breath. "They…" she paused, sucking in another deep breath, "are coming!"

Ashes quietly shut the door to the room. "Correction. They're here."

Ember caught her breath. "I'm sorry," she said. "They were driving with their lights out. I didn't see them until it was too late."

I grabbed Tara by her shoulders. "Who's keeping you here? Is it Atmoro?"

Tara used the bottom of her shirt to wipe the tears from her eyes. "A vampire named Jake," she said, wiping the blood from under her nose. "He works for Atmoro. A day or so ago, he left, saying he'd be back to finish us off."

"I assume I know what they were after." I said, not needing an answer.

Tara summed it up with one word, "Jade."

She fought through the pain of her injured arm and tied her hair back. "Although, I don't believe neither Jake nor Atmoro know what they're looking for exactly. Jake kept screaming about finding him the stone. He wanted to know who I was working for and what information I had about it. I tested him by asking what he wanted with a stupid rock, and he didn't correct me. He just kept screaming about the stone as if it were an inanimate object, not a person. I didn't give her up, Erone, or you."

"I'm so sorry I got you involved in this mess," I said, hugging her. "You did great."

Ashes held her hand up for us to be quiet. "There are two vehicles," she said softly. "They've stopped in front of the house. I can hear six sets of feet on the gravel. Three of them walk lightly—vampires. That's why they were driving with the lights out. The others are heavy footed, most likely werewolves in human form. They do not seem to be in a hurry." Ashes paused to listen. "They've stopped on the porch. They're discussing what to do with the girl. The one in charge told the other two that he has a fresh meal ready for them."

Ian's eyes shot open, knowing he was the meal. Rain wrapped his powerful arm around Ian, covering his mouth as he tried to speak.

Ashes cracked the door open and peered inside the main room. She waved for us to follow her out. We made our way inside and started up the stairs to the second floor. Halfway up, a board creaked loudly under Tara's feet. We all froze. Tara looked at me, her eyes wide.

Two men rushed in through the front door; Ashes was right— werewolves. The two men were gigantic, at least seven feet tall with big, barrel chests and long, shaggy hair. Their arms and necks were as thick as tree trunks.

Ashes knelt down on the stairs and fired two shots at the werewolves, hitting one in the head and the other one in the arm. The werewolf with the wounded arm retreated out the door, transforming into his wolf form as he escaped. The other werewolf lay still but wasn't dead. It would recover from the head wound quickly.

"Move!" Ashes ordered us.

We ducked into side bedroom at the top of the stairs. Ashes fired several shots at the vampires trying to enter the house.

"I can't hold them off forever!" she hollered back.

Rain's eyes blazed a deep dark crimson. He released his grasp on Ian. I had seen this look on Rain's face before. His lips curled into a smile, exposing his deadly, white fangs.

"No!" I yelled, but I was too late.

Rain crashed through the bedroom window, landing on the roof of the porch. Hearing the glass shatter, one of the vampires from outside leapt up to confront him. The vampire was no match for Rain's incredible strength and speed. He sidestepped and spun backwards behind the vampire, breaking his arm in the process. Once behind him, Rain grabbed him by the chin, forcing his head back to expose his neck. The vampire hissed loudly. He was clearly overpowered and outmatched by Rain.

Enormous arms crashed through the porch's wooden roof. A werewolf grabbed Rain by the ankles, pulling him and the vampire down through the splinters. They disappeared into a pile of broken boards.

I grabbed Tara and looked her right in the eyes. "Ember will take you and Ian down the hall to the furthest room. Find a window and climb out the back."

"I'm not leaving without you, Erone!" Tara urged back.

I admired her courage, but it was a fight she could never win. "It wasn't a question!" I said forcefully. "When you hit the ground, run. You'll find my sister at the end of the dirt road."

Tara tried to argue more, but I wouldn't let her. "Go! Now!" I yelled. "Ember, get them out of here!"

"He's right, Tara!" Ian yelled, pulling her hand. "Let's get out of here!"

With Ember leading the way, Ian pulled Tara out of the room and down the hallway towards the back of the house. I closed my eyes and drew in a breath, pulling in all the energy around me. A second later, I was at the stairs. Two werewolves were in their wolf form, one black and the other light brown. The two snarling beasts had Ashes cornered at the bottom of the stairs, blocking her retreat. It didn't seem to faze her. She ran straight at the wall, using it as a springboard to kick herself up and back over the werewolves. She floated above their heads, the muzzles of her guns firing rapidly.

I don't think the landing was what Ashes had expected. Her foot caught an old light fixture on the ceiling, and she tumbled down to the floor, crashing into an old wooden case full of a ceramic bell collection. The werewolves wasted no time and were on Ashes in an instant, pinning her down. She let out a forceful growl, knocking the werewolves back. One of her blows struck the black werewolf, sending it tumbling through the air. It hit the wall and yelped, but in an instant, it was back on his feet and back on Ashes.

Instead of trying to pull the werewolves off, I threw my hands out and grabbed Ashes with my mind, yanking her from under the werewolves and splintered wood, flinging her to the other side of the room. She hit the wall hard, knocking the guns from her hands. She was back on her feet before the dust could settle.

The werewolves were now circling each side of the room, keeping one eye on me as they stalked Ashes. She ripped the legs off a broken chair near her. The two wooden clubs were useless against the werewolves, but any weapon in a Shadow Vampire's hands was a deadly one.

The werewolf at the furthest distance attacked Ashes. The beast sprung from its hind legs, lunging with razor sharp fangs open wide. Ashes smashed one of the chair legs into the hard wooden door frame next to her, shattering it at the tip, leaving a deadly sharp spear tip. She swung the other chair leg, connecting with the werewolf's head. The werewolf yelped in pain as she crushed it against its skull. Ashes forced the jagged end of the spear-tipped chair leg into the werewolf's chest, until the bloody tip of the wooden dagger punctured through its back.

The second werewolf attacked me on the stairs. Saliva dripped from its mouth. Its eyes were black as night and showed no apprehension. These creatures were bred to be unafraid of death. My hands may not move as fast as Ashes, but my mind could run circles around any werewolf. I raised my right hand beside me, the palm facing out. The werewolf leapt up the stairs, snarling like a beast. Halfway up the stairs, the wolf's snout crushed against the invisible wall I had created. The werewolf backed up and tried a second time with the same result. I placed another transparent wall behind it. The werewolf was confounded by the invisible walls. I created a wall on either side of the werewolf, and one more on top to complete the enclosure.

The werewolf was puzzled, trapped in a virtual glass cage. It threw itself into all four sides of the enclosure and tried to break free. Streaks of blood smeared the invisible walls. Realizing it was trapped, the werewolf began to claw at the wooden steps, attempting to dig its way out.

Ashes retrieved her guns from the pile of splintered wood in the corner. "Stop messing around!" she yelled. "Kill it!"

I used Aerona's trick of squeezing water molecules from the atmosphere to create a rainstorm inside the glass cage. The cage filled rapidly with water. The werewolf floated to the top of the cage, kicking its legs furiously, trying to swim free as it gulped for air. It didn't take long for the werewolf to drown and transform back to its human form.

The werewolf transformed into a young, dark-skinned woman with jet black hair and an athletic muscular body. I released the invisible walls. Water gushed down to the main room, leaving the woman's soaking wet nude body on the stairs.

Ashes quickly fired two bullets into the woman's head. "Where's Rain?" she asked, firing a third shot.

"He went out the window," I said, rushing down the stairs and out the door.

Outside, another werewolf lay dead on the porch alongside two vampires with pieces of the wooden swing protruding from their chests. Rain had a third vampire pinned against a police car in the driveway.

Ashes, with both guns drawn, covered us from the sides.

"This," Rain said, squeezing the vampire's neck, "is Jake."

Jake struggled to say something under Rain's powerful grip. He released Jake's throat, then forced him to his knees.

"Fuck you!" Jake cried, spitting blood on the ground.

Rain grabbed Jake by his jaw and pulled his head back.

"Wait!" I yelled to Rain. "We need him."

Jake, not realizing who he was dealing with, tried to flee as soon as Rain released his grip. Jake's reactions were fast, but he was definitely created in this world. Rain caught him effortlessly within the first five steps. He grabbed hold of Jake from the back, tossing him through the air into the side of the police car. The passenger side door caved in from the impact. Jake shook his head, dazed.

"Don't move," Rain warned him.

I turned to Ashes to help find the others. "Ember, Tara, and Ian made it out the back. Please find them and bring them back here."

Ashes disappeared around the corner of the farmhouse.

I bent down to Jake's level. "Where's Atmoro?" I demanded.

Jake hung his head down and shook it from side to side. "Go to hell," he said, breaking into an evil, hysterical laugh. "Go to hell!"

Rain's arm moved too fast for me to see, slamming Jake's head back into the car's door.

"Let's try this again," I said. "Has Atmoro found the stone?"

Jake rested his head back against the car. "Are you deaf? I said go—"

Rain stepped on Jake's leg just below the knee, pinning him to the ground. Jake showed his fangs and snarled. Rain pressed on the leg, snapping it like a twig. I winced from the sound of the bone breaking.

Tara, Ian, and Ashes came walking out of the darkness. A flash of light shined from the corner of the house, followed by Ember. A shower of sparkling dust fell to the ground around her.

"Why is he still alive?" Tara asked.

"We need him to tell us Atmoro's location," I said, walking away from Jake, irritated by his loyalty to Atmoro.

"Atmoro doesn't know shit!" Jake shouted. "I'll kill him myself if I ever see him again! I never asked for him to make me a vampire! I'll kill him!"

I gave Jake another chance. "Tell us what you know, and we'll make this painless."

Rain put his foot on Jake's other leg.

"OK! OK! OK!" Jake pleaded. "I'll tell you everything I know."

Rain grabbed Jake by his shirt and lifted him up to his feet.

"Atmoro has a mole in your operation," Jake said, cringing from the pain of his broken, healing leg. "He's using the mole to track your movements, hoping you'll find the stone for him."

"A mole?" I said in disbelief. "That's impossible."

Jake laughed. "How else do you think he's been able to find you across the country and back?"

I looked at Rain, then at Ashes, trying to piece together Jake's allegation. No one in our team could possibly be feeding Atmoro information. We didn't run across Ashes until we were in Montana, and we found Rain and Ember in Erie; they didn't come to us. The only thing that made sense was Jake making a last effort to save himself.

I turned back to Jake. "Does Atmoro have the location of the hidden door to the Shadow World?"

"I don't know," he snapped. "Google it."

Jake held up his hands in defense as Rain moved in again to grab hold of him. "Whoa!" Jake begged. "Tell your super vampire to back off, and I'll tell what I know."

"Let him go," I instructed. "Jake, you better start talking. Now!"

Jake straightened his shirt. "Atmoro told me this one thing. I'll be breaking his trust if I tell you, and he'll be pissed. It's like top secret information, but you guys are my friends, so I'll tell you." Jake cracked a smile. "Erone, he said your sister is a nice piece—"

Ashes fired two shots into Jake's stomach. He fell to his knees.

"Shit!" he gurgled, spitting more blood. "Don't kill the messenger!"

Ashes moved in closer. "Wrong," she declared. "Killing the messenger sends a message."

Jake forced his head up to look at Ashes. "You bitch!"

Ashes fired two shots into Jake's forehead. "We were wasting time." Jake's body toppled over. "He was never going to tell us anything."

Rain popped the trunk of the police cruiser. He pulled out a small red gas container in one hand and an orange road flare in the other. Ashes dragged Jake's body away from the car, dropping it next to the other two vampires and the werewolf. Rain poured gasoline over the bodies, then ripped off the top from the flare to ignite a red-hot spray of sparks. He tossed the flare, setting fire to the bodies.

Without a warning, a sharp pain squeezed my head from the inside. The pain intensified, knocking me to my knees. I clinched my head from both sides and screamed.

Tara ran to my side. "What is it, Erone?"

This pain was something I had never felt before. It was as if a tiny demon was sitting on my brain, poking my eyeballs with a knife. I couldn't see straight. I couldn't think. My brain was on fire.

I heard Tara's voice, but it sounded as though she was yelling from miles away. "Erone!" she shouted. "What's wrong with him?"

And then, just as suddenly as the pain appeared, it vanished. I lay on the ground in a cold sweat, and that's when it hit me. "AERONA!"

Rain and Ashes vanished in a flash.

"Get in the car!" I barked to Tara, Ember, and Ian. "Now!"

The police cruiser screeched onto the pavement as we turned off the dirt road. I floored the accelerator. A mile down the road, the black Raptor was parked in plain view. Aerona's cloaking spell was down.

I skidded the police car to a stop at the center of the road, leaving the car running as I jumped out and ran to where Rain and Ashes were kneeling over a body wearing a bright pink shirt.

"Get back!" I ordered them.

Rain held me back with his iron grip. "Erone, she's gone."

"NO!" I screamed. "I can feel her! She's still here!"

Ashes touched Rain's shoulder. "Let him go."

I collapsed next to my sister's lifeless body. She was on her back. Thick lines of blood ran down her nostrils and the corner of her mouth. Rain was right; her heart had stopped, but I could feel her energy. There wasn't much there, but I could feel her. I had to work quickly. I ripped her pink shirt open, exposing her black bra. Removing the stun gun from Aerona's side pocket, I yanked out the electrodes with wires attached, placing one just below each of her breasts. I pulled the trigger.

Aerona's body thrashed violently from the high voltage.

I released the trigger, but Aerona's body lay lifeless.

I pulled the trigger a second time.

Aerona's muscles contracted, and her body shook violently again.

I released the trigger, and Aerona's body went still.

"She's gone," Ashes said from behind me.

"NO!" I yelled. "She wouldn't give up on me!"

I placed my hands just above her head and shut my eyes. I felt my energy pass from me to my sister. I opened my eyes and saw Aerona's body begin to glow bright white. I pulled in every ounce of energy I could manage to control, passing it all to Aerona. Her body began to rise up off the road, hovering a few inches above the pavement as energy passed between us. Gradually, I began to lose control. I felt my mind losing its connection with Aerona, and I set her back down gently.

She lay motionless on the pavement, and for the first time in nearly a century, a tear rolled down my face. I lowered my head and shut my eyes.

Hayley flashed through my mind. I finally understood the pain Kasiah had felt when she lost her sister.

"Are you crying?" Aerona asked in a weak voice.

I thought for sure my mind was burned out, playing tricks on me. I opened my eyes to see Aerona's smiling face looking back at me. She brushed the hair from her eyes.

"Awe, you're the little sister I've never wanted," she said, sitting up and looking down at her torn shirt. "You ripped my shirt *and* shot me with a stun gun?"

Ready to pass out from exhaustion, I gave Aerona the biggest hug I could manage. "You are one of a kind."

"Erone," Rain cut in from beside us, "you need to see this."

"It's alright," Tara said, holding her hand out to Aerona. "I've got her, Erone."

"Are you OK?" I asked her.

"Better than new, little brother."

Rain helped me up and took me over to the Raptor. A body lay on the ground next to the truck's driver side door. Rain bent down and rolled the body over—it was Damien. His eyes were open, frozen in shock after capturing his last breath of life. His neck was ripped open, and the front of his shirt was soaked with blood from a violent vampire attack.

I didn't want to look inside the truck or ask the next question, but I did anyway. "Jade and Kasiah?"

"There's no sign of either one," Rain said. "They're gone."

I placed my hand on the truck to prop myself up. "I should have listened to Kasiah," I said in sadness. "She was right. We served Jade up on a silver platter, and Kasiah is probably—"

I couldn't get the words out. I walked away from Damien's body and back to Aerona, where Tara and Ian had pulled the police cruiser off the road. Ian was handing Tara a jacket with POLICE stenciled in bold letters on the back.

"What happened here?" I asked Aerona.

She stuck her arms into the jacket and wrapped it around her shoulders. "I don't know," she said, rubbing her forehead. "I don't remember a single moment from when you guys left to just now. It's like my memory has been erased. There's an empty hole where these memories should be."

I leaned against the car next to Aerona. "Atmoro has a warlock working with him," I said, finally making sense of how Atmoro was able to track us. "I should have seen this."

"How could you have possibly known Atmoro had recruited a warlock?" Aerona disputed, zipping up the police jacket. "Don't beat yourself up. Use that energy to find Jade and Kasiah."

I thought about it for a minute. I knew what we had to do. "Atmoro will keep Jade alive until the last possible minute. He won't risk losing her blood. He'll sacrifice her at the secret door to the Forgotten Shadow City." I looked at Tara. "We need to find how Atmoro plans on crossing into the Shadow World."

"I think," Ian added hesitantly, "I may know the place you're looking for."

FORTY

"You sure know how to travel in style," Ian commented, climbing the stairs into Ember's Star II.

"Welcome aboard," Andrea greeted him. "A computer is ready at the table. It's linked to a secure fairy satellite."

Ian thanked Andrea, then sat down to get to work. On the way to the airport, Ian had explained to us that Atmoro employed him as a freelance hacker. Several weeks back, Atmoro contacted Ian to hack the U.S. Social Security database to compile a list of names and addresses of anyone with a name related to rare stones. Less than a week after Ian provided Atmoro the final list, he had requested Ian to hack the U.S. Geological Society database to compile a detailed list of their entire inventory and locations around the country. Atmoro seemed particularly interested in finding a rare, glowing nodule.

According to Ian, Atmoro always paid on time through wire transfers. Ian had assumed Atmoro was a typical white-collar criminal, trying to build his rare stone collection with unusual pieces that would make his rich friends jealous. He had no idea the stone Atmoro coveted was a flesh and blood human, one he intended to sacrifice in order to open a secret door to an inescapable prison deep within a different world.

As Ember's Star II rocketed down the runway, I watched Tara hovering over Ian's shoulder as lines of code streamed down the laptop's screen.

"Tell the pilot to head south toward Arizona," Ian directed, hacking through cyberspace. "As a precautionary measure, I always destroy all original information for all my customers, including Atmoro. It's basically a safety step, in case they get any ideas about incriminating me in their crimes."

"That's understandable," I said, watching the runway grow smaller out my window. "Any information will be useful."

Ian typed a few more commands. "Got it," he said, excitedly, leaning back in his chair. "Atmoro's smart, very smart. He did make one mistake, though, assuming he was smarter than me. I destroy any data trails to my front door, but I also build backdoors for future access of any server I touch. Atmoro always used the same e-mail server to receive my files, and apparently, he never permanently deleted any of my e-mails or files. Sedona, Arizona is our target."

"Sedona, Arizona?" I asked. "Are you sure?"

"Positive," Ian stated, typing in a few more commands, then pointing at the screen. "According to these e-mail confirmations, Atmoro chartered a plane to Sedona from right here in Chicago. The plane departed an hour ago."

I nodded to Andrea. She rushed to the cockpit to inform Candice of our destination.

"Good work, Ian," I said, standing up. "Copy everything from that server but do it discreetly. We don't want Atmoro knowing we can track his movements."

Rain and Ashes were seated at the rear of the plane. Rain had his headphones on and stared into the emptiness of the night sky. Drained of energy, Aerona was already fast asleep in the seat next to Rain.

"We have a location," I said, sitting beside Ashes. "Sedona, Arizona."

Ashes nodded. "We're going to need a recharge when we land."

"A recharge?" I asked, swallowing hard, realizing what she had meant. She and Rain needed human blood to supercharge their strength before taking on Atmoro.

I looked towards the front of the jet at Tara and Ian. "You don't mean?" I asked quietly.

"No," she reassured me. "We'll hunt once we land... find someone local. Rain has considerable control over his thirst for human blood. Don't worry, we won't kill them."

"I don't want to know the details," I said, sighing heavily. "I'm going to get some rest. Please wake me before we land."

It was a five-hour flight to Sedona. I spent most of the flight trying to push thoughts of what Atmoro must be doing to Kasiah out of my head. The chance that Atmoro had kept Kasiah alive was slim. I fought off sleep for as long as I could, knowing it would surely bring nightmares. Eventually, the weight of my eyelids was too much to hold back; my mind and body were both drained of energy, and just like Ashes and Rain, I needed a recharge.

It seemed as if it were only a few seconds from when I let myself drift into dreamland to when my eyes shot open from Aerona shaking me awake.

"We'll be on the ground in thirty minutes," Aerona said.

I was momentarily disoriented, my head pounding. If I had dreamt, I couldn't remember a single second of it. I rubbed the back of my stiff neck and glanced out the window. The sun was just appearing over the horizon, stretching its deep, dark orange rays over unique crimson and rust-colored mountains. I wondered if it was the Grand Canyon. Wherever we were, it was one of the most beautiful landscapes I had ever seen.

"And you drool," Aerona snapped, buckling herself into the seat next to me.

I ran the back of my hand along the sides of my mouth, and sure enough, I had been drooling. "Any new information?" I asked her; she was now wearing a black T-shirt with "Ninja" stenciled on the chest.

"Tara said she wanted to talk to you as soon as you woke. She's up front," Aerona said, staring out the window. "Isn't that beautiful? The colors are breathtaking. I've never seen a red like that."

I took one last look out the window before catching up to what Tara and Ian had discovered in cyberspace.

"Here, Erone," Ian said, standing up as he saw me. "You can have my seat."

"Thank you, Ian, but if I sit down, I'm falling right back asleep."

"Just one minute," Tara said, typing incredibly fast.

Streams of digital code scrolled down the screen alongside a typical webpage. Tara was accessing the source code that composed the webpage, essentially looking behind the scenes. She entered two more quick commands, then pressed the enter key, closing the secondary code screen. The main webpage appeared to be part of a cell phone provider's site. Tara clicked on the "My Account" link, opening a new window that displayed a list of phone numbers, dates, and times.

"What are we looking at?" I asked.

"This is Atmoro's phone account," Tara explained, highlighting a specific phone number before applying a filter to isolate that number in each row through the long list. "Well, one of his accounts. Do you recognize this number?"

"No," I said, running the number through my head. "Should I?"

"I'm not sure, but over the past few days, this is how Atmoro has been receiving updates of your location."

Tara expanded each highlighted row with the associated text message listing our specific time and location, matching our exact movements over the past few days.

"And the phone number?" I asked.

"It's a ghost phone," she replied. "The number has been cloned and sent through too many towers to track the origin."

"Any good news?" I asked, hoping for something, anything.

"Yes," Ian added from behind me. "The messages have stopped. There hasn't been a communication in over six hours."

"How is that good news?" I asked.

Ian started grinning, "It means Atmoro is unaware we are about to touch down in Sedona, only an hour after he arrived."

I thought about that for a few seconds. This was the first time we had been able to make a move without Atmoro being one step ahead of us.

I looked past Tara to the front of the jet, motioning to Andrea.

Andrea jumped up and hurried over to our seats. "Yes, Erone, how can I help you?"

"Please inform Candice that we'll be landing in Flagstaff instead of Sedona."

"Yes, sir," she nodded, hurrying to the cockpit.

"Flagstaff?" Tara questioned. "Won't that put us another hour behind Atmoro?"

"Yes," I said, considering, "but it's necessary. Atmoro's been able to track every move we made, even in the air. I don't want to take the chance. He may have a team on the ground waiting for us to land. The Sedona airport is small—located on the top of a mountain—and we'll be trapped in the jet without options. Plus, flagstaff is closer to us. We'll be on the ground in just a few minutes."

"He's right," Ian agreed. "We would be sitting ducks."

The plane banked slightly to the right, then leveled out on our new flight path to Flagstaff.

"Wheel's down in ten minutes," Candice announced over the intercom. "Please take your seats at this time."

The plane touched down on the runway with nothing more than a slight bounce. Candice steered towards the north end of the runway. The Flagstaff airport didn't look much larger than Sedona, but chances were that it wouldn't be swarming with vampires waiting for us to arrive.

With our last-minute change of destination, we didn't have time to reserve a hanger or transportation. We had to improvise.

As we neared the end of the airport, Candice spun the nose of the jet around, jolting to a stop only fifteen feet away from the last doorway at the end of the terminal.

"We'll need to move quickly," Ember said, unlocking and opening the cabin door. "Atmoro touched down little over an hour ago, and we have an hour's drive to Sedona."

Tara stopped me at the door and handed me a tablet. "Here, take this. Ian downloaded all the satellite images and GPS coordinates he had provided Atmoro."

I swiped my finger across the tablet's screen, waking it up. The screen came to life, displaying a wide-view satellite image of dark red mountains. I touched a bright yellow push pin icon, and the image zoomed in. The resolution was so clear it was as if I was flying just above the rocks.

"That's the location where the nodule was found by the geologist," Ian said. "It's very secluded. You won't be able to drive that deep into the mountains, not even with a modified four-wheel drive. You'll have to tackle the last two miles on foot."

Ian swiped his finger across the screen. The image we had been reviewing flipped behind another image. "The road ends at a trailhead. Atmoro chose this route since it would get him closer to ground zero than any other."

"Tick tock," Ashes reminded us from outside the jet.

I turned to Tara. "Thanks," I said, hugging her. "I owe you for this."

"Don't worry about it," she responded, squeezing me back. "You say it like I had anything else to do besides being tortured by a vampire. Just get the girls back."

"We will," I assured her, hoping I could.

As soon as Andrea shut the Jet's door, Candice throttled up the powerful engines, leaving Ashes, Rain, Ember, Aerona, and me behind. They would refuel the jet and get back in the air to circle Sedona, just in case we needed to be extracted in a hurry.

There was no time to fill out the huge stack of paperwork involved with renting a car from the airport, so we made our way to the passenger drop off area instead. The sun was racing into the sky, heating up a nice summer day in Arizona. I slid my sunglasses on and scanned the large parking lot.

Aerona, in her "Ninja" shirt, stopped beside me. "Why don't we just snag one of the cars in long-term parking?" she suggested. "We'll be long gone by the time they do the nightly count and license plate verification."

"That's not a bad idea," I said, still scanning the parking lot. "As long as we can get past the security gate."

Before we could decide one way or the other, a large, older white car pulled right up to the curb in front of us. The car's front right tire hit the curb hard, jarring the driver back and forth. Rain had to step back to avoid being hit as it bounced back off the curb, stopping abruptly.

"We're taking this one," Rain said, peering at me over the top of his sunglasses.

296

I didn't have time to argue. He stepped off the curb and walked around the front of the car. The driver's door swung open, blocking Rain's path, and a woman, maybe seventy years old, stepped out. She had on a crisp, clean, cream-colored skirt and matching suit jacket. An oversized brimmed hat, complete with brightly decorated flowers, was balanced on top of her neatly done hair. A gaudy diamond necklace matched her large dangling earrings.

"The bags are in the trunk," the woman said, tossing the car keys to Rain. "And if you bring them to the gate for me, there's a crisp five-dollar bill in it for you. Oh, and when you park the car, use the garage. I don't want it left out in the sun. I'll be gone a month."

The woman waddled around the rear of the car and into the airport. The look on Rain's face was priceless; he just stood there holding the keys, shocked.

I opened the passenger side door, then slapped the roof with my hand to snap Rain out of his trance. "Let's go, cabby!"

"This car smells," Aerona remarked, pinching her nose. "I think she has a cat. Maybe two."

"Ashes," I said, ignoring my sister as usual, "we'll make a stop outside the city for you and Rain to recharge your batteries."

"Recharge their batteries?" Aerona asked, confused. "What the hell does that mean?" Then it struck her. "Wait... that doesn't mean?"

Ashes flashed a smile and ran her tongue along her razor sharp fangs. "We can settle for a snack in the car."

"Not funny," Aerona muttered. "Not funny."

Within a few minutes, we were on driving south toward Sedona, leaving Flagstaff and Route 66 behind us. Thick evergreen forests lined both sides of the winding road. The landscape wasn't what I had envisioned the desert state of Arizona to be like. As we continued south down the Colorado Plateau into the Coconino National Forest, the forest blended together with scattered, bright green desert vegetation.

Halfway down a zig-zag set of switchbacks, Rain drove off the road unexpectedly, right in the middle of a sharp curve, sliding to a stop in a cloud of dust behind a compact red sports car parked at a hiker's pull off.

Rain looked back at Ashes, and she nodded her head.

"Oh my God," Aerona exclaimed, disgusted.

"We'll be back shortly," Ashes said.

Ashes and rain vanished into the forest in search of the hikers.

"Am I the only one who doesn't approve of this?" Aerona complained.

"It's a necessary evil," Ember replied. "Rain has incredible control over his thirst. They won't kill the hikers. We knew the intense Arizona sunlight would drain them both. If we're to take on Atmoro, we need them at their best."

FORTY-ONE

Within ten minutes, we were back on the road. Rain and Ashes now had enough human blood in their system to beat the intense Arizona sun climbing high into the sky, determined to show us a hundred degrees before noon.

I scanned the satellite image on the tablet's screen. "Rain, in two miles, there should be a turn to your right that will take us a few miles off the main road into the mountains." I zoomed in on the image. "It looks like that trail will dead end at a canyon. We'll have to go on foot from there."

"What happens if we're too late?" Aerona asked, always the cynic. "And Atmoro's already crossed over to the Shadow World?"

"We're going after him," I said, without looking at her. "We can't let him reach the Forgotten Shadow City with Jade."

She turned to Ashes. "And you?"

"I am a warrior of the Shadow World," Ashes replied. "I have taken an oath to protect my world and its people. If successful, Atmoro will risk the safety of everyone in my world. Therefore, your goal is now mine. We must stop Atmoro from reaching the city and sacrificing the girl."

Aerona stared out the window. "And when we do?"

Ashes did not hesitate or attempt to sugarcoat her answer. "I am to deliver you and your brother to Malance for the crime of jumping to the Light World. You will be sentenced accordingly."

Aerona did not respond.

At the base of the Colorado Plateau, just north of Sedona, the thick, evergreen forests gave way to deep, dark, red mountains with veins of lighter oranges and gray limestone surrounded by desert vegetation. The iconic prickly pear cacti and agaves were scattered throughout the massive red rock formations, carved meticulously by the elements over centuries.

"The turn off is coming up," I directed Rain.

Rain slowed the car, then turned off the main road. After two miles or so, the road changed from pavement to a simple, red-dirt access road barely wide enough for one vehicle. A mile later, we passed by a large yellow caution sign with bold, black letters: *"ROAD NOT MAINTAINED. 4-WHEEL DRIVE VEHICLES ONLY. CAUTION: WATCH FOR FALLING ROCKS."*

The dusty dirt road wound deep into the mountains, slowly transitioning to more of a rugged trail than a road. Rain struggled with the steering wheel, spinning it left and right to avoid large rocks and deep washed-out sections. The tires spun gravel, pushing us up a slight incline and closer and closer toward a steep mountain face. Dried branches of small desert trees and plants brushed down sides of the car, scratching off the white paint. The car's undercarriage scraped loudly as we passed over a large, exposed flat rock that spanned the width of the trail. Then, just after a nearly 180 degree turn in the trail, Rain brought the car to a sudden halt.

"No way!" Aerona exclaimed, judging the obstacle ahead. "There's no way we're making it around that."

The trail ahead was nothing more than a narrow ledge wrapping its way around the mountain. A massive, red rock wall bordered the left side, and a sheer drop, at least a thousand feet deep, lined our right.

Rain looked at me for approval.

"We don't have a choice," I said, reluctantly. "We're still ten miles out."

Rain inched the car forward. "Keep an eye on that ledge, Erone."

I had a death grip on the armrest as Rain crept along the trail. Aerona gripped the back of my seat tightly. The driver's side mirror struck the rock wall, which cracked the glass. I heard several small rocks tumbling over the ledge outside my window. At one point, the car's front right tire fell into a large rut, rocking the car to the right down the edge. Rain floored the accelerator, spinning the tires on the loose rocks, lurching the car forward out of the rut and closer to the rock wall. The sound of metal grinding against rock sent a shiver down my spine. The wall gained patches of white automobile paint.

After a hundred yards of tense stunt driving, the trail widened again, weaving its way through thicker vegetation and smaller trees, ultimately ending at the base of a tall mountain.

"Which way, Magellan?" Rain asked jokingly.

"According to the satellite image," I said, zooming in, "Atmoro is to crossover on the other side of this mountain." I turned to Ember. "Do you feel comfortable flying?"

Ember's eyes scanned the mountain, calculating the risks. "You believe Atmoro has a warlock working with him?" she asked.

"Yes. That's the only way he could have possibly erased Aerona's memory."

"If I'm not back in two minutes," Ember cautioned, removing a tiny, leather pouch from under her shirt, "assume that I've been compromised."

I nodded. "Be safe."

Rain gave Ember a quick hug. "Fly high. Fly fast."

Ember disappeared around two large boulders, and then, in a flash of white light, she was off into the sky, moving faster than my eyes could follow.

The rest of us hiked through the mountains, blazing our own trail. We moved quickly with Ashes leading the way. She navigated through the rough terrain with ease, even leaping onto a twelve-foot tall boulder that blocked our way. It surprised me that she still had on her full-length leather jacket in the Arizona heat. Although, I guessed heat wouldn't bother a Shadow Vampire as much as direct sunlight, and the jacket probably blocked most of the sun.

Casting a levitation spell, Aerona and I lifted ourselves off the ground, floating to meet Ashes on top of the boulder.

"The mind is a powerful weapon," Ashes remarked, studying us closely as we lowered ourselves.

"You haven't seen anything yet," Aerona countered, stepping past Ashes.

Rain stopped. "Ember has returned," he said.

Ember walked out from behind a tree to our right, discreetly tucking her pouch back under her shirt. She was out of breath.

"Any sign of Atmoro or the girls?" I asked, handing her a bottle of water.

Ember downed a long gulp. "Not exactly," she said, "but there are two Jeep Wranglers parked half a mile from here. It looks like they drove in on a newer, but still extreme, trail from the east." She handed the bottle back to me. "There's more. About halfway up the mountain, there's a cave guarded by two trolls and some creature I've never seen before."

"What does this other creature look like?" Ashes asked.

"This is going to sound weird," Ember said, doubting her own thoughts, "but it looks like a saber-toothed tiger."

"A grawl," Ashes declared, not surprised.

"A grawl?" Ember asked. "I've never heard of a grawl."

"Saber-toothed tigers are extinct in your world," Ashes explained, removing her jacket, "not ours. Grawls are a species of saber that has been bred for centuries with one purpose, to be guardians of the gates to the Shadow World. Their speed will match Rain's, and they can span fifty feet in a single leap. Their dagger-like fangs can puncture through the steel of a car door, then release a potent venom that will burn your veins from the inside."

"Can we survive the venom?" Rain asked.

Ashes unbuckled the silver clasp and handed her belt to Rain. "Not without losing your mind from the excruciating pain."

"Oh, great," Rain said. "So avoid the sharp end of a grawl?"

"Avoid every end of a grawl," she emphasized. "You've never seen a creature like this one. They are not to be played with or taken lightly. This is no joke. Do not mess around with them."

"Looks like you have a plan," I said.

Ashes unbuckled the leather strap around her neck. "The plan," she continued, removing the strap and unzipping her tight, leather body suit down to her chest, "is to not get bitten."

"I like it," Rain added. "It's a simple plan."

Ashes smiled as though she was eager to run out on the field for her next soccer match. "I'll take care of the grawl. You guys get passed the trolls and reach Jade."

"You just said that you'll die if it bites you," I reminded her.

"I did," she said, tightening her boots. "I also said I am sworn to protect the people of the Shadow World. If it preserves the safety of my people, my life is expendable."

Aerona placed her hand on my shoulder. "Erone, there is no use arguing with her. She's a soldier, and she will do whatever is necessary to protect her people. Besides, this is our only chance at getting out of her sight."

I won't lie; it hurt me to see Ashes taking such a huge risk, but as much as I hated to admit it, Aerona was right. When the time comes, Ashes would not hesitate to turn us over to Malance.

"I don't wish her harm," I whispered to Aerona.

"Me neither," Aerona admitted, "but I do wish I would not end up in the very prison we are trying to prevent Atmoro from compromising."

"We must move swiftly," Ashes advised. "Once I lead the grawl away from the entrance, the trolls will be caught by surprise, making them easy targets for you."

We carefully made our way to where Ember had seen the trolls and the grawl, stopping a couple hundred feet west of the cave. Several large, rust-colored boulders had been moved to expose the cave's entrance. Two ugly trolls, armed with heavy broadswords, were guarding the cave's entrance. One held onto a length of steel chain—the size typically used to pull logs out of forests—as a leash to control the grawl. Ember was right; the grawl's copper color fur and wide, commanding stance resembled a saber-toothed tiger. The beast was at least four feet tall at the shoulders and twice as long. It must have weighed close to five hundred pounds. Two large, ten-inch-long poison filled fangs protruded from the sides of its mouth. Its piercing eyes scanned the mountain below, searching for any signs of movement.

Ashes pointed to herself and then to her right. The rest of us nodded. We watched her maneuverer silently down into position below the cave's entrance. Once she was satisfied that she had a clear escape route behind her, she intentionally stepped on a large, dead branch to attract the grawl's attention.

The beast's head snapped in the direction of the cracked branch, voicing a low rumble from its powerful chest, searching for whatever caused the noise. Ashes stepped into plain view, locking eyes with it. The troll on the other end of the leash stumbled forward, struggling to hold on; and after two more hard yanks, the troll released the chain. The grawl tore down the mountain with incredible speed straight for Ashes.

Ashes didn't move a muscle.

"What's she waiting for?" Aerona whispered.

I nudged her with my elbow, holding my finger to my lips; though, I wondered the same, since the grawl would be on Ashes in another three or four strides.

Only milliseconds before the grawl could reach her, Ashes took off like a jack rabbit. Her movements were a blur. She moved much faster without her jacket and weapons. The grawl moved as though it was fixed to rails, turning sharply to align itself right behind her. The two raced down the mountain side, weaving through a maze of cactus and bush.

Ashes must have sensed the grawl closing in. She leapt high into the air to clear a large boulder and twisted her body in midair to face the grawl, catching it off guard. She grabbed the grawl by its front legs, then yanked it to the ground, slamming them both down hard into a cloud of dust.

The trolls strained to see what the grawl was after. Ashes's plan had worked—the trolls were distracted.

"Now!" I yelled to Rain.

Rain and I moved in on the trolls from the side. Rain dodged the first troll, crashing into the second one, knocking it backwards. The troll swung its long broadsword, but missed Rain completely. The sword crashed against an enormous boulder with a loud clang, spraying sparks. Rain struck the troll again, low in the legs, and knocked it back further towards the ledge.

The other troll turned its attention to me and raised its sword to attack. I narrowed my eyes and pulled in energy, then used my mind to lift a large red boulder into the air. The troll swung its sword at the hovering boulder, hitting it on the first try. The boulder cracked in half and crumbled to the ground.

Rain soared past my face, crashing on his back into the mountain next to the cave's entrance. Loose rocks dropped from above, burying him. The trolls were much faster and stronger than the other trolls I had ever seen, but they were no match for my mind. I exhaled slowly, settling my heartrate, working my way into one of the troll's minds. With my hands gripping the hilt of an invisible sword, I raised my arms up high, compelling the troll to mimic my movement. The troll's mind was a dark place, but it was easy to manipulate. I swung my arms down diagonally to my side, making the troll follow. Blood spilled onto the rocks as the long sword sliced deep into the other troll's arm. It released a high-pitched screech from the pain. I raised my arms again, lifting the troll's arms and sword high into the air. The wounded troll, in an effort to defend itself, rammed the tip of its sword straight into the torso of the troll I was controlling. I slammed my arms down to the ground, burying the sword into the other's shoulder. They both shrieked out in pain. The two trolls began fighting between themselves, pushing themselves back and over the cliff's edge together.

I helped Rain out from the pile of fallen rocks. His face was bloodied, and his left arm suffered a compound fracture; a sharp piece of bone stuck out through a gaping wound. He pressed his palm on the end of the broken bone, then screaming in pain, he shoved it back into his arm. I almost passed out from just the thought of his agony.

Ember ran toward Rain as he collapsed to his knees.

"NO!" I yelled, grabbing Ember, holding her back. "He's in his own world right now! It's too dangerous!"

Rain's deadly fangs dripped with saliva like a wild beast. His face cringed as he repositioned his broken bone before using his uninjured arm to set the broken arm straight. The energy Rain gained from the hikers' blood flowed through his veins, energizing him like a dose of adrenaline. I turned Ember's head away as he let out another fierce cry.

When I turned back around, I was not expecting to see Rain on his feet. His eyes were shut, and he was breathing heavily, but the wound on his arm was nothing more than a thin red line on his skin. His eyes snapped open, and his breathing steadied. He ran the back of his hand over his lips to wipe the blood from under his nose.

Ember ran toward Rain, wrapping her arms around him.

Rain embraced Ember. "Ashes?" he asked.

"I don't see her," I said, scanning the terrain below us for any signs of Ashes or the grawl. "We can't wait. She's on her own."

The sunrays didn't penetrate beyond the first turn inside the cave. A tiny blue flame floating over Aerona's palm lit our way along the tunnel. It was shockingly cold beneath the mountain, probably a drop of twenty degrees. The tunnel appeared to have been dug out by hand long ago. The walls narrowed to a point where we had to walk in a single file. Rain led the way with Aerona and her tiny light right behind him.

"How will we know when we cross over?" Rain asked. "What if this goes on for… wait, I see a light ahead."

We all froze.

"Is there movement?' I whispered. "Can you hear voices?"

"No and no," Rain answered. "It's a blue haze, similar to Aerona's light."

Aerona curled her palm, extinguishing the tiny flame, and we moved forward cautiously.

A minute later, around the final curve, the tunnel ended at an opening. One by one, we stepped out and onto a ledge, a mirror image of the one we had just entered from. The sky was velvet black and almost nonexistent. It was dark and empty. The blue glowing light was shining up from below the ledge.

I knew at once what was emitting the soft, blue light—sapphire trees.

We had crossed over to the Shadow World.

FORTY-TWO

I felt a wave of anxiety pass through Aerona; her heart was racing like a scared rabbit being chased by a hungry fox. Aerona knew the risks of us being in the Shadow World as well as what would happen if we were apprehended. I'm sure she felt my own hesitation about stepping back into our forgotten lives.

"I thought the elves built a backdoor to the prison?" Aerona asked. "All we did was cross over to the Shadow World."

I stepped closer to the ledge. "The Shadow Council must have opened this unprotected transport tunnel to allow the elves to come and go as they built the secret entrance to the Forgotten Shadow City. We need to make our way to the prison, quickly."

Ember sat down gently against the rock wall, curling her arms around her knees. "I'm not supposed to be here," she sobbed. "I can feel it."

I knelt down next to Ember. "Ember, what do you mean you can feel it?"

"I feel nothing," she said, her voice melancholic, "and that's the problem. In the Light World, I felt alive... wonderful energy. But here..." Ember stopped. A tear rolled down her cheek. She turned her face away. "I feel nothing. I feel dead."

I reached out and placed my hand on Ember's arm. She flinched. I didn't know what to do or say. I had never met anyone from the Light World who had crossed over to the Shadow World.

Aerona knelt down next to us. "It's OK," she said softly. "You are very much alive. It's the lack of the sun's energy that you are feeling... or rather not feeling."

Ember looked up into the darkness where the sun would have been in the Light World.

"When I first jumped to the Light World," Aerona explained, "I felt the same way—as if an enormous weight had been placed on my shoulders. My mind was full of energy, and I was scared it was about to explode at any moment. The energy of the sun from your world is very powerful."

Ember's eyes filled with tears. "Are we dead?" she asked. "Did we have to die to cross over?"

"No," Aerona replied calmly, "you're not dead. That's just a myth told to people from your world to keep them from being curious of the Shadow World."

"But I am," Rain added, standing at the ledge's edge. "Or, at least, I was dead in the Light World. I can feel a new kind of energy, and my blood-thirst is gone."

"You're home, Rain,' I said. "This is where you belong. You don't have a thirst for blood because the sun is no longer draining your energy. Your strength will grow considerably here."

Rain looked over at the forest of beautiful sapphire trees; their blue leaves lit the valley as though the trees were a soft, glowing carpet. The valley below the ledge was alive with color. A small kaleidoscope of cobalt butterflies flew passed us, gently flapping their bright blue wings. The Shadow World's lack of sunlight allowed the natural beauty of many species to flourish.

I went back to check Ember's condition. "We need to move quickly," I said, placing my hand on her shoulder. "If you don't feel comfortable, now is the time to go back."

Ember's arms were still wrapped tightly around her legs. "I'm OK," she said, lifting her head up before standing. "Let's get Jade and Kasiah, and go home."

"How do we find Atmoro?" Rain asked, peering down over the ledge.

"Atmoro won't waste any time," I said. "He'll head straight for the Forgotten Shadow City. According to the elf scrolls that Tara had found, they built a secondary gate at the base of the east mountain near Arcadia."

"Arcadia?" Ember asked. She was now back in the game.

"The small town of Arcadia guards the entrance to the Forgotten Shadow City," Aerona explained. "Arcadia is the mirror image of Sedona in your world."

"That would be twenty miles from here," Ember exclaimed. "How do we get there?"

I nodded to my sister. "Aerona will handle our travel arrangements."

A smile spread across Aerona's face as she moved to the very edge of the ledge. Tilting her head back and gracefully spread her arms far out to her sides. She closed her eyes and opened her mind, stretching her hands wide with her palms up.

"What are you doing?" Rain asked, taking a step toward Aerona. "Aerona, you're too close to the edge. You're going to fall!"

"She's making a phone call," I said. "If I were you, I'd stand back."

"A phone call?" Ember asked, confused. "Who's she calling all the way out here and without a phone?"

Before I could explain, Aerona bent down, then leapt off the ledge down into the darkness with her arms spread far apart and her legs pressed tightly together. It was as if she was making a picture-perfect Olympic dive into an invisible pool far below.

Rain's reflexes kicked in, but he was too late. "Aerona!" he screamed, racing to the edge only to see her disappear into the darkness.

Ember grabbed my arm. "What has she done?" she cried.

I pulled Ember back toward the rock wall. "Rain, you might want to—"

A rush of air erupted from below the ledge, knocking Rain off his feet and onto his back in a cloud of dust. An enormous, black dragon soared straight up passed the ledge; its impressive twenty-foot wingspan created strong gusts with each motion. The burning tip of the dragon's long tail snapped like a whip as it vanished into the black sky.

Rain was back on his feet instantly. "What the hell was that?" he shouted, searching the sky for whatever had just knocked him off his feet.

The dragon reappeared from the darkness above, landing hard on its powerful hind legs in front of Rain. Its front legs slammed down, blowing up a large cloud of dust. The beast tucked its massive wings in, then curled its tail around to extinguish the flaming tip.

Rain shifted his position to his fighting stance, flashing his deadly, white fangs.

In a burst of light, Ember transformed into her tiny fairy form.

I tried to stay as still as possible. "Be calm," I whispered to Rain and Ember. "She can sense your fear."

"That's because we *are* terrified," Ember said, landing on my shoulder. "How do you know it's a she?"

The dragon lowered its head and stepped towards us, shaking the ledge with every step. An intricate pattern of glistening, black scales—stronger than any steel armor—covered the dragon from head to tail. The scales smoldered bright scarlet along the edges, and as the dragon's heart slowed to conserve energy, the scarlet edges began to transition to a darker maroon. Stopping in front of me, the dragon's three-foot wide head was now only inches away from my own. It exhaled a warm breath through its nostrils, blinking its baseball-sized, stone-grey eyes slowly. I reached out and touched the center of the dragon's snout. The intricate pattern of scales felt unexpectedly cool.

"It's been a long time, Jasmine," I said, gently massaging my hand up and down between her nostrils.

Aerona leapt down from Jasmine's back, landing gracefully beside her old, dragon friend. She held out a handful of small green berries for Jasmine. A long tongue shot out from Jasmine's mouth, exposing her rows of long, dagger-like teeth. The small treat vanished in a second, but the energy from the berries would satisfy Jasmine for hours.

"I have missed you, my friend," Aerona said, rubbing Jasmine's long neck.

Jasmine snorted and blinked her eyes twice at Aerona.

I recalled when my father brought Jasmine home for Aerona's tenth birthday. At that time, Jasmine could fit in Aerona's palm. She flapped her tiny wings, trying to take flight as she looked up at Aerona for the first time. Attempting to burn Aerona's hand, a small puff of fire shot out of Jasmine's mouth. Aerona returned fire with a tiny flame from the tip of her finger, and from that day on, they were inseparable.

"We don't have time for a proper reunion," I said to Aerona and Jasmine. "We need to move quickly."

Aerona whispered reassurances to Jasmine as we climbed on her back.

For the first time since I met Rain, he looked scared.

"You're not afraid of heights, are you?" I asked Rain.

He didn't respond.

Aerona jumped up and sat in the old, leather saddle with metal buckles strapped around Jasmine. The saddle was made of a thin piece of padded leather wrapped with beautiful, braided, leather ties.

Aerona turned to Rain. "Feel free to cry," she joked and broke out in a laugh.

"Just fly the plane," he snapped.

"Jasmine!" Aerona shouted.

The edges of Jasmine's armored scales brightened, and like a rocket, she launched herself into the black sky. Aerona used her mind to communicate with Jasmine, swooping to the left, then diving down low to the sapphire trees before gliding just above the forest. Several small goblins darted behind the trees to hide from the dragon. We circled a small emerald field of maize ready for harvest, then blasted over a short mountain full of colorful vegetation in full bloom. Aerona and Jasmine avoided areas where homes were illuminated with nodules; we hoped not to be seen or reported. I had nearly forgotten the Shadow World's beautiful landscape. In spite of my reluctance, it was good to be home.

Several minutes later, using the thrust of her powerful wings to slow her descent, Jasmine landed softly in a small clearing outside Arcadia, surrounded by towering, thick sapphire trees.

"Welcome to Arcadia," I said, climbing down from Jasmine's back. "We should be less than a mile south from the secret back door to the Forgotten Shadow City."

As everyone else climbed down, Aerona rubbed Jasmine's head, thanking her for her help. Once we were all clear, Jasmine launched back into the sky, vanishing into the darkness.

"Jasmine is going to sweep the area around Arcadia," Aerona said. "If she finds anything, I'll be able to hear her thoughts."

We headed toward north of the clearing.

"Thank you for calling her," I said to Aerona. "I know how much it hurt you to lose Jasmine when we jumped to the Light World."

The faint blue light of the sapphire trees lit our way through the forest as we walked.

"It's difficult seeing her again," Aerona admitted, "knowing I will have to leave her for a second time."

Sensing something awry, Rain froze and signaled for us to be quiet. He was too late; a pack of four ferocious werewolves attacked from the trees, two on either side. They were all easily five feet tall at their shoulders.

Ember took flight straight into the night sky, leaving sparkling white dust trailing behind her. Rain met one of the werewolves in midair. It sank its powerful jaw into Rain's shoulder, igniting a fire inside Rain. In excruciating pain from the werewolf's bite, he slammed the werewolf to the ground, planted his feet firmly, and ripped its head clean off. The werewolves body changed back to its human form, and then to a pile of ash.

Rain's swift victory over the first werewolf did not slow down the other three. Two of them were now circling me, and the third snapped its dangerous jaws at Aerona.

Earlier, Aerona had explained to Ember how the Light World's sun had weighed down on our minds when we jumped from the Shadow World; we basically had to learn how to use our gifts all over again with that new type energy. In the Shadow World, however, Aerona and I were right at home. I reached out and touched the sapphire tree to my right, surprising the werewolves as roots grew out and upwards from the dirt underneath them.

The roots weaved and wrapped themselves around their legs, working their way around their bodies. The wolves howled and growled in frustration as the roots squeezed the wolves, pinning them to the ground.

I heard a tiny yelping behind me. When I turned to see what it was, I saw Aerona cuddling a small, black wolf pup in her arms. The pup's little ears wiggled excitedly as Aerona ran her hand along its spine.

"No," I scolded Aerona, "you cannot keep it."

As soon as Aerona let the little, furry pup down, its little legs hurried it into the forest, toppling over twice along the way.

"Aren't we worried that thing will head straight for more werewolves?" Rain asked.

"Don't worry," Aerona reassured him. "In another hundred feet, that pup will be curled up and sleeping."

"I assume those were sent courtesy of Atmoro," Rain remarked.

"I believe so," I nodded. "There's no other reason why werewolves would be out here. The gates to the Forgotten Shadow City are heavily guarded by Shadow Vampires, and as far as everyone else knows, there is only one way in and no way out."

Ember landed on Rain's shoulder to inspect his wound; it was nearly healed.

"Are you alright?" Aerona asked.

"I'll survive," Rain said, checking his wound, which was now nothing more than a scratch. "We better keep moving. I'll be good in a few minutes."

The trees thinned as we neared Arcadia. We stopped on a ridge overlooking the small town nestled in a valley between two mountains. Most of Arcadia's inhabitants were Shadow Vampires assigned to guard the entrance to the Forgotten Shadow City. From our vantage point, we could see several guards standing watch outside the largest building at the base of the colossal mountain range that held the prison.

"That's the entrance," I said, pointing to a large, guarded structure. "There are many more guards inside, and more at every level down to the main prison gate."

"It doesn't look like they are on high alert," Aerona observed. "If Atmoro's here, he hasn't been detected."

"Let's follow his lead and keep our distance," I suggested. "The elf door should be around the east side of the mountain."

Cautiously, we made our way around the face of the mountain, stopping often so Rain could listen for any hidden threats deep in the darkness.

"Jade's been here," Rain said, stopping in a small clearing. "Her scent is unmistakable."

My heart skipped a beat. "Kasiah?" I asked.

Rain turned his head toward the breeze blowing along the face of the mountain. "No, but it's difficult to tell with all these new scents in the air that I've never experienced."

"Can you tell which way they left the clearing?"

Rain raised his head into the breeze. "Through there," he said, pointing to the north.

Two miles later, we stopped at a forty-foot tall sheer flat rock face that formed a massive wall. The deep, dark red rocks were not unlike those in the Light World.

"The trail ends here," Rain said, staring up at the rock wall.

"What do you mean it ends here?" Aerona questioned, waving her hands around in a circle at the rock wall. "They didn't just vanish."

Rain placed his hand on the wall. "Well, they did. The trail runs right into this rock wall, then ends."

I broke a branch off a nearby sapphire tree. "He's right," I said, holding the blue light of the leaves near the ground. "Look at the footprints."

Several sets of footprints ended right at the rock wall. We all looked up at the same time.

"Do you think they climbed up?" Ember asked.

I turned to Aerona. "Have you received anything from Jasmine?"

"No," she said, "Jasmine flew over this very spot five minutes ago, and she didn't notice anything out of the ordinary."

I placed my hand on the cold rock wall. "The secret entrance to the Forgotten Shadow City was designed and constructed by elves," I said, thinking.

"And?" Aerona asked.

"Elves don't like to be found. They are experts in camouflage techniques. The Shadow Council chose elves for a good reason. Elves would be able to construct a secret door that could never be seen by the naked eye."

I pressed both of my hands against the wall and closed my eyes, pushing through with my mind. "Dammit!" I yelled, jumping back and rubbing my hands. "This is it!"

"This is the secret door designed and constructed by elves?" Ember asked, pointing to the wall.

I leaned close, giving the wall a thorough inspection. "No," I said, "this isn't the actual door to the Forgotten Shadow City, but I'm willing to bet there is a tunnel behind this wall that leads there."

I reached out and held my finger an inch from the wall. A small stream of electricity jolted out from the wall and touched my finger. "This is no ordinary rock wall," I explained, letting the tiny bolt of lightning dance back and forth. "It looks like a cloaking spell has been cast here recently."

"Can you break it?" Ember asked.

"No," I said, disappointed. "The spell has been cast by elves, then reinforced by a warlock—one who is much more powerful than me. We'll need the key to the spell to break it."

"There's another way," Aerona mentioned.

I raised an eyebrow. "Another way?"

Aerona pulled out our mother's necklace from under her shirt, then unlatched it from around her neck. She held the pendant up in her hand. "This."

"Mother's necklace?" I inquired, unsure of what Aerona intended.

"When she gave this to me," Aerona said, clasping her hand around the necklace, "she said it was the key to all magic and that this stone has the power to map a spell and show me its root."

"You got a dragon *and* a magic stone?" I asked, envious. "Can you say spoiled?"

"No," Aerona countered, "but I can say jealous."

"Hey," Rain interrupted, "are you two children going to open this door or what?"

"Well," Aerona said, showing me her middle finger, once again, "Mom did ask me to give you this."

"Aren't you clever," I said wryly. "Get with the spell breaking, big sister."

Aerona held the pendant in one hand and pressed her other against the rock wall. She then closed her eyes and lowered her head.

After a few seconds, smoke started emerging from the rock wall. Aerona's head wrenched from side to side as she was deep within the cloaking spell, trying to find the key. Puffs of smoke exited the thin crevasses on the wall's face. Then, to the left of Aerona, right where the trail of footprints had ended, a rectangular, wooden door came into view. The door was covered from top to bottom with finely detailed elf carvings.

"Go!" Aerona screamed. "I can't keep this open forever!"

I didn't think twice; I shoved the wooden door open and stepped through, followed by Rain and Ember. The door slammed shut behind Aerona as soon as she stepped in, trapping us in total darkness.

FORTY-THREE

Aerona and I ignited flames in our palms, illuminating the dark, narrow tunnel. The ceiling was low, barely tall enough to stand in without hitting our heads. The tunnel twisted and turned under the mountain. The air pressure increased, and the temperature dropped. I lost count of the many corners we turned before finally noticing a dim light around the next corner.

"There's light ahead," I said quietly, dousing my flame. "It looks like the tunnel may open."

"Something is running toward us," Rain whispered. "I can feel the vibrations."

"We can't go back," I replied, peering into the darkness. "We have to stand our ground."

Rain squeezed ahead of me, taking the forward position. "Move back around the last corner," he instructed, crouching in the darkness.

We retreated to the last corner we had turned from, watching as a shadowy figure blocked the light from down the tunnel. They were moving fast. Rain waited until the last possible second, then pounced down the tunnel.

Hearing Kasiah's screams, I ran out from our hiding spot.

"It's me!" Kasiah yelled, gasping for breath, trapped in Rain's iron grip. "It's me Kasiah!"

Rain released Kasiah and helped her up.

"Are you alright?" I asked, wrapping my arms around Kasiah, ecstatic to see her alive.

A thin stream of fresh blood from an open wound ran down her cheek. Her clothes were tattered and filthy, as though she'd been rolling in the dirt for hours.

Kasiah struggled to catch her breath. "Atmoro has Jade," she said, filling her lungs with air.

"How many Shadows are with Atmoro?" I asked.

Kasiah wiped the back of her hand across her bloody cheek, still trying to catch her breath and calm down. "Just Atmoro," she said.

"Just Atmoro?" Aerona probed. "He's here alone?"

Kasiah wiped the blood on her shirt. "Yes, just Atmoro. As soon as we crossed over, he killed the other two vampires who were helping him. Apparently, he didn't need them anymore."

"Why did he keep you alive?" Aerona asked, always the cynic.

"Glad to see you too," Kasiah responded. "From what I gathered, Atmoro wanted to keep me alive as a bargaining chip in case you guys somehow tracked him down."

"What about Jade?" I asked, staring into the dark tunnel. "Has Atmoro performed the sacrifice to open the prison?"

"No, but he's close. He turned his attention away from me for only a second. He was focused on strapping Jade in position against a gigantic and intricately carved wooden door."

"That must be the elf door to the Forgotten Shadow City!" I exclaimed. "Can you show us the way?"

Kasiah hung her head low, and a tear rolled down her face. "I can't go back there," she said, sobbing and shaking. "He's too powerful! He'll kill us all!"

I pulled Kasiah close and embraced her. "You say he's alone?" I asked. "We can handle Atmoro. You just need to point us in the right direction."

Kasiah sniffled. "I… I… I can't remember. I was running so fast. I never thought I'd see you again."

"It's OK, Kasiah," I said, comforting her. "We can do this. We have to do this. Hayley died in order for us to stop Atmoro from releasing these monsters into our worlds. Your sister is here with us."

With the back of her dirty hand, Kasiah wiped away her tears. "If we even have a chance at stopping Atmoro," she continued, "we'll need to move quickly."

"Which way?" Rain asked, eager to save Jade and end this madness.

Kasiah pointed down the dark tunnel. "The tunnel splits into two around the next bend. I came from the left, but I don't know how far. I was running. I was so scared."

"You can do this," I reassured her.

Kasiah took a step forward and tried to recall the route. "I remember the tunnel opening into a cavern. A massive cavern with very high ceilings. A small stream of water trickled down one wall, and some strange blue and green plants lit the whole cavern."

"This is all good information," I urged her on. "You're doing great. Is Atmoro in that cavern?"

"Yes," Kasiah continued. "At the center of the far wall, there is a tall, wooden door with detailed carvings. When I ran, Atmoro was strapping Jade to the door with thick, leather straps. He turned his attention away from me for only a second. I took the chance and I ran so hard, so fast."

"Erone," Rain prompted, "time is not on our side."

I nodded back. "Kasiah, will you be able to show us the way?"

"Let's go get her," she said, stepping forward and suddenly reenergized.

Aerona fell in step behind me. "I don't like this, Erone. We're going in blind."

I glanced over my shoulder. "Well, Aerona, unless you have a map, we don't have a choice."

The tunnel twisted twice, and then we came up to the split in the tunnel that Kasiah had told us about. We followed the left side of the tunnel. The dirt floor slanted downward at a very steep angle, and I could hear everyone's feet sliding to keep traction along the loose dirt.

Rain led the way down the tunnel. "How much further?" he asked Kasiah.

"We're close," she replied, holding my hand. "The cavern should be just around the next corner."

The tunnel opened into a small, dark cavern. I released her hand as we entered, brightening my flame to reveal an empty cavern. It appeared as if construction had been halted, and the cavern was never finished. The walls were only twenty feet square, and I didn't see markings or carvings that Kasiah had described.

"I think we took a wrong turn," I said, looking up at the ceiling. "This is a dead end. Are you sure we had to take the left tunnel?"

Kasiah didn't answer.

I turned back toward the entrance. "Kasiah?" I asked, searching the darkness.

"I'm sorry, Erone," Kasiah whispered. "You weren't supposed to make it this far."

My flame was extinguished, and I was flung through the air, slamming my back hard against the rock wall. I fell to the floor, unable to breathe. Rain let out a thunderous growl and slammed into the wall beside me. Aerona screamed as she collided with the solid rock wall. A flash of light exploded in front of us; Ember transformed and fled to the tunnel.

The cavern went dark.

"Is this all of them?" came a man's voice.

My brain strained to focus. I had heard that man's voice before; it wasn't Atmoro's.

"Yes," Kasiah answered, "sadly, this is their entire crew."

"And the one that escaped?"

"Don't worry about the dumb, little fairy," Kasiah said crudely. "The guards will find her in the tunnel maze."

Slowly, a single white light began to brighten the cavern. I was shocked when I saw an evil grin on Kasiah's face, but I was even more shocked to see her speaking with Noshimo, the same warlock who betrayed my parents by helping Malance, the corrupt council member, to take over the Shadow Council. He hadn't aged a day since the terrifying night that destroyed my family. He was tall, nearly seven feet, and lanky with spiked, white hair. I don't know how he could manage down that little tunnel. His facial features were sunken in, accenting his cheek bones. The rest of his thin body was hidden behind an extended, leather robe tied at the waist.

"You've done well, human," Noshimo said to Kasiah. He released the oxygen around us and allowed us to breathe.

"You bitch!" Aerona yelled with her first breath. "I'm going to slit your throat!"

Kasiah walked over to where Aerona was held against the wall, frozen in place from Noshimo's spell, then kicked Aerona in the jaw, snapping her head back. Aerona held back a scream as blood sprayed from her lips.

My head was throbbing; Noshimo had control of my mind. I was frozen in place, only able to watch Kasiah lean down and grab a handful of Aerona's hair, yanking her head back to expose her neck.

"You've had this coming from the moment I met you," Kasiah said as she pulled out a glistening blade. She slid the back of the blade across Aerona's neck. "What is it that you said to me when you held a knife to my throat? Oh yes, I remember. 'Give me one good reason why I shouldn't spill your blood.'"

From deep down inside Kasiah, the woman I thought I knew and cared for, an overdramatic, evil laugh erupted—I was clearly wrong.

"Stop this!" I screamed. "You don't need to do this!"

Kasiah let go of Aerona's hair. "How sweet," she replied, standing. "Her little brother comes to the rescue."

"Let us go!" Aerona demanded. "So we can have a fair fight, you psycho!"

Ignoring Aerona's threat, Kasiah ran the steel blade of her knife up my chest, propping my chin up with its tip. Her soft lips touched mine, passionately kissing me for several seconds. Memories of our first kiss flashed through my weakened mind. Her lips were still as soft as that first kiss.

"We could have been so good together," Kasiah grinned. "You have more passion and heart than ten mortal men, but you're fighting a losing battle."

I held back my emotions which were killing me from the inside out. "You don't have to do this, Kasiah," I pleaded. "They're filling your head with lies."

Kasiah threw her head back and laughed. "You're so pathetic," she said, securing the blade back into her pocket.

"What about Hayley?" I asked, trying to pull her into reality. "They killed your sister. They killed Damien. Are you just going to let all of that go?"

"The loss of their lives was a necessary evil," Kasiah said, turning away from me.

The reality of Kasiah's words struck me; she had played me from day one. She was already involved in Atmoro's plan before I had met her in Madison. She was there when Atmoro's vampire killed Hayley, and she let it happen. For all I knew, she may even have helped. Kasiah had been leaking information to Atmoro the whole time, which explains how she was able to survive the poison dart from the troll in Erie. She must have already had the antidote in her system. Kasiah was the reason Atmoro was one step ahead of us. She was the mole who Jake warned us about. Kasiah led Noshimo right up to the farmhouse in the woods where we found Tara.

How could I have been so foolish? I thought to myself. How could I have let my feelings for a beautiful woman cloud my mind that I couldn't see what was right in front of me?

"Karma will catch you for this," I warned her. "Maybe not today or tomorrow, but you will answer for this evil."

Kasiah ignored me. "Let's get them to the other cavern," she told Noshimo. "We have many more fun things planned for tonight's celebration."

Noshimo released enough of the spell to allow us to walk, but only where he could lead us. We had no choice but to follow him and Kasiah through the tunnel. Rain protested at first, until Noshimo stole the air around him, burning his lungs till he fell to his knees. Noshimo had shown him the full potential of a seasoned warlock.

The next cavern was much larger, exactly as Kasiah had explained—at least she wasn't a total liar. The ceilings were high, maybe twenty feet at the center and another hundred feet of space between each wall. A sparkling stream flowed down the far wall. Tiny blue and green plants grew on either side of the stream, illuminating the entire cavern. On the opposite side of the stream, Atmoro stood next to a twelve-foot-tall, intricately carved wooden door. Jade was strapped to the door with thick leather straps and steel shackles. Her eyes were saturated with fear as she fought against the shackles that locked her wrists and ankles. A cloth gag held back her screams.

What happened next was even more surprising than Kasiah's betrayal or Noshimo's presence. Malance, wearing a thick cloak fit for a king, emerged from the shadows. He was flanked by six typical Shadow Vampire protectors. Resembling a king's guards, they wore full armor with sleek, black medieval helmets. Each had a deadly sword sheathed at their side. I suspected there were more of Malance's guards across the tunnels. We fell right into their trap. They probably saw this coming from a mile away.

"Welcome!" Malance said, as though he was greeting visitors to his home. "I see you've taken care of our uninvited guests."

"Yes, sir," Noshimo nodded, tightening his grip on our minds.

Malance stopped in front of me. "It's been a long time, Erone. You've grown. Yet I see you are still fighting the same losing battle of your late father. With proper training, you could have made a great addition to my alliance."

"Traitor," I cursed through gritted teeth, anger lurching inside me.

Malance smiled. "You are as foolish as your father once was."

Kasiah approached Malance and planted the same forceful kiss she had given me not five minutes prior.

"Maybe we could keep this one as a pet," Kasiah proposed, embracing him again, tracing her fingers down his arms.

Malance separated from Kasiah and laughed. "If you wish," he said, moving on to Aerona, eyeing her up and down. "Well, well, well, you've grown into such a beautiful woman. You're an exact copy of your gorgeous mother."

Aerona spat at Malance.

323

Kasiah stepped in front of him and slapped Aerona across her face. "We're not keeping this one!" she hollered.

Malance laughed at Aerona the same way he had laughed at me. "I like this game!" he said, clapping his hands excitedly.

"Enough games!" Atmoro ordered from across the cavern standing at the large wooden door. "I brought you the girl, now let's get this exchange over with. Get me Christine."

Malance turned his attention to Atmoro, and his tone became serious "Yes, the deal was Christine for the blood of a stone. I must say, Atmoro, I'm pleased, yet surprised you were able to deliver this impossible key. Kasiah had provided me with updates of your progress along the way. Your use of the warlock twins was wise, but was it within the rules of the game?"

"How I obtained the angel is not in question," Atmoro disputed, his anger surging. "The deal was the blood of a stone for my wife!"

It was obvious Atmoro was holding back his anger; at any moment, this situation could take a sharp right turn into chaos. Malance may have underestimated Atmoro's true capability as one of the strongest Shadow Vampires ever to have existed. Add Atmoro's power to the rage he was holding in from when Malance left him for dead, and you have an unstable bomb ready to explode.

Malance thought about their arrangement for a minute and spoke again. "You are correct. You have delivered the stone, and I shall deliver Christine back to your arms the moment the gate to the Forgotten Shadow City is opened."

Malance motioned to one of his Shadow Vampire guards. "Spill the girl's blood and open the gate to the prison," he commanded.

"Wait!" I yelled. "You can't do this!"

Malance held his hand up to stop the vampire. "I can't do this?" he asked, laughing. "I am doing this."

"You must realize," I continued, trying to buy some time, "once opened, there is no going back. You'll release thousands of lost souls into our two worlds."

Malance smiled. "Yes, young Erone, I realize that, and by the way, that is the plan."

"What is the point of this madness?" I asked. "What do you gain by doing this?"

"The point," he explained, taking his attention off Jade and Atmoro, "is the Shadow Council is in need of reform. The Shadows I release today will kneel to my command tomorrow. Today is the day the Shadow Council embraces their true leader."

"You're insane!" Aerona shouted. "The Shadow Council was formed to keep Shadows like you from becoming powerful enough to make these foolish decisions!"

Aerona had struck a nerve in Malance.

"The Shadow Council is foolish!" Malance shouted back. "The Council was created centuries ago by elders with no vision of the future! They were fools to think we should stay hidden from the Light World! We are the superior race! The mortals of that world will bow to our rule!"

Aerona laughed out loud. "Because that didn't just prove my point," she taunted, shaking her head, maddening Malance even more.

Noshimo's mind knocked Aerona down to the ground, stealing the air from her lungs. She gasped for a breath that wasn't there. Rain dug his feet into the wall behind him, pushing with all his might to free himself from Noshimo's powerful mind. The wall behind him began to crack. He stopped pushing, but spun around instead, slamming his fist into the wall. A large crack shot up the rock wall, splitting it right up to the ceiling. Rain swung a second time, impacting the wall with enough force to fracture solid rock. A second crack shot across the floor.

"Stop this foolishness!" Atmoro bellowed from the elf door. "They will all be dead soon enough! Show me Christine, or our deal is off!"

Malance nodded to Noshimo, and he released his grasp on the air around Aerona, allowing her to breathe again.

I looked around the cavern, searching my mind for answers on how I had allowed myself to be taken advantage of by Kasiah. If we had any chance of getting out of that mess, we needed to take out Noshimo.

"Noshimo," Malance said, turning his attention back to Atmoro and Jade, "show Atmoro why he shall not betray me."

Noshimo sent a single beam of light to the elf door, shining slightly left of Jade's leg. The door transformed from solid to transparent, and I saw hundreds, thousands of Forgotten Shadows far beyond the door. There were vampires, warlocks, werewolves, demons, trolls, and many more imprisoned Forgotten Shadows. A young, beautiful blonde made her way to the front and placed her hand flat on the transparent door. On the other side, Atmoro placed his hand flat against the door, mirroring the woman's—it was Christine.

I swear I could feel their love passing through the thick elf door.

Christine, in melancholy, shook her head back and forth. She did not approve of what Malance was about to do. She knew what would happen to our two worlds if the Forgotten Shadows were released.

Atmoro hung his head, understanding that Christine did not want to be freed. I felt his heart sink as he realized he was about to lose her forever again. Atmoro raised his head and looked into his wife's eyes. She smiled back, and I saw her lips move to say "I love you."

Malance, realizing what was happening, ordered his guards to kill Jade. "Spill the angel's blood!" he shouted. "Every single drop!"

Atmoro spun around to face Malance. "We have made a mistake, Malance! We cannot allow this to happen! Our worlds will collide! War will destroy us!"

"That's the whole point!" Malance argued. "Kill the angel!"

The Shadow Vampires moved in, their weapons drawn. Atmoro shifted into defensive mode. He reached his arm over to his shoulder sheath and pulled out a long sword that shimmered in the light. Atmoro defended Jade, cutting apart the first Shadow Vampire to reach her. His sword sliced the vampire in half diagonally across the chest. Jade screamed through her gag as the vampire fell at her feet.

"Atmoro!" I hollered. "Free us from Noshimo, and we will help you stop this madness!"

Without hesitation, Atmoro yanked a dagger from under his jacket, then hurled it at Noshimo. The dagger, inches from Noshimo's face, froze midair.

Two more of Malance's vampire guards attacked Atmoro. The vampires were young and, despite their heavy armor, were fast, but they lacked the training required to effectively engage an angry, seasoned Shadow Vampire.

Running, the first of the two vampires drew out an automatic crossbow, firing two arrows one after another. Atmoro leapt toward the vampire, catching one arrow as the other passed an inch from his face. Atmoro swung the head of the arrow he had caught, driving it through the helmet and into the skull of the Shadow Vampire. An instant later, he swung his shimmering sword, decapitating the other Shadow Vampire. Atmoro ripped the crossbow from the dead vampire's hands, then fired three arrows into his chest, just to be sure.

"Noshimo!" I screamed. "You don't have to do this! Malance is going to destroy your world if he releases these Shadows! You betrayed my father, but you have the chance to redeem yourself now!"

Noshimo didn't take the bait. He smiled, tightening his grip on my mind and squeezing the energy from me as he held Rain tightly against the wall. Rain continued to try and wrestle his way free. The cracks in the wall grew behind him.

Atmoro had his hands full. The remaining three Shadow Vampires attacked at once, driving Atmoro away from Jade. I fell to my knees as Noshimo held me in intense agony. Aerona and I could do nothing but watch Malance approach the elf door, his dagger in hand. Jade's green eyes looked to me for help. She was beyond terrified.

"Do something!" Aerona shouted to me.

I reached deep down inside myself, searching for any amount of energy that Noshimo had not stolen. The pain in my chest was excruciating. I couldn't breathe. My father's memory flashed briefly through my mind. I was letting him down.

Malance stepped in front of Jade and raised the dagger high above his head. "The blood of a stone will release them alone!" he recited before swinging the blade down toward Jade.

My father's memory gave me the energy to lift my right hand. I fired a single small burst of blue flame at Malance—I hoped it was enough. The fireball caught Malance in this shoulder, twisting him around as he swung the blade. The sharp blade fell from Malance's hand, slicing across Jade's arm as it tumbled to the ground.

Blood flowed from Jade's wound, trickling down her arm to her finger tips before dripping to the floor. The elf door began to smoke. It had started opening. Rocks began falling from the ceiling.

Unexpectedly, my mind was free of Noshimo's grasp. I fell to the ground, sucking in my breath. Aerona collapsed to the ground next to me. I rolled on my back just in time to see Ashes driving a second long, broken grawl fang into Noshimo's back, forcing him to the ground. He screamed in pain as the venom began burning his veins.

A spark of light flashed over my head; Ember had returned. I noticed the trail of fairy light flying to Jade. Ember began working on releasing the straps that held Jade to the door.

Malance had recovered from the fireball and stumbled backwards, brushing the last of the fire from his cloak. He tripped over a boulder and fell into the shallow stream.

Kasiah backed up against the far wall, alone and afraid.

The ground beneath us shook violently; the elf door was beginning to open.

Rain dashed across the cavern and slammed into the door like a freight train. He slowed the door down, but it continued to inch its way open. It wouldn't be long before it was open wide enough to release Shadows trapped within the prison.

"I can't hold it!" Rain hollered, his face tense as he struggled to hold the door. His feet slid along the ground.

Atmoro threw his entire body into the door next to Rain, digging his feet into the dirt floor of the cavern. The two worked together to hold the door from opening any further as Christine fought off the Shadows who were trying to push the door open from the other side.

I reached Jade and helped Ember with the shackles. I ripped the bottom of my shirt off and wrapped it around the wound on Jade's arm, using my belt to hold the makeshift bandage in place.

Ember removed the cloth gag tied around Jade's mouth. Her face was splattered with blood from the first Shadow Vampire Atmoro had slayed.

"I'm sorry," Jade muttered, tears forming in her eyes.

"Jade," I said, wiping the blood from her face, "this is not your fault. Kasiah betrayed us all. She used us to find you for Atmoro."

"How can we stop this?" Ember asked, helping her down from the door.

"I'm not sure we can reverse this door," I said, hoping it wasn't true. "We need to get Jade out of here."

More rocks fell from the ceiling as the cracks widened. A large boulder crashed down next to us, shaking the entire cavern.

"We need to move!" I shouted to Rain. "Atmoro! We have to go before we're crushed in here!"

"Get the angel out of here!" Atmoro ordered, without turning his head from the door. "If she is crushed, and more of her blood is spilled, we will not be able to stop this door from opening!"

Aerona grabbed my arm. "Erone, the whole ceiling is about to cave in! We have to get out of here! The elves knew they could never allow the release of these Shadows. They designed this room to cave in if the blood of an angel ever found its way in here."

Kasiah started to make her way to the entrance to the cavern, dodging the falling rocks. The sound was deafening. An entire column fell from the far wall, sounding a thunderous roar as it crashed. A ten foot wide crevasse formed between us and the elf door.

"Take Jade and get her out of here!" I shouted to Aerona. "Ashes will defend you!"

Kasiah slid to a stop at the edge of the crevasse. "Erone!" she yelled across to me. "You can't leave me here!"

Aerona pulled Jade free from my arm, and then, using her gift to slow time, she weaved her way toward the entrance with Ashes right behind.

I turned to Kasiah. Images of us rolling naked in bed on Ember's yacht raced through my mind. Kasiah's once sweet smile and intoxicating perfume blinded my senses. Her beauty was a weapon—a weapon I was not trained to defend against.

I threw as much energy as I could find at the prison's opening door. "You'll have to jump to me!" I yelled to Kasiah. "You can make it!"

Kasiah took several steps back, and judging the distance, she sprinted to the edge of the crevasse, leaping just as another tremor shook the cavern. The crevasse widened before Kasiah could reach halfway across. Releasing my mind's hold on the elf door, I reached out, catching her by the wrists as though she was a circus flyer.

I fell on my stomach, which knocked the wind from my chest as Kasiah's weight yanked on my wrists. It took everything I had to keep hold of her. My arms extended down into the crevasse with Kasiah. She had struck her head in the sharp rocks, and fresh blood trickled down the side of her head.

"Erone!" she cried. "Don't let go!"

"I'm drained of energy," I said, fighting to hold on. "You have to climb up."

Kasiah kicked her feet in an attempt to find a foothold. "Don't you let me go!"

I looked down at Kasiah, sliding further toward the edge. Kasiah slipped further down my arms, and her hands slid down to mine. I saw the terror on her face as her seemingly innocent, brown eyes stared back at me.

"I'm sorry, Erone," she said, weakening. "I never meant to hurt you."

I fought to hold my grip. "Hang on!"

"I love you," Kasiah said, tears filling her eyes, and then without warning, she let go.

My heart ached as I watched her fall into the darkness. I screamed after her, but she was gone. The sound of my voice echoed down into the emptiness. My eyes welled up as I climbed back to my feet, forcing the last image of Kasiah to the back of my mind. I concentrated on the elf door. "Rain, it's now or never! Let's go!"

"I'm staying!" he shouted back. "Atmoro can't hold this door alone!"

I caught a glimpse of something shimmering in the light as it zoomed through the air. A spear struck Rain's shoulder, forcing a fierce growl from deep within him, but he did not release the door. Instead, he reached back and pulled out the silver-tipped spear thrown by another Shadow Vampire near the entrance with Malance.

"Kill them!" Malance ordered his guard. "Kill them all!"

Malance's guard was dressed in the same armor as the others but was much larger and moved with Rain's speed. He raced across the cavern. I didn't dare risk pulling my mind away from the door, or it would open.

Rain turned just in time to see the guard leap over the crevasse, sword in hand. Rain flipped around, pushing his back against the door, digging his heels into the rock floor. He sidestepped, and the sword ricocheted off the elf door. The guard recovered and swung a second time at Rain, lower this time.

Again, Rain shifted his position to miss the sword. Sparks flew wide as the sword hit the solid rock below the door. The vampire guard was incredibly fast and handled the sword as if he was born with it in his hands. Behind the helmet, I could see the fierceness in his eyes as they followed Rain's movements, ready for a third attempt.

For the first time since Rain was freed from Noshimo's spell, he stepped away from the door. Atmoro turned his back and dug his heels into the ground. I fell to my knees with my hands stretched out, trying to keep the door from opening further. On the other side, I could see Christine ripping the head off a werewolf. The legends were true—she was a fierce warrior.

Rain and the guard circled each other as the guard expertly flipped the sword from one hand to the next, calculating his next move.

"Drop the sword and let's finish this like men," Rain challenged, antagonizing the guard. "You coward!"

"That's where you make your mistake, fool," the guard responded. "You think we are men."

The guard raised the sword high above his right shoulder to strike. Rain, anticipating the next move, moved to the guard's left. Then, the guard changed his momentum and spun around completely, catching Rain in the left arm as he swept past.

Rain hissed in pain, flashing his deadly fangs. His wound was deep.

I was helpless but did not release my hold on the prison's door.

The guard and Rain faced off again as blood poured from Rain's wound. His wound would not heal as quickly that close to the prison. A large boulder dropped from the ceiling, crashing on the floor between them. This disoriented the guard as he took his eyes off Rain to look up for more falling rocks. Rain took advantage of this split-second opportunity and leapt up the boulder, then toward the vampire guard, grabbing hold of a large falling rock as he flew. The guard noticed Rain soaring through the air, but he was too late; Rain crushed the rock on the guard's helmet, knocking it off his head. They both fell to the ground.

The guard's sword clanged on the ground. He was now on his back, dazed from the rock's blow. Rain, with the guard's sword in hand, lifted the hilt high above his head, pointing the tip downward to make the kill.

Rain hesitated.

"Do it!" I shouted.

The sword fell from Rain's hands.

The face of Malance's guard was a mirror image of Rain. Every facial feature was carved perfectly from the same mold as his.

I momentarily lost my hold on the door.

"Two warriors created equally," Malance stated from behind us, admiring the secret only he had known for so many years.

Rain backed away from the guard, holding his chest, feeling the only place on his body that had never fully healed—a small scar over his heart. Memories flooded his mind as he fell to his knees. He recalled diving through the air as a child, attempting to save his father, an arrow striking his heart.

Atmoro couldn't believe his eyes, and Christine stopped fighting off the Shadows inside the prison. For many decades they had believed their sons were killed by Malance, then burned along with their home.

The door pushed harder against Atmoro.

Malance's guard, Rain's twin brother, stood up and picked up his sword, raising it high.

"Your father commands you to stop!" Atmoro shouted to Rain's brother. "He is your brother! Your blood!"

The sword plunged through Rain's chest and came out through his back.

332

Rain's brother had been brainwashed by Malance, who used the newborn Shadow Vampire's strengths as an evil weapon.

"Come!" Malance commanded. "We must leave before the door is fully opened!"

Rain's twin brother released the sword and leapt over the wide crevasse, following his master. He bolted for the entrance behind Malance, and together with him, vanished into the tunnel.

I focused my energy on the ceiling above the door. "Atmoro! Move! Now!"

Atmoro looked at the ceiling and, understanding what I was about to do, released the door. A boulder the size of a truck fell from the ceiling, crashing down in front of the door, taking Atmoro's place. It was by no means a permanent solution, but would hold for a few minutes. My mind shook loose a part of the cavern wall, collapsing a large rectangular boulder across the crevasse in front of me—a makeshift bridge.

Atmoro fell to Rain's side. "My son," he cried in pain. "I have found you only to lose you again."

I ran across the rock bridge to Atmoro and Rain. Rain lay lifeless in Atmoro's arms. "We have to go, Atmoro."

"I am staying," Atmoro insisted, not lifting his head. "I've had enough of this life."

"Those boulders will not hold the door for long," I warned.

Atmoro stood up with Rain in his arms, pulling out the blood stained sword from his chest. "Take my son with you. Take him to the Light World. He does not deserve a grave under this rubble."

I didn't have time to argue, nor did I think Atmoro was asking. I let him drape Rain's surprisingly light, lifeless body over my shoulder.

"You are a gifted warlock, Erone," Atmoro said. "Your father would have been proud. I am sorry for the chaos I created."

I looked at Christine behind the elf door. "I understand why you did what you did, Atmoro. There are higher powers that will sentence you for your crimes." I handed Atmoro the pouch with the grimlight from Whisper. "Use this to push them back."

The cavern shook violently several times, nearly knocking us off our feet, and more rocks fell from the ceiling.

"Go!" Atmoro ordered, picked up the sword that had killed his son. "I will hold back the Shadows."

I ran towards the entrance of the cavern, only turning to see Atmoro force the boulders to the side to enter the prison. He and Christine fought their way into the sea of Shadows, pushing them back away from the elf door. A blast of intense light chased after me as I ran from the collapsing cavern—he had used the grimlight.

Thunderous roars of falling rock chased me down the tunnel, echoing off the walls. I felt the pressure changing as the tunnels sealed off. I could only hope that the tunnels in front of me were still clear.

FORTY-FOUR

A final, deafening roar sealed off the tunnel behind me as I raced out of the mountain through the wooden door Aerona had opened with our mother's necklace. A massive cloud of dirt and dust settled around the foot of the mountain where the camouflaged door was now closed forever.

I lowered Rain's body gently to the ground.

Aerona ran over to me. "Erone, what happened?"

I rested Rain's head down. "One of Malance's guards attacked us," I said, running my fingers over his face to shut his eyelids. "He caught Rain in the chest with a sword."

Ember dropped to her knees next to Rain's body, placing her hand on his blood-soaked chest. She sobbed at the loss of her dear friend, who had saved her life on more than one occasion.

Ashes stood silently nearby with Jade at her side.

I looked to where the door had once been. "The tunnels caved in all the way back to the cavern. I don't know if Malance was able to escape."

"What about the elf door to the Forgotten Shadow City?" Ashes asked.

"Thanks to you, Ashes, we were able to limit the amount of Jade's blood that was spilled. It slowed the opening of the door. The entire cavern caved in around the prison's door, and it is sealed forever."

Aerona placed a small bouquet of dimly glowing blue flowers on Rain's chest. "Kasiah and Atmoro?" she asked.

The last image of Kasiah falling away from me into the darkness kept blazing through my mind. "Kasiah is dead," I said grimly, not elaborating.

335

"Atmoro sacrificed himself to ensure no Shadows could escape before the collapse. The door has been resealed, and Atmoro has been reunited with Christine, his long, lost wife. They will spend eternity together within the prison walls."

"You speak of Atmoro as if he's a hero," Ashes said, sounding a little defensive.

"Atmoro may not be a hero, but he was only trying to save the woman he loved, Rain's mother."

Aerona stared at me with a blank expression on her face, piecing together what I had just said. "Are you telling us that Atmoro is Rain's... father?" she asked, her eyes opening wide. "Like Darth Vader and Luke Skywalker?"

"Yes," I said, finding it hard to believe myself. "It's very Star Wars, but there's more. Rain caught Malance's guard in the head with a large rock and removed his helmet. The guard's face was exactly like Rain's, except for his blonde hair; it was his twin brother. Atmoro and Christine must have had no idea that their young sons had survived Malance's attack."

"His brother?" Ember asked, crying. "How can that be?"

I explained what I had put together only moments ago. "Not unlike Jade's parents, while in the Light World, Atmoro and Christine gave birth to the first true-blood Shadow Vampires. Their existence was never known to anyone else, because Malance covered it up by killing Atmoro and imprisoning Christine. Then, I suspect, Malance kidnapped the blonde twin and raised him in secret. Rain must have been injured badly while trying to save his parents from Malance's attack. A large amount of blood loss would have shut down Rain's brain. That's why he could never remember any of his past. Atmoro and Christine must have thought Malance had killed the twins when their home was invaded."

Jade knelt next to Rain. "I'm sorry, my new friend," she said, resting her hand on his forehead, "you gave your life for mine. You are a hero, and I shall never forget you."

Amazingly, Jade's hand began to glow with a soft white light. She snapped her hand back away from Rain. "What was that?" she exclaimed, shaken by what had just happened. "I'm so sorry! I shouldn't have touched him!"

I reached out and grabbed Jade by her arm. "Look," I said, turning her hand over, "your palm is stained with the blood from your wound."

Jade tugged her arm back and tried rubbing the blood off on her shirt.

"No!" I shouted. "Take off your bandage!

"What?" she asked, confused. "My bandage?"

"Your blood!" I yelled, hastily pulling the bandage from Jade's arm. "It's the blood of an angel!"

"What does that mean?" Ember asked, as confused as everyone else.

"I have no idea!" I shouted, placing Jade's arm over Rain's face.

We all watched as a red line of blood trickled along the knife wound on Jade's arm. A drop of blood ran around Jade's arm, then dripped off on Rain's lips, which began to radiate the same soft light as when Jade's bloody hand touched his head.

Jade gripped her arm near the wound and squeezed, causing the blood to flow faster. Several more drops touched Rain's lips, and his veins began glowing softly. The light traced down his neck under his shirt, and within seconds, Rain's entire body radiated with the same soft light. Jade continued letting her blood flow into Rain's mouth. Her face grimaced from the pain of her wound, but she kept squeezing. The gash left by the sword on Rain's chest was shining brightly. His back arched as a beam of bright white light shot into the dark sky, knocking us all off our feet as though a percussion grenade had just been detonated.

I shielded my eyes from the tower of light now beaming high into the sky. Rain's body hovered several inches off the ground beside Jade, and her long, blonde hair blew back as if was caught in a whirlwind of energy. Her green eyes shined like emeralds as the column of explosive white light shot higher into the sky, illuminating the Shadow World from above.

Rain's arms lifted and grabbed hold of Jade's arm, forcing it to his lips. Jade didn't scream; instead, she closed her eyes and allowed Rain's fangs to sink into her flesh. I had to turn my eyes away from the intensifying light.

As quickly as the column of light had burst into the sky, it receded, and the Shadow World was once again thrust into darkness. Rain's body collapsed on the ground, and Jade fell on her side next to him.

Standing up, I blinked away the white spots from my eye. Jade lay immobile next to Rain as he slowly sat up, shaking his head from side to side, as if waking from a restful sleep. He touched his chest where his brother's sword had punctured his heart. The wound had healed. He ran the back of his hand across his bloodied lips.

Jade's green eyes slowly opened. She smiled at the sight of Rain, now alive and looking back at her. "I saved you," she said softly. "The blood of a stone saved you."

Rain brushed the blonde hair away from Jade's face and kissed her lips tenderly.

Jade kissed him back.

EPILOGUE - JADE

The stage lights went out, and the crowd erupted in excitement for Kate's Mind to take the stage. I heard guitar amps click on and noticed the silhouettes of band members moving around on the stage. The energy of the crowd grew louder as the hum of guitar feedback ramped up through a massive sound system. The stage lights turned steadily brighter. Jimmy and his lead guitarist were in front of their amps, their guitars in hand and their backs to the crowd. The drummer began a nice, slow groove that the bass and the guitars matched perfectly. The music intensified with every measure, and the volume slowly amplified louder and louder.

I felt Aerona's heart race a bit faster to keep pace with the music.

The music stopped, and the speakers became silent as Jimmy stepped up to the mic. He brushed a few long, dark strands of hair away from his face and smiled as he yelled, "Pick it up, Madison!"

The whole band kicked back in with perfect time.

My muscles tensed, and my mind froze. I was almost knocked off my feet by someone slamming into me from the back.

"Sorry, babe!" a guy shouted to Ashes, struggling to keep his balance from her powerful push that forced him into me. "You're bound to attract a few guys like me when you look like... damn... like you."

Ashes stared the guy down until he stumbled backwards, turned, and then pushed his way through the crowd. I'm pretty sure he doesn't know how close he came to being a statistic.

I pointed to Ashes's tight T-shirt, compliments of Aerona's private collection. "You'd think a shirt stenciled with 'I Bite!' would say enough."

Ashes opened her mouth to respond, but before she could, Aerona grabbed her by the arm and pulled her towards the stage. Ashes could have easily resisted Aerona's grip; but over the past few weeks, she had learned it's pointless to argue with Aerona. I smiled and waved to Ashes as she looked back at me for help while she was pulled into the crowd.

It had been almost a month since we stopped Malance's insane plan of releasing the Shadows from the Forgotten Shadow City. I was surprised by Ashes's decision to jump with us back to the Light World. She couldn't bring herself to serve under a corrupt council in the Shadow World.

Safely back in the Light World, with a little help of Ember's bottomless bag of money, we vanished. Destiny and Kate's Mind brought us back to Madison, where our adventure first began. Aerona and I, impersonating federal agents, visited Damien's family to notify them of his sad demise in the line of duty. They were devastated but proud at the same time.

Standing close to the stage, Rain smiled with excitement as he told Jade all about Kate's Mind. Over the past few weeks, Jade and Rain had become quite close—her blood had bonded them together like I have never seen. Their minds were connected somehow, and Rain seemed to have a new outlook in life. Although, he never mentioned a word about his twin brother, who essentially killed him back in the Shadow World.

Ember's hand rested on my shoulder. She leaned in close to my ear and said, "Whisper just sent me a text. They have his location."

My mind started spinning. I caught Aerona's eye from across the room; she must have felt my heart skip a beat. Ashes picked up on Aerona's sudden change of mood.

"Is he sure?" I asked Ember.

"He and Tara are confident," Ember confirmed. "They intercepted an encrypted e-mail from Malance to the elves. I've instructed Candice to ready the jet."

ABOUT THE AUTHOR

RICHARD BRAINE JR spends his nights writing about a new world of fantasy as summer monsoons chase the sunset across the mountains surrounding Phoenix Arizona into the Sonoran Desert of the Southwestern United States.

Other than writing contemporary vampire and fantasy books, Richard also enjoys driving his Jeep off-road to explore the Grand Canyon and Arizona's mountains with his beautiful wife and two children. Their smiles are his greatest inspiration.

Did you enjoy this book? Leave a review on Amazon to help others find and enjoy this unique story.